Blood is Thicker Than Lots of Stuff

ALSO BY CHRIS TULLBANE

<u>The Murder of Crows</u>

See These Bones
Red Right Hand
One Tin Soldier *

<u>Stories from a Post-Break World</u>

The Stars That Sing
The Storm in Her Smile
A Sure Thing
Fire of Unknown Origin *

<u>The Many Travails of John Smith</u>

Investigation, Mediation, Vindication
Blood is Thicker Than Lots of Stuff
Ghost of a Chance *
The Italian Screwjob *
A Dead Man's Favor *
Godswar *
John Smith Doesn't Work Here Anymore *

*Forthcoming

Blood is Thicker Than Lots of Stuff

CHRIS TULLBANE

GHOST FALLS PRESS

NEVADA

First published by Ghost Falls Press 2021

GHOST FALLS PRESS

Publisher's Cataloging-in-Publication Data
provided by Five Rainbows Cataloging Services

Names: Tullbane, Chris, author.
Title: Blood is thicker than lots of stuff / Chris Tullbane.
Description: Henderson, NV : Ghost Falls Press, 2021. | Series: The many travails of John Smith, bk. 2.
Identifiers: ISBN 978-1-955081-00-9 (paperback) | ISBN 978-1-7334824-9-3 (ebook)
Subjects: LCSH: Vampires--Fiction. | Mediators (Persons)--Fiction. | San Diego (Calif.)--Fiction. | Humorous stories. | Paranormal fiction. | Fantasy fiction. | BISAC: FICTION / Fantasy / Urban. | FICTION / Fantasy / Humorous. | FICTION / Occult & Supernatural. | GSAFD: Fantasy fiction. | Humorous fiction.
Classification: LCC PS3620.U45 B56 2021 (print) | LCC PS3620.U45 (ebook) | DDC 813/.6--dc23.

Book cover design by Jake @ jcalebdesign.com

FIRST EDITION

For Nami,
the reason for everything

ACKNOWLEDGMENTS

Thank you to all the usual suspects:

Nami, my angel-wife.

Johanna, my whisky buddy and John's long-time #1 fan.

Jamie, protector of the free world, who, against all odds, continues to be both the best and the only brother I've ever had.

Keith and Shawn, who don't get paid to beta read my nonsense.

Simon, great poet and better friend.

Kerri, Sam, and Mark, for their eagle eyes and for making Twitter fun.

And last but never least, my mom and dad.

PROLOGUE

I was cold.

No, that's an understatement; I was freezing, like I'd been cuddling an ice-covered pillow while tucked into a snow drift. It was the shivering that finally woke me, interrupting my dream of a half-dozen Valkyries, Frosty the Snowman, and a castle-sized Twinkie. It was a frequently recurring dream, and I was unhappy to have it disrupted, especially before Frosty had reached his song and dance number.

My unhappiness doubled when I tried to rub my eyes and couldn't, then doubled yet again when those eyes finally opened. I blearily looked into pitch black darkness through a film of eye goo. Where was I? And why couldn't I move my arms or legs?

I struggled to sit up but ended up just flopping about like a fish on what appeared to be a cold, hard surface. It might have been marble, or tile, or even simple, boring concrete. It was even possible that I'd been trussed up like a Thanksgiving Day turkey and dropped in the middle of an ice-skating rink. I didn't know, and I didn't care, because two other things had just become apparent: I was naked and I was in a serious amount of pain.

I wish I could say I'd seen this coming, but foresight had never been my forte. It was the sort of character flaw that was going to get me killed someday.

Someday might have finally arrived.

CHAPTER 1

IN WHICH THERE IS NEVER A SECOND CHANCE TO
MAKE A FIRST IMPRESSION

I was having a pretty good date until the vampires showed up.

Mister A's was something of an institution in San Diego, located at the top of a tower just north of downtown, its windows and deck giving panoramic views of the city and harbor. It wasn't the sort of place I could normally afford, but I'd just finished a job for one of San Diego's goblin tribes, and even after paying my office rent, I'd had enough left over for wining and dining.

Carly looked just like she had online: tall and slim with short black hair and brown eyes. Given how weird my life had become, she was just what I was looking for: cute, perfectly normal, and most importantly, non-homicidal.

Granted, it usually took multiple dates to verify that last bit.

We'd met at the restaurant, per her request, which had allowed me to keep my graffiti-stricken Corolla out of sight. I'd come with flowers in my hand and product in my hair, wearing the suit my parents had bought me back when they thought I'd get a real job instead of going into business as a private investigator.

This was my first date in a long time, but I was killing it.

Mostly.

"Wait." Carly wrinkled her nose in confusion. "You still live with your parents?"

I coughed as eight-dollar beer went down the wrong pipe. By the time I could breathe again, I'd convinced myself that letting that small detail slip in our first few moments of conversation was a good thing. After all, honesty was key in relationships, right?

"Yeah," I admitted. "They live over in Chula Vista and have let me stay with them while I get my business off the ground."

I didn't mention that I'd started that business more than three years earlier and still couldn't afford to move out. There was such a thing as being *too* honest.

"Starting a business must be tough in this economy," said Carly, closing her menu with a snap.

"There've been some rough patches, but things are starting to turn around."

"You said you're a private eye, right? Like Sherlock Holmes?"

"Kind of." Most of my business still revolved around missing people or cheating spouses. I didn't remember Sherlock having to stoop quite so low. "Recently, I've also started handling mediations."

"Like, for divorce settlements and stuff?"

"And stuff, yeah. Intellectual property disputes, labor strikes, inheritance… that sort of thing. Sometimes, it's cheaper and faster to go through a mediator than to hire lawyers and go to court."

Especially since my mediation clients would rather eat their lawyers than pay them. It had been four months since I'd learned that humans weren't the dominant species on the planet. Vampires, pixies, goblins, immortals, weird amoeba looking things… it was a big damn world out there and humans were near the bottom of the food chain.

The waiter swooped in to take our orders. When he was gone, I decided it was my turn to show an interest. "What about you? I don't know anything about the tech industry. What's it like being a recruiter?"

"It has its moments. When Qualcomm went under last year, things were tough, but the industry seems to be bouncing back already. I get to meet a lot of people, which can be…"

Her words trailed off as someone behind me caught her eye. Given the infamous Smith luck, we must have run into an ex-boyfriend or something. I could only hope he was balding and out of shape.

"Hello, little bird."

Or maybe it was someone from *my* past instead. I tried not to grit my teeth as I turned around.

"Hello, Juliette."

There was something about Juliette that just screamed *trouble*. Maybe it was the feral cast of her otherwise lovely features. Or the almond-shaped eyes that glowed distinctly yellow in the restaurant's dim lighting. Or the short, ever-spiky hair and cheekbones sharp enough to shave with.

Or maybe it was the fact that she was a vampire, the youngest member of the San Diego House's Council, and cars and people both tended to explode in her vicinity.

Yeah, it was probably that last one.

Usually, Juliette had two styles, punk rock chic and borderline indecent exposure, but tonight, she was sheathed in an elegant black dress. The plunging neckline was classic Juliette. The hem, which extended to her knees, was anything but.

She strutted to our table, giving me a sweet smile. That was just as weird as the dress. Juliette's default expression was a smirk. Friendly smiles were almost always precursors to violence. Or humiliation, usually mine.

"Juliette, what are you doing here?"

"Well, John…"

Another warning sign. I could count on one hand the number of times Juliette had called me by name. Usually, it was *little bird* or *moron*.

"You never write, you never call…" Her eyes darted over to appraise my date. "I'm starting to think you don't want this marriage of ours to work."

Well, shit.

ooo

Carly went from bemusement to outrage in three seconds flat. "What? You're *married?!*"

"Oh, I *like* this one, Daddy," cooed Juliette. "Can we keep her longer than our last toy?"

My date seemed dangerously close to having a conniption. "Juliette…"

"Oh, fine." She turned to Carly. "Zip it up, buttercup. Everything is golden and you're having a grand old time."

Just like that, the recruiter lost her scowl and sat back in her chair with a contented smile.

"I hate it when you do that." Fiction had gotten a lot of things wrong about vampires—like that whole sun allergy thing—but one thing our authors had nailed was a vampire's ability to cloud human minds. The People—as vamps unhelpfully called themselves—named it compulsion or glamour. I called it annoying.

"Would you rather I allow our little chickadee to make a scene and go storming off instead?" Juliette's yellow eyes sparkled. "Because that would be hilarious."

I'd rather she hadn't interrupted my date at all but saying so would get me in more trouble than it was worth. It had been months since I'd last seen Juliette—that much, at least, she hadn't been lying about—and I was hoping to get out with my skin and dignity intact.

"I'm just glad she's not a freak like you. One human who can resist compulsion is enough for a lifetime. I hear pixie dust doesn't work on you either?"

"Or goblin tricksiness or whatever it is they're calling it this week." For some reason, I was immune to most of the other species' so-called mind magic. Hell if I knew why, but it was one of the reasons I'd been able to continue in my role as supernatural mediator. That and my winning personality, obviously. "I guess I'm just special."

"That's not the word I was going to use."

"Juliette, it's actually nice to see you again, sort of, but if you hadn't already noticed, *I'm on a date*. Is it too much to ask for some privacy?"

"Sometimes, you're positively adorable. *This* is supposed to be a date? No skydiving? No mosh pit? Are you at least going dancing afterwards?"

Okay, so maybe it wasn't a date by Juliette's standards. But I was half a century younger than she was, and despite my best efforts, dramatically poorer.

"She's in a dress and I'm in a suit." I waved at the city skyline. "We're at an expensive restaurant with a great view. This is a *quality* date. I'm kicking *all kinds* of dating ass."

Carly kept drinking her wine, blissfully unconcerned with the dialogue happening in front of her.

"Maybe you get some credit for the effort," Juliette admitted, "even if it *is* doomed to failure."

"What?"

"You told her you lived with your parents."

The fact that Juliette had been at Mister A's long enough to overhear my screwup was yet another warning sign that slipped right past me.

"That's water under the bridge. We've moved on."

"Sure you have." Juliette turned to Carly. "Honey, why don't you tell Mr. Smith how *you* think the date is going?"

"Of course, Mistress." I suspected it was the first time Carly had ever called someone Mistress. Unless her personal life was way more interesting than she'd been willing to admit online. Her brown eyes sparkled as she looked in my direction. "I think you're cute…ish—" Juliette loudly gagged in the background. "—and a nice enough guy, but we're a terrible match."

"And why is that, chili bean?" Juliette's blood-red lips curved in a predatory smile.

"I'm a grown woman. I have a career and an apartment in the Gaslamp. I'm looking for a man who can keep up with me, personally and professionally. John doesn't seem to qualify. To be honest, I was on the fence about even coming out tonight."

"So, why did you?" I asked, feeling my ego deflate to match my bank account.

"I just got out of a long-term relationship. This seemed like a way to dip my feet back into the dating pool. And you never know; we might have had a spark."

"But instead…" prompted Juliette.

"*He lives with his parents*, Mistress." Carly shook her head.

"So, no conciliatory roll in the hay? Not even a good night kiss?" Juliette's smile only widened as my humiliation continued.

"Not a chance. But the lobster here is amazing. An hour or so of small talk seems like a fair trade."

"Thank you, my dear. Go powder your nose or something." Juliette shooed Carly away and the recruiter obediently headed in the direction of what I hoped was the restroom. The yellow-eyed date wrecker sat down in her place. "You're welcome."

"For *what?*"

"Saving you from the awkward embarrassment of the next hour, obviously. What if you'd tried to kiss her?"

"You don't think *this* was equally embarrassing?"

"Nope. She won't remember a thing she said, and gods know *I've* seen worse from you."

That was sad but true.

"You still haven't told me what you're doing here. You can't possibly have come down from Scripps Ranch just to tell me my internet date was doomed to failure."

I watched the yellow-eyed femmepire—short for female vampire; a linguistic construction I remained justly proud of—mouth the words *internet date*, but she refrained from mocking me further. In fact, she lost her smirk entirely. "First of all, you ran away from the House in July. It's November now and have I gotten a single call? An email? A freaking postcard? Even a *thank-you-Juliette-for-saving-my-life-all-those-times* singing telegram?" Her eyes glowed dangerously.

"Well, no, but I didn't want to get you in tr—"

"Second, you really need to get over yourself. The world doesn't revolve around you."

"What?"

"I didn't come here to speak with you or even to interfere with this pathetic excuse for a date. I came for *dinner*."

"Oh." My persecution fantasies notwithstanding, that almost made sense. "Then why did—?"

"*She*, on the other hand—" She pointed over my shoulder, her smirk making its triumphant return. "—came to speak with you."

It was like that scene from a horror movie, where one of the soon-to-be-dead teenagers stops, turns around, and finds the killer at their back. Except instead of an axe murderer standing behind me, there were two extravagantly beautiful women seated in a prime spot by the window.

The auburn-haired, jade-eyed goddess with the billion-dollar poker face was Lady Anastasia Dumenyova—enigmatic, elegant, and more deadly than Ebola. The other woman, the one Juliette was pointing to, was a golden-skinned blonde whose beauty somehow eclipsed even Anastasia's. She wiggled the tips of her fingers at me and offered a smile that could have chilled a volcano.

"Shit," I breathed. "Lucia."

I'd have preferred the axe murderer.

CHAPTER 2

Queen Lucia Borghesi, Lady of Winter, was the most beautiful woman I'd ever met. She was also the richest and the most arrogant. Like Anastasia and Juliette, she was a vampire. Unlike them, she had a stick the size of an aircraft carrier lodged up her curvaceous ass.

My first supernatural mediation had been on behalf of Lucia's House. Against all odds, I'd succeeded. I'd *also* exposed a traitor within the vampire ranks and helped Lucia's subjects stop a bloody coup in the process.

And then one argument had sent everything sideways.

Next thing I knew, the queen had me pinned to the wall. She'd then gnawed on my throat like a rabid dog and torn her way through my supposedly impregnable mental defenses to make me her human servant.

The only good news was that the process hadn't taken. Not entirely, anyway. A proper thrall spent the rest of their no-doubt-terrible life in service to their master. It wasn't like that for me. A bond had been forged between us, but Lucia hadn't been able to use it to make me do anything.

I was the worst thrall in vampire history. For once, me sucking at something was actually a good thing.

Unfortunately, the queen was also unable to remove the bond. I'd be stuck with her in my head until the day I died. Worse, there was a chance our bond would continue to strengthen over time. If the books were correct, the femmepire might even be able to take sustenance from me *without* blood someday, making me a two-legged battery pack for a woman I'd be happy to see starve.

This early in what promised to be many decades of awfulness, the only thing our bond *did* do was allow us to sense each other's presence. After giving me a month to get over my petty irritation and return to her House's service—her words, not mine—Lucia had used that bond to stalk me across San Diego, trying to force a face-to-face confrontation.

I'd been doing the exact opposite. Whenever I felt the queen coming closer, I'd run like hell in the opposite direction. It had worked for two months now, and there was no way Lucia should have been able to approach Banker's Hill—let alone Mister A's—without me noticing. Unless…

I mentally fumbled about in my head for the sense of her, feeling the first stirrings of hope. Had our bond dissolved on its own? Had my natural immunity finally come to the rescue?

Nope. I could still feel Lucia, like a cold lump (or tumor) in the back of my brain. However, when I tried to get a location or a direction, I felt… nothing. If Lucia had figured out a way to mask her presence, my days of running were over.

I shivered and gave the queen a half-hearted wave of acknowledgment. "You could have warned me she was coming."

"And miss out on seeing that look on your face? Please!" Juliette took another sip of Carly's wine. "Honestly, when the queen invited me on a hunt, this wasn't what I had in mind."

"What does she want? If she thinks I'm going back to the House like a proper thrall, she's even crazier than I thought." I kept my voice quiet, not that it did any good. Private conversations were an impossibility among the People, given that the whole damn species had super hearing.

"Little bird, I don't think you could be a proper anything, except by accident." Juliette smirked, then softened it into a smile. "As for what she wants? Ask her yourself; she's coming this way."

ooo

I turned around yet again and saw that Juliette was right. Lucia moved through Mister A's in a bubble of silence. Conversations stilled, eyes widened, and mouths gaped open as she dropped whatever glamour she'd been using to cloak herself from the masses.

As much as I loathed the vampire queen, there was a part of me that understood the crowd's reaction. Lucia truly was indescribably beautiful, a golden-skinned, platinum-blonde angel with a body right out of a comic book, her jaw-dropping form straddling the borderline between lushness and voluptuous excess. As always, she was wearing white. Tonight, it was a sleeveless silk blouse atop a bandage style pencil skirt that hugged her hips and thighs. Her A-line bob was perfectly styled, hair tucked behind one of her ears to expose no less than three glittering diamonds. Similar stones marked her fingers, and the platinum band around one golden arm. Eyes the pale blue of an arctic sky sparkled invitingly, and raspberry-colored lips slowly spread in…

Wait.

Was that a *smile?* At me? Usually, the queen looked at me like I was a particularly loathsome bug splattered across her windshield.

I waited for Lucia to speak, my clenched fists hidden under the tablecloth, but she turned instead to her spiky-haired femmepire subordinate. "Thank you, Lady Middleton. Perhaps you should go in search of Mr. Smith's date? I would like a moment alone with my thrall." Her voice was cold and clear, the auditory equivalent of fine crystal.

I'm not sure which of us bristled more at the queen's words, but Juliette, at least, was bound to obey. She clamped down on her irritation with obvious effort and stalked off in the same direction Carly had gone.

Lucia took the now twice-vacated seat, her strangely warm smile making a reappearance. "Mr. Smith, I was hoping we could reach an understanding. I come under a flag of truce."

"You're basically *wearing* a flag of truce," I pointed out, distracted by the sudden mental image of a giant waving the white-clad vampire queen about in the air. Did giants even exist? The research I'd done in the past few months had been nebulous on that point. Apparently, even Google didn't know everything. "And us finding an *understanding* seems unlikely when you keep calling me a thrall."

"Why is that? It is what you are."

"Great talk, Lucia. Enjoy your dinner." I started to rise but was stopped by the queen's hand on my wrist. Literally stopped. My imaginary giant would have struggled to break her grip, and *I* didn't even lift weights.

"Sit down, Mr. Smith. I would hate to tear your arm from its socket."

"I'd hate it even more." I dropped back into my seat and waited until she'd let go of my wrist. "Look, I think we've said all there is to say. Can't we just agree to go our own separate ways for the next seven or so decades until I die?"

"That would be a waste of the opportunity presented to us."

"See, every time you say *opportunity*, all I hear is *slavery*."

Lucia's eyes narrowed and a thin film of frost formed over Carly's wine glass in a physical manifestation of her displeasure. Like many of the older vampires, Lucia had a magical ability, called a Talent. Hers involved ice and snow. When she was irritated, temperatures plummeted. When she was truly angry, blizzards were not out of the question, even in San Diego. During the attempted coup, she had frozen several of her attackers solid and then shattered them like ice sculptures.

That had been the moment I stopped referring to her as Lady Snow Cone behind her back. I was an idiot, but I wasn't suicidal.

"Why must you insist on making this a struggle? If you had the decency to behave like a normal thrall, none of this would be necessary! Instead, you invariably perform like an uneducated and poorly mannered monkey!" Her annoyed sigh was a bitterly cold wind on my skin. *This* was the femmepire queen I was used to.

"Members of my House insist that I acted precipitously in claiming you as my thrall," she continued. "I have considered the matter at length and believe they are correct. However, what has happened cannot be undone. The bond between us is an admitted inconvenience, but you *are* this city's mediator. If my House requires your services, I must be able to trust in your willingness to provide them, uncolored by bias due to past squabbles. I have come to you tonight that we might put our unpleasantness behind us." She ended with a smile that would have brought the statue of David to its knees.

I was less impressed. Her calling me an uneducated monkey probably had something to do with it. Just because it was true didn't mean she was allowed to say it.

"*After much thought, Mr. Smith,*" I parroted, "*it has occurred to me that matters beyond my control may have led to an action that could potentially have been somewhat hasty and left us bonded for life, but you know… bygones.* Seriously? Worst. Apology. Ever."

Lucia's control, never solid at the best of times, didn't so much splinter as shatter. Frost coated the table, silverware, and glasses. It occurred to me—far too late, as usual—that, even in the middle of a crowded restaurant, there was absolutely nothing preventing Lucia from killing me.

Maybe I was both an idiot *and* suicidal.

The femmepire queen rose from her chair, like an exceedingly short, white-clad angel of death—

—which was when our waiter arrived, bearing food. He didn't blink at finding Lucia in Carly's place, which told me the queen's glamour was back in full effect. With a bow and a smile, he placed a large, steaming bowl of soup in front of her, heedless of the frost-covered table. To me, he gave a smaller plate, piled high with greens.

I dug in as soon as he left. I even remembered to use the proper fork, despite being well past the point of trying to impress anyone. After one bite, I looked over at Lucia. "I would take it as a personal favor if you waited to kill me until after he brings out my lamb."

The waiter's interruption, coming when it did, had almost certainly saved my life. Lucia's voice was quiet, almost tired. "I did not come to kill you. I have subjects who would happily do so on my behalf. Instead…" She trailed off. "Very well. I apologize. You performed a great service for my House, and it was inconsiderate of me to claim you as my own."

Her Royal Majesty, Queen freaking Borghesi, apologizing to a lowly human? That was something of a stunner. It was also nowhere near as satisfying as I'd hoped it would be. An unbreakable bond went a long way past inconsiderate, and all the words in the world wouldn't change that.

But an apology was better than nothing.

"What about Jee Sun?" I asked, citing the name of the little girl who'd been at the heart of our original argument.

"Lady Middleton explained that the child's value as leverage against Lord Beel-Kasan had been grossly overstated." The femmepire frowned. "The girl has nothing to fear from my House."

"Good." If Juliette, aka the recently titled Lady Middleton, had shared that information *before* I lost my temper with Lucia, we might have avoided the whole confrontation. Of course, the same could have been said of me mouthing off to a room of vampires. Unfortunately, Lucia and I had a way of pushing each other's buttons. Rational thought too often took a back seat with us… when it wasn't left stranded on the curb entirely.

The femmepire queen sampled her soup, glacial blue eyes trained on my face. "I am over four hundred years old, Mr. Smith. I have had a dozen thralls over the centuries, and not a one resented being claimed. In truth, the most trying aspect of the process was choosing from the pool of applicants. Until you."

She seemed confused and a little bit lost. It was a rare moment of vulnerability for the queen, and more devastating than all the low-cut outfits in her wardrobe put together.

"Americans have a thing about freedom," I said. "It's kind of what our country was founded on. That and something about tea, I think. It was different in Italy?" For the first time, I spared a thought about how awful it must have been for her to be stripped of her throne, exiled from Rome, and forced to travel across the world in search of sanctuary.

"It was. However, this is the New World, and like all the long-lived, I must adapt or perish." Eyes glowing like cut sapphires, she extended a golden hand across the table. "Will you accept my apology, and renew your association with my House? I know that the Ladies Middleton and Dumenyova have missed your presence."

My heart did a little backflip at the mention of Anastasia, who'd owned a place in my heart ever since she saved me from crabman assassins during Comic-Con. Even so, I couldn't bring myself to take Lucia's outstretched hand.

"I'll think about it."

The femmepire's expression was equal parts shock and… something darker, bloody, and violent. I hurried to explain myself before that second emotion could take over.

"I appreciate the apology. Seriously. But working for your House again, after what happened last time? That's not something I can just agree to without a lot of consideration. I'll have an answer by Monday if that's acceptable?"

To a woman who was used to having people (not to mention People) jump whenever she snapped her fingers, the delay clearly *wasn't* acceptable, but Lucia nodded anyway. Which was so unlike her that I couldn't help but worry.

"Is there already something going on that needs mediating?"

It was the most logical explanation for the queen's behavior, but she shook her head. "Not at present. A short time ago, there was a minor squabble where we could have used your services, but that situation has since been resolved."

"What happened?"

"What often happens in our world when mediation fails, Mr. Smith," Lucia replied tiredly. "People died."

೦೦೦

I *did* get to eat my lamb. It was every bit as good as I'd hoped, even if my latest and greatest attempt at internet dating had been blown to hell. Lucia ate the soup and lobster Carly had ordered and we had what was, on the surface at least, a nice and relaxed dinner. When she finally took her leave, joined by a silent but always-fabulous Anastasia, I had almost come to peace with the idea of working with the People again.

Given how things had ended in July, that said a lot.

Then the waiter delivered our bill, and I discovered I'd been stuck paying for the meal the ultra-rich vampire queen had just eaten. Worse, Juliette had never come back, so I still had no idea where Carly had gone. I sighed, painstakingly calculated a twenty percent tip, and left to search for the brainwashed technical recruiter.

I wish I could say it was the worst date I'd ever had.

The sad truth is it didn't even crack my top five.

CHAPTER 3

IN WHICH CELL PHONES ARE A
FRATMAN'S BEST FRIEND…

I sat in my Corolla outside Mister A's, caught between frustration and confusion. According to the hostess, Carly had left shortly after emerging from the restroom, and well before the vampires' own departure. If nothing else, that told me she was okay. But it was clear I wouldn't be seeing her again.

The benefits of wearing a suit had apparently been overstated.

As for Lucia? I had a lot to think about, but there were better places to do that than in my car. With a sigh, I pulled onto 5th Avenue. Some cars roared, like the mid-60s Mustang that my friend Mike was constantly working on. Other cars purred, like the ultra-plush Mercedes E class sedans and Escalades the House utilized. Then there was my Corolla, which sounded a little bit like a seventy-year-old man with emphysema. I wish I could say it at least handled well, but it lurched from pothole to pothole like a drunkard after last call as I made my way over and onto 6th Avenue.

I dodged a pedestrian and pulled out my new phone. When I'd found myself flush with cash after mediating for the House, the first thing I had done was pay off my overdue bills. The second thing had involved a trip to the Chula Vista Best Buy. I'd lost my phone during the crabman attack and when I was finally able to replace it, I went all-in. I'd shelled out several hundred dollars for a brand new, top of the line iPhone with a ludicrously large screen, more processing power than it knew what to do with, and a surplus of genuinely enjoyable time-wasting apps, including the one I'd met Carly on. It felt good to finally be part of the modern crowd. After all, it was almost 2014 and the whole world ran on smartphones. I didn't know how I'd ever survived before buying mine.

I looked up just long enough to turn *back* onto 5th Avenue—most streets in downtown San Diego were one-way, making navigation a giant pain in the ass for the tourists—before taking the on-ramp to head southbound on the 5. My parents' home was fifteen minutes away, and I could drive it blindfolded. Or drunk… not that I'd ever tried. With one hand on the wheel, I reviewed my missed text messages. One was from my mom. The other half-dozen were from my friend, Kayla. They read, in order:

7:05PM: luck 2night with C!! B interested! B entertaining!
7:06PM: But don't try 2 hard 2 b funny
7:06PM: Maybe skip being funny at all until 2nd date
7:10PM: D wants u to call when date is over. Hopes 2 hear from u tmrw ;-) ;-)!
7:30PM: Heard L is downtown. Might b hunting 4 u
7:35PM: Def hunting. B careful! Call us!

I did the mental gymnastics required to translate her messages back into English while careening around a battered old pickup truck that was dumping sod and greenery onto the highway. Kayla was another femmepire, the newly promoted Captain of the House Watch. Like virtually every vampire other than Lucia, the Aussie had saved my life once. During the coup, I'd gotten a chance to return the favor.

Granted, all I'd done was take her to Darlene, Kayla's diminutive human firecracker of a girlfriend and blood donor, and the "D" referenced in her texts. On the heroism scale, that ranked slightly above putting on my shoes in the morning and below pretty much everything else. Still, it had sown the seeds of a friendship that survived my estrangement from the House and its queen.

In fact, along with my now-useless bond sense, Kayla and D had been instrumental in alerting me to Lucia's whereabouts for the past few months. They'd also put an insane amount of effort into getting me ready for my date with Carly. That night had seen both projects ultimately fail, but still. They were good people.

I wasn't excited to rehash the night's events, but my friends deserved a response. I cut over into the slow lane and typed out a short message:

9:25: Done with date. No chance of 2nd. Ran into L. Still alive.

There. That seemed sufficient.

It was time to pay attention to my drive home.

Safety first, California!

ooo

I somehow managed to avoid the post-date, motherly inquisition and was headed down to my basement bedroom when my wonderphone rang. I answered it without thinking.

"This is John."

"If you think you can send a text like that and then not follow it up with all the juicy details, then you are an absolute…" Kayla lapsed into a series of Aussie slang words, not a one of which I'd heard before. I looked around for a pen and paper to take notes, but it was impossible to find anything in the disaster zone of my bedroom.

"Are you still there?" the femmepire finally asked, her accent still strong. I could hear Darlene giggling in the background. She loved it when Kayla got on a roll.

"Of course I am," I teased, "I wasn't sure if you were done or just catching your breath."

"That's *exactly* the kind of unfunny joke I hope you avoided on your date," Kayla said tartly. "Anyway, I'm putting you on speaker. We want to hear exactly how things went down."

The retelling took almost as long as the dinner itself, largely because Kayla and Darlene wanted to know every single detail of the night. *How was the restaurant? What did you eat? What was Carly wearing? Upon meeting, did you shake her hand, or give her a hug?* When I reached the point in the date where I'd let my housing situation slip, there was a funereal silence on the other end of the line. It was quickly followed by a whispered conversation that I couldn't quite decipher, although the words *told you* were both intelligible and prominent.

"You don't have to say anything," I grumbled, "Juliette already rubbed it in my face." I shrugged out of my suit jacket and hung it next to the glorious leather jacket I'd inherited from the city's previous mediator.

"So, you *did* run into the Council dinner party? They're not back yet, so I haven't gotten Steve's report." Steve was Kayla's mohawked second-in-command, who had apparently been heading up the security detail for the night's excursion. I liked Steve a lot, and not just because he was ninety percent ninja, but he was still getting a spot on my shit list for having left me to Lucia's tender mercies.

"Run into? That's one way of putting it, I guess. Another would be that Juliette interrupted my dinner, mojoed Carly into telling me exactly why she had no interest in a second date, and then sent her away to, and I quote, *powder her nose.*"

"I hope Carly interpreted that as *go freshen up in the restroom* and not *go find a key of coke and party like it's '85.*"

"Me too, D," I admitted. Not that Darlene or I had been alive in 1985. "I think she's fine though. Whatever happened, she was lucid enough to have already blocked me."

I'd made that discovery very soon after parking my Corolla. "Ouch."

"Yeah." I flopped onto my unmade bed with a sigh. "Anyway, after Juliette dismissed Carly, Lucia dismissed Juliette. Then your lovely queen ate Carly's dinner. And stuck me with the bill."

There was another long pause. "We did try to warn you she was on her way."

"I know, although I would have had a hard time convincing Carly to leave Mister A's. Apparently, it was one of the only reasons she even showed up. Regardless, I'd turned off my phone so I could be *attentive* and *engaged.*"

Those had been just a few of the watchwords drilled into my brain over the past few days by my two friends.

"What about your Spidey sense?" Darlene had never read a comic in her short life but loved superhero movies. The fact that she went to bed every night with a real-life superheroine probably had a lot to do with it.

"I don't know what's going on. I was looking straight at Lucia, but she still didn't show up on my Queendar."

"Well, *that's* not good." Darlene echoed my own sentiment from earlier in the night. "What are you going to do? And what did she say? And did you kiss *anyone* tonight?"

"I have no idea, I'll get to that in a second, and absolutely not." I paused to reconsider the last answer. "Unless you count my mom. She gave me a kiss on the cheek for good luck on my way out."

"You are never getting laid," sighed Darlene.

I resumed my blow-by-blow recap. Juliette's conversation provoked more than a few laughs at my expense, but Lucia's two apologies—both the mediocre pseudo-attempt and the apparently genuine follow-up—were met with stunned silence.

"In my twenty years with this House, I don't think I've ever heard Queen Lucia apologize… for anything," murmured Kayla.

"Maybe that's why she sucks at it? How bad have things been up there anyway? She said something about an incident?"

"Well, yes. We had a little snafu with a tribe of gnomes that were in town just before Halloween."

"Why didn't you ask for my help?" I dimly recalled Kayla being busy that weekend but had assumed it was normal job stuff. I mean, she *was* Captain of the Watch. Her position came with innumerable responsibilities, and her predecessor had been a workaholic. And a perfectionist.

And a traitor, which was how Kayla had inherited the role.

"You'd made it clear you were done working for the House."

"Yeah, because Lucia tried to make me her thrall! But I wouldn't have just sat back and let people die!"

"Whoa! Hold on a second! Who said anything about people dying? It was a business meeting, John. When it became obvious that we weren't going to come to an agreement with the foul-mouthed pygmies, we shipped their arses back to Idaho. I'm sure they'll organize an angry letter-writing campaign in retaliation or something, but violence really *isn't* the gnome way."

"Nobody died?" Lucia was, quite literally, unbelievable.

"That's what I said." Kayla's voice changed. "Have you been drinking, John? Because we're happy to call you a cab. Are you still at Mister A's?"

I shook my head, forgetting that she couldn't see the motion. "I'm home, and I haven't been drinking… much. Let's just say someone may have stretched the truth a bit while trying to make me feel needed."

Silence. Then Kayla spoke. "Oh."

"Oops." That was Darlene.

"Yeah. When magical conscription doesn't work, lies are clearly a queen's next best tactic." I sighed heavily. "Anyway, that was my night. If you ladies don't have any more questions, I'm going to get some sleep. I've got a new case starting tomorrow."

"No worries, John. Do you think you'll still be able to make brunch on Sunday?" I could hear the hopeful smile in Kayla's voice. "We can wander South Park afterward and find you a woman that puts this Carly to shame."

"Someone who *doesn't* mind me living in my parents' basement? That's a big ask, K. Anyway, I'm going to have to skip brunch this weekend. I'll be on stakeout for that new case."

"Sounds exciting!" chirped Darlene.

"If only. I'll bring you along sometime so you can see for yourself, but I start bright and early tomorrow and really need to get some sleep first. You ladies sleep well, okay?"

"Oh, John," purred Darlene, "you're on the phone with two mostly-naked women, who are at this very moment lying in bed together. Do you really think we're going to *sleep*?"

"Yes," I said firmly, conjuring up an image of the two fully clothed in burkas and muumuus. "And I don't want to hear anything to the contrary, or I'll never get to bed."

With much laughter, the two ended the call.

Tomorrow's stakeout was going to be boring, but it would be a day without awkward first dates, manipulative vampire queens, or letter-writing gnomes.

That sounded an awful lot like heaven.

INTERLUDE

I read once that the human body is an amazing thing. Given time and sufficient resources, it can adapt to nearly anything.

My body seemed to be the lone exception; I'd been huddled in the cold darkness for somewhere between ten minutes and thirty years, but it hadn't adapted one bit.

A spontaneous covering of fur would have gone a long way to protecting me from the cold, but my naked skin was just skin— presumably still pale and pudgy, though it was impossible to verify either detail without light or free hands. The extra appendages that would have allowed me to untie those hands or feet had likewise failed to magically appear.

As I continued to lie there in the cold and dark, I came to the sad conclusion that there was equally little chance of my developing phosphorescent eye beams or the ability to teleport like Nightcrawler. That left me with two options. I could wait for someone—probably my captor—to come finish what they had started or I could use the big mouth that God had cursed me with in the hopes of summoning help.

As usual, I went with option B.

"Hello?" My voice was weak and reedy. It had never developed into the rich baritone that sex ed and puberty had promised me, but this was a whole new level of bad. I cleared my throat and tried again.

"Hello? Can anyone hear me?"

In the darkness to my right, something stirred, like Yeats' horrible beast, or a purple polka-dotted people eater.

I really should have stuck with option A.

CHAPTER 4

My alarm rang at the ungodly hour of 6:30 A.M., waking me from a dream that involved three gnomes, whipped cream, and a circus bear in a tuxedo. I rolled out of bed and trudged over to the shower. My new client, Phil Thompsen, worked construction, which required him to be on site by eight, even on a Saturday. And I needed to be at his house sometime before that to set up my stakeout. The crack of dawn was anything but a prime hour for adultery, but if his wife, whose recent unexplained absences had brought Phil to my office, left again, I needed to be ready to follow her.

Really, I told myself, *you should be grateful your date went as badly as it did. At least this way, you'll be on time and mostly rested.*

Because promptness was so much more important than finding love or at least ending my long national nightmare of undesired abstinence.

My parents were still asleep. I poured myself a glass of orange juice from the refrigerator, choked down a slice of bread, and put together a bag of food for later: two granola bars, an apple, and a small bottle of water. My dad had left his camera out for me in the entryway. Beneath it was a note from my mom, asking me to buy eggs on the way back. I tucked that note—and the ten-dollar bill that came with it—into my wallet, grabbed the camera, and headed out into the morning.

We had recently gained an hour thanks to the end of daylight savings, and the sun was already up in the sky. I saluted it, plastic bag in hand, and walked to my Corolla. Mr. Brown, the bitter retiree who lived across the street from us, had complained to the HOA about my car's penis-and-expletives graffiti, so I'd been parking it around the corner. The fact that it was now closer to the house of Ms. Givens, the extremely attractive and not particularly old divorcee, was purely coincidental. Honest.

Sadly, Ms. Givens was still asleep, like everyone else in the neighborhood. I grabbed a large, empty water bottle from my trunk for when nature would inevitably call later that day. That was one of the less glamorous parts of running a one-man stakeout. I'd thoroughly bleached the bottle, of course, but even so… I put my lunch bag in the passenger seat and my pee bottle in the back.

The Corolla only took a couple of tries to start, which made it a very fine morning indeed. I gave it some gas and eased away from the curb.

○○○

The Thompsens were renting a home in North Clairemont, just west of the 805. According to Phil, he and his wife, Melissa, had fallen in love with the neighborhood when they'd moved from Minnesota a few months earlier. Their house was small, only slightly larger than the attached garage, and occupied an equally small plot of land. A short driveway was all that separated it from the street.

I knew I'd stick out like a sore thumb if I parked in front, so I circled the block until I found a spot on the nearby cross street that gave me a passable view of their front door and garage. My vantage point lacked sight lines on the two front windows, but the blinds were down anyway. Besides, I only cared what happened inside the house if someone else showed up. At that point, I'd have to move in for a closer view, and hope that none of the neighbors noticed.

I parallel-parked behind a rusty old truck that, judging by the oil stains beneath it, hadn't been driven in months. Tucking my camera beneath the chair, I put on my sunglasses and crawled over the emergency brake and stick shift to sit in the passenger seat. With my feet extended back across the driver's seat and onto the door's armrest, I looked like someone who had simply pulled over to take a nap.

That was the hope anyway. The last thing I wanted was neighbors calling the police to report a suspicious individual. Thankfully, the Logan Heights gangs had made sure my car fit in well with some of the other beaters on the street.

God bless the recession.

Shortly after my arrival, Phil left for work. He was a big man, headed toward fat, a baseball cap protecting his few remaining strands of hair. Given the picture he'd brought me of Melissa, it was easy to understand why he was worried; she was at least a decade younger and attractive in a rangy, former-cowgirl sort of way.

In my professional experience, that sort of age discrepancy rarely boded well for a relationship. Then again, I was probably biased. By the nature of our business, private investigators didn't run into a lot of happily married couples. Or happy people, in general.

Phil looked around for a minute before climbing into a truck that was a newer, shinier twin to the one I'd parked behind. I tried not to envy the masculine rumble of his truck's engine as I settled in for the day.

Staking out a house isn't difficult. All it takes is a camera, a good vantage point, and superhuman levels of resistance to boredom. It's a lot easier if you bring a co-worker. A second pair of eyes lets you take turns napping. One of you can even leave the car on occasion which helps avoid the indignity of a water bottle urinal.

When I was first getting my agency started, Mike had come on stakeouts with me, but his tendency to bring a six-pack of beer and turn the whole thing into a party had proven counterproductive. Nothing spoils the element of stealth like a two-hundred-and-fifty-pound man yelling drunkenly out the window. His obvious Mexican heritage worked against us too. For whatever reason, people became suspicious when they saw him lurking for hours at a time. It seemed like textbook racism to me, but Mike had called it *an unconscious reaction to his inherent alpha dog status.*

That was my best friend in a nutshell.

I made it almost two hours before my stomach finally woke up with a loud grumble. The first of several granola bars was shoveled into my mouth with the table manners that had my mother sighing and casting her eyes upward in silent conversation with Jesus. Either she was asking him to intercede on my behalf, or she was blaming him for the eternal trial that was her son. Either way, the son of God had never responded, which told me he secretly *liked* a messy eater.

I mentally bumped knuckles with him.

Bros before Moms, J-man.

The problem with granola bars, and the reason I'd put off eating this one, was that they made me thirsty. The problem with being thirsty was that I inevitably had to drink something. And the problem with drinking something was that it hastened my need to use the hand-held urinal, something I still tried to avoid as much as humanly possible. So, when I cracked open my water, the sip I drank was very, very small.

Hours later, I checked the clock, ignoring my growing thirst. Ten past eleven. There appeared to be at least one light on now inside the residence, but the blinds were still down, and I had yet to catch even a glimpse of Melissa Thompsen.

I pulled out my phone, taking the usual moment to admire its gleaming shell. I scrolled past contact numbers for way too many people I hadn't spoken to since high school, found the number I was looking for, pressed dial, and held the phone to my ear. Careful observers would realize I couldn't both be sleeping and on my phone, but I'd yet to see a single person on my cross street.

Plus, I was really bored.

The phone rang once on the other end before a bright, lightly accented voice spoke. "Good morning, Borghesi residence. How may I direct your call?"

Celeste was one of several operators that worked the switchboards at the vampire House. The other I knew of was Akiko. I'd never actually met either of them, but that hadn't kept me from falling in love with both just a tiny bit, whether it was for the French accent that colored all of Celeste's speech, or the way Akiko flirted with me relentlessly, despite already having *two* boyfriends. Both women could have made a fortune as voice actors, but were, like many vampires, already comfortably rich.

I'd be lying if I said that little fact didn't make them even *more* attractive.

"Hi Celeste! Could you please connect me to Lady Middleton's cell?" As Juliette had pointed out, I hadn't called her even once since fleeing the House, which meant I didn't have her cell number—or the number for her land line in the House—programmed into my fancy wonderphone.

"Mr. Smith, is that you?" Celeste purred. "Does this mean you're coming back to us? It's been *so* dull since you left!"

"Celeste, I was there for a week, and during that time, you guys had to fend off an angry demigod, suffer through a room-by-room search of the mansion, *and* fight off a bloody coup orchestrated by the European courts."

"Exactly! And in these last few months?" She sighed, hamming it up for the phone call. "Absolutely nothing of excitement."

Vampires were crazy. That's all there was to it.

"What about the gnomes?"

"Oh, you heard about them? Well, gnomes are gnomes, *non*? Dried up little sticks in the mud. We had them out to the House for a dinner, but it was all so formal I wanted to cry." Like most of the vampires who had flocked to Lucia's banner, Celeste was young—likely under a century in age—and had little patience for the formality of her elders.

"Well, I'm not sure yet if I'll be coming back, but Juliette gave me hell for being incommunicado, so I'm trying to unburn *that* bridge."

"Good luck. She has not been in the greatest of moods since Lucia assigned her Andrés' former duties." Celeste chuckled, and even that somehow sounded French, reminding me of Aurélie, the exchange student I'd mooned over for several semesters in high school. "I can't *wait* to hear how it goes!"

With a quick goodbye, she transferred me to Juliette's phone.

"What?!?" Yeah, Juliette was definitely pissed off about something. In the background, I could hear loud music blaring. It sounded suspiciously like the Sex Pistols' *God Save the Queen*.

"Is that how you *always* answer your phone, Duchess?" Duchess was short for *Duchess of Snark*, a nickname I'd given her several days before Lucia bestowed the more official—and far less creative—title of Lady Middleton.

"Little bird, is that you?" There was a long pause, as she went somewhere quieter, or turned down the music, and then Juliette spoke again. "What kind of trouble have you gotten yourself into?"

"A lowly human can't just call you out of the blue to chat?"

"Seriously… I'm up to my eyeteeth in crap here. Whatever your crisis is, it had better be urgent. And involve lots of bloodshed."

"Juliette," I said soothingly, "I'm not in any trouble." And if I were, I very carefully did *not* add, I'd be calling Anastasia instead. Juliette was wild and crazy and fun, but Ana was, by far, the more capable of the two. She made the Japanese seem inefficient by comparison. "You complained last night that I hadn't called you… so, that's what I'm doing."

"Oh." Another long moment of silence. "Huh."

"I can call back later if you want?" This was not how I'd envisioned the conversation going. I glanced at the Thompsens' house. Still no movement. I could always play a few more games on my phone while I had battery life left…

"Yeah, that might be for the—actually, you know what? Screw it! I'm sick of slaving away on House duties." I could hear a door slam in the background, and then Juliette came back on. "You're practically unemployed, right? Let's go do something."

"I'm on the job at the moment," I said apologetically.

"Seriously? Anastasia hiring you was the best thing that ever happened to your career. It's not the pixies again, is it? Trust me, those winged freaks are a lot less sweet than you might think."

"I figured that out right after one of them swore a blood feud against me for eating a berry off her family shrub." And even then, the pixies had still been way better than the goblins. "Anyway, I'm doing P.I. work. For a human, this time. I'm on a stakeout over in Clairemont."

"Oh." Juliette chewed that over for a while. "That sounds dull."

"You're not wrong."

"Another cheater?"

"I've got a week to find out for sure."

"And you finally got so bored that calling me seemed like the less terrible option?"

"Pretty much," I teased, hoping that Juliette could hear the smile in my voice. She might be less capable than Anastasia, but that still put her in a stratosphere that I couldn't even see with binoculars. "Plus, Kayla and Darlene were busy."

"Asshole!" She laughed, and I breathed a silent sigh of relief.

I would live to torment her another day.

ooo

Juliette and I chatted for an hour before she had to go. Her role in foiling the coup had earned her prestige, but she'd also inherited the duties of Andrés, the Council member slain in the assault. The Duchess of Snark was now responsible for the entirety of the House's human relations, from the outside security they contracted as drivers, to the on-site staff—the maid service, the gardeners, and the garage mechanics. I didn't think she was regretting that change—reputation, to a vampire, was everything—but it was clear she was struggling to find her footing. And the mountains of paperwork were making her irritable.

My absence hadn't helped matters any. I lost count of how many times I had to both apologize and remind her I'd avoided contacting both her and Anastasia for their own good. Kayla was bad enough, but if members of Lucia's own Council had been in touch with me even as I continued to dodge the queen herself? It didn't bear thinking about. The exiled royal had tried to crush my mind just for saying no to her; I didn't want to see what she would do when she felt betrayed.

After our phone call, it was back to the stakeout grind. Foot traffic on my street had picked up, but nobody seemed inclined to call the cops on me. I spent the remainder of the day playing on my phone while keeping one eye on the Thompsens' house. My battery life had dwindled into the low teens by the time Phil returned home. After twelve long hours, my first glimpse of Melissa came when she opened the door and greeted her husband. She was prettier than she'd appeared in the photographs, even dressed simply in jeans and a t-shirt. Her greeting seemed genuine, but I'd never been the greatest judge of human character.

Only time—and a hopeful mountain of billable hours—would tell if Phil's fears were unfounded.

I was on my way home when the man in question called. Apparently, he was going to be one of *those* clients. I reminded him that I would have a full report at the end of the week, but he wanted to know what, if anything I had seen so far. The undercurrent of worry in his voice kept me from being too annoyed. If I were in his situation—which would first require finding someone who wanted to marry me—I'd be desperate for information too.

By the time I ended the call, the sun was starting to set. The freeways were packed with cars; people returning home after a day at the beach, or headed up to Los Angeles, or going downtown to start their Saturday night early. I'd spent my day literally doing nothing, but was exhausted anyway. I stopped at the grocery store to buy some eggs, added a king size Butterfinger, and drove home.

CHAPTER 5

IN WHICH TRIPS ARE TAKEN, SIGHTS ARE SEEN,
AND AN UNEXPECTED VISITOR SHOWS UP

By Wednesday, I was sick of Clairemont. Mrs. Thompsen had left the house a grand total of three times that week, twice to go to Von's for groceries, and once to wander through the closest Barnes & Noble. After the bookstore, she'd eaten lunch at a nearby Panera, where I carefully recorded her selection of a cup of soup and half-salad on the off chance that Phil would ask. The rest of the time, my target had stayed cooped up inside her home.

This was like watching paint dry, except *less* exciting.

On Tuesday, one of the neighbors had finally taken notice of me. Specifically, an old woman who lived on the cross street where I'd been parking. The movement of her white lacy curtains had initially caught my eye. A minute or so later, I glimpsed a round, bespectacled face peeking out through the window in my direction.

I ignored her for an hour or so, but when she checked on me for the fourth time, I decided discretion was the better part of valor and looked for a new place to park. Unfortunately, the spot I eventually chose was located on the Thompsens' far busier street, where the Corolla stuck out like a sore thumb.

By lunchtime the next day, it was a toss-up whether a neighbor was going to call the cops on me or Melissa herself was going to cross the street to ask who I was. I was mentally preparing my *Mom, Dad… I'm in jail* speech when the Thompsens' garage door began to open.

The woman herself backed down the short driveway in her white Jeep Cherokee. The Jeep was starting to show its age but had been detailed recently—on Monday, right after the second Von's trip—and gleamed in the bright sunlight. I waited as she turned toward Clairemont Mesa Blvd., and then pulled away from the curb. Someday, I would have a car that shiny. Maybe a Corolla that had been built in the last decade, even.

I thought back to my failed date with Carly and rearranged my priorities. First, I'd move out of my parents' house. Then, I'd worry about buying a car.

The good part about following someone in San Diego was the sheer number of vehicles on the road at any given time. Unless someone was expecting a tail, it was unlikely they'd notice one car among thousands. The bad part about following someone in San Diego was… well, the same thing, really. It was hard to tail anyone through an ocean of other people. Especially since many of my fellow San Diegans drove like they were late for the birth of a child. I tried to stay close enough to see the Jeep, but far enough away to not be too obvious, a technique I'd gleaned from the spy movies of my youth.

A few blocks to the north, Genesee crossed the 52, a freeway that would take us out of Clairemont for the first time all week. I eased over into the right-hand lane as we neared the on-ramp… and then pulled back into the left lane, as Melissa rolled right past the freeway. Where was she going this time?

"You've got to be kidding me." I watched the Jeep turn into yet *another* shopping center, this one on the corner of Genesee and

Governor. If she was going to the grocery store for the *third* time in five days, I was going to charge Phil hazard pay for extreme boredom.

In the parking lot, a stoner pushed his shopping cart full of Cheetos across the street in front of me. In those old spy movies, Melissa would have taken advantage of our momentary separation and sped out of the parking lot, snickering at the KGB's inevitably shoddy tradecraft. Instead, she parked in front of the Goodwill that took up one entire corner of the shopping center. Walking to the rear of the Jeep, she lifted out two bags of clothes from the trunk. Donations, by the looks of them.

I almost wept, not even realizing the stoner was out of my way until the driver of the Mercedes behind me laid on her horn. It's not that I *wanted* Melissa to be having an affair… it's just that I was *so* bored with the alternative. After five days, even my wonderphone was running out of ways to keep me entertained. I gave the donut shop next to Goodwill a longing glance, but Melissa was already coming back, ready to embark on her next mission of diabolical domesticity.

Plus… I looked down at the slight belly that I seemed incapable of completely banishing. I could stand to lay off the donuts for a day or two. Maybe even all the way to New Year's. My current regimen of three to five crunches a month just wasn't working.

ooo

When Mrs. Thompsen left the shopping center parking lot, she predictably headed back south on Genesee. I checked my clock. Five more hours of surveillance to go, followed by another two days. God help me. I was in the middle of a wild fantasy about blowing off the rest of the day's stakeout—maybe I could convince Mike to leave work early for a beer or seven—when… was that…? Could it be?! Yes, that was Melissa's Jeep, two cars ahead of me, *turning onto the 52!*

I perked up and followed her onto the eastbound freeway, grinning like an idiot. Beer could wait; the game was afoot!

After surviving another of San Diego's typically hair-raising merges, I firmly resolved to never again even *think* that phrase. Sherlock Holmes might be able to get away with foot-related sayings, but I was no Sherlock. More's the pity. Dude had cheekbones like bladed weapons—he and Juliette could have themselves a duel—and he rocked long coats like nobody's business.

Melissa crossed over the 805 and then the 15, putting us squarely into what I considered eastern San Diego. We were still twenty-five miles or so from the ocean, but you would never have known it from the scrub grass and desiccated shrubbery that dotted the hills on either side of the road.

When most people think of California, they think of palm trees, bikinis, and movie stars, or of Silicon Valley, trolleys, and the Golden Gate bridge. Truth is, most of the state is arid and desolate, a desert without the sandy dunes. Just don't call it ugly. Please.

You'll hurt the rattlesnakes' feelings.

The number of cars on the freeway dwindled as we went east, but never reached a point where Melissa's Jeep and my Corolla were the only cars in sight. I tailed her off the highway and into Tierrasanta, where she parked in the driveway of a residence on Portobelo. The house was a clone of its neighbors: over-sized and with only a narrow strip of grass separating it from the next such unit. It always amazed me that people would pay half a million dollars for a house and not care that it had been built on a lot the size of a postage stamp.

Then again, I lived in my parents' basement. I wasn't in a position to throw stones.

Unfortunately, the houses being squashed together made for a serious lack of curb-side parking, even on a Wednesday. I finally just pulled into the driveway of the house across the street, hoping that the absence of cars there signified a corresponding lack of people inside. I threw on the emergency brake and squeezed into the Corolla's back seat with my camera. Taking pictures through a windshield, let alone one that hadn't been washed in a long while, wasn't ideal, but I didn't have the time to explore other options.

I started with a wide shot of the house itself, so I could both record its address and clearly show Melissa's Jeep in the driveway. Then, I snapped a succession of shots as the woman in question walked from her car to the house's front door. Despite being at least thirty-five, she moved with the grace and energy of someone in their early twenties. Phil was a lucky man.

Except for the whole cheating-on-him part.

Melissa rang the doorbell and waited, her relaxed stance at odds with the behavior of someone out for afternoon nookie. Usually, there was some sort of excitement or nervous anticipation. And usually, the cheating spouse wore something other than just jeans and a shirt. Either this affair had been going on long enough for the two to get comfortable or this wasn't what I'd thought it was.

If Melissa had driven all the way out to Tierrasanta for a book club meeting, I was going to be *really* annoyed. Relieved for Phil, but annoyed.

Unfortunately for my client, the man that opened the door didn't seem like book club material. He was closer to *book cover* material, in the age-old tradition of models like Fabio: tall and deeply tanned, with a full beard and long, black hair that had been pulled out of his face but still reached down to absurdly broad shoulders. A thickly muscled chest was displayed to full effect by a white tank top, and those bulging arms were obnoxiously intimidating even from across the road. His features were rough but well-defined.

Some women would probably have found him handsome, but only if they were into rugged manly men who looked like Thor's dark-haired older brother.

The man didn't smile when he saw Melissa, but they clearly knew each other. He ushered her inside with a wave of one arm, and I decided the only way his bicep could be popping like that was if he were consciously flexing it. Which made him kind of a tool.

I felt better about myself almost immediately. Dude was probably a lousy conversationalist too.

I had the whole exchange on camera, but it was a long way from the conclusive evidence that Phil would demand. I was debating whether I wanted to truly live down to my profession's seedy reputation by finding a vantage point with a clear shot *into* the house, when the front door swung back open. The man stepped out, his eyes meeting mine from across the street.

He couldn't possibly have seen me, could he?

Oh. Yes. He could. And had. He strolled unhurriedly in my direction, bearing down on me like a one-man Ragnarok.

That was my cue to leave. I bruised easily and I sure as hell wasn't getting paid to be pummeled by barbarians.

The engine started on the very first try—as if the demigod of gently used Toyotas had heard my plea—and I pulled away with a squeal of tires. When I was around the corner and safely out of sight, I flipped Tierrasanta the bird, and sped away.

I kept an eye on the rearview mirror during my long trip back west, but my keen detective instincts told me I'd made good on my escape. Further surveillance seemed out of the question, so I headed to the office instead to spend the remainder of my day digging up information on Melissa's Wednesday afternoon beefcake appointment. Those were the sort of details that would help pad the report I was going to give Phil.

As the adrenaline faded from my system, replaced with a vague sense of success, I almost felt like a real detective. John Smith, gumshoe-for-hire. I straightened an imaginary fedora and resolved to toss down two fingers of whiskey as soon as I reached the office. Like the fedora, the whiskey would be imaginary. Bourbon was expensive and made me act like an idiot.

Beer, on the other hand… beer was nature's blessing.

My office was on the second floor of a four-story building that squatted like a mangy dog on the least nice street of Logan Heights. At any given time, there was at least one vacancy, and the 'Space Available for Lease' sign in the window had acquired both a layer of dust and a sense of permanence. Without a garage to call our own, parking was a problem; there was plenty of space on the street, but any car left curbside was considered fair game to the gangbangers who occasionally rolled through the neighborhood.

That wasn't a concern anymore with the Corolla—I'd had a Jehovah's witness leave a dollar on the windshield out of pity—so I parked directly in front of the building. I checked my mailbox in the run-down lobby, but it was empty, as usual. The good part about paying my overdue bills was that companies had stopped trying to drown me in threatening letters. The bad part was realizing that those letters had been the only mail I got.

When even the debt recovery agencies don't write or call anymore, life starts to get a little bit lonely.

I shrugged away those dreary thoughts and took the stairs two at a time, whistling something that totally wasn't a song from Frozen. The insurance broker across the hall had already gone home for the day, his shaky work ethic explaining why he was stuck renting office space in Logan Heights. Someday, I'd have my own office tower in La Jolla or downtown. All I needed was time.

And money. A lot of money.

Keys in hand, I went to open my office door, only to have it swing open at a touch. Crap. It was never a good sign when someone broke into my office. A sudden noise from inside told me I might have caught my burglar in the act. I set my dad's camera down in the hall, clenched my fists, and rushed into the office with a roar that was unlikely to scare even the smallest of children.

Case in point: the bespectacled Korean girl sitting in my visitor's chair didn't even twitch at the noise. Her legs swinging for all they were worth, she turned and smiled at me. "Hi, Mr. John!"

CHAPTER 6

IN WHICH THINGS GET HAIRY

"Jee Sun?" I retrieved my camera, stepped into the small office, and closed the door behind me. "What are you doing here?"

She offered a shrug and a blinding smile, dressed in her standard Catholic school girl uniform, even though, to the best of my knowledge, she didn't attend Catholic school. Or school at all for that matter. She was somewhere between five and ten years old, but her behavior made it hard to be sure. This was the first time I had ever seen her without her guardian.

"Where's Bill?"

Jee Sun jumped down and skipped over to me. Over her uniform, she was wearing a slightly faded red cape with a stylized yellow S on it. That cape flowed behind her in a nonexistent breeze, one of the many troubling details about her that I tried not to pay too much attention to. She handed me a piece of paper that had been folded roughly ten billion times and retreated to the chair. I unfolded the note to find a message written in green crayon:

Howdy-doody, AMIGO!
I will be OUT OF TOWN for a few
MICKEY ROTATIONS, and need you

TO WATCH Tiny Flower for me!
She likes ice cream BEST and
DOES NOT LIKE squirrels <u>AT ALL!</u>

-Yours in Love,
Bill

"AT ALL" had been underlined five times with crayons of a different color.

Bill was short for Lord Beel-Kasan, Demigod of Nightmares, Terror, and Vindication. *Tiny Flower* was one of his many nicknames for the girl sitting in my office. In my mediation for the vampire House, Bill had been the second party. To most people, he appeared in the shape of whatever their greatest fear might be, but I saw him as a seven-foot-tall asparagus, with two pieces of coal for eyes, a carrot nose, and a mouth that had been drawn on with magic marker.

I had no idea if that was his natural form or not. He'd been vague on that front—and pretty much every other front—when questioned. Bill was at least a few screwdrivers short of a toolbox, but during our initial meeting, and for reasons known only to him, the demigod had taken a liking to me.

In the time since, we'd gotten drunk together, sipped milkshakes on his boathouse, and even watched old Winnie the Pooh episodes with Jee Sun. Most recently, he had pitched in on an investigation, looking into a goblin's impossible nightmare. While he and sanity were distant acquaintances, he remained, in his own nutty, frequently terrifying way, my friend.

I looked up from the note to find Jee Sun back in her chair, now sipping from a fruit punch Capri-Sun. "Bill's gone away for a few days?"

"Yes, Mr. John," the little girl confirmed with a small pout, her dark eyes enormous behind the thick lenses of her plastic-framed glasses. "Gehenna went boom." She waved the Capri-Sun around as she pantomimed an explosion, sending droplets of flavored juice across the carpeted floor of my office.

I stared at Jee Sun, at a rare loss for words. Gehenna was Bill's private hell dimension, a land of red sand and purple storms, absent of any free-standing structures beyond the fields of human candelabras. I didn't want to even hazard a guess what *Gehenna went boom* might mean. Or how it could have happened. How long would Bill be gone for? And what was I supposed to do with Jee Sun in the meantime? The last thing my life needed was another complication.

A knock on the hallway door told me that I had a visitor… and that God had a twisted sense of humor.

Which God?

Every damn one of them, as far as I could tell.

ooo

There had only been one knock, but I could hear someone waiting in the hallway. How they'd made it to my office at all without being buzzed in was a real question. I was starting to lose faith in the building's security.

Jee Sun was back to work on her juice, drinking it loudly through the small plastic straw. With a shrug, I opened the door and took two quick steps back as Thor's dark-haired cousin pushed his way into my office.

The first thought that went through my brain was worry that he'd somehow seen me flip him off as I drove away, but right after that was the question of how he had found me, and what he was doing here.

"How can I help you?" I still had a slim hope that this was all an unfortunate coincidence.

"You can start by telling me what you were doing outside my house today, Mr. Smith." His answer pretty much shredded that small hope, but I wasn't going to give up so easily.

"House? I'm afraid you must be mistaken."

"Yes, and I'm sure that's not your Corolla downstairs either, with the license plate 4CP…" He rattled off my license plate number without the use of a cheat sheet or anything. Bastard. *I* couldn't even remember it, half the time. "And that there's another person who looks exactly like you and drives that car in San Diego."

"Ohhhh," I replied, pasting a happy grin on my face. "You must be looking for my twin brother, John." I pointed back at the door. "I don't know how, but you *just* missed him. If you hurry—"

"You're so silly, Mr. John!" chirped Jee Sun.

"Drink your juice, sweetie." I turned back to Thor. "Look, I'm not sure who you are, but this is private property, and I'm going to have to ask you to leave."

"Not until you answer my question." He brushed past me and took a seat in the executive chair behind my desk with the confidence of a man who both owned *and* used a gym membership.

It was clear I was going to have to throw him out.

A voice in my head snickered. I couldn't even *think* that with a straight face. Thor was only a little bit taller than I was, but we looked like the before and after pictures of a bodybuilder's Instagram, and I was not the aspirational photo in that pairing.

With a sigh, I took a seat in the second of my two client chairs. Jee Sun had finished her juice and was now fiddling with the pleats in her knee-length wool skirt. I met Thor's implacable gaze. "I'm a private investigator, Mr. Too-damn-rude-to-give-me-his-name. I'm sure you understand that both the nature of my investigation and the identity of my client are confidential."

"So, my husband *didn't* hire you to follow me around town?"

I looked to my right and found Melissa Thompsen stepping through the doorway. She looked unamused.

I eyed the exit wistfully but refused to be chased out of my own office. Mostly because they would have caught me if I tried to escape; Phil's wife looked like a runner.

On the bright side, my office only had three chairs, all presently occupied, so Melissa had to stand. Vengeance was petty, but it was all I had at that moment.

The silence lengthened uncomfortably before my visitors realized I wasn't going to answer the question. Thor spoke again. "Mr. Smith, the relationship between Mrs. Thompsen and myself isn't what you think it is."

"I can't tell you how many times I've heard *that* one, Mr. Still-anonymous-and-kind-of-pissing-me-off."

"No doubt, but this time it's tr—" I assume he was going to say *true*, but something flew through the air and struck him in the head. The projectile bounced off his cheek and onto my desktop, and I recognized the wadded up remains of a Capri-Sun. I looked to my right, where Jee Sun was on her feet, dark eyes wide and angry, one arm outstretched and pointed at the other man.

"Red!" she shouted.

I looked down at Jee Sun. "Red?"

She nodded, jutting her chin out pugnaciously, and then spun to face Melissa in the doorway. "Red!" she cried again, pointing at the confused woman.

Thor looked bemused. "Mr. Smith," he asked carefully, "would you please tell your daughter to settle down?"

Jee Sun responded in time-honored fashion, extending both middle fingers in the man's direction. Being raised by Lord Beel-Kasan had left its mark on her, but it was still better than the alternative. Bill was a seven-foot-tall, insane, immortal, asparagus demigod, but it was Jee Sun's real father who had been the monster. His body was one of those permanently mounted on candelabras in Gehenna. When it came to vindication, Bill subscribed to the original definition—revenge—and he did not mess around.

"She's not my daughter," I said absently, my thoughts racing. I looked from Thor to Melissa and back, gaze speculative. Jee Sun was special in a lot of ways, but the most distinctive was that she saw supernatural species as specific colors. If Thor and Melissa were both showing as red … "What are you?"

"I beg your pardon?" That was from Melissa, who crossed the room to join the other man. They kept a careful distance from one another, the sort of spacing you might see with strangers, or co-workers. It *really* didn't fit the narrative of them being lovers.

I shrugged and ticked off the possibilities on my fingers. "You're not human. You're not vampires. You're not immortals. You're *clearly* not pixies or goblins. So, I'll ask again: what are you?"

"How could…" Melissa's voice trailed off. I watched her flesh ripple, as if something stirred underneath. Gross.

"Ah," murmured Thor. "You're *that* John Smith? The one who replaced the Rook as San Diego's mediator?"

"I am," I said, feeling just a bit smug. Four months on the job, and I was already famous.

"I don't understand. Who is the Rook? What mediator?"

He turned to Melissa. "It goes back to the history you've been learning. Remember the Toulon Concordat? One of its provisions is that we make every effort to avoid outright war in our world." By *our world*, he clearly meant that of the supernatural. "Mediation is one of the proscribed tools for doing so." He eyed me with a fresh consideration. I found it especially unnerving now that I knew he wasn't human.

"But why would a *mediator* be following me?"

"Well," I explained, "I'm *also* a private detective. The whole mediation thing is kind of a side business." I gave the two of them my best hard-eyed stare. "So, you two really *aren't* having an affair?"

Melissa drove her fist a solid inch into the heavy wooden surface of my desk. Yikes. "I love my husband, whatever you and he might think," she growled, her skin rippling again. The color drained out of her dark eyes, leaving them as pale as dried bone.

Jee Sun carefully retreated behind me, Supergirl cape tucked around her like a blanket. I don't think the little girl realized that I was every bit as mortal as she was. In her mind, bigger meant stronger.

Sadly, I was the exception to that rule.

"Melissa," said Thor, capturing the woman's gaze. "Calm yourself. Remember your breathing."

She took several deep breaths, shaking her head slowly as if to clear it. Her eyes reverted to their usual brown. Her skin stopped rippling like Jell-O. Color stained her cheeks when she saw the fist-sized dent she'd left in my furniture.

"As you've somehow discovered, Mr. Smith," the other man continued, as if nothing had happened, "we aren't human. We are members of the San Diego Pack."

I ran over the possibilities in my head. When I first learned that humanity had company, I had quizzed Anastasia and Juliette about what else was out there. And in the months since, I'd done my own research. Pack sounded like… "Infected?"

He grimaced. "That is not a label we care for. Especially those of us who are naturally born, rather than turned."

"Would you prefer werewolf?"

He shrugged his broad shoulders and ignored my question. "Mrs. Thompsen came to me for help in controlling the beast. Our relationship is—" He smiled, his teeth shockingly white against his tan, "—strictly professional."

Melissa took up the story. "I was attacked and turned a few months ago, back in Minnesota. When we moved to San Diego, I looked to the local pack for aid. Davis has been working with me for the past month."

Davis? I eyed the burly werewolf.

"What?" he growled.

"Nothing. You just look more like a Brutus to me. Or maybe an Igor." I smirked, then looked to Melissa. "So, your husband doesn't know…?"

"That I'm no longer human?" She shook her head, dark hair swaying with the motion. "It's not the sort of thing you discuss over dinner."

I nodded. The majority of what I knew about werewolves came from books and movies. If real-life vampires were any indication, that information was wildly inaccurate, but my experience with San Diego's creepy crawlies told me that this wasn't the time or the place to educate myself. Instead, I tried to figure out how to handle my very first ethical dilemma as a private investigator.

Honestly, I'd been waiting for just this sort of thing to happen. The werewolves were a new touch though.

I waved to the chair Jee Sun had vacated. "Would you like to sit down, Mrs. Thompsen?" As she did so, I quirked an eyebrow at Davis. With an easy grin, he stood, and we changed seats. I felt better almost immediately back on my side of the desk.

Past the werewolves, Jee Sun had forgotten us and was now rummaging through a black duffel bag almost as large as she was. Inside, I could see a stack of schoolgirl uniforms, in addition to various Marriott-branded articles. Everything a little girl might need for a prolonged stay. Awesome.

"Okay," I continued, once we were all seated again, "I think we need to figure out where to go from here."

"I'd say the solution is obvious. Tell Mr. Thompsen that his concerns are misplaced."

"It's not that easy, dude."

"I understand," Davis acknowledged, "but I'm sure we could agree on a dollar figure to compensate you for the difficulty."

"It's not about the money," I started to say, but the date with Carly was still fresh in my mind. "Exactly how much money are we talking about?"

Before he could respond, I waved him off, already feeling guilty. "Sorry. Unprofessional. Forget I asked."

I turned to Melissa. "By the time someone comes to me, they're already pretty sure their spouse is having an affair. I might be able to tell Phil otherwise, but he's still going to want to know where you've been going." I gave her a pointed look. "Your husband is not blind."

"I know he isn't. Stubborn as an old goat, but not blind." She sighed. "What do *you* think I should do then?"

"I'm not really a solutions guy," I admitted, "but have you thought about maybe... just telling him the truth?"

The reaction was swift. Davis sprang to his feet in one sinuous motion. If I hadn't already known he was inhuman, that alone would have proven it. A man his size simply shouldn't have been able to move like that. His bark of dissent was echoed by that of Mrs. Thompsen, who had also leaped to her feet.

Jee Sun straightened up from where she'd been digging through her bag. The handgun she pointed at Davis' back looked ludicrously huge in her tiny hands.

I stayed in my seat... partly because my desk offered some degree of protection, and partly because my own attempt to stand would have just looked slow and clumsy by comparison. I ignored the two angry werewolves and spoke to the young girl behind them. "Jee Sun, honey. Please put the gun down."

She did so slowly and with the greatest of reluctance. When held at her side, the weapon's barrel almost scraped the floor. I couldn't believe she'd even been able to lift the thing. God only knew what the recoil would have done if she'd fired it.

At my words, Melissa and Davis had both spun around to look at Jee Sun and were only now turning back to me. Melissa looked horrified… Davis, bemused. "Where on earth did you find this girl?"

I waved off the question, taking some measure of satisfaction in his frustrated growl, and looked at Melissa. "It's your relationship, not mine, but this seems like the sort of secret that could destroy a marriage."

A thump interrupted us all, and we looked to find that Jee Sun had dropped the gun at her own feet. Thankfully, it hadn't discharged in the process. The little girl was back to digging through her bag. Whenever the werewolves left, she and I were going to have a long talk about gun safety.

"You're right," said Melissa. She looked at Davis, the emotion naked on her face. "It's my marriage. I didn't leave Phil when it happened; I don't want to drive him away either."

"Telling him the truth might do just that," he rumbled in response.

"I know."

"And if that happens, he will know about us," Davis continued implacably, "which would make him a threat to the pack."

"He wouldn't be the first divorcee to claim his ex-wife was a monster," I interjected, "but I have a few ideas on that front."

Both werewolves took their seats, and we began to hash out exactly how to proceed. Whatever might happen, I took comfort in one thing; my days staking out the Thompsens' home were officially over.

CHAPTER 7

IN WHICH MISERY SEEKS COMPANY AND
HOME IS WHERE THE BEER IS

It took about twenty minutes to formulate a plan that everyone could be satisfied with. Melissa left immediately after, but Davis didn't seem to be in any hurry to go. Instead, he lurked by my office door, watching as I re-packed Jee Sun's duffel bag and cleaned up the half-dozen messes she had somehow already managed to make.

His continued presence was irritating—and not just because I lacked the physical ability to evict him. It felt… judgmental, somehow. It wasn't *my* fault that Jee Sun was a walking disaster zone in size two shoes. By the time she was ready to go, fully packed and wearing her jacket—an oversized, pink satin thing that looked like a relic from the 1950s—I'd had just about enough of our werewolf intruder.

"Is there something else you need, dude?" I hoisted Jee Sun's duffel bag with one arm and took her hand in mine with the other. As far as I was concerned, office hours were over. I'd somehow been shanghaied into being the 'neutral party' at Melissa's official werewolf coming-out party the following afternoon, which meant I'd swapped a boring stakeout for what might be a first-row seat to the end of a marriage.

Not to mention the very real possibility that, should Phil react badly to his wife's confession, Melissa would snap, transform, and eat us all.

"This isn't the greatest of neighborhoods," I continued. "If you're parked out front, you've got about two minutes before someone steals your hubcaps."

The big man flashed another dazzling smile. "I think my car will be fine, John. There's something I wanted to discuss with you."

I made a show of looking at the bag in one of my hands and the girl holding onto the other one.

"Why don't I walk the two of you down?" he suggested. "We can speak of it on the way."

Traveling any distance with a small child is… a learned skill. Thankfully, it was one I had mastered over the many years of visits from my little cousin. I carefully shepherded Jee Sun to the stairwell, Davis pacing beside us. The werewolf didn't offer to help.

Some people have no manners whatsoever.

"So, what was it you needed?" I asked as we started down the stairs.

"I might have a job opportunity for you, actually."

I perked up immediately. Lost in all the hubbub about Melissa's marriage was the minor question of whether I'd get to keep my advance. After all, I'd only worked five of the seven days that Phil was paying me for. If their reconciliation went poorly, I could easily see him wanting at least some of that money back. And that was both sad and a potentially devastating blow to my dreams of residential independence. "What sort of job are we talking about?"

"A mediation."

My inner child pumped his fist in glee. I started thinking about the color of paint I'd request for my future apartment's walls. Maybe eggshell. What color was that anyway? Yellow? White?

"Should I set up an appointment to come back here to discuss the details?" He held the front door open so that Jee Sun and I could exit. Between that bare slice of courtesy and the possibility of a lucrative contract, I found myself warming to the burly werewolf. Sort of.

"Actually," I countered, "if you meet me at the Thompsens' house tomorrow, you could support your packmate *and* we could discuss this other case afterward." Inside, I snickered. Misery does love company.

Davis frowned, beard bristling, but I hadn't left him a graceful way to decline, and he seemed unwilling to admit to outright cowardice. Sucker. "That would work," he admitted.

"Awesome!" My odds of survival would rise dramatically with Davis there to talk Melissa out of eating her husband and his well-meaning private detective. I walked to my battered Corolla. A gleaming black Dodge Ram was parked just behind. "Is that yours?"

At his nod, I deposited Jee Sun and her bag into my car, and wandered closer, surprised that the local gang had left his vehicle undisturbed. It must have been a street holiday or something. "Nice truck. What sort of mileage—?"

I jumped back as two hundred pounds of slavering, growling beast tried to force its way out through the window to get to me.

"Holy shit!" I picked myself up off the sidewalk, keeping a careful distance from the vehicle. Inside, an enormous, black-furred animal prowled about on the passenger seat, watching me with malevolent eyes. It was either the largest dog I'd ever seen or...

I turned to Davis, who was watching me without even trying to disguise his amusement. Bastard! "Is that..." I stopped, at a loss for words or intelligible gestures. "You know..."

"A dog?" He smiled that easy grin of his. "Yes, Mr. Smith, it is." He took a step past me and gently rapped his knuckles on the window. Fido the demon dog immediately quieted. "Werewolves are much, much larger."

"I see." I took a careful step further away from the werewolf and his dog. "What's his name?"

"Brutus."

Of course it was.

○○○

Once Davis had finally departed, the only question left was what I was going to do with Jee Sun. During my brief conversation with the werewolf, she had climbed from the back seat of my car into the front and was rooting through the glove compartment.

"Jee Sun, shouldn't you ride in the back sea—?" She looked up at me with her usual slightly off-kilter smile, and I sighed. "Never mind. Buckle yourself in." She did so, turning back to her exploration of the random junk and papers I'd stuffed away and forgotten over the years. "Let me know if you find any money in there."

I started up the Corolla, listening to make sure the emphysema-stricken wheeze of its engine hadn't worsened in the past hour. "Is there a reason Bill brought you to me, instead of having me come to the boat?" Bill and Jee Sun lived on a small yacht moored in the San Diego harbor. The boat's cabin was surprisingly homey, even if a good portion of the cabin furnishings—in addition to the glassware, robes, and towels—had been stolen from the nearby Marriott.

"Mr. Bill took the boat with him," she said cheerily, chewing on a strand of her hair.

"To Gehenna?!?"

She giggled in response but said nothing.

Apparently, we wouldn't be crashing on the houseboat. I'd already dismissed my office as a suitable spot for Jee Sun to stay, and Mike's girlfriend, Suzanne, was still holding a grudge against me for our most recent all-nighter. That left only one option. I took off the parking brake and pulled into the street.

"Tiny Flower," I murmured, "it's time to meet the parents."

Introducing Jee Sun to my parents was the last thing I wanted to do. There are some things that you just know won't end well. I spent the entire drive to Chula Vista fabricating increasingly ridiculous strategies to sneak her in past my parents, but when we arrived at my house, I was still lacking a plan. A workable one, anyway.

I parked in my usual spot around the corner and took both the little girl and her bag in hand once more. A quick—and no doubt subtle—glance to my right determined that the lovely Ms. Givens remained out of sight. Pity. Maybe she would have been up for a short-term adoption.

The walk to my house took almost five minutes, which was—sadly—about average speed for little kids. The lights were off, and my parents' minivan was nowhere to be seen. That seemed entirely *too* convenient, until I remembered that it was Wednesday. My dad would be playing in his over-forty intramural basketball league. My absence would be both noted and commented on, but that was par for the course. There were few things more depressing than being one of a handful of spectators watching—and sporadically cheering for—out-of-shape, middle-aged men struggling to make it up and down a basketball court.

Even worse were the times when some of the players *were* in shape. There's nothing like having someone your father's age make you feel bad about your own conditioning.

I unlocked the front door and ushered Jee Sun inside. We had at least an hour before my parents returned, so I abandoned my original plan to smuggle her into the basement, and instead took her to the kitchen. The refrigerator was well stocked, as always. I pulled out the cold cuts and bread and began making myself a sandwich. Jee Sun plopped down on top of her duffel bag and looked up at me with big eyes.

"Are you hungry?"

She nodded, and I opened the refrigerator door again.

"Well, you can have anything in here that looks good to you." After a long pause, during which chilled air escaped into the house, I prompted her further. "Does anything look good?" She nodded happily, but still didn't budge. "Okay then… *what* looks good?"

"Burgers!" she said excitedly, clapping her hands together.

"Uhm." I took another careful inventory of the refrigerator. "We don't have any burgers, sweetie."

"Ice cream!" That cape of hers was doing its weird flapping-in-the-nonexistent-breeze thing yet again.

"How about a cheese sandwich?" I countered. She thought about that one for a while before finally agreeing. My all-too-frequent abstinence over the past… well, twenty-five years… suddenly seemed less dire. At the very least, it meant I wasn't going to have to worry about fatherhood any time soon.

Intramural basketball league or no, I breathed a sigh of relief once Jee Sun and I were safely ensconced in my basement bedroom. I still had no idea how I was going to keep her presence a secret from my parents—particularly given my mother's near-supernatural ability to divine everything that ever happened in my life—but that was a problem for another day. For now, my stomach was comfortably full, Jee Sun was watching Nickelodeon on my television, and things were peaceful. There was no point in ruining that peace with idle speculation.

"Are you okay over there?" She nodded without taking her eyes off of… whatever it was that SpongeBob was doing. "Okay then." I grabbed the now well-worn copy of <u>Success as a Mediator for</u>

<u>Dummies</u> from my bedside table and flopped down onto the bed. "I'm going to just read for a while. If you need anything, let me know."

ooo

When I woke up, the blinking digits on my alarm clock informed me that several hours had passed. SpongeBob had been replaced by Uncle Jessie from Full House… and Jee Sun was nowhere to be found.

Damn it.

I rolled out of bed and my half-read book tumbled to the floor. I should have known better than to study on a full stomach. If something happened to Jee Sun… my mind conjured up images of giant mushroom clouds and a Pacific Ocean the color of blood. My friendship with Bill only went so far.

I double-checked my bedroom and the adjoined bathroom, but the little girl wasn't there. So, I triple-checked. Still nothing. I cautiously crept up the basement stairs. As I reached the hallway door, I heard voices. My parents had returned while I was sleeping. I straightened up, assumed my best 'no, I didn't misplace a little girl, because there was no little girl' pose, and headed for the living room.

"There you are, John," said my mother, looking up with a smile. Jee Sun sat next to her on the couch, scribbling with a black crayon on a sketchpad. From where I stood, it looked like she was drawing a series of meaningless loops and swirls. Or a black bear in a dark cave at midnight… it was impossible to be sure. "Did you have a nice nap?"

"Uhm… yes?" There was a trap there. I could sense it.

"I'm glad to hear it. I've just been talking to…" she broke off, and patted Jee Sun's hand. "What was your name again, dear?"

"Jee Sun!" came the response, although the girl in question didn't look up from her sketchpad.

"Yes… Jee Sun. A delightful little girl." My mom's eyes sharpened, like missile guidance systems locking in on their target. "Is there something you forgot to tell us?"

"She's not mine, Mom," I rushed to reassure her. My mother was still a few years away from pressuring me about grandchildren, but that would in no way lessen her wrath if I had been hiding one from her all this time. "A friend of mine had to go out of town for a few days, and he asked me to watch Jee Sun."

"A friend?"

"Yes. Uhm… you don't know him, but his name is Bill."

"Mr. Bill!" chimed in Jee Sun.

"So, she'll be staying with us then?"

I nodded.

"Did Bill give you power of attorney, in case anything goes wrong?"

Power of *what?*

I might as well have said the words out loud.

"I see. Well, you'll want to give him a call then to have him do so. Better safe than sorry."

"Right." I did, in fact, have a number for Bill, but I highly doubted he could get a signal in an entirely different dimension. AT&T barely even worked across county lines. "That's what I figured."

"Hmm." My mom glanced over at Jee Sun again, and then rose from the couch. Her long multicolored skirt—one half of what my dad always referred to as her artsy outfit—swooshed audibly with every step she took toward me. In function, if not form, the noise was eerily reminiscent of the theme music to Jaws.

She took me into the hallway, where her pale green eyes—one of the few physical traits we shared—stared earnestly into my own. "John, honey… you know your father and I love you, right?"

"Sure." That much had never been in doubt. Which made me luckier than most of my classmates, growing up.

"And you know you can tell us anything, and we're not going to stop loving you?"

"Mom," I groaned, "*she's not my daughter.*" Parents never listened.

"That's not what I'm talking about, dear." My mom was eight inches shorter than me but had a way of looming that could made her seem ten feet tall. She was doing it now, and I worried that her head would brush the ceiling at any moment.

I fled for the kitchen. It was time for some liquid courage.

I managed to snag a beer from the refrigerator before being herded to the dining room table. My mother pointed to a chair with one imperious finger, lowering it only after I had taken my seat like the dutiful son she kept asking Jesus for. She sat on the other side of the table, gaze intent upon my face.

I steeled myself for whatever it was she wanted to talk about. We'd never had the birds and the bees discussion, but she had to realize I'd figured that stuff out, right? More or less, anyway. I hadn't received any complaints, but I hadn't had a lot of repeat business either. Regardless, wasn't the sex and pregnancy talk a father's responsibility? Speaking of which…

"Where's Dad?" Rule number twenty-seven for resisting parental interrogations is *change the subject.* And if that doesn't work, change it again.

"He's taking a shower."

"I'm sorry I couldn't make it to the game," I told her, placing the cold beer bottle on a coaster. "I was busy with work again. Did they win?"

"You can ask him about it when he comes down, John. I'm sure he'd like that. But first, you and I are going to finish our conversation."

My mother could teach the KGB lessons in focus. "Sorry, Mom. I'm not sure what it is you want to talk about." I reached for my beer, but she swiped it before I could get there.

"I want to know what's going on with you!" She took a long sip of beer and sighed at my confused expression. "Ever since your father and I came back from Las Vegas this summer, you've been acting weird. Weirder than normal, I mean. Now, you're watching a little girl for a friend I've never even met? It feels like you're hiding things from us."

Me? Acting weird? Hiding things? Whatever could she mean? I certainly wasn't going to explain that their 'free' Vegas trip had been paid for by the vampire House, to get them out of the city while I handled the mediation between Lucia and Bill. Nor was I going to tell them that their hometown of San Diego hosted all manner of ghosts, ghouls, and goblins. That was *at least* a three-beer conversation.

"You're not… doing drugs, are you?"

"What? No!" I gazed at her in injured disbelief. "Hell no!"

"John Smith, I will not have you blaspheming in my house!" She took another sip of my beer. "If it's not drugs, then what are you keeping from us?"

"I don't know what to tell you, Mom," I lied. "Business has picked up, but I don't really—" A thought occurred to me. "Wait… you're not *still* upset that I didn't tell you what happened on my date, are you?"

"I'm your mother, John!" She growled, as fierce as any werewolf or vampire. "I deserve to know these things!"

I didn't want to relive my humiliation with Carly—even if I got to gloss over the vampire parts of it—but if it would distract my mom from asking about all the other oddities in my life, I was willing to make the sacrifice. My parents' ignorance about the supernatural world was one of the only things keeping them safe from it. As safe as any of us could be, anyway, in a world where humans were at the very bottom of the food chain.

"You win, Mom." I held out my hand, and she reluctantly passed the beer bottle back over. "So, I met Carly at Mister A's…"

INTERLUDE

I did my best to recoil from the shuffling, slavering hell beast sharing the darkness with me, but mostly I just ended up repeating my award-winning impression of a flopping fish. Which was when I remembered reading that predators were often attracted to noise and motion.

Well, shit.

That same article had said something about animals using their natural defenses to scare away those predators. Lacking anything that would work as a weapon, and very much aware that my dude-parts were dangling in the nonexistent breeze, I gritted my teeth against the pain in my shoulder, and once again opened my mouth.

"I hope that, whatever you are, you understand English, because I've got you dead in my sights with the biggest, baddest—"

I struggled to recall a gun model, any gun model, but struck out. I really wasn't great under pressure. Or naked.

"—gun," I finished lamely, "and will blow you sky high if you even twitch."

"Little bird," came a tired voice from the darkness, "what the hell are you talking about?"

"Juliette? Thank God. Help me out here."

I heard her move again, but it was impossible to see her. Still, if the noise was any indication, she wasn't getting any closer. When she shifted a third time, I heard another sound, deep and heavy.

Clink.

Clink.

My heart sank.

"Duchess… are you in chains?"

CHAPTER 8

I'd been woken up by hungry vampires. I'd been woken up by my dad, who was, in a crime against nature, a morning person. I'd even been woken up by the sound of someone puking in my shoe. But nothing in my life prepared me for being woken up by Jee Sun.

"Mr. John! Mr. John!" I cracked an eye open, and through sheer willpower, cast it skyward. *Gah!* An enormous brown eye stared back at me, separated from my own by thick plastic and mere millimeters of open space. As I watched, that eye retreated and the rest of Jee Sun's face came into view. A small knee dug into my ribcage. "Breakfast time!"

"Guh."

Apparently, that one syllable was sufficient to communicate that I was awake and would be upstairs shortly; Jee Sun jumped down to the carpet. She had acquired a yellow bow at some point, the ribbon almost lost within her thick black hair.

"We're having toast!"

"Awesome." I scrubbed my eyes and yawned. "We didn't get a chance to talk about it last night, but I want you to know: you're safe here. My parents are good people and would never do anything to hurt you." I wasn't sure how much Jee Sun remembered of her life before Bill, but it was something that needed to be said.

"Of course not, Mr. John," she replied happily. "Mr. Bill would destroy them if they did!"

With a bright smile, she scampered up the stairs.

ooo

I had just finished my shower when I heard heavy footsteps on the basement stairs. My dad called down to me. "John, are you up? You've got a *visitor.*" He put a special emphasis on the last word, the sort of emphasis that told me—and anyone with ears and half a brain—that my visitor was both female and attractive. At my mumbled acknowledgment, he shuffled down to see me.

My dad is… my dad. John Smith the sixth, internet neophyte, accounting nerd, and devoted husband. From him, I'd inherited a mop of unruly brown hair, a reasonably cheery disposition, and a love of Star Wars. There was some question as to whether that last bit was genetic or just a result of prenatal brainwashing—my mother claimed the score for A New Hope was on constant rotation while she was pregnant—but that was a debate best left to the historians and scientists.

Thursday was the one day of the week where my dad worked from home, and he was wearing his usual attire: an oversized Hawaiian shirt, board shorts, flip flops, and a delighted smile.

"Your mom told me you crashed and burned on your date." He waggled his thick eyebrows playfully. "But I guess things didn't go as bad as you thought! You can never count out that old Smith charm."

I tossed the towel back into the bathroom and pulled on a clean shirt. "Are you telling me *Carly* is here?" How had she even gotten my address?

"Was that her name?" He frowned and shrugged, ushering me up the stairs. "She's a lot prettier than you said."

Well, shit. My dad had two volume settings: loud and louder. There was no way Carly *hadn't* heard that. I took the stairs two at a time in a desperate attempt to mitigate further father-inflicted damage.

Behind me, he chortled. "Go get her, you sly dog!"

Shoot me now. After all this time, I still had no idea how he'd convinced my mom to date—let alone marry—him. I hadn't ruled out black magic or mind control. Especially now that I knew both things existed.

I rounded the corner, proceeded down the hall past the kitchen, and took a left into the living room, where I stopped dead. Seated on the couch, clothed in a sapphire blouse and an ankle-length black skirt was...

"Anastasia?" The auburn-haired femmepire and House Secundus was sipping from the cup of tea that my mother had conjured on demand. Our good china, I couldn't help but notice. "What are you doing here?"

"John Smith!" My mom's voice was pleasant, but her usage of my full name was a sure sign that I'd done something wrong. "Is that how we greet guests in this house?"

"Sorry, Mom." I was twenty-five, but she could still make me feel like I was in kindergarten.

My dad finally caught up with me, huffing and puffing just a bit, and took a seat in his overstuffed easy chair by the couch. Jee Sun was curled up in the second and final chair, munching happily on a handful of blueberry jam. There may have also been a piece of toast somewhere in there, but it was difficult to tell.

"Everyone, this is Anastasia Dumenyova, a... friend. Anastasia, these are my parents, John and Maria Smith. Who I guess you've already met." I stood there awkwardly, my initial question still echoing in my head. *What was Anastasia doing in my parents' house?*

"It is a pleasure, Mr. and Mrs. Smith." I'd once described Anastasia's voice as chocolate-drizzled cheesecake, low, rich, and sweet. Even after so many months, the sound of it made me weak in the knees. "I apologize for intruding on your day but wanted to catch John before he left for work this morning."

"Not at all, dear." My mom patted Anastasia's knee. "The pleasure is all ours." She smiled sweetly, like a medieval torturer preparing to go to work. Or a gleeful dentist, I guess. The metaphor kind of worked, either way.

My dad flashed me a thumbs-up sign from across the room.

I darted a look at Anastasia to see if she had noticed.

She had. Her lips quirked.

Parents. Can't live with them… can't afford *not* to live with them. Before my dad could say anything more, I cut in. "Actually, I really will need to get to work soon. Mom, Dad, do you mind giving us some privacy?"

My mother's pursed lips told me that she *minded awfully much, thank you very much,* but she nodded with regal grace. "Of course, honey. You two talk as much as you need to. I need to get your father his breakfast anyway."

She bent down to give Anastasia a hug. My mother was big on hugs. "It was lovely to meet you, dear."

The mention of food was perhaps the only thing that could have pried my father from his easy chair. He trailed after my mom, a hopeful expression on his face. "Do we have any bacon?"

Mom's voice floated back down the hall to us. "No, sweetie. I threw it out after your bloodwork came back. But I did pick up some lovely bran muffins at the store…"

Dad's inevitable protest was too quiet for us to hear over the gruesome noises Jee Sun was making as she sucked jam from her fingers. I handed the girl a napkin before she could wipe her hands on the chair.

Anastasia took another sip of tea. The cup she was drinking from was part of a set that had been passed down through multiple generations of my mother's family. The fact that my mom had brought it out from its place of honor on the top shelf of the credenza was like a neon sign announcing her approval. Humorously, that antique china set was at least three centuries younger than the woman currently drinking from it.

Ah, Anastasia. What could I say about her that wouldn't make me sound like some sort of deranged stalker? Pale skin, auburn hair, and jade eyes to die for. She was tall, maybe four inches shorter than my own six feet, and always impeccably dressed in expensive, tailored clothing. I'd watched her catch a sword blade with one hand and perforate her former lover's body with the other, but she was also quiet and thoughtful, considerate and calculating, professional and impossibly alone.

My parents' assumption that she and I were dating said a lot about the power of parental love to blind someone. All vampires were physically gorgeous—Steve had women tripping over themselves to talk to him and Kayla had literally stopped traffic during one of our brunches—but Anastasia was something else. Next to her, I was a grubby, unwashed troglodyte.

Seeing her again, for the second time in a week, reminded me how much I'd missed her.

The femmepire's voice broke the silence.

"Again, I apologize for the intrusion, Mr. Smith. Do you need to leave immediately for work?"

"I don't have to be anywhere for a few hours, actually. That was just the only way to get them to leave us alone. Want to chat outside?" At her nod, I turned to Bill's ward. "Jee Sun, do you want to come with us or go get more breakfast?"

The little girl sprinted toward the kitchen.

That answered that.

I escorted Anastasia to the front porch, where we took a seat on the bench swing, the femmepire's closeness every bit as intoxicating as her subtle fragrance.

"Your mother is formidable," said Anastasia.

"She'd be happy to hear you say so. For as long as I can remember, she's ruled our house with an iron fist. And platefuls of cookies."

"I like her very much."

"Everyone does, eventually."

"And the child? That *is* Lord Beel-Kasan's human ward?"

"Yeah. I'm babysitting her for the next few…" I trailed off, realizing yet again that neither Bill nor Jee Sun had given me any sort of timetable.

"I see."

We sat there awkwardly as the neighborhood slowly woke up around us. This time, I broke the silence. "It's fantastic to see you, Ana. Really. But—"

"What am I doing here?"

"Yeah. This wasn't how I expected my Thursday to start."

"Today being Thursday is one of the reasons I am here."

"What?" Even after my shower, I was still half-asleep. Maybe that's why it took me so long to put it together. "Oh crap. Lucia."

She nodded. "You told her you would have an answer by Monday."

"I didn't say *which* Monday," I muttered.

Anastasia did me the favor of pretending she hadn't heard.

"Honestly, I forgot. I've been on a stakeout for the past week and the whole thing kind of blew up in my face yesterday." I frowned. "Wait. Why did Lucia send *you*?"

"*Queen Lucia*, Mr. Smith," she reminded me. "And I am her Secundus."

Which, as far as I'd been able to tell, just meant second-in-command.

"In truth, I volunteered to come speak with you." Anastasia's sharp eyes scanned the houses across the street. "It seems judicious to keep your interactions with my queen as brief and infrequent as possible."

Given how my last few meetings with Lucia had gone, I couldn't argue with that. If the femmepire queen had shown up at my house, I'd have lost it. Anastasia, on the other hand… well, there were worse ways to spend a morning. Billions of them.

"I drove to your office on Tuesday," she continued, "but you were away. On this stakeout, I presume."

"Yeah. You could have called, you know. You're always welcome to call." I didn't have Anastasia's number, but had no doubt she could get mine if she wanted.

"I wanted to speak with you in person."

That was enough to give me warm tinglies, even if she almost definitely didn't mean it the way it sounded.

"Last night, I went by your office again, but you had visitors." Anastasia gave me an unreadable look. "John, you do know that both the man and woman are…"

"Infected? Yeah." Every now and then, Ana slipped up and called me John instead of Mr. Smith. It was ridiculous how good that made me feel. "What started out as a standard cheating-spouse investigation now looks like it might result in a mediation for the San Diego Pack."

Even her frown was lovely. "The Infected can be dangerous."

"Like vampires? Or insane demigods?" My grin failed to prompt an answering smile.

"Perhaps more so, especially when angered."

"I'll avoid angering them then," I replied, willfully disregarding my own recent history.

"I fear that it is too late for that. Do you remember the creature that Zorana killed during Xavier's failed coup?" Her tone was gently chiding.

"The hulking thing that chewed its way through the House Watch? Yeah." Zorana was a thousand-year-old vampire Blood Witch, stuck in the body of a twelve-year-old girl. The Infected had out-massed her by a factor of ten-to-one, but that hadn't prevented her from tearing its head from its shoulders and then carrying that head around with her as a bloody trophy. Normal vampires were scary enough, but Zorana was in a whole different league. "What about it?"

"Which pack do you think he came from?"

"Oh." That was bad.

"He was, in fact, Davis Hawthorne's older brother."

"Oh," I said again. That was *really* bad.

"As well as the former leader of the San Diego Pack."

Well, shit.

CHAPTER 9

IN WHICH EVEN A PAWN CAN THREATEN THE QUEEN

"Davis didn't seem hell-bent on revenge," I decided, making a mental note of the werewolf's apparent last name, "but thanks for letting me know. I'll have a talk with him before I agree to do anything for the pack."

"When last we spoke, you said you were done with our world."

By *our world*, she meant the supernatural one. It really needed a snappier title. One more thing for me to work on in my spare time.

"I was therefore surprised to discover," Anastasia continued, "that less than a week later, you were mediating for Kristin and her congregation."

"She was literally waiting in my office when I got there. I was going to say no, but… she was persuasive." The fact that Kristin was ten inches tall with sparkly wings didn't hurt. Only an asshole would say no to Tinkerbell. Especially when she'd come bearing cash.

"There is a reason her species has thrived in the modern age."

"Kind of like the People, you mean?"

"Precisely. In their own fashion, the pixies are as much predators as we are."

"Yeah, I found that much out during the mediation. Although I'll take pixies every time over goblins."

"Yes. I heard that your investigation for the Superchargers had some difficulties."

I didn't even find it creepy anymore that Anastasia always seemed to know exactly what was going on in my life. If anything, it was almost comforting, like a safety blanket that could beat a half-dozen enemies to death in the blink of an eye.

"Three brawls and a handful of dead, yeah, but Chief Tikky-Wokka Tomlinson's son is no longer having nightmares. He seemed happy with the outcome."

"That makes two jobs for the non-human species of San Diego in a span of months. Three, if you include your work for the House. Perhaps we have different definitions of what it means to retire from this world." Anastasia had a world-champion poker face, but I was pretty sure she was teasing me.

"Word got out that I had replaced the Rook." I shrugged. "Given the state of my P.I. practice, I can't really afford to turn down large sums of money."

Money that kept the office rent paid *and* financed disastrous first dates… and Lucia's lobster.

"I see." Anastasia was quiet for a long time. "As good as it is to see you doing well, John, I wish you had not taken Kristin's case."

I responded with my award-winning, patent-pending look of confusion.

"If you had left our world permanently," Anastasia explained, "it very well might have been the end of things with Queen Lucia."

"Except for this freaking bond in my head, you mean."

"Even with the bond, I had convinced my queen to leave you to your own affairs, and that choosing to do otherwise would only lead to further discord within our House."

I frowned. "Apparently, we also have *different definitions* of being left alone. Lucia's been stalking me across San Diego for months now."

"Precisely."

For the second time in less than a minute, I just stared at the femmepire in confusion.

"In taking on additional cases, Mr. Smith, you accepted the mantle of city mediator and forced my queen's hand. A wayward thrall is one thing, but a city mediator who bears a public grudge against the queen's House? That is something else entirely."

"Why does she even care? It's not like the House has had any actual cases since Bill." Before she could speak, I cut her off with an irritable wave of my hand. "And please don't try to feed me that same lie about the gnomes."

Anastasia went still, the way only the older vampires seemed to do. "When have I ever lied to you, Mr. Smith?"

It was a fair point.

"Never," I admitted, "but your queen was fibbing through her pointy eyeteeth at Mister A's, so it doesn't seem all that unreasonable to—"

"And am I she?" The femmepire's eyes glittered like polished glass. It was one of a handful of times I'd seen her angry. Even when she decapitated her ex-boyfriend, she'd mostly just seemed sad.

I had a special talent for pissing off femmepires.

Or maybe just women in general.

I shook my head. "You're nothing like Lucia. And thank God for that. Or Gods, I guess. But..." I trailed off. Where had I been going with this, and was it worth insulting one of my three favorite vampires? It sure didn't seem like it. "I'm sorry. I don't know what the hell I'm talking about. It's been a weird couple of days."

"It was I who brought you into this world, Mr. Smith," said Anastasia, in that moment as distant and remote as an unclimbable peak. "The pain you have suffered is upon my head, and I will forever be cognizant of that fact. While my duties are what they are, please believe that I am trying to be your ally in these matters."

"You weren't the person who hired the karkino to kill me, Anastasia. I'd have died that first day if it weren't for you. As for the rest of it?" I shrugged. "None of it was your fault. I could have found a better way to convince Lucia that using Jee Sun as leverage was insanely stupid. Lucia could have exhibited an ounce of self-control for once in her life. Our choices aren't on you."

Anastasia said nothing.

"And while you've already shown me how awesome an ally you can be," I concluded, "I'd rather be your friend."

It was one of the rare times I'd ever seen Anastasia Dumenyova, House Secundus and Stone Lady, at a loss for words. Almost by their own volition, her lips quirked in that half-smile I liked so much.

"My position does not often afford me the luxury of friendship."

"Because everyone's scared of you," I pointed out.

"And you are not?"

"Maybe I should be, but no. I think you're incredible. I'd be lucky to be your friend."

It was the sort of line that could have come straight out of a cheesy novel, but I meant every word, and her smile said she knew it.

"I would like that," she said quietly.

"Anyway," I said, coughing to clear the sudden lump in my throat, "what were you saying about Lucia?"

"*Queen* Lucia, John. Remember that in her company, if nowhere else. As for the present predicament... what do you know about the power structure in San Diego?"

Again, I was pretty sure she was talking about the supernatural world, and again, I wished there was a cool term for it. The Dark World? No, too easy. The Underworld? Too Beckinsale. What did that leave?

"Not a whole lot. I know the vampires and the Mer and some third party are at the top of the pyramid, with goblins, pixies, chupacabras, and other species somewhere beneath. And the local demigods mostly do their own thing. Why?"

"It is germane to the current situation. Thanks to the Toulon Concordat, open warfare is seen as a last resort. Military might continues to matter, of course, but few will strike openly for fear of reprisal."

"Like nuclear deterrence?"

"Where the nuclear weapons are deities and ancients, yes." The early morning breeze tugged at a strand of her auburn hair and it was all I could do not to reach out and tuck it back into place. "In lieu of actual battle, power struggles now play out in other arenas."

"Like what?"

"Politics, business, and—most pertinent to our discussion—public relations."

"I'm still confused." It was becoming a habit.

"I know." She gave a short sigh and tried again. "Her Majesty is a queen-in-exile, yes?"

"Right." Although nobody had ever told me what Lucia had been exiled for. I was guessing it was her personality.

"When we came to this country, the established Houses refused us sanctuary rather than risk the ire of the Italian Court. We arrived in San Diego with few allies and a great number of enemies."

I nodded. Either she'd explain where she was going with all of this, or I'd have an opportunity to ask yet another stupid question.

"So why do you think it is that, despite *two* separate attacks on the House in the past fifteen years, recruits continue to flock to our banner?" Anastasia arched one elegant eyebrow as she posed the question.

"Well, some of those recruits ended up being spies and traitors. As for the rest, I just assumed they were outcasts like Juliette." Although none of the other vampires I knew—from Steve to Kayla to sweet-voiced Akiko—seemed like the sort of people who would get kicked out of their own Houses.

"There is some truth to that," she acknowledged, "although many of our members remain in good standing with the Houses they grew up in. Perhaps I should rephrase the question; why have so many younglings come specifically to *Queen Lucia's* House?"

"I don't know… maybe because she's still famous? Being a formal member of royalty has to count for something." Hell, Americans still went nuts over the British royal family.

"Precisely. Our House has twice survived what should have been its death blow because our liege continues to attract new supporters."

"Only because they've never met her," I muttered. "So, what does that have to do with me?"

"You are an uncontrolled thrall. Should that ever become public knowledge, it will be a blot on her reputation, a reputation that shields our House even in its weakest moments."

"I haven't been running around telling everyone I have a vampire stuck in my head."

"Be that as it may, word is spreading. The greater issue is that you are now considered to be the city mediator, as the Rook was before you. And when the city mediator holds a grudge against Her Majesty's House—"

"It hurts your recruitment efforts and fuels new plots against the House," I finished. "That's messed up."

"The weak are culled from the herd, Mr. Smith. It has always been the way of things."

"So, *I'm* Lucia's weakness? All of this cat and mouse stuff has been about Lucia trying to protect her House?"

"My queen has her flaws, as you well know. But she also understands that she is responsible for the safety of her people."

"Then why hasn't she just killed me?" I winced, immediately filing that question away under the heading *Ideas Not to Give to Vampires.* "Hypothetically-speaking, of course."

"Of course." Anastasia's voice was bone dry. "In addition to the risk of fallout from those of us who do not wish you dead, killing you would be a public admission that she lacked the skill or statecraft to arrive at a peaceful resolution."

"Which would *also* hurt her reputation, and therefore weaken her House." Vampire politics were bizarre, but Ana's explanation made a twisted sort of sense. "I get it."

There was a difference between understanding what was going on and being at peace with it though. I didn't want anything to happen to Darlene, Kayla, or Juliette. Or Anastasia, for that matter, although she seemed more than capable of protecting herself. But Lucia was stuck in my head. The vampire queen had forced that on me, and the fact that I had managed to hold onto my free will didn't change her original intent.

Would I be willing to work with Lucia again?

I still didn't know.

"I'll give *Queen* Lucia a call when I'm done with work."

"That is all I can ask, Mr. Smith."

We were back to Mr. Smith. That wasn't great.

"If I forget—again—will you come back over to remind me?"

"I suspect she will send someone else in my stead." Ana's eyes glowed in the early morning light.

I winced. "Then I'll definitely call tonight."

CHAPTER 10

IN WHICH CARS ARE SWOONWORTHY BUT
RESEARCH PAYS THE BILLS

We talked for a while longer before the femmepire had to leave, our conversation free of any further awkward silences. I escorted her down the driveway, looking in vain for one of the House's gleaming black Mercedes. Had a driver dropped her off?

The answer soon became apparent. On the right-hand curb, several houses over, a deep burgundy Jaguar convertible was parked. Even from half a block away, I could hear it whispering sweet nothings in my ear.

"That is the sexiest thing I have ever seen," I murmured. "Car-wise, anyway. Is it yours?"

"Indeed." Her voice glowed with a possessive pride that I totally understood.

"If I owned a car like that, I would never bother with the House fleet."

"There are advantages to being driven, the ability to do work en route being one of them. However, in the wake of this summer's assault, we have scaled back our usage of human security firms."

"No more burly drivers?"

"Not until we can keep them from being used against us."

"Makes sense." In the supernatural world, human security was essentially well-paid cannon fodder. Unfortunately, Xavier had used compulsion to turn that cannon fodder against his own House. "Is Lucia pissed at not having someone to drive her around?"

"Quite the opposite. There are few things my queen enjoys more than being behind the wheel."

The Jag was even more beautiful up close. I was absurdly grateful that my Corolla was parked around the corner, where it couldn't see me drooling. Was automotive adultery a thing? And if so, were there private investigators who specialized in it?

"She has one just like this," continued Anastasia, "albeit in—"

"—white," I finished. Lucia was nothing if not predictable with color schemes.

"Indeed. However, she prefers the Ferrari."

"I bet she does."

"Our tastes have always differed in a number of areas." Anastasia unlocked the driver-side door and looked at me over the soft top. "It was good to see you again, Mr. Smith."

"John, Anastasia. Friends call each other by their first names."

"I will have to remember that." Her jade eyes sparkled.

Standing there, a marvel of automotive engineering between us, the morning sun painting her pristine features in a hundred shades of color, I was struck again by just how much I'd missed her and how desperately I now wanted her to stay. When we'd first met, I'd joked about marrying her. While that was obviously never happening, there was still something that set her apart from anyone else I'd ever met.

"Hey… do you want to get dinner?"

"I beg your pardon?"

"Not now. Some other time, I mean. Like in the evening. When people actually eat dinner." I rallied desperately. "After all, you kind of owe me; I introduced you to the wonders of In-n-Out."

"An experience I will always cherish." Her almost-smile evolved into something playful and wicked. "Need I remind you that *my* favorite restaurant requires a suit and tie?"

"You saw me at Mister A's. I can do formal, Lady Dumenyova."

Only with a lot of primping and help from Kayla and Darlene, but she didn't need to know that.

After a moment of careful consideration, briefly interrupted by a car backfiring several blocks away, she nodded. "Give me a call and we will establish a time and date."

I'd never hit a game-winning home run, but right then, I knew exactly how it felt. I tried and failed to keep the shit-eating grin off my face as I stepped back onto the curb. The Jaguar's engine came to life with a roar befitting its namesake, and the soft top retreated and folded into the trunk.

It was only then that I saw the fatal flaw in the plan.

"Hey, wait a second… I don't have your number!" I fished the wonderphone out of my pocket.

"Surely, acquiring such information won't be a problem for someone in your profession?" Anastasia slid on a pair of wraparound shades, smiled that wicked smile again, and pulled away from the curb at a speed my poor Corolla could never hope to match.

That would have been a great time to announce to the world that the game was afoot, but I'd recently sworn off doing so. Instead, I just shook my head and kept on grinning as I walked back to my house and the coffee that was hopefully waiting for me inside.

Halfway up the driveway, my cheerful saunter transformed into a panicked run as the sound of glass breaking was drowned out by Jee Sun's high-pitched voice at full volume.

ooo

I rushed through the front door of my house, lungs burning even from the short run, only to find my parents and Jee Sun calmly seated around the dining room table. They all watched me with confused expressions on their faces as I struggled to find my breath.

"Is… everything okay?" I wheezed. "I heard… noises."

"Just a minor accident with a mug, honey. It's already taken care of." Over my mom's shoulder, I saw a dustpan and broom leaning against the wall. On the table, Jee Sun's own mug was conspicuously missing.

"Are you okay, Jee Sun?" My breath was starting to come back, but my head was spinning. Damn it, I really *did* need to start exercising.

"Yes, Mr. John!" She smiled brightly. "Coffee went boom!" She giggled in a manner that I hoped came across as charming and girlish rather than creepy.

"Really, Mom?" I eyed my mother. "Caffeine?" I hadn't even been allowed *soda* until I was a teenager.

"It was supposed to be yours."

Of course it was.

My mother rose from her chair and took me aside into the kitchen, while my dad said something that sent Jee Sun into peals of laughter. "How old is Jee Sun anyway, dear?"

"Uhm… six or seven… ish? I think?" I winced, certain that the non-answer wouldn't please my mom.

"She's a special sort, isn't she?"

"You have no idea." And she really, really didn't.

"Are you sure it's a great idea for you to be watching her? You're not trained for this sort of thing, and some children require a lot of attention and care."

"Mom, it's just for a few days." I hoped. "Bill will be back then, and she'll be out of our hair long before Thanksgiving. I'm sorry about the mug."

"Don't be." She waved a hand dismissively. "That was your father's fault. He should know better than to make a little girl laugh while she's carrying something heavy."

I felt better immediately. It was always easier when something could be blamed on Dad. Maybe my paranoia about Jee Sun interacting with my family had been unreasonable.

"I am curious though," continued my mom, her green eyes boring into my own, "what is this Gehenna she keeps talking about?"

Or maybe it had been entirely justified. "I don't know, Mom… just typical kid stuff."

"She told your father it was some sort of hell dimension." My mother's voice was calm and reasonable, like she was discussing the price of eggs or her most recent visit to the Salvation Army. "I don't think I've ever heard Father Peter mention it in one of his homilies."

"I think it's from a cartoon," I lied hastily. "You know how crazy Japanese anime can be."

"I see." She chewed that over in silence for a moment, before changing subjects with the practiced ease of a sharpshooter switching targets. "Anastasia seemed nice. And quite attractive!"

That was a conversation I wasn't ready to have. Not with my mom, and *definitely* not so soon after the Carly inquisition. "Yeah, she's great. Anyway, I'd love to stay and chat, but Jee Sun and I need to get going. Especially since it takes like an hour to get her ready."

My mom's expression cleared instantly, replaced by fond nostalgia. "I remember what that was like." The moment passed, and her eyes regained their laser-like focus. "We'll talk more tonight."

"Yes, Mom." I fled to the basement, where I gathered up Jee Sun's jacket, socks, and shoes. The possibility of death by werewolf was gaining a certain appeal.

ooo

Despite what I'd told my parents, the meeting with Phil and Melissa was still a few hours away, so I took Jee Sun to my office, where she began another black-on-black-on-black crayon masterpiece on the notepad my mom had sent along. As for me? I decided to dig up some information on one Mr. Davis Hawthorne.

In my admittedly limited experience, access to personal data operated on a hierarchical level. At the very top were government organizations like the FBI and NSA, both of whom no doubt had agents listening to me type at that very moment. The next tier consisted of other agencies and the police; people who could run a license plate or do a background check with relative impunity. Then there were the security firms or high-priced investigators who supplemented whatever information their police contacts might provide with more mundane research like credit or employment checks. The final level belonged to the general public, as well as particularly poor private investigators like me. Our tool of choice was powerful and all-seeing, its name consisting of a single word comprised of two syllables.

I opened a browser tab and pulled up Google.

An hour later, I could definitively state that there were a lot of Hawthornes in the world. Including the author, of course, and a short-lived TNT television show that had starred Will Smith's wife. There was even a Hawthorne elementary school, located—in an apparent coincidence—less than a mile from the Thompsens' rental.

Information on Davis the werewolf was considerably harder to find. Neither he nor his family had any connection to the school. A brief article in the Union Tribune suggested he had once been the owner of a small architecture firm but had sold it several years ago. The article was focused on the new owners, and Davis only warranted one paragraph with little in the way of usable information. There was no mention of the brother Zorana had killed, or any other family for that matter.

I shrugged, not too concerned with my failure. Over the past few years, I had learned that Google was better at some tasks than others. Ten thousand fan theories on the latest hit movie? Google was the place to go. Biographical data on Thor-look-alike werewolves? Technology couldn't do *everything*.

On a whim, I did an image search on werewolves, but what came back bore little resemblance to the furred, bipedal monstrosity I'd seen in the House. That creature had been half again Davis' already impressive size, which meant either his brother had been part giant or werewolf transformations ignored purely human theories like the conservation of mass and energy. And since I still didn't know if giants were a thing, I was betting on the latter. Once magic entered the fray, all bets were off. Zorana's own spells had made that much clear.

Jee Sun tore out her finished sketch and handed it to me with a happy smile. A few solitary specks of white paper shined through what was otherwise an entirely black page. She had dark smudges all over her hands and the crayon itself had shrunk to a nub.

"Thank you, Jee Sun." I went to tuck her artwork into a desk drawer, but the resulting pout stopped me in my tracks. Instead, I looked around the room, finally settling on the corkboard near the door. "Why don't I hang it here, so I can see it whenever I'm sitting down?" I pinned the paper to the cork board. "What do you think?"

She offered a dazzling smile but said nothing. The page was so heavily coated in crayon that it seemed to tug downward on its pushpin. It was the kind of artwork Wednesday Addams would hang on her refrigerator door. In fact, the whole office seemed darker, as if Jee Sun's sketch was slowly consuming the light. But that was crazy, right?

I shivered. "Let's get your jacket, sweetie." We still had time before we had to be at the Thompsens', but I was suddenly in need of coffee. And sunshine. And plenty of each.

CHAPTER 11

IN WHICH CONFESSION IS GOOD FOR THE SOUL,
BUT BAD FOR THE SPLEEN

"What are *you* doing here?" Phil Thompsen was barely contained by the frame of his house's front door. Despite his age and the steady expansion of his waistline, he remained an intimidatingly big dude.

Luckily, I'd brought a werewolf as backup.

"I invited him, dear." Over Phil's shoulder, Melissa appeared in the foyer, greeting me with a nervous wave.

"I also invited Mr. Hawthorne." I motioned to Davis. Out of the corner of my eye, I saw the werewolf twitch when I used his last name. It served him right for underestimating my badass detective skills. Or the information-gathering abilities of my friends and allies, anyway.

"What the hell is going on? Is this how you do business, Mr. Smith?" Spots of color appeared in Phil's cheeks, and his large hands clenched into meaty fists. In anger, he bore little resemblance to the defeated man who had come to my office.

"Not usually," I admitted, "but this is a really special case. Can we come in?"

"Honey, please let them inside," Melissa pleaded. Her tone reached her husband in a way my words had not, and he stepped aside, still scowling. I glanced back at my Corolla, making sure Jee Sun was still there and happily drawing, and then entered the house. As I squeezed by Phil, I heard him mutter something under his breath: words that sounded suspiciously like *contract* and *refund.*

People always shoot the messenger.

What followed was one of the most uncomfortable hours of my life. First came the admission that Davis and Melissa had not only spotted me on my stakeout but then tracked me back to my office. That disclosure both obliterated my already-shaky professional reputation and led to a few rounds of recriminations being tossed between husband and wife. Meanwhile, Davis and I sat like mute stumps in the wildly overdecorated crochet wonderland the Thompsens called a living room.

When that storm had finally died down, I gave a short recap of my actions in tailing Melissa to Tierrasanta. That went about as well as expected, with Phil angry at Melissa, Melissa angry at me, and Davis doing his best surfer-zen impression. Eventually, we managed to convince Phil that there'd been nothing sexual going on between the two of them.

Which brought us to the far thornier question of exactly why she'd been visiting Davis.

Between Jee Sun and Anastasia, I hadn't had much time to think about Melissa's confession, but a small part of my mind had still wondered what the plan would be at this point. How do you tell your husband that you're a werewolf when everyone knows they don't exist? Insanity might be an acceptable courtroom defense, but it didn't play well in couples counseling.

It turned out that Melissa was a hands-on demonstration sort of woman. She rose from the couch that she and Phil were seated on and turned to her husband. "I have something to show you." And then, she began to shift.

I'd seen my share of werewolf movies. An American Werewolf in London… Brotherhood of the Wolf… all of the Underworld films, even the older movie with Jack Nicholson and Michelle Pfeiffer. Whatever it was called. I was used to the general idea of what the shape change would look like. Skin bulging, muscles tearing, bones reshaping… basically, like when Bruce Banner became the Hulk, except grosser and less green. I thought I'd even caught a small glimpse of it the day before, when Melissa was struggling to control her temper.

This was nothing at all like that. Instead, the general shape of the woman blurred and condensed, like flesh and bone had become mist and fog. As if to reinforce that point, her clothing fell to a heap on the rug-covered floor.

"What the fu—" Phil nearly jumped out of his seat, eyes wide as saucers in his suddenly pale face.

The mist settled closer to the ground, congealing into a mass roughly four feet high and six feet long. As I watched, the air solidified further. Four limbs appeared and then the grey-furred body. Last of all was the head, and by the time the mist had faded, it left behind what was very recognizably a wolf.

A really, really big wolf. She was half again the size of a St. Bernard. Normal wolves didn't get that large, did they? My only frame of reference was coyotes, and they were pretty small.

Melissa sat back on her hind legs, large enough to look her husband in the face. Her eyes still appeared strangely human, but the brown had washed away, leaving orbs the color of bleached bone. She trotted over to lick her husband's hand, a move which very nearly caused him to upend the couch in his haste to get away. With a low whine, she retreated to the pile of her clothes. And then the transformation started to reverse.

"Mr. Smith?"

I ignored Davis, watching with fascination as the mist shaped into a column almost six feet tall, and then slowly began to condense into the general figure of a woman. It was kind of how I imagined a female genie might take form.

A firm hand on my shoulder got my attention. "Perhaps we should look the other way until Mrs. Thompsen has gotten dressed?"

"Oh. Right." Davis and I turned to gaze out the living room window, conscious of the sound of clothes being hurriedly pulled on behind us. When the creak of the couch told us Melissa had taken her seat, we turned back around. All eyes turned to Phil.

"What…" He cleared his throat. "What *are you?*"

I winced. I was the furthest thing from an expert on relationships, but this seemed like a bad sign.

"I'm your wife, Phil," she replied, her voice so full of emotion that it almost hurt to listen to, "and I love you, and nothing will change that."

"But you just… you… it's not possible." He gestured wildly at the carpet where the wolf had stood, momentarily at a loss for words. His body tensed, and I thought for a moment that he'd run. Instead, he slumped on his couch, looking old and confused. "Have you always…?"

"Been like this? No. Remember when you had that job in Minneapolis? The one that kept you away for almost the whole month because of on-site problems?" When he nodded slowly, she hurried on. "While you were gone, I was… attacked. By something I would never have believed could exist. A wolf, but larger than any wolf I'd seen. The next day, the bite was gone, like it had never happened. I thought I was losing my mind. Then, it happened again. And again. The third bite was apparently enough to change me."

"Into a… a…"

"Werewolf," I supplied helpfully, earning glares from both Thompsens and another heavy hand from Davis. I leaned over to the older werewolf, keeping my voice to a low whisper. "Dude, if you keep tugging on my shoulder like that, it might fall off. And that would be bad news for your mediation."

Davis' brilliant white smile seemed supremely unconcerned, but he released my shoulder. I turned back to my client and his wife, who had continued talking without us.

"Why didn't you call me?"

"I tried. But you were dealing with a supplier that had fallen through and didn't have the time to listen to what I was pretty much convinced was the product of a nervous breakdown."

"But why would that… thing… want to change you?"

"In all likelihood, he was a rogue wolf, Mr. Thompsen. One looking for a mate." Davis' voice was smooth and reasonable, like he had to explain random rogue werewolf attacks all the time.

"And who exactly are you? Mr… Hawthorne, is it? What do you have to do with all of this?"

"I've been trying to teach your wife how to adapt to the changes in her physiology," he replied easily. "So that she would not be a danger to you."

"So you're a *werewolf* too?" Phil's mouth twisted, as if even saying the word hurt. "Wait. What do you mean… a danger to me?"

"The wolf is…" Melissa paused, her lips moving slightly as if she were trying out different sentences in her head. "…in some ways, a separate entity. It's not bloodthirsty, or particularly violent, but it doesn't always understand human interaction, and sometimes responds… inappropriately. Davis has been teaching me the control I need to keep living my life."

Phil had the thousand-yard stare of someone who'd served in a half-dozen world wars. I flashed back to my own reaction when I learned that the monsters of our mythology actually existed. There'd been shock and surprise, yeah, especially after two bipedal crabs tried to kill me, but in the end, I'd mostly been disappointed. Vampires were okay, but aliens would have been so much cooler. Phil didn't seem to be taking things nearly as well. But as my mother often told me, I was a special sort of person.

Which was, I suddenly realized, the exact same phrase she had used to describe Jee Sun.

Melissa was doing most of the talking, with the occasional question from Phil or comment from Davis. I listened closely and learned a lot. Like vampires, werewolves were very different from their depictions in fiction. Unlike vampires, as Melissa herself had discovered, new werewolves could be created from humans. Davis didn't like the term Infected, but it seemed fitting. In fact, each pack could be divided into two groups; the naturally born and the turned. Werewolf cubs could only be born to a couple that consisted of at least one natural werewolf. The child of a turned werewolf and another turned werewolf—or a vanilla human, for that matter—was always purely human. It felt like the classic chicken and egg scenario. If natural werewolves could only be born to natural werewolves, how had the first werewolf come into existence?

Nobody seemed to appreciate that philosophical quandary when I voiced it aloud.

Philistines.

Again, I was nobody's idea of an expert on… well, anything, but even I could tell that Melissa was leaving details out. For example, her wolf form bore little resemblance to the two-legged engine of destruction that had been Davis' brother. Clearly, werewolves had a hybrid shape that bridged the gap between wolf and human. Was that something all werewolves could do? I had no idea, and I kept my mouth shut. The last thing I wanted to do was get further involved in their marital conflict.

From my seat near the window, I could just barely see Jee Sun's head bobbing inside the Corolla. I'd left the keys in the car, with the engine and A/C running, and the windows slightly cracked. I wasn't going to be one of those people who got in trouble for leaving their child unattended. Even if she wasn't my child.

Or… was that more of an issue with dogs? Whatever. She seemed to be doing fine, regardless.

The conversation dragged on and on, but eventually, Melissa turned to us. "Thank you both for being here, but I think my husband and I need some time alone to talk things through."

I was out of my seat by the word *time*, more than happy to put some distance between myself and the emotional maelstrom that was their living room. I didn't even like that sort of scene in *movies*; the real thing was a hundred times worse.

Davis rose more slowly but gave a solemn nod. "Of course. Mr. and Mrs. Thompsen, if I or any of the San Diego Pack can assist you, please do not hesitate to call. I greatly regret the actions of that one rogue. His madness reflects poorly on our kind." With a half-bow, he strode past me to the front door.

"Uhm, yeah," I said. "The same goes for me. You both know where I work, so… well… call if you need anything." I thought about giving a half-bow of my own, but there was no way I could follow Davis' graceful rendition. Instead, I offered a hesitant wave, which made me look every bit as stupid as the bow would have, and left.

Outside, I was greeted by the loud thumping of bass and the almost inaudible words of Eminem's latest single. The Corolla was shuddering under the onslaught of its own speakers and Jee Sun had her hands up in the air as she bounced about to the music. Perhaps leaving her the keys had been a mistake. At least she hadn't tried to drive away.

I hurried over and turned down the volume, Davis on my heels. "That went about as well as could be expected."

"We'll see," he replied, shrugging his broad shoulders. "This was her choice, not mine."

"True. So… you said something about another job?" I didn't want to press, but the sooner I started my next mediation, the sooner I'd be able to move out of my parents' house. It was bad enough that I pretty much embodied the cliché of the low-rent private eye… I'd prefer to not *also* lay claim to the cliché of being a single, twenty-something comic book lover who still lived in his mother's basement.

"Yes." He nodded to his truck, which gleamed even more than it had the day before, as if he had gotten it detailed in the time since. "If you'd like, I can drive you out to our pack's hunting grounds. We can discuss the specifics of the matter on the way."

"Before we do, maybe we should talk about your brother."

"I wondered when you would bring him up. I understand you were present at the vampire House when he was killed?"

I carefully inched away from him, as if that would do anything at all to save me should he attack. "Yes. Sort of. I mean, I saw him, but wasn't there when he actually died."

"Ah." A long moment of silence followed. "Do you know if it was a good death?"

"What?" When he started to repeat the question, I waved him to silence. "Sorry, I heard you; I just don't know how to answer that. He died in combat with Zorana, after tearing through more than a few of the House Watch."

"Zorana is the Blood Witch?" At my nod, he smiled. "Then it was a good death."

"That's not the reaction I expected."

He waved one hand. I managed not to flinch, but it was close. "Anthony would have known from the start that his chances of survival were low. It's why he took the job."

"You'll have to explain that one to me."

"Our kind does not live long, Mr. Smith, even by human standards. Forty years, forty-five at the most, and those last years are typified by madness and wanton slaughter. It has become tradition for us to seek our deaths in a manner that will benefit the pack. Often, this involves mercenary work. The more dangerous the better, both because the risk of death is higher, and the fee is greater."

"That seems extreme." I mean, nobody liked to age, including humans, but violent suicide for the greater glory of our people? Yeah… no thanks.

"Does it? We consider it a mercy. If one of the pack survives into madness, it is the responsibility of their kin to perform the killing."

"And Anthony—"

"His forty-second birthday was in June, but he could already feel the madness nibbling away at the edges of his brain. In my opinion, he only held on as long as he did to see his child wed."

"Jesus."

"We do not choose the lives we are given, John. All we can do is make the best of them." He shrugged. "Regardless, I assure you that I bear you no ill will for whatever small part you played in Anthony's sacrifice." He motioned again to his shiny truck. "Shall we?"

"Actually," I countered, "why don't we take my car? I have some blank contracts in there, and there's a back seat for Jee Sun." It would also ensure I wasn't left without transportation if something went wrong. Davis seemed sincere, but I'd already been kidnapped once, and that filled my quota for the decade.

He eyed my graffiti-stricken Corolla with distaste but nodded anyway. Which left me with the challenge of explaining to Jee Sun that she would no longer be riding shotgun.

INTERLUDE

"Can't you break the chains?" I'd seen Juliette practically kill a man just by opening a car door.

"I'm a vampire, damn it, not Wonder Woman." I heard the rattle of metal on metal, followed quickly by an exasperated sigh. *"Not gonna happen."*

"Wonder Woman does poorly when tied up, anyway. Now, She-Hulk on the other hand…"

"Do you really think this is the time for that tired DC and Marvel debate?" She hid it from the rest of the House, but I'd learned that Juliette was an avid comic book reader. She just happened to read the wrong publisher's comics.

"If you can't get out of those chains, we've got a lot of spare time on our hands. Let's start with how Thor would totally kick Superman's ass…" Thank God for company. It was much easier to be bravely nonchalant when there was an audience to appreciate it.

"That does it," she hissed. *"First, I'm going to find a way out of these chains, then I'm going to stuff your precious comic collection down your throat."*

"So, there's hope of escape, after all! You just needed the proper motivation."

"Ha." Even Juliette's laugh was tired. "How are you holding up, asshole?"

"Oh, you know. It's not sipping mai tais on the beach, but few things are." Whatever the hell a mai tai was; I mostly stuck to beer. "I think I've been hogtied with rope instead of chains, but it's hard to tell since I can't see a thing."

"Rope is good!" she said, a sudden spark of hope in her voice. "It can be stretched or severed. Try to reach into your pockets and tell me what you have available. We'll MacGyver our way out of this shit hole."

"Uhm."

"What is it?"

"I don't have any pockets." I winced.

"What do you mean you don't have… Little bird, are you naked?"

"Kind of," I muttered, struggling futilely against my bonds. As far as I could tell, the ropes hadn't loosened in the slightest. The pain in my shoulder, on the other hand, was now worse.

"John," murmured Juliette in the darkness, her voice suddenly thick. "You're also bleeding."

CHAPTER 12

The route we took was almost an exact match for the one Melissa had driven the previous day. We merged onto the 52 and headed east. In the rearview mirror, I could see Jee Sun, safely buckled in and still pouting. I was glad I'd locked her gun away in my office safe. And that she would forget and forgive as soon as she got hungry.

"…and so, while many of us do have our own homes, some members of the pack live on our hunting grounds," Davis continued.

"Which is where we're headed?"

"Yes." He finished reviewing the printed contract form in his hands, and then flipped it over to scan the small print on the back. "This looks acceptable. Nothing like what the Rook had, but functional enough."

"Did the pack use him often?"

"Not if we could help it. He was a bit of a sleaze, if you know what I mean."

"I really do." I'd never met the Rook, whose murder had occurred before Anastasia found and saved me, but I *had* searched his home, and if the décor and magical sex bots had been any indication, sleaze was putting it mildly. "So, what exactly am I going to be mediating?" After dealing with the Thompsens and their marriage, I was ready to sink my teeth into something interesting. "Land usage debates? Pack discrimination? A blood feud with wandering zombies?"

I was joking about that last one; everyone knew zombies didn't bleed. Or exist.

"Actually, it's a rather bitter divorce."

I tried to stifle my groan, but a small sigh leaked out anyway. *More* relationship stuff? *Really?* Whenever you added heartache or feelings of betrayal to the mix, things got messy. And that was even before you considered the supernatural aspect. "Werewolves get married?"

"It depends on the individual, of course, but yes. We're people, John."

"Just not *the* People."

"I beg your pardon?"

I waved him off. "Never mind. So, they're trying to determine who gets what in the divorce?"

"In a way. This marriage was intended to bind two packs together. The pack territory in San Diego was given to the couple as a wedding present, so ownership of that land is now in question." We crossed the 15, once again headed in the direction of Tierrasanta. I kept an eye on Davis in case he had any new directions for me, but he seemed content to have me driving east.

"That sort of wedding gift seems a little bit… short-sighted," I commented carefully.

"Yes. My brother was always the sentimental sort."

Oh. Come to think of it, Davis had said something about that. "So, the groom—?"

"The bride, actually. Carolyn Hawthorne was his daughter and is now my ward." He turned to look at me, and I could feel the weight of that gaze.

We drove in silence for another few minutes. The exit to Tierrasanta came and went, but we remained on the 52. Were we seriously heading all the way out to Santee?

"Shouldn't the land revert back to Carolyn, since she's Anthony's daughter?" As far as I could tell, werewolves didn't do the whole royalty thing, but still… leadership had its perks.

"Not when it was freely gifted to both the bride and her groom. The concept of inheritance is a little bit tricky. While they were married for only a short time, Jason is within his rights to insist that he not come away from their union empty-handed."

"And I suppose the unhappily married pair aren't cool with the idea of splitting the land right down the middle?"

"They are not. Nor am I, to be fair."

"Awesome. Anything else I should know?"

"Only that tensions are high. Most of Jason's pack remains in their New Mexico territory, but he has a few friends here with him, all of them young males, easily bored, and prone to violence. The longer this drags on, the more likely that someone does something dumb, and then…"

"War?"

"It's possible," he confirmed.

Awesome. I'd seen the sort of damage one older—and apparently insane—werewolf could wreak. I was not looking forward to seeing that on a larger scale.

Messy divorce? *Check.*

Emotional stability of the involved parties? *Questionable.*

Possibility of bloodshed? *High.*

Yep, it was definitely starting to sound like one of my cases.

ooo

"This is it?" I peered out through my now-dusty windshield at a hill covered in scrub grass, indistinguishable from any of the hundred other similar hills in eastern San Diego.

"It's just over that ridge." Davis pointed. "This is the closest we can get by car." He gestured at the vehicles that had been parked haphazardly around us, where the loose gravel that was a poor excuse for a road had finally petered out into the dry underbrush that made so much of San Diego a fire hazard.

If my car had GPS, it would have told me that we were located somewhere in the endless hills northwest of Santee. But my car didn't have GPS. I felt fortunate that it even had a CD player, honestly. I was pretty sure that the local gang in Logan Heights had left the decade-old device untouched out of pity rather than any recognition of my inherent worth as a neighbor. Thankfully, I didn't need a nav system in my car. That's what my wonderphone was for.

I turned off the engine, stepped out into dry heat that was uncharacteristic for November, and turned the phone on with a swipe, curious to see exactly where we were. The dirt and gravel road I'd been following had twisted and turned like it had a mind of its own, a mind fully bent on confusing the hell out of me. Sadly, when I brought up the map app, I was greeted by the two little words every cell phone user has learned to fear: no service.

Thanks for nothing, AT&T.

Jee Sun scooted out of the back seat, shrugged off her pink jacket, and skipped over to look at some sort of wildflower nearby, her superman cape flapping behind her to give the illusion of great speed. I picked up the jacket and tucked it under my arm.

"Let's go, Tiny Flower." She came back at a significantly reduced speed, but at least she came. Taking her hand in my own, I turned to Davis. "Lay on, Macduff!"

He gave me a blank look. "Come again?"

"Uh… it's Shakespeare." Now, even the wolf thought I was a nerd. "You know what? Never mind. Let's go meet your niece."

In the nebulous future, if a werewolf ever again told me something to the effect of *our destination lies just beyond that ridge* or *we're closer than you think* or even *we're making good time now*, I was going to request a map and visual confirmation before agreeing to set out on the journey. We hiked past the ridge in question, and then a second ridge, and then a third, until I was deeply regretting my decision to bring Jee Sun. Even a girl her size can get heavy, and we had only made it halfway up the *first* ridge before she decided she needed to be carried the rest of the way. As the early afternoon sun beat down on us, I was also regretting that I had left my sombrero—a relic of a past Cinco de Mayo gone horribly right—at home. If I ended up with a sunburn, someone was going to pay.

And that someone would almost certainly be me. As usual.

Finally, a circle of dilapidated structures came into view, clustered at the bottom of one of the hills in the area. We were still some distance away, but I could see a crowd milling about in the large courtyard at the circle's center. Actually, *courtyard* was more than it deserved. It was just a big dirt field, surrounded by shacks that needed to be repainted, if not bulldozed and replaced entirely.

"I can see why everyone's fighting to keep this place," I muttered under my breath.

"This is simply the meeting area," replied Davis tersely. "*The fight* is over the land around us. Land in which a pack can roam together without concern or interference from your species."

It's easy to tell when you've offended a supernatural critter; just wait for them to whip out the 'humans suck' card. Unfortunately, the fact that our species *does* kind of suck makes it hard to argue. I followed Davis in silence, searching in vain for an appropriate comeback. Jee Sun's light snores provided a weird harmony to the sound of dry brush crunching under our shoes.

And speaking of shoes… I frowned down at my formerly white Air Jordans. If the dirt had stained them permanently, I was going to add the cost of a new pair to Davis' bill.

As if he'd heard my thoughts, the werewolf slowed until we were walking together again. He gave me the side-eye for a good dozen paces. Finally, I'd had enough.

"Can I help you, dude?"

"I've been trying to identify your talisman, but I'm honestly stumped. That ring seems like the only possible candidate, but… I mean, just look at it."

Maybe a twenty-five-year-old shouldn't still have been wearing their high school graduation ring, but it had cost a lot of money. I was trying to get as much use out of it as I could before I hit thirty. Plus, my birthstone—diamond—looked classy, even in a setting of low-quality white gold. "What's wrong with my ring? And what are you even talking about? What talisman?"

Jee Sun shifted in my arms, but I patted her back soothingly until she returned to sleep.

"I mean the artifact that keeps you free of the vampires' influence. Unless those rumors aren't true?" Before I could reply, he shook his head. "No, they must be. Neither the pixies nor goblins would have hired you if you were the vampires' patsy."

"I'm nobody's patsy," I quickly confirmed. It was important to get in front of that sort of thing. Otherwise, people would talk, rumors would spread, and the next thing you knew, your reputation would be in shambles. Or more of one, anyway. Shamblesier? No, that didn't sound right. "But my ring's also not a talisman. Well, not in the way you're thinking, anyway." I had originally dug it out as a sort of good luck charm for my date with Carly. Over the objections of both Kayla and Darlene. "This is my high school ring."

"I know what it is, John. I went to school too, you know. And college. And grad school. I just figured you wouldn't still be wearing it unless it had some sort of magical power." By this time, we were within a hundred feet of the outer circle of buildings, but he stopped to give me another once-over. Finally, he tossed up his hands. "I give up. I have no idea what item it might be."

Ha! Sucker. I'd have rubbed it in some more, but I was hot, sweaty, and tired, and had a pair of feuding werewolves to speak with. "I don't have any talismans or artifacts or magical doodads, dude. My ability is one-hundred percent all-natural."

"Really?" His eyes widened and then narrowed, a play of emotions racing across his face. "You're saying that you're just… innately immune to compulsion?"

"And glamour and tricksiness and hoodoo and anything else that's intended to mess with my head," I confirmed with an undeniable sense of pride. "Well, almost anything." Lucia's enthrallment ambush hadn't been successful, but it hadn't been a complete failure either.

With that thought, I became aware that the queen was currently some distance to our northwest. Whatever she had done to hide herself from the bond was clearly no longer in effect.

"That's fascinating," he murmured. He gave me a respectful nod, regarding me for the first time as someone of actual interest. Unconsciously, I stood up a little bit straighter. God of Thunder or not, he had that sort of a presence. "Were you blessed or cursed as an infant, or is it just some sort of random thing?"

"No idea," I replied cheerfully. "The vampires seem to think it's a genetic quirk."

"If anyone would know, it would be them. Still," he concluded, "that's pretty cool."

Yeah, it was. I decided I could get used to this new, more appreciative werewolf. I even magnanimously offered him an olive branch. "I'm sure your kind has something similar, right?"

"Of course," he agreed, "but the wolf only protects us when we let it out to play." He noted my blank look and elaborated. "When we are in one of our wolf forms, I mean. In our human shape, even the natural-born have only limited protection. It's one reason we avoid vampires whenever possible."

"If it makes you feel better, even with this *immunity*," I made air quotes around the word, "the vampires have still been able to screw with my life in every other possible way."

"A common complaint regarding their kind. I think it's the overly long lifespan. It creates a sense of entitlement."

"You have no idea." We bumped fists, which practically made us brothers. I resolved to give this mediation case one-hundred-and-ten percent of my usual effort, and not just because I desperately wanted to move out of my parents' basement.

People were gathering in the center square. "Are these all…?"

"Yes, Mr. Smith." As we neared the others, Davis cast off his easy-going surfer attitude, as easily as Jee Sun had removed her jacket. His spine stiffened, his words became terse, and the nods he gave to the people around us seemed precisely measured. I wasn't sure how he was doing it, but suddenly he looked every inch a leader. "This is the pack."

I looked about me in interest. After the vampires, pixies, and goblins, I had expected a sort of homogeneity. Every vampire I'd ever met (other than Zorana, who was her own kind of very special person) ranked at least an eleven on the one-to-ten scale of attractiveness. Some, like Lucia and Anastasia, were solid fifteens. While there was significant variance in ethnicity, in style, and in hair, they were all, when it came right down to it, disgustingly fit and disturbingly good looking. They could pass for human, but if you ever saw two vampires together, their similarities became undeniable.

That was less true of pixies, who seemed to vary wildly in shape and disposition… but the fact that they were all less than a foot high and sported iridescent butterfly wings was itself a strong indicator of what you were looking at.

As for goblins… well, the less said about goblins, the better.

But the pack? Beyond their presence here, a mile away from that little back road to nowhere, there was nothing to suggest they were from the same species, or that each of them had an unstoppable killing engine buried just beneath the human shell. The woman closest to us was bow-legged and almost as wide as she was tall, with an untamed mass of curly blonde hair pulled back into what was supposed to be a ponytail but ended up looking like a puff ball. She held hands with a Latino guy who could have been Mike's much shorter and older brother. His pale grey tank top strained over a small round belly, but his most outstanding feature was the thick, black handlebar mustache… a mustache so effortlessly old-school that I immediately wanted to go home and grow one myself.

Looking around us, I found short people, tall people, fat people, skinny people…

"Is something wrong?" Davis murmured in a low voice. I realized I was staring at the werewolves, eyes and mouth wide open like a moron or, God forbid, tourist.

"I just assumed they were all going to look like you," I muttered back. In truth, it was kind of nice to not *automatically* be the ugliest person in the room, purely by virtue of my species. At the same time, it meant Davis had come by his rugged lumberjack, Son of Odin handsomeness without the benefit of magic or supernatural breeding, which made me kind of hate him. Or would have, had we not so recently bonded.

"Does Melissa Thompsen look anything like me?"

"Fair point. Although that could have been because she was turned, instead of born." All told, there had to be at least thirty werewolves in the clearing. They parted before us like Moses' Red Sea, revealing a group of five werewolves at the center.

No, I reconsidered almost immediately; *not a group of five. One group of four and one separate individual.* The divide became more obvious the longer I looked; stiff postures, angry gazes, and a fixed boundary of open space that might as well have been patrolled by armed guards.

The foursome were all men; old enough to vote, but probably *not* old enough for the beer bottles in their hands. They wore white muscle shirts and ripped, low-hanging jeans, but that was the extent of their conformity. The biggest had a large metal chain looped about his thick neck, his shaved head an odd contrast to the bushy black eyebrows that left his eyes in shadow. On either side of him, standing shoulder-to-elbow, were two skinny dudes that looked like they'd crawled right out of central casting for a trailer park movie. One of them even had an honest-to-God mullet. The second had covered his head with a dark blue bandana, but the hair that spilled out from underneath was dyed a virulent green.

The fourth member of their gang stood slightly in front of the others, and I didn't need the wedding ring on his finger to identify him as Jason, Carolyn's soon-to-be ex. His aura of command was a far cry from Davis' own, but still noticeable. He was also the only one of the four who looked like they'd ever met a stylist.

"Carolyn." Davis nodded to the fifth werewolf, who stood opposite the frightful four. What might have been a formal gesture was made less so by the obvious affection in his voice. "Jason." His nod to the werewolf I'd correctly identified contained significantly less warmth. "I believe I have found a way to resolve your ongoing dispute."

"For real?" Carolyn looked nothing like her uncle, save perhaps for a slight similarity in facial bone structure. She also didn't look anything like her dad, by virtue of not being a slavering, drooling, million-foot-tall hell monster. Instead, she was… well, not plump, exactly, but borderline so, with long straight hair of a red so dark it almost had to be dyed. Like her husband, she was somewhere in that nebulous college age range, casually dressed in a yellow t-shirt with a red star on its chest, faded jeans, and a pair of hiking boots that had probably cost half what my significantly less practical Air Jordans had gone for. She seemed nice enough, and when she smiled in my direction, it was almost impossible not to return it.

"Who is this, Uncle Davis?" She sniffed delicately, as if testing the air, and then gave me a second, more considering look. "You do know he's human, right?" She peered at Jee Sun, still snoozing in my arms, jacket wrapped about her like a blanket. "And the girl, too."

"My nose works as well as yours," replied Davis easily. He ignored my muttered excuse about deodorant and the lengthy hike, his voice raised so that it would carry to the pack around us. "This is the new mediator for San Diego. I've hired him to help you and Jason work out the details of your separation. Everyone, meet John Smith. John Smith, this is the San Diego Pack."

I lifted one hand and gave an awkward wave, getting a few in return. Jason smirked at me with the casual insolence of someone who hadn't quite left his teenage years behind. It was like looking at myself, half a decade earlier. We'd probably get along fine. As for Carolyn…

The blood drained from her face, leaving it oddly pale despite what was clearly a grade-A beach tan. Her eyes lasered in on my face. "You're John Smith?"

I nodded confidently.

"The human who helped the vampires?"

I nodded again, slightly less confidently.

Bright spots of color appeared on her cheeks. "The vampires who killed Daddy?!"

At that point, I'd realized continued nodding was not in my best interest, but she wasn't waiting for a reply. One second, she was slouching a good five feet away, the very image of a mildly irritated college freshman. The next, she was airborne and coming directly at me, eyes shining like polished bone, fingers lengthening into flesh-rending claws.

CHAPTER 13

I dropped to my knees and spun, shielding Jee Sun as best as I could, but the expected blow never fell. Davis had stepped in front of his niece and caught her about the waist in mid-leap. She struggled in his grasp but couldn't shake free.

"Carolyn," he rumbled, "control yourself. Mr. Smith is not your enemy."

"He and his friends killed Daddy!" she protested, the words garbled by what appeared to be a mouth full of razor sharp teeth. She made another run at me, but her uncle calmly kept himself between us, leaving the angry werewolf to snarl at me over his shoulder.

"Anthony sought out his death, as is our tradition. You diminish his choice by holding the human responsible." He pulled her into a tight embrace. "I miss him too, Cara."

After a moment, she returned the hug, bone-white eyes squeezed shut as tears rolled down her face.

A solid kick to my ribs told me that Jee Sun had woken up and was displeased to find me on top of her. With the danger apparently behind us, I rose to my feet, setting the little girl on the ground next to me. She clutched my hand tightly with one of her own and rubbed her eyes with the other, blinking as she looked about us. And then…

"Red! Red! Red!" She spun about, repeating the color as she pointed out each individual werewolf about us. By the time she was done, the crowd was dead silent. Even Davis and his niece had turned to regard us.

"Who's the midget, and what do I have to do to shut her up?" Mr. Mullet had a deep, gravelly voice entirely at odds with his appearance.

"I am JEE SUN!" She stomped one foot, raising a cloud of dirt and dust, and scowled in his direction. "I am not a midget!"

"Don't worry about that guy, Tiny Flower," I muttered down to her. "Let's just focus on not getting killed for a little bit, okay?"

She looked up at me, and smiled, her thick glasses still askew from my not-so-evasive maneuvers. "Don't worry, Mr. John. Mr. Bill will make them go away."

"Mr. Bill's not here right now, sweetie," I reminded her. "So, let's not piss the nice werewolves off, if we can help it."

She thought about it for a moment, her small face contorting with the effort, and then finally nodded her acceptance. She looked back at the werewolves and waved robotically, looking for all the world like a miniature Korean prom queen. She then beamed a huge smile at Mr. Mullet. "Your hair is ugly!"

I met Jason's amused gaze and shrugged. "Sorry."

"No worries, hombre. We've been telling Travis the same thing ever since he grew it out." The two other werewolves with him snickered, even as Mr. Mull—I mean, Travis—went beet red.

"Now that you've met everyone, Mr. Smith," Davis interjected, arms still wrapped about his niece, "perhaps you'd like to speak to Carolyn and Jason in a more private setting?" His eyes swept the crowd, and it immediately started to disperse. That impressed me far more than the fangs and talons his niece had flashed.

I'd have to bring the older werewolf with me on my next trip to the DMV. Or Disneyland.

"That works." I wiped the sweat from my eyes, once again lamenting my absent sombrero. "I wouldn't turn down some water either, if you have it."

"Of course." He ushered me toward the largest shack. Up close, it was just as rundown as it had seemed from a distance. Rusted aluminum siding covered the frame haphazardly, and the "door" was simply another sheet of metal, pulled to one side. It was hard to believe Davis had been an architect. If I hadn't seen his real house in Tierrasanta, I'd have also started to question his ability to pay my fee. "We have some lemonade for the little one too, if you can convince her to stop yelling out random colors."

I wasn't going to explain that there was nothing random about the colors Jee Sun was shouting to Davis or anyone else in the pack. I didn't think the idea of a human that could pick werewolves out of a crowd would go over well, and her vegetable demigod guardian wasn't around to protect her. Or me.

And anyway, she seemed excited about the lemonade, so I figured we were safe for the time being.

The interior of the shack was nicer than expected. A long wooden table—simple but well-crafted—sat in the middle of what I took to be the living room, surrounded by matching chairs. A low couch occupied the wall to my left and a door in the far wall led to the rest of the house. Just stepping out of the sun lowered the temperature by at least five degrees, and for a building that lacked windows, there was surprisingly good air flow. I looked up and saw three ceiling fans hung from the central beam, their blades rotating slowly.

"We have a generator out back," explained Davis, when he saw the direction of my gaze. "We're not barbarians." He looked over at Jason's crew, who had tagged along. "Travis, why don't you go back to the kitchen and grab us some drinks?"

"I don't answer to you, old man," sneered Travis. My opinion of him, which had already been scraping rock bottom between the mullet and his words to Jee Sun, continued to plummet.

"Just do it already, dude," sighed Jason, rolling his eyes as he took a seat at the table. "And then you guys can bounce if you want to. There's no point in us *all* having to suffer through this."

Travis and his bad attitude stomped through the doorway in the far wall. He returned shortly after, attitude miraculously intact, with an armload of water bottles and one lemonade flavored vitamin water. He dumped the bottles onto the table and stalked outside. With matching shrugs, the other two—who, in lieu of formal introductions, I had dubbed Chains and Skullcap—followed him out.

Davis and Carolyn took their seats across from Jason, leaving the head of the table to me and Jee Sun. I snagged a bottle of gloriously cold water, opened Jee Sun's equally cold lemonade, and sat down in one of the two available chairs. There was a long moment of silence, during which all three werewolves looked at me expectantly.

Oh, right. This was where I did the mediation thing.

"How long is this going to take anyway?" Jason drummed his fingers on the table and scowled at me. "I'm missing *Madden* for this, bro."

"You guys come out to the middle of nowhere and then spend your days playing X-Box?"

"You have no idea," muttered Carolyn.

"Pardon me, if we don't all go in for earth mother shit."

"Okay, okay," I drowned out the rest of their bickering. "Forget I asked. To answer your question, Jason, it kind of depends on you two. I've had a mediation that was resolved in a week, and one that took the full month."

That last one had been the pixies. By the end, I no longer found any of them cute.

"A month?!" Carolyn and Jason spoke up at the same time. Neither of them looked at all happy.

"And just like that, you've already found common ground," I cheerily announced. "That's what we call progress."

Carolyn looked over at Davis. "I think I hate him, Uncle."

"Now, as I was going to say before *someone* derailed the whole conversation—" I rolled my eyes in Jason's direction. "—my role here is not to make decisions, but to help the two of you come to a compromise that you can both live with. That means we're going to have to do a lot of talking, both separately and as a group. The only way that works is if we agree to a certain level of respect. You don't have to—"

A now-empty lemonade-flavored vitamin water bottle rolled away from me, and down the full length of the table. Next to me, Jee Sun was tossing the plastic cap up in the air.

I looked back at three visibly amused werewolves. Awesome. Nothing like having my carefully planned speech undercut by an eight-year-old. Or whatever age she was.

"Anyway, let's try to keep the shouting to a minimum, and agree that each of you has the right to voice their opin—"

The plastic cap hit the table, miraculously landing on its edge. It rolled in a wide loop before dropping off onto the floor. I looked down at Jee Sun.

"Is there anything you'd like to add, Tiny Flower?" She shook her head from side to side. "Do you want to maybe go play in the corner over there?" I looked about for her crayons and sketch pad, before realizing that we'd left them back in my car. It was quite possibly an even more egregious error than my failure to bring the sombrero.

"Is there pizza there?"

"No, honey, there isn't. But if you're extra quiet for the next little while, we can maybe get some for dinner tonight. Okay?" I knew my dad, at least, would be thrilled with the idea.

Jee Sun nodded and put her arms on the table and her head in her arms. Almost immediately, she was snoring quietly.

"Your daughter is really cute," said Carolyn quietly, the words stiff, as if it pained her to say anything nice to me.

"She's not my daughter, but thanks." I eyed the redheaded werewolf and her ex-husband for a moment. "Before we go any further, I really should ask. Are you two okay with this mediation? And with me specifically as a mediator?" I regretted the latter question, even as I asked it. In my mind, I had already spent the fat check this case was going to earn me.

"Sure," answered Jason with a shrug. "Whatever it takes to get it all over with, y'know?"

"Carolyn?" When she didn't reply, I looked down the long table and into her pale blue eyes. "I understand how you must feel. If it matters at all, I am sorry about your father. A lot of my friends died that day too, some of them at his hands. As I understand it, the purpose of mediation, and the Toulon Concordat in general, is to minimize exactly that sort of pointless killing. Nobody wins in war."

It was possible I'd cribbed that last line from a movie.

Fresh tears slid down her cheeks. "I…" She cleared her throat, and tried again. "I don't see how something as small as my divorce would ever end in war, or how it necessitates the Concordat being invoked, but I'm okay with you as our mediator. For now, anyway."

"Fair enough. My understanding of the situation is that Anthony owned the rights to the land we're currently on, and made it a wedding gift to the pair of you? And now that you're separating, the question becomes what to do with the land?" They both started to speak at once, but I waved them to silence. "Let's go one at a time. Jason, you start."

"Tony didn't give *us* the land. He gave it to *me*. It was one of those… whatchamacallit dowry things. It was part of the arrangement between our packs."

"That's not true!" protested Carolyn. "Daddy was trying to strengthen the San Diego Pack by bringing in fresh blood. He wasn't giving our territory away!"

I looked down the table at Davis. "I don't suppose there's some sort of written record of the agreement?"

"Of the agreement? No. But the land deed does reflect the change in ownership."

Oh. That made sense. It hadn't really occurred to me that the pack's so-called 'ownership' of the area would actually be reflected in human court documents. "And who does the deed list as owner?"

"Both Jason and Carolyn."

"Okay. So, from a legal perspective, it's both of yours. Whatever the late Mr. Hawthorne may or may not have said is meaningless in this case. Unless one of you has written proof of his words to the contrary?" Two disgruntled young werewolves shook their heads angrily. "Alright. Well, I'm not a lawyer—"

"Obviously," muttered Jason, under his breath.

"—but even I know that California law says the land is communal property, meaning you each get half of it, if you separate. Is there a reason that arrangement wouldn't be—"

"I'm not going to give half of my pack's land away to this poser and his hick friends," growled Carolyn.

"It's not your land anymore," fired back Jason. "It's mine. And there's no way in hell I'm going to let your scruffy little band of mongrels keep squatting on it!"

With a loud roar, Davis brought one fist down on the wooden table, causing the entire thing to shake and shudder. Jee Sun bolted out of her chair even before she had fully woken up. Cracking her eyes open, she looked up and saw the three werewolves.

"Red!" she shouted.

Things went downhill from there.

CHAPTER 14

"That could have gone better."

"You think so?" Davis took a long pull on his beer. I'd regretfully had to decline when he offered me one of my own. *Some of us* were going to have to drive home, and having a beer on an otherwise empty stomach was not a winner of an idea.

A pile of candy bar wrappers littered the table's surface in front of me, all that was left of Jee Sun's snack. The little girl was now racing around the room, holding a giant pillow she had liberated from deeper in the house, but we were otherwise alone.

The meeting had basically been a succession of arguments and outbursts. If we had made any progress at all, it could be measured in inches. Jason's attempt to slam the door as he stalked out—mere minutes before Carolyn also departed—had been defeated by the door's shoddy construction and complete lack of hinges, but that was the only thing that had worked in my favor. Through the still-open portal, I could see the residue of what must have been a spectacular sunset.

"I'm trying to think of a diplomatic way to ask this, but it's late, I'm tired, and I used up all of my diplomacy several hours ago.

What the hell was your brother thinking in pairing those two together? It's obvious they can't stand each other, and they have absolutely nothing in common."

"As my niece said, Anthony's main goal was to strengthen the pack. In my grandfather's time, our kind had free reign over much of Southern California. Since then, the human population has quintupled, while our power and numbers have only declined. The few wolves you saw today are almost the entirety of our current pack." He drained his beer and set the empty bottle on the table in front of him.

In the corner, Jee Sun began to spin in a circle, like a ballerina, a figure skater, or Wonder Woman.

"I don't follow. I mean, I know San Diego's a lot bigger than it was, what… fifty years ago? But most humans don't even know you exist. How are we linked to your pack's decline?"

"I don't really feel up to explaining the full intricacies of pack history to you tonight, John. You're not the only one who's tired."

"No worries," I replied. "I'm sure my continued ignorance won't be at all problematic for the ongoing mediation." I smirked and waited.

He grinned tiredly. "You really are a bastard, you know?"

Jee Sun fell over, giggling.

"It's not that humans themselves are such a problem. Loud, smelly, and incapable of living in harmony with the world around them, sure… but we've learned to cope with all that."

I didn't bother to defend my species, given that I'd been sitting in a cloud of my own sweaty stench all afternoon.

"The real problem is that humans are… a vector."

"For disease?" Every werewolf I'd seen so far had seemed healthy. If we'd been killing them off with swine flu or measles outbreaks, the evidence was well hidden.

"For other supernatural species."

"You've lost me again."

"It may have escaped your notice, Mr. Smith, but many of the races in San Diego have a symbiotic relationship with your own. The vampires drink your blood. The goblin tribes claim your sports franchises as their totems. The pixies develop marketing schemes that convince you to pay triple the usual price for *new and improved* products which are secretly the same, but less durable. Even the immortals…" He paused, giving that a bit of thought. "Well, they do whatever it is they do."

"And that's bad how? For you guys, I mean." I'd lost sight of Jee Sun and had a few seconds of panic before I found her crawling along under the table, like a Green Beret sneaking up on an enemy fortification.

"As San Diego's human population has continued to grow, the number of other species has too. And that means increased competition for territory and space. Even in my life, there've been four minor wars between various races, to say nothing of the conflicts your predecessor *was* able to resolve peacefully."

"Four? I'd only heard of one." The Cedar Fire of 2003 had been a smokescreen for a major assault on the vampire House, although I was still uncertain as to who the attackers had been. According to Anastasia, it didn't matter, as they no longer existed. War was serious business. "I wouldn't think anybody would be anxious to pick a fight with you. I saw the sort of carnage your brother left in his wake."

"Yes." He smiled smugly, for just a moment, before that smile flickered like a candle flame, and went out. "There's no question that we can kick some serious ass. So, our enemies strike at us from the shadows, when we are alone, or in our human forms and vulnerable. So-called accidents and mishaps." He placed his beer bottle on its side, and nudged it with one hand, watching it slowly roll off the table. It tumbled to the floor, next to Jee Sun's own discard. "Half of the pack doesn't even live in San Diego anymore. They live across the border, in Tijuana and further south, where the mundane dangers are greater, but the supernatural ones less so."

"So, when you're not all—" I made a vague growly noise that would have embarrassed even Buster, my parents' long-departed Cocker Spaniel. "—you're basically human?"

"Of course not. But we are strongest as wolves, or in our hybrid shapes. In this form, we are slower, weaker, and…"

"And you lose your immunity to glamour," I finished. He peered at me, clearly startled. "You mentioned that on our hike over here."

"Ah." He rubbed his face tiredly. In the dim light, he no longer looked like a young God of Thunder. Now, he was a little bit more like Daniel Day-Lewis as Lincoln. Still good looking, but worn down by the weight of responsibility, and a future that seemed inescapably bleak. "I guess I did."

"And the marriage…?" I prompted.

"Was an arranged union, to promote an alliance between the San Diego and New Mexico packs, and to bring new blood to our numbers."

"I didn't know people still did arranged marriages. In the U.S., at least." The concept had always seemed odd to me, even in a time when bloodlines and family alliances might determine who would rule a given kingdom. In the modern era of short-lived relationships, where divorce was only ever a phone call away, the idea was positively archaic.

Davis offered another tired smile. "Believe it or not, when Carolyn and Jason first met, they couldn't get enough of each other. It was all we could do to keep them apart until the details of the union could be finalized."

"So, what happened?" I had a hard time reconciling the picture Davis was painting with the non-couple I'd spent the afternoon with.

"What often happens." He met my eyes again, his face thick with shadow, as the last remnants of sunlight finally vanished from the sky. "You're single, right? I'm sure you've had more than your fair share of failed relationships."

"I wouldn't say *more* than my fair share," I muttered.

"And in those relationships, there was a honeymoon phase, then a period of time where maybe everything was comfortable but not as awesome as it had been, and then…"

"You wake up and your girlfriend is pissed because you were breathing loudly in your sleep," I finished. "Okay. Yeah, I get it." Truthfully, it had been a long time since I'd been in a relationship at all, and my last one had skipped the honeymoon stage and jumped right to the point where I was the most irritating person on the planet. But I understood what he was saying.

"Exactly. If there had been time for them to truly get to know each other first, perhaps even a trial run as a couple…" He shook his head. "I don't know. Would any amount of time have been sufficient? My brother knew his end was near and wanted to see the pack in a better place before he died. Perhaps his decision was short-sighted, but I understand the motivation." He shook his head again, and this time, there was something of a dog shaking himself awake in the motion. "Now that you've met them, do you think you can help?"

"I'm not a marriage counselor," I cautioned, "but if I can get them talking to me… hell, I have no idea. It's going to take some time, but hopefully we can figure out a solution that everyone will be satisfied with." I paused, trying to think of a way to phrase the next question delicately. But once again, I was too tired for delicacy or diplomacy. "As far as my fee is concerned…"

"You'll have the deposit in your bank account by morning"

"Sweet." I felt better about things already. "Can I speak with Carolyn sometime tomorrow? Somewhere away from her ex-husband?"

In the short term, it was clear that nothing would be accomplished with the two of them in the same room.

Davis nodded. "Absolutely. We can use my house in Tierrasanta. How does eleven sound?"

It sounded like I wasn't going to get to sleep in at all, but I didn't say that out loud. With Jee Sun around, early morning wakeups were practically guaranteed. I flashed back to that morning, and the giant brown eye staring me in the face, and shivered. "Yeah, eleven works."

"Excellent." He rose to his feet and shook my hand. "I'm going to stay here and speak with some of the pack. I'll get someone to drive me home later tonight. Will you be able to find your own way back to the car?"

I managed not to laugh in his face, but it was a close thing. "Sure thing," I said blandly, sticking my arm out to point in a totally random direction. "It's just over that ridge, right?"

"Ah. I'll find you a guide then."

"That would probably be for the best."

He disappeared into the darkness, presumably to do just that, and I began the laborious process of trying to coax Jee Sun out from under the table and into her jacket for the long walk—or in her case, ride—back to the car. When she was finally dressed, I took her hand and we left together.

Outside, the area was mostly deserted, although a few lights indicated occupied buildings. Just across the way, I could hear simulated football being played. Travis' whine was particularly irritating, even at a distance. Jason was smoking just outside that house. He flashed a peace sign in my direction but kept silent.

"John?" I turned and found Davis coming in our direction, accompanied by the werewolf with the glorious handlebar mustache. "This is Emilio. He's volunteered to see you back to your car."

Emilio was almost lost in Davis' enormous shadow, but nothing could keep that mustache from looking badass. One part Kurt Russell in Tombstone and one part the guy on the Pringles can, it dominated his face. If Emilio smiled or even said hello, I totally missed it, my attention reserved entirely for his facial hair.

I was never going to shave again.

Without further ado, Davis took his leave. Emilio headed in the opposite direction, motioning for me to follow. This time, we only made it twenty steps before Jee Sun demanded that I carry her. I picked her up in my arms and followed behind our guide. She rubbed her face against my shirt and went right to sleep. I didn't remember my cousin sleeping even half as much at that age, but Jee Sun's childhood had been anything but normal. I was willing to cut her an enormous amount of slack.

I took one last look back as we crossed the ridge. The werewolf town was already vanishing from view, with only a handful of lights to indicate its presence amongst the dark and empty hills. A few more steps, and even those lights were lost, as if they'd never been there at all.

I held Jee Sun tighter and followed Emilio into the darkness.

CHAPTER 15

IN WHICH THE JOURNEY HOME IS ALWAYS LONGER
AND A CASSEROLE IS NARROWLY AVOIDED

The hike back was ten times worse in the dark. Emilio seemed to glide across the pitch-black hills, but I couldn't take a step without stumbling over unseen rocks, bushes, and desert gremlins. The taciturn werewolf said nothing as we traveled, and our footsteps and Jee Sun's light snores were the only sounds to disrupt an otherwise silent night. Where were the crickets? Or the birds? Or the bugs? I'd been camping a few times as a boy, and I remembered nature being a lot noisier than this.

After what seemed like an hour, but was probably closer to thirty minutes, we topped the final hill, and saw the solitary streetlight that towered over the parking lot. Only a few vehicles remained, but I was unsurprised to see that my Corolla was among them. Even if the pack didn't keep eyes on the lot—and I was pretty sure they did—there wasn't a car thief in San Diego desperate enough to steal mine.

I moved from scrub grass to gravel and fished my keys out of my pocket, trying not to wake Jee Sun in the process. "That's me, over there." I nodded in the direction of the Corolla, relieved to see that its graffiti was invisible in the darkness. "Thanks for showing me the way back."

I was almost positive that Emilio and his mustache were the proud owners of the sweet Harley parked just past my vehicle. Maybe I'd get a bike when the Corolla finally called it quits. Motorcycles were cheaper than cars, right? And they looked easy enough to ride.

Emilio gave a casual wave as he turned and headed back toward the camp. Before he even reached the hill, he was just another shadow in the night.

"Looks like it's the two of us again, Tiny Flower. Let's go home and get some pizza."

The engine started with its usual phlegmy burble. Thank God Emilio had already left. I flipped on my high beams and drove south on the dirt and gravel road.

I did my best to avoid the more obvious ruts and dips, but visibility was crap and we bounced and slid our way down the unpaved path. The pothole-ridden streets around my office were awful, but night-time driving in the desert was a whole new level of bad. After one particularly bone-rattling bump, Jee Sun woke again. She removed her glasses to regard me with a baleful eye.

"I know, I know. But unlike Bill, I can't just teleport us around. Mortals have to make do with cars. Someday, you will too."

She scowled, clearly unsatisfied with my answer, or my car's depressingly bad shocks, or both, and spun to gaze out her window, kicking her Mary Janes up and onto the dashboard.

"We'll be on the 52 soon, Tiny Flower. Then it'll be a smooth shot over and down to Chula Vista, where we can order our pizza. What should we get? Pepperoni? Sausage?"

"Anchovies!"

"Sounds like we'll be getting *two* pizzas. And tomorrow, we'll figure out something for you to do instead of hanging out with me while I interview Carolyn."

"Red!"

"Yes, sweetie, I know. She and her ex-husband are both werewolves. So was everyone else we met tonight."

"Red!"

I sighed. "We're going to be seeing a lot of werewolves over the next few days. You might want to stop shouting the color every time you—" I took my eyes off the road for just long enough to realize that she was pointing out the window. Dark shapes were pacing our car along the side of the road. "Wait, do you mean red *now?*"

"Red!" she screamed, this time pointing straight ahead. I looked back to the road and found an enormous wolf standing directly in our path. The high beams reflected off its eyes.

"Shit!" I pulled the wheel hard to the right, and we skidded past the werewolf. Another hard turn back left kept us from barreling off the road. "Okay, I think we're…"

The car bounced to the side as a heavy impact thudded into my door. I wrestled with the wheel and looked over to find multiple wolves running full-out next to my car. I was exceeding thirty miles an hour, which skirted the boundaries of safety as it was, but they were easily keeping pace. As I watched, another wolf turned and smashed into my Corolla with its shoulder.

"Shit!" I said again, as we left the road entirely for a moment, desert shrubs scraping the underside of the car. My high beams were barely sufficient to find where the road curved back in front of us. I slammed down the gas pedal and we shot forward, barreling through the underbrush. We reached the road more quickly than I had anticipated, and I spun the wheel to keep from driving over the path and back into the desert on the other side.

"Red!" Jee Sun's shout was my only warning before the car was struck heavily again. This time, the impact was on her side. As I struggled to compensate, another impact came. The little girl screamed as her window shattered, and glass sprayed across the interior.

"You know what? If that's what you want…!" I pulled the car to the left and then spun it back to the right just before the anticipated impact could come. There was a satisfying thud and a yelp, as one of the wolves was knocked off its feet. In the distance, lights on the horizon suggested we might be nearing the 52.

I accelerated again. We were now pushing almost fifty, which was well past dangerous and approaching suicidal on a road like this and in a car like mine. It seemed to be doing the trick though; a quick glance to the side showed the wolves falling behind. "I think we're almost—"

I looked up and found the road ahead of me blocked by what appeared to be ATVs. In front of those vehicles were another two wolves, staring us down as we barreled toward them. The werewolves were so large that they made the ATVs seem kid-sized.

As quickly as we were going, there was little chance of stopping—not that I could afford to do so anyway with the other wolves in hot pursuit. I blindly spun the wheel to the left and we shot off the road, hurtling past the roadblock. My headlights picked out a good-sized boulder directly in my path and I barely managed to turn the car back to the right to avoid it. I drove through an enormous tumbleweed and a handful of additional bushes, but somehow found myself back on the dirt road, headed in the right direction.

The 52 was the most beautiful thing I'd seen since Anastasia that morning, displacing even Emilio's mustache in my immediate recollection. I skidded onto the on-ramp with a squeal of tires and badly abused brakes and headed west at the Corolla's top speed of seventy-three, leaving my attackers in the literal dust.

Jee Sun picked shards of glass off her pink jacket and looked up at me reproachfully. Maybe we'd be having pizza *and* ice cream.

"Well, that was something," I told her with forced cheer.

"Shit," she agreed solemnly.

○○○

We stopped briefly along the side of the road to sweep glass out of the car, and move Jee Sun to the back seat behind me, where she would be better shielded from the cold night air. Then, I drove home, keeping an eye out for anyone who might be following us. Given that I'd failed to spot Davis or Melissa tailing me to my office the day before, it was a tense half-hour. It didn't help that every car looked alike in the dark.

It was only when I drove into my parents' neighborhood without any cars at all in my rearview mirror that I breathed a sigh of relief. There was still no sign of Ms. Givens, not that I expected her to be out in the yard at eight on a Thursday night. Jee Sun unbuckled herself and hopped out into the street to take my hand. We rounded the corner, and she pointed.

"Re—"

I clamped my hand over her mouth before the word could escape, and quickly reversed directions to take shelter behind the closest house. The Davidsons were on vacation somewhere in the Midwest, and their home was dark, its driveway clear of cars. I peeked around the house and looked where Jee Sun had been pointing.

There was a car across the street from my house. With its lights and engine off, there was, at first, nothing to distinguish it from any of the other cars parked along the curb. A second glance revealed one important difference; there were people inside, their dim silhouettes outlined by the nearby streetlight. Seriously? Werewolves were staking out *my parents' house?* The day's mediation had gone poorly, but this was an epic overreaction.

"Ow!" I hissed, as Jee Sun bit the fingers of the hand still clasped across her mouth. She glared up again at me, but I put my finger to my own lips before she could speak. "We have to get out of here."

I backed slowly away until we were entirely out of view, and then hurried her to the Corolla. With the car's lights still off, we backed up to the intersection behind us, took a left, and got the hell away from my parents' house. I found an out-of-the-way parking space a good ten blocks over and stopped to think.

Were my parents okay? I decided they must be. There was no reason for the werewolves to wait outside my house, where they might be spotted, if they had already broken in and were holding my parents hostage. Still… I dug my phone out and dialed their land line. My dad picked up after a few rings.

"Hello?"

"Dad, this is John."

"Hey John! I was wondering when we'd hear from you. Your mom is keeping a casserole warm in the crockpot. When are you coming home? It's a new recipe, and I would hate to die alone." A loud smack could be heard. "I was kidding, dear! I'm sure it's going to be lovely." He lowered his voice. "Help me, my favorite son. You're my only hope!"

If my dad was quoting Star Wars, they were fine. "I'm your *only* son, Dad."

"Which is why you're my only hope!"

"Uh huh. Actually," I continued once his laughter had died down, "this case I'm on is going to take Jee Sun and I out of town for a few days. I just wanted to check in and make sure everything was okay."

"Always, my boy! But…" his voice trailed off. I could hear my mother in the background, though her words were indistinct. "Your mom says to make sure that Jee Sun gets plenty of rest. And she's got *that look* in her eyes, so you know she really means it."

"Tell her I will," I replied, with a smile he couldn't see. "I'll see you guys later." I hung up the phone and looked in the rearview mirror. Jee Sun looked back at me, swaddled in her enormous pink coat. Now what? And why was it that every mediation seemed to end—or even start—with my clients trying to kill me? "Maybe this isn't the safest line of work after all."

"Shit," she agreed.

I was really going to have to start watching my language.

Putting the car back into drive, I pulled away. If there were werewolves at my house, then there were probably a few staking out my office too. Maybe they would at least eat some of the gangbangers while they waited. But I needed to lie low until I figured out what the hell was going on. Who in the pack was trying to kill me? Emilio and his mustache were obviously innocent; if the wolf had wanted to end my life, our mile-long hike through the desert would have been the ideal opportunity. That made me think Davis was okay too. Especially since he'd hired me in the first place.

As I rolled along the street, I looked through my phone for the werewolf's contact info and dialed him. The phone rang and rang, but nobody picked up. I ended the call when the prerecorded message came on. Either something had happened to him, or he was still out at the camp, where the reception sucked. I was betting on the latter.

E Street took me to the Best Western just off the 5, where I checked in for the night. I really hoped Davis came through with his promised bank deposit or I was going to run out of money. Especially since it looked like I'd be the one paying for pizza tonight. At least I wasn't in my dad's shoes, doomed to taste-test my mother's casserole surprise. I snickered.

That laugh petered out when I realized the werewolves at my house might do something stupid if I never showed up. Like heading inside to look for me. My mom was a force of nature, but I didn't like her odds against a pair of Infected. (One of them, sure, but two…?)

I collected my room key with a terse nod of thanks to the clerk and stepped back outside. For the third time that night, I flipped through contacts on my phone, finally dialing the number I'd promised to call. "This is John. I need your help."

INTERLUDE

"I know I'm bleeding," I growled back at Juliette. "My shoulder's completely screwed up! I'm naked and my shoulder is screwed up."

My facade of calm was crumbling fast.

"I can smell it," murmured Juliette, in a dreamy voice entirely unlike her usual tone. "Thick and warm and rich."

For a second, disgust warred with pride. Yeah, it was gross that she was talking about my blood that way, but still… it was my blood she was drooling over. Not every guy could say that.

Then both emotions were washed away by a third: fear.

"Juliette, how long have we been here?"

"I don't know," she replied, her words slightly mangled by what were clearly protruding fangs. "A day, maybe?"

"Shit. How long has it been since you fed?"

"Smells good," she murmured again. Her chains rattled loudly, and I suddenly found myself praying they would hold. Juliette had already fed on me once, when she was injured, and I'd had a hell of a time prying her off. I did not want to repeat the experience with her starving and me neatly wrapped up like a very early Christmas present.

"Earlier, you were telling me about Wonder Woman," I said, my voice shaking with a combination of fear and naked-man-on-a-cold-floor chill. "Since you're almost a hundred, I'm guessing you watched the tv show too? What was your favorite episode?"

The slow grind of metal against metal was my only reply.

CHAPTER 16

IN WHICH ICE CREAM ALWAYS WINS

I woke to the sun on my face, light streaming through our hotel room window. It took me a moment to remember why I was there and not in my wonderfully dark basement bedroom, then I rolled out of bed in a panic, and began looking for Jee Sun. It wasn't like I *wanted* to wake up with the girl staring me in the face again, but if something had happened while I was asleep…

Oh. There she was. Jee Sun sat on the end of her own bed, blanket wrapped about her as if it were a nest, watching the room's small television with unwavering focus. Tom was once again trying to teach Jerry a lesson.

Given their respective track records over the past fifty years, my money was on the mouse.

"How long have you been up?" I asked, getting only a shrug in response. "Have you eaten yet?" A shake of her head. "Are you hungry?" A vigorous nod, but her eyes stayed glued to the screen. "Purple polka-dotted people-eater catch your tongue?"

She giggled and spun about to look at me for the first time. "There's no such thing, Mr. John!"

I wished I shared her confidence. Once upon a time, I would have said the same thing about vampires, werewolves, and demigods.

I left her to her cartoons and fumbled my way to the bathroom where I took care of my morning business. Then, I cranked on the hot water in the tub, locked the bathroom door, and took a much-needed shower. The water pressure was low, and what came out of the shower head was San Diego's usual, borderline disgusting, tap water, but it felt good to scrub the prior day's dirt, sweat, and fear from my skin.

It felt considerably *less* good to pull on the same clothing I'd worn yesterday, but with my clothes at the house with my parents, I wasn't spoiled for choice. I had secured some temporary protection for the two of them, but I was reasonably sure that all bets would be off if I showed my face. At least until my side of the arrangement was finalized.

I combed through my hair, which only made things worse. When I came out, Jee Sun was still in the same spot, but Tom & Jerry had been replaced by some cartoon I'd never seen before.

"Come wash up, Tiny Flower." The look she gave me left no doubt as to how she felt about that idea. "You don't have to shower, since we don't have any fresh clothes for you to change into anyway, but at least wash your hands and face, okay? You look like a raccoon, and raccoons don't get breakfast." I dumped the messy remains of the previous night's small pizza—half anchovies, half pepperoni—into the trash can.

"Okay!" She untangled herself from the blanket, sprang to her feet, and ran to the bathroom, cape streaming behind her. I returned the blanket to its bed, turned off the television, and rescued her jacket from where it had been tossed into a heap at the bottom of the room's single closet, resolving yet again to never, ever have children of my own.

Half an hour and three Egg McMuffins later, we were on our way. As usual for ten on a Friday morning, traffic was light as I took the 5 up to the 52 and then over to the 15. I tried calling Davis again, but there was still no answer. This time, I left a message. "Davis, this is John. Something's come up, and I'm going to be very, very late for our meeting. Could we reschedule for later in the day? Like, two or three? Let me know."

Jee Sun was still banished to the back seat, thanks to the broken window on the passenger side, but I could hear her humming. It sounded suspiciously like the Eminem song she'd been blasting the day before. I kept one eye on her in the rearview mirror, and one eye on the road ahead.

○○○

At some point in San Diego's distant past, Scripps Ranch really had been a ranch; a twelve-hundred-acre property owned by a newspaper publisher named E.W. Scripps. Both the man and his ranch were long gone, as far as I knew, and the neighborhood was now home to a number of wealthy families. I'd never actually driven to our destination, but I knew the way by heart. They say you always remember your first.

First *prison*, in this case, but the adage still worked.

I pulled up at the iron gate to the estate grounds. Through its bars, I could see an enormous mansion, perched atop a grass-covered hill. In the daylight, it looked like a giant-sized version of the cookie-cutter houses we'd just traveled past. Its sole distinguishing feature was the tower that rose into the sky on one end, unbalancing the symmetry of the house, and lending it a quasi-medieval-fortress vibe. Even so, a few minutes on any real estate website would yield far more interesting looking mansions.

Appearances were deceiving.

On my last visit, the gatehouse had been staffed by human security guards, all equipped with assault rifles and flak jackets. This time, there was only a single individual. Even without visible weapons, he was far more dangerous than the humans he'd replaced. Like all members of the House Watch, he was in black, from his sneakers to his slacks to the button-up shirt that somehow managed to show off his physique while allowing full freedom of motion. Long blonde hair was tugged back into a ponytail, and wraparound shades adorned his face. He approached the car with sinuous grace.

"Yellow!" muttered Jee Sun.

"Yes, Tiny Flower, I know. You're going to be seeing a *lot* of vampires here."

"Hmpgh." She didn't seem pleased by the notion.

I rolled down the window and pasted on my best non-threatening smile. "Party of two, good sir. I called ahead for reservations."

He looked at me for a long moment and my smile started to slip. "You must be John Smith." His voice was deep and unaccented, in stark contrast to his appearance. The ponytail alone practically screamed European.

"That's me." I had met a lot of Lucia's vampires during my last stay at the House, but Ponytail-Boy was new to me. "And you are…?"

"Disinterested," he replied, stalking back to the gatehouse, where he smacked the button with unnecessary force. The gate slid aside, allowing us entry. As we drove past, I could see his lips moving silently, as he read the various slogans spray-painted on my car.

Never had I been so grateful for the filthy minds of my gangbanger neighbors.

I drove up the long, curved driveway, winding past an orchard on one side and a man-made duck pond—with actual ducks in it—on the other. The humans that had patrolled the grounds on previous visits were absent, again replaced by individual vampires. Given the losses the House had taken in the coup, I had no idea how Kayla and her Watch were managing to guard the entire property by themselves.

The House had an expansive underground garage, but I drove past its entry and parked instead at the circle that marked the very end of the driveway. A flight of stone stairs led up to the ancient wooden doors that served as the mansion's front entrance. It was only when Jee Sun and I had reached those doors that she balked, setting her feet as if fully prepared to resist any attempts to drag her inside. I crouched down to look her in the eye.

"I know you don't like vampires, Jee Sun, but I have some unfinished business with Lucia. You're safe here. I won't let anyone hurt you, and neither will Mr. Bill. Okay?"

She shook her head stubbornly. I was conscious of one of the large doors opening but kept my focus on the girl. "It'll be fun," I implored, desperately hunting for a winning argument. "They have great big televisions and a basketball court and all the food you could possibly want to eat."

That caught her attention. "Ice cream?"

"Absolutely."

"*Chocolate* ice cream?" She eyed me suspiciously, as if she'd just requested gold-flaked ice cream with diamond marshmallows.

"Of course." I recognized the accent immediately and looked over to find Kayla squatting next to us, a warm smile on her face. "But my girlfriend and I prefer chocolate double-fudge brownie."

"Okay," agreed Jee Sun tentatively. Without further prompting, she stepped inside.

"Lucia told us you were on your way," murmured Kayla. "I'm here to take you to her."

We both stood and I was reminded again of how tall Kayla was for someone old enough to be my grandmother. Like the guard at the gate, she wore the all-black uniform that identified members of the House Watch. She just made it look good.

"John, are you sure you know what you're doing?"

"I don't have a lot of options. My current case has gone pear shaped, and I have no idea how or why. And now, my family and—" I nodded in Jee Sun's direction. "—friends are in danger."

We moved deeper into the house, Jee Sun trying to look in all directions at once. Leaving the foyer behind, we passed both the stately staircase that led up to the second floor and the banquet hall that had been full of the dead and dying on my last visit.

"You know I'll help any way I can," Kayla began, her voice hushed.

"I know," I whispered back, "and I appreciate it. But for how long? You already have way too much on your plate, and I have no idea how long this will all take." We reached the elevators, and she pressed the button to summon one to our floor. "Besides, most of my friends live in this House, and it sucks not being able to visit you guys. This game of hide and seek I've been playing with Lucia was never going to work as a permanent solution."

"As long as you're sure." The elevator doors finally opened, and Jee Sun rushed inside, all reservations forgotten. She wrapped her hands around the brass bar at the back of the elevator and kicked her legs up around it until she was hanging upside down like a monkey.

Kayla quirked one eyebrow, brushing a strand of ash blonde hair out of her face. "How old is she again?"

"At this point, I have no idea." It was the third question I'd ask Bill when he returned—the first and second being where he'd gone and what he'd been thinking in giving Jee Sun a gun—but any answer I received would involve an indeterminate number of rotations on his Mickey Mouse clock. Which was even less helpful than it seemed. "Oh, that's right... you two have never actually met, have you?"

I waved a hand to get Jee Sun's attention. "Jee Sun, this is Kayla. She and Darlene are two of my best friends in San Diego. Kayla, this is Jee Sun, also known as Tiny Flower. She is Lord Beel-Kasan's best friend in at least two worlds."

Jee Sun dropped to her feet with a thud. She peered at Kayla and then back at me. "She's yellow, Mr. John," she said quietly, which was at least a marked improvement over her tendency to shout.

"Yes, she is," I agreed. "But she is still a friend, just like Juliette, who you had milkshakes with, and Anastasia, who you met yesterday."

She thought about that for a moment and shrugged. "Okay." The elevator began to rise, and she looked about her. "Are we going to the ice cream?"

"Soon," I promised, "but I have to speak with Lucia first." Her fierce expression told me that she remembered exactly who Lucia was. This was *such* a bad idea. "We'll get ice cream together afterward. And whipped cream."

She wrinkled her nose at the last suggestion, leaving me scratching my head. What sort of little girl didn't like whipped cream? It was downright un-American.

The elevator doors opened onto the House's third floor waiting room, where we were ushered through the checkpoint of armed Watch members. Behind me, Jee Sun had started humming again.

Yeah, that was *definitely* Eminem.

CHAPTER 17
IN WHICH GOOD HELP ISN'T FREE

The House's third floor was reserved for the living quarters of Lucia and her Council, but additional suites had been set aside for the Captain of the Watch and Zorana. As we walked past the first two rooms, I nodded to the door on our left, where Xavier had lived before his ill-fated coup. "Have you and D moved up yet?"

"No." She shook her head at my look of surprise. "D's not thrilled about abandoning our old rooms on the second floor. Especially with all the added security up here."

"Well, it *would* make her late-night kitchen raids more difficult." I grinned. "So, both Xavier and Andrés' rooms are just… empty?" Andrés had been another casualty of the coup.

"At the moment. Queen Lucia has found a replacement for Andrés in one of the Brazilian Houses, but he or she won't arrive to take their seat on the Council until early next year."

"And in the meantime, you're short-staffed?"

"Badly, and at every level." Kayla's voice was uncharacteristically grim. "I'm sure you saw how many of us are being used just to patrol the exterior. There's too much ground to cover, and too few of us to do it, even with the new recruits."

We finally reached the end of the hallway. The door there opened in response to Jee Sun's eager knocking, and she scowled as the individual within was revealed.

"Mr. Smith. Human child. Captain. Enter and be welcome." Lucia was sticking with her standard color scheme. A cropped white leather halter clung to her shapely torso, exposing tanned shoulders and an acre of cleavage, while butter-soft leather pants in matching white showcased her narrow waist and every last curve of her hips.

I blinked. I'd seen that outfit before. This was how Lucia dressed for war, which made the sight every bit as alarming as it was appealing. Despite the femmepire's courteous words—and her welcoming smile—I entered the room on high alert.

Lucia's suite was, as might be expected, palatial, larger than my parents' entire house. It had six rooms, although I'd only ever seen two of them. We followed her through the first—the entry hall—and into the second—the living room. The rest of the Council had assembled there, standing in a line along the far wall, with the enormous bay window at their backs. I nodded to each of them in turn.

Anastasia was clad in the twin to Lucia's outfit, although hers was black instead of white. The dark leather set off the red in Ana's hair, and I drank her image in like a man who'd been lost for weeks in the desert.

To Ana's left was Marcus, the vampire accountant, dressed in another of his thousand-dollar tailored suits. To look at him, you'd never guess that the GQ cover model was capable of sprouting bat-like wings and flying. As Talents went, his was admittedly cool… it was just his personality that sucked.

We traded sneers from across the room.

Juliette stood on Anastasia's right, dressed in a pastel pantsuit rather than her usual punk rock t-shirt and skintight jeans. She looked fantastic too—like an ice-cream-and-attitude sundae—but I was starting to wonder if her promotion had come with a mandatory wardrobe upgrade. I missed her usual style.

Last but certainly not least was Zorana, who had paired a cheap yellow cotton sundress with ruby slippers likely stolen from the set of the Wizard of Oz. The Blood Witch wore what she wanted, when she wanted, and woe to the individual who suggested otherwise. She flashed fangs at me in an expression that could never be mistaken for a smile.

Jee Sun squeaked and hid behind my leg, once again exhibiting terrible taste in human shields. Her reaction did prompt an actual smile from Zorana but even that was the sort of smile a leopard would save for the gazelle.

Lucia reached the center of the room and turned, clearly prepared to launch into whatever formalities she'd unearthed for the occasion.

I didn't have time for that. "Are my parents okay?"

Marcus growled something under his breath about protocol and manners, but Lucia took my interruption with surprising grace. "They are unharmed, Mr. Smith. Per last night's agreement, members of the Watch are there even now, guarding your domicile. The Infected fled as soon as my forces made their appearance." Her lip curled as she mentioned the werewolves.

I felt a knot of tension inside me suddenly loosen. I guess I could have swung by for a change of clothes after all. Oh well. The vampire elders (and Kayla) would just have to put up with me in my not-so-best.

"However," Lucia cautioned, "as my Captain has no doubt informed you, my House's strength is stretched thin. We cannot watch your residence for an extended length of time. When we depart, it seems likely that the beasts will return." Her glacial blue eyes met my own, and the sweet smile turned sharp. "I would suggest you conclude your business as quickly as possible or instruct your family to leave town."

"As much as my mom and dad love Vegas, I doubt they're ready to head back so soon," I mused, "but thanks for the warning. How much time can you give me?"

"A day, maybe two at most." She saw my reaction, and spread her hands wide, palms up. "In the aftermath of Xavier's betrayal, we are far below our usual strength, and must worry about further attacks. My primary concern will always be the safety and well-being of my subjects."

I nodded absently. While I wasn't inclined to believe *anything* Lucia told me anymore, Kayla, Anastasia, and my own walk through the empty building had all made the House's situation abundantly clear. The traitors might have been killed, but the driving force behind that attack—Lucia's brother, the king of the Italian court she had been exiled from—remained a threat, his power undiminished. At some point, he would try again to destroy his sister and her House. The only questions were when and how.

Technically, I was a little bit fuzzy on the why too, other than that it had something to do with vampire politics. Maybe Lucia irritated her brother as much as she did me?

The obvious snag in this entire situation was that the werewolf mediation was nowhere near complete. Hell, it had barely even started, and as I had recently told Carolyn and Jason, the process could take the full month that the Toulon Concordat allowed. A day or two of protection was not going to cut it.

"There is perhaps another solution," mused Lucia, her eyes tracking every emotion as it skated across my face. She tapped one long finger against her plush lower lip, a gesture of thoughtfulness that was as pretentious as it was premeditated.

"Such as?" It was clear that the blonde queen had a plan, and equally clear that I wouldn't like that plan. But beggars couldn't afford to be choosers.

"If you formalized your relationship with my House…"

"My queen—" Anastasia began to protest, but Lucia held up a hand for silence. Next to me, I felt Kayla stiffen. Marcus remained expressionless, while Juliette looked almost as confused as I was. That left only Zorana, and I very carefully did not look in the Blood Witch's direction. Doing so would just encourage her, and the next thing you knew, she'd be biting the heads off live rats on stage or something.

"Isn't that what we're doing right now?" I waved a hand, the gesture encompassing myself, the queen, and her Council. "You're helping me out, I'm agreeing to let bygones be bygones, and we're resuming the professional relationship that ended—" *When you decided to enslave me.* "—when we had our disagreement."

The initial source of that disagreement plopped down onto my foot, still humming to herself. I glanced down, relieved to see that Jee Sun had retreated into her own little world. Her brand of chaos was not going to be helpful in this sort of situation.

As for myself… diplomacy wasn't something that came easily to me, particularly when dealing with someone like Lucia. But these were my parents' lives at stake; I would do whatever it took.

Lucia glanced over one golden shoulder at Anastasia. The auburn-haired femmepire stepped forward, her lovely green eyes reflecting the soft glow of the room's many lamps.

"What you've described is simply a business arrangement, Mr. Smith, such as we had with the Rook before you. An understanding that your mediation services remain available to us, should we require them."

"Right. So, what's the difference between that and a formalized relationship?"

"The latter would involve House Borghesi officially putting their political weight behind your position," said Lucia. "It would also make an attack on you the same as an attack on my House, and one that, by the provisions of the Concordat, the People would be free to defend or avenge."

That sounded pretty good too. My own private vampire army? I could work with that. And yet... "How would that help my parents? Would they get the same protection?"

"No, Mr. Smith," said Lucia, "but our allies in San Diego would be far more willing to defend the family of someone formally affiliated with our House."

"Ah." I didn't ask where those supposed allies had been over the summer. Maybe coups didn't count. And again, this was a time for diplomacy. "So, the House doesn't have the numbers to run security for my parents, but someone else could—"

The sound of running feet in the hallway cut me off in mid-question. I spun just in time to intercept the dark-haired missile that sprinted around the corner and launched herself at my chest.

"John! You came back!"

I looked down into the big blue eyes of the House's lone child, a now six-year-old vampire who had her arms and legs wrapped around my mid-section in a python-like grip that was slowly depriving me of air. While she was a good twelve years from her first feeding and the powers that would come with it, she was still way stronger than a human child.

"Hello, Tea Leaf." I returned the hug, and then slowly peeled her off, placing her on her feet. Her wild mop of curly brown hair barely reached my waist, but she beamed up at me. Just seeing her made me smile. "I like your dress. Are those dragonflies?" I teased.

She glanced down at her dress and giggled. "No, silly! They're ladybugs!" She started to speak again, but stopped, looking past me.

Her eyes widened until they were the size of small saucers. "Who are *you*?"

"I am JEE SUN!" replied Bill's ward, who had somehow managed to avoid being trampled in the chaos of Tea Leaf's entrance.

"My name is Summer. John calls me Tea Leaf!"

The two girls regarded each other warily for a long moment. All we needed to turn their standoff into a spaghetti western was harmonica music and a tumbleweed. I heard movement from the Council members behind me but didn't dare look away. "Now, girls…" I began, hesitantly.

"John is going to be my donor!" Tea Leaf told Jee Sun brightly. "Do *you* have a donor?"

"I have Mr. Bill," said Jee Sun, who thankfully had no idea what a donor was. "We eat pizza and watch Winnie the Pooh."

"Oh." Tea Leaf digested that for a little bit, before shrugging and smiling happily. "Do you wanna play tea with me and Sir Floppy?"

"Are there cookies?"

"Yes! And pie!" cheered Tea Leaf. She darted forward and grabbed Jee Sun's hand, and the two of them tore back out of the room. Tea Leaf's voice echoed down the hall to us. "Why are you wearing *that*? Did your mommy make you go to church?"

"I think it might be best if I watched over the girls, my queen," offered Kayla, hurriedly heading off in pursuit. I wasn't sure if Kayla wanted children—the People had a notoriously difficult time conceiving—but a few hours with those two would probably cure her of that desire. They were *almost* cute enough to be worth the trouble…

But only almost.

I turned back to Lucia in time to catch a fond smile on her face. Summer tended to have that sort of effect on people.

"Did Tea Leaf—I mean Summer—just ask Jee Sun if she'd been to *church*? I didn't think your kind attended mass."

"We do not, Mr. Smith. We understand that there are a multitude of gods, and that they deserve respect but not worship."

"But…?"

"But I have a responsibility to Summer's family to educate her in the realities of the world. Human religions have changed the balance of power on this planet on multiple occasions. It would be foolish of me *not* to educate her about such things." She smiled again, a far warmer smile than I had ever earned. "She quite liked church, but was mystified as to why the parishioners would drink wine and pretend it was blood, when there was so much blood readily available. I explained that your species has all manner of illogical rituals."

On the far left, Zorana coughed pointedly; a neat trick, since vampires didn't suffer from phlegm. Or colds. Or sickness of any kind.

Lucia shot Zorana a look as cold as the arctic snow. "As our Blood Witch reminds me, time is short, and we have strayed a good distance from the original thrust of our conversation. I believe you had further questions about my proposal?"

"Uhm…" I'll be honest, I'd lost my train of thought, and finding it again took a minute or two. What had we been talking about before Summer came in…? Oh, right.

"Just one question, actually. You've done your best to tell me how this arrangement helps me… but what does the House get out of it?" The vampire queen was many things, but charitable was not one of them.

Again, Lucia gestured to Anastasia, and again, her Secundus stepped forward to respond.

"As you are aware, Mr. Smith, one of the primary currencies in our world is prestige. Claiming you is something that would gain my queen a great deal of it and put an end to any lingering stories of a rift between our House and yours."

"It would do more than just end them," corrected Lucia. "The ability to improve one's position even after what initially appears to be failure—to turn weakness into strength—is a mark of power and of wisdom."

"Seriously?" I would have laughed, but neither Anastasia nor Lucia cracked a smile. "But I'm just a human! I have a home, not a house, and I've heard—at considerable length—what most of your world thinks of my species."

"You are the mediator for San Diego," replied Anastasia calmly. "While you hold that position, you are no mere human."

"In fact," said Lucia, "your short-lived rebellion has gained you a measure of respect, which means the net gain for my House will be even greater than if you had just originally submitted."

I didn't like the idea that my daring not to jump at Lucia's orders might have actually benefited the queen. But it did explain why she was pushing this proposition so hard.

"Alright. So, this would net you bonus rep points, which would shore up the House's footing at the top of San Diego's power pyramid."

"Precisely." Lucia's lips curved upward into a smile that, even directed elsewhere, left me weak in the knees.

"Got it." I didn't care about Lucia's prestige, but I *did* like the idea of making things safer for my friends at the House. Especially if it also allowed me to protect my parents and wasn't going to cost me a thing. Hell, they could declare me the Sacred Cow of Scripps Ranch, if they wanted. "Where do I sign?"

"There is no written contract, Mr. Smith." Anastasia's voice was as composed as ever, but an undecipherable emotion flitted across her face.

"Okay. So… what? We shake on it?"

"We can do so, if you like," replied Lucia, "but the agreement must be witnessed by a neutral party and sealed in blood."

"Sealed in *what* now?"

"I will partake of your blood and provide you with a taste of my own. Our energies will intertwine, and our forces will align. Symbolically, at least."

"Oh, hell no!" I shook my head vigorously. "I've fed enough of you vampires to last me two lifetimes."

"What?!" Lucia's beautiful mask cracked, and her blue eyes flared like tiny suns. A cool wind blew through the suite, as if someone had just opened a window directly to the North Pole. *"Who dared feed on my thrall…?!"*

"I did." Juliette stepped forward, shoulders tight and eyes worried. "After the car bombing, John and I were stranded in Lord Beel-Kasan's home world. My wounds weren't healing sufficiently on their own. I swear I didn't have any other choice. And technically, he wasn't your thrall yet."

I winced at the memory. I had survived a car bomb, only to awaken in Gehenna, body riddled with shrapnel. As painful as those wounds had been, they had paled in comparison to Juliette feeding from my wrist. But without my blood, she would never have been able to carry me through Gehenna while we searched for an exit. And the tourniquet she had tied around my leg while I was unconscious—despite having a solid foot of steel scrap through her own abdomen at the time—had unquestionably saved my life. It had all balanced out, more or less.

I wasn't going to explain any of that to Lucia though… not when she was doing spooky things with the temperature. Nobody had warned me that she was so possessive of her toys.

The cold wind continued to howl through the suite as Lucia pondered her Council member's words. Marcus shifted uneasily from foot to foot. It might have been honest concern for Juliette, but I was betting he just didn't want to be caught in the blast… or saddled with Lady Middleton's duties, should the queen decide to downsize the Council by one.

Zorana's sugar-sweet smirk, on the other hand, suggested she was actively enjoying the chaos and discord. Sometimes, it felt like the Blood Witch was *trying* to be over-the-top evil. I guess everyone needed a hobby.

"If you had not fed," Lucia finally concluded, "it is likely that neither you nor Mr. Smith would have survived to escape Gehenna and unravel the truth behind Xavier's conspiracy." She nodded sharply, and the wind died, as if it had never existed. "And as you said, he was not yet my thrall. I accept your explanation, Lady Middleton."

Juliette sagged as the tension left her.

I was really getting tired of the t-word being tossed around. "Regardless, having you and Juliette each feed on me once was enough. Never again."

Lucia took a step toward me, somehow rolling her hips in a way that drew the eye. She looked more perplexed than angry, which made no sense. Worse, I was struck by the sudden realization that I actually *preferred* her angry. A nuanced Lucia wrinkled my brain. Before you knew it, I'd be stuck paying for dinner. Again.

"My queen…" began Anastasia again, her voice touched with a note of concern. Unable to see Lucia's expression, the femmepire clearly feared the worst.

"Worry not, Secundus." Lucia's voice was calm, and the look she gave me reflected that same cool serenity. "It is *your* decision, Mr. Smith. I will not risk discord in my House a second time by forcing you to my will."

Behind her, Anastasia's expression cleared.

"I appreciate that," I allowed, "but my answer is still *hell no.*"

"You have an alternate plan then?" Lucia's voice was soft, but the sweetly spoken words cut like knives. "To protect your parents, yourself, and Lord Beel-Kasan's ward?"

That raised an obnoxiously good point. In the aftermath of the werewolves' assault, I hadn't even *thought* of what to do with Jee Sun. After the previous night's narrow escape, keeping her with me was no longer an option. And even if I could convince my parents to leave the city for a week or two, asking them to take the little girl with them was a terrible idea. Bill might return for her at any time, and I did *not* want my parents making the acquaintance of Southern California's demigod of nightmares. Ever.

I could stash Jee Sun at the Best Western during the day, but the television wasn't going to keep her occupied full-time, and I didn't think even Davis' deposit would be sufficient to cover the damage Bill's ward might inflict on her surroundings when bored.

For that matter, what was I going to do if my werewolf attackers decided that trying to run me off the road had been too subtle a ploy and they needed to kick things up a notch? It was going to be difficult for me to hide when I was meeting with the pack every day, especially since I had absolutely no clue which of the two factions was gunning for me.

I kept spiraling, conscious of the weighty gazes of the entire freaking House Council. I worked my way up and down every possible approach, examined every angle, and finally realized the simple truth wasn't going to change. Without help, I was well and truly screwed.

Lucia was watching my face and knew immediately when I had reached my conclusion. Her red lips slowly widened into a shark's toothy smile.

Well, shit.

CHAPTER 18

IN WHICH A JAWA BEARS WITNESS

"Tell me again why Lucia has to *bite* me?"

We had moved what I was starting to think of as the *worst party ever* into the Midnight Tower, the medieval looking structure that rose ominously into the sky on one end of the mansion. The tower got its name from the fact that its open roof looked out onto a starscape of perpetual night. I still didn't know how that was possible. I stood by the raised altar that was the tower's only furnishing, and awaited Lucia's arrival with the neutral witness.

"Couldn't we just slice my finger or have Zorana pull my blood out through my nose or something?"

"As appetizing as you make that last possibility sound," Anastasia's voice was dry, "the act of feeding is an important part of the ritual."

"Could I have her feed from my wrist then?" Every repetition of the word *feed* made me want to curl into a small ball. My fight or flight instinct was heavily predisposed toward the second option.

"When the head of a House accepts fealty from their members, she gifts those vassals with a single sip from her wrist. For Lucia to feed from *your* wrist would be a declaration of submission." She caught my sudden look of consideration. "There is no chance of that happening, John."

"Seriously," I grumbled, "is there anything in vampire culture that *isn't* ridiculously over-complicated?"

"Beer," chimed in Juliette helpfully, joining us by the altar. "There's nothing complex about beer. Although who drinks first, pays for it, and what type of beer it is …" She ran a hand through her spiky hair and smirked, yellow eyes dancing. "Okay, scratch that. Even beer is a bit of a mine field."

"Of course it is." I matched Juliette's smirk, before a new thought occurred to me. "If the wrist is out, and I don't want her gnawing on my throat like an angry badger, what other options are there?"

There was a moment of silence, and then both femmepires' gazes flickered down to…

"Oh, hell no!" I didn't even care that my protestations were starting to get repetitive. I covered my crotch with both hands.

"Actually, she would take it from your femoral vein. Which," Anastasia clarified, "is in your thigh. Your manhood would be left untouched."

"Something I'm sure it's used to," added Juliette.

"Lady Dumenyova," I addressed Anastasia formally, ignoring the snickering Juliette to the best of my abilities, "please inform the Lady Middleton that, as someone who *did* feed from my wrist and is therefore clearly submissive to me, she will henceforth no longer be allowed to mock me."

"I'd have an easier time giving up blood for good, little bird," said Juliette.

So much for that. I swear, vampires only cared about the rules when they stood to benefit from them.

"Anyway," I continued stiffly, "while my dude parts and I thank you for the clarification, I'm still not particularly crazy about the idea of someone drinking from my thigh."

"That is understandable, John." Anastasia's mouth quirked briefly, as if a smile were trying to peek out. "Such locations are often reserved for more private settings."

"Oh." I looked down at my thigh, and the jeans that covered it. "Oh! Right." Yeah, I was not going to be disrobing any time soon if I could help it. Especially not in front of an audience. I let out another defeated sigh. "I guess she'll be slurping from my neck, after all."

"I do not *slurp*, Mr. Smith."

We turned to find Lucia crossing the tower's marble floor, a robed and cowled individual following her. Freaking vampire hearing. There was no such thing as a private conversation in the House. And I would never get over how quietly they could move, even when wrapped in leather.

"Sorry, Lucia," I retorted, ignoring Anastasia's disapproving look as I intentionally dropped the queen's title, "but the last time you fed on me, I was a little bit too busy trying not to scream to take note of your *technique*."

"Sadly, this feeding will be far swifter than the last, Mr. Smith, so I cannot promise the same level of pleasure." She smiled at the look on my face. "But you may still scream if you are so inclined."

"Just don't moan," pleaded Juliette. "It's such a cliché."

"On the contrary," retorted Lucia, "a good moan can be just the thing to put a cap on the entire experience."

I looked from Lucia's pleased expression to Juliette's. "What?!?" I turned to Anastasia, who had removed herself slightly from the conversation upon Lucia's arrival. "What the hell are they talking about?"

The auburn-haired femmepire raised an eyebrow. "They are talking about the sexual pleasure engendered in a donor when one of the People feeds."

"Wait… it's supposed to feel *good?*"

"Are you suggesting that it doesn't?" Lucia's voice was chilly. Offended, even.

"I'm not suggesting anything," I said, "I'm *telling you* it doesn't. In fact, it hurts like hell." And I'd been to hell—or at least a hell dimension—so I knew what I was talking about.

There was another long moment of silence.

"Fascinating," the queen finally said, her voice anything but amused. "In your own peculiar fashion, you are a very interesting specimen, Mr. Smith."

I replayed that last line in my head. Yep; she really *had* managed to take a backwards-compliment, pair it with an actual compliment, and then finish it with the obvious insult of referring to me as a specimen. And all in only eleven words. Maybe contempt was another of her secret vampire powers.

"It has been theorized that the pleasurable sensation is the result of a subconscious utilization of compulsion during the bite," Anastasia mused. "If so, then Mr. Smith's immunity—"

"—would explain the result," Lucia finished, with a nod of agreement. Her cold blue-eyed gaze ensnared my own. "At last, I understand why you objected so strongly to my actions."

"Clearly, you don't," I sighed. "If it was just about the pain, I'd have been equally pissed at the Duchess of Snark over there." I nodded to Juliette, who was looking a little bit green. She must have eaten something that disagreed with her prior to my arrival. "Instead, I just punched her in the face, and we put the event behind us."

"You punched her in the face?" This time, Anastasia's smile surfaced entirely, brightening the room—if not the world—in the process. Juliette scowled, which brightened the room even further. I so rarely came out ahead of her in these conversations.

"She wouldn't let go of my arm," I explained. It had been like punching a boulder. While the blow had been sufficient to snap Juliette out of her feeding frenzy, the femmepire had otherwise shown no ill effects. And she was the *youngest and weakest* of the Council.

It was a sobering thought.

I looked back over at Lucia. "Like I said, it wasn't about the pain. I can handle pain." Usually with lots of tears and expletives, but I wasn't going to tell them that. A man had to have some pride, right?

"So, your primary objection really *is* that whole *free will* thing you were prattling on about at the restaurant?"

That whole free will thing? Prattling on? God, I hated vampires. I looked at the two ladies flanking the queen, and begrudgingly amended the thought. *Some* vampires. "Obviously."

Lucia shook her head, her platinum blonde hair shimmering like silk. "I shall never understand Americans." She turned to address the robed figure who had been waiting in silence. "Are you ready for us to begin?"

The figure nodded slowly in response, and I took my first good look at him/her/it. Whoever or whatever they might have been, they were taller than I was, which meant they towered above the blonde queen. Every inch of that height was wrapped in a thick brown material that looked suspiciously like burlap. The robe hid the lines of the creature underneath, and the large hood cloaked their features in darkness. They might have been human, they might have been vampire, or they might have been some weird soul-sucking fiend I'd never heard of. Did chupacabras wear clothes? My knowledge of myth and legend was admittedly fuzzy, but the only inhuman creature I knew of that wandered around the desert in a brown hood and robe was...

I had to bite back a laugh. If this was a Jawa, it was the biggest damn one the Star Wars universe had ever seen.

"Very well then." Lucia repositioned me several feet to my left, putting the altar at my right hip. She stood at the other end, with the altar between us. Anastasia and Juliette joined Marcus and Zorana on the far side of the room, and the enormous would-be Jawa took its place directly in front of the queen and me.

When Lucia spoke next, it was in a language I'd heard only once before, filled with bizarre rises and falls, hisses and moans. The only words that were recognizably English were John and Smith. Everything before and after—and the after part showed no signs of stopping—was gobbledygook.

After thirty seconds of unintelligible vampire monologue, I abandoned any hope that the ritual would be a short one and settled in for a long wait. I was going to have to reschedule with Davis, yet again, or risk being a no-show to the afternoon meeting. Neither option would do anything for my steadily plummeting professional reputation, and both were likely to piss off one of the few werewolves that I knew was *not* already trying to kill me.

At least, I told myself, as Lucia droned on and on, I'd always have Emilio, and his magnificent mustache.

ooo

Finally, Lucia finished her seemingly interminable speech. Either that or she was as bored as I was and had decided to call it a day. She had gestured at me more than once during her monologue as I pretended to be attentive. Maybe she'd been singing my praises in whatever weird language that had been. Or maybe the entire group— vampires and Jawa both—was having a laugh at my expense. Either way, when she turned to face me, I knew we'd reached the biting stage.

"Mr. Smith, please repeat after me."

Or not. "Okay, but I've got to warn you; I don't speak whatever that click-hiss language is, so this needs to be in English."

"Obviously." Lucia gave me a look like I was the dumbest human on the planet. I knew I was closer to average, but her expression gave me some real doubts. That was a Grade-A look of contempt, the kind that usually came with an advanced degree.

I was so glad we were going to be friends.

"Now, then…"

My speaking part was considerably shorter than the queen's. Basically, it stated that, as a result of the deep admiration and trust I held for them yadda yadda yadda, friendship blah blah blah work as a group etc. etc. etc. I stopped in the middle of the recitation, suddenly worried.

"This isn't going to make people less likely to hire me as a mediator, is it? I can't imagine anyone would be too thrilled with the idea of the House having a say in my cases."

The queen let out an exasperated sigh, drumming her long nails on the surface of the altar next to her. I snuck a glance at Zorana to see how she felt about that—it was her altar after all—but the Blood Witch and Marcus were busy talking to one another. Sensing my gaze, they both turned to regard me with flat, hostile expressions.

Oh yes, we were one big, happy family.

"Mr. Smith, if I thought this was going to compromise your position as mediator, I would not have suggested it," said Lucia. "At that point, you would be of little use to my House. We'd be better off just letting you die."

"Sure, but—"

"A mediator is not a magistrate," she continued, with her usual blend of impatience and superiority. "You do not issue judgments, so your ability to enforce an agenda—whether yours or that of your allies—is largely nonexistent." Her voice sharpened. "Now, shall we continue?"

The blonde queen did not even wait for my nod to resume putting overly pretentious words into my mouth. It seemed we had already been almost to the end, as she fell silent shortly after I repeated the line about a pact sealed in blood. We both turned to look at the mutant Jawa.

After a long pause, the figure stirred. For all I knew, it had been sleeping off the previous night's bender while the rest of us were pretending to listen to Lucia's speech. It nodded to Lucia and then to me. I broke out in immediate goose bumps, knowing what was coming.

This time, I was right. Lucia took a step forward to stand directly in front of the altar. She waited, glacial blue eyes alight with a rather worrying fire.

I waited too, until a sharp gesture from the queen informed me that I was supposed to have mirrored her movement. How anyone expected me to know that was a mystery even Sherlock could never have cracked. With a shrug, I took a tentative step forward, leaving a healthy amount of space between us.

That space vanished as she crossed it in an instant, my personal space invaded—and conquered—by the vampire queen. Lucia was quite a bit shorter than I was, despite the skyscraper heels on her white leather boots, but she had no difficulty placing one hand at the back of my neck and tugging me down until her fangs were at my throat. Both her hand and lips were feverishly warm.

"I will make this quick, my thrall," she murmured softly, and then, before I could protest being called her thrall, her fangs drove into my flesh.

I stiffened at the sudden pain, and then…

OH MY GOD.

That pain was rapidly replaced by glorious heat, like warm apple pie pouring through my veins. My eyes fluttered shut, and I clutched her to me, completely forgetting where we were and how many people were watching. I wanted that feeling to last forever. Sex was good—or so I vaguely remembered—but this was on a whole different level. It was all I could do to keep standing as Lucia had her vampiric way with me.

When the queen finally released me, only her inhumanly strong arm at my elbow kept me from melting into a puddle on the floor. She ran her tongue over the bite marks, sending a fresh spasm of delight through my body. The pleasure was fading, but I remained lightheaded and weak in the knees. I looked down into the queen's blue eyes and saw the solid ring of gold that had emerged about her pupil. Her smile was wide and satisfied.

Something about that smile reminded me where I was and that I really didn't like this woman. I jerked out of her grip.

Lucia extended one shapely arm toward me. With the other hand, she drew a nail across her wrist, slicing through the skin as if it were rice paper. Through that incision, thick, golden-hued blood languorously bubbled to the surface. "Drink, Mr. Smith, and the ritual will be complete."

I took her hand in mine, the wrist still facing upward, and lifted it to my mouth. I eyed her across the small space, my equilibrium slowly returning. "That was the last time you will be tasting my blood, Your Majesty."

I blinked. *Your Majesty? Where the hell had that come from?*

"If you say so, my thrall." Glacial blue eyes laughed at me. "Now drink."

And I did, wrapping my mouth around the wound. I'd been punched enough in the face to know what blood tasted like. Human blood, anyway. This was different. Spicy instead of salty, sweet instead of bitter. Only a small amount of blood trickled to the surface and into my mouth. I swallowed and tried to not think about what I was doing, helped considerably by the post-bite afterglow.

I'd be damned if I was going to lick her wrist afterward though.

Finally, it was over. The queen and I separated. The giant Jawa spun on its heel and headed for the stairs. Lucia reclaimed her arm, shaking free of my grasp, and followed the robed Jawa.

The ringing of heels on the marble floor told me someone was coming my way. I looked up to find Juliette scowling at me.

"So, biting doesn't feel good, does it? I cannot *believe* you actually made me feel bad about biting you!"

"I don't know what happened," I protested. "That was totally different than the other times."

"And what did I tell you about moaning?"

"Well—"

"I said *don't do it!* and yet there you were!"

"I didn't moan! Did I?" The whole episode was already a rosy haze in my memory.

"Like a twenty-dollar prostitute, little bird, within seconds of her latching on."

"Oh." I blushed.

"And then again, even louder," the spiky-haired femmepire continued mercilessly, "right around the time you grabbed her ass."

And that was when I decided to move to someplace far away, where I could live out the remainder of my life in embarrassed solitude.

Somewhere like Montana, Antarctica, or Fresno.

CHAPTER 19
IN WHICH ONE GOOD BITE DESERVES ANOTHER

I didn't see Lucia again that afternoon. The femmepire queen was apparently a bite-them-and-leave-them sort of woman. I was okay with that. In fact, I was kind of hoping we wouldn't see each other again for another decade or two.

It would take at least that long for me to stop blushing.

Anastasia and the rest of the Council had cleared out while Juliette was reading me the riot act. I followed the Duchess of Snark down the tower's spiral staircase and out onto the second floor. Despite it being the primary dormitory level for the entire house, it was mostly empty. I permitted myself a satisfied nod as we walked past the vacant room of a vampire who had tried to kill me during the coup. He hadn't been a part of that coup... he just really, really hadn't liked me. Zorana had turned him into roadkill in her angry rush to defend the House. My own salvation had been entirely incidental.

We continued past Kayla and Darlene's room and the room I had used for the week I'd been a guest/prisoner in the House. Eventually, we reached the kitchen and Juliette pushed me inside.

"Eating time. You need to replace some of what Lucia took from you."

"Is it still bleeding?" I didn't want to touch my neck, but no matter how I turned, I couldn't make out any details in the toaster oven's reflective surface.

"Of course not." The femmepire extracted a cold beer from the refrigerator and popped the bottle cap off with one thumb. "We would be spectacularly inefficient predators if our food kept bleeding after we were done with it." She peered closely at my neck, smelling faintly of spices and jasmine. "Even the marks will fade shortly. Especially if you actually eat like I just told you to."

The vampire kitchen was a marvel of technological advancement. The fact that I barely even noticed it anymore said a lot about how quickly I had adjusted to extravagance. Clearly, I was meant to be rich. Among the twelve different artisanal loaves of bread in the pantry, I found one that was just plain wheat. Two slabs of bread later, I was building a sandwich.

"More beef," said Juliette. "You want foods rich in iron. I'd also recommend you avoid serious exercise for at least a few hours, but I don't think that will be a problem for you." She smirked.

"Beef and inactivity? I've been training to be a donor all my life." I returned the cold cuts to the refrigerator and snagged a can of Coke, carrying sandwich and drink over to the small table where Juliette was already seated.

"Soda? Really?"

"We don't all get to drink beer in the middle of the day. I'm going to have to drive home at some point."

"That is true, little bird." Juliette drained the entire bottle in one long pull. It was damn impressive. She then turned and pitched it underhand the entire length of the kitchen and into the recycling bin against the far wall, which was even more so. Her yellow eyes sparkled. "I forget that some of you have to toddle on with your mundane little lives."

"Kind of like that femmepire who got stuck being the House's human relations correspondent." I made a great show of checking the clock on the near wall. "I wonder how many new issues were added to your plate while you were drinking that beer."

Juliette made a sound halfway between a laugh and a wail. "I should have left you in Gehenna." She grinned wearily. "Nobody ever told me that being a full-fledged Council member was so much damn work!"

As we chatted, numerous vampires wandered in and out of the kitchen. I waved to the familiar faces, traded scowls with the few obvious anti-human racists, and broke out into an enormous smile when Kayla's girlfriend, Darlene, made her appearance.

I had called Darlene a pixie before I knew pixies were a thing. As a human, she towered over members of the diminutive race, but the description otherwise still worked. Five-foot-nothing, with short, flaming red hair and a dusting of freckles across her button nose, she was the epitome of cute innocence. Until she opened her very filthy mouth. She took one look at me and squealed, throwing herself into the other chair at our table.

"Finally! Kayla was convinced it was never going to happen, but I told her you'd find someone to take pity on you!" She leaned close and peered into my eyes. "So, who was she? When did you meet her? How was the sex? Did you do that thing I told you about with your fingers and your thumb…" She made a gesture with her hand.

"Twenty-five and he still blushes like a schoolgirl," marveled Juliette.

"Please stop doing that," I begged, taking refuge in my sandwich until the moment had passed. "Now, what the hell are you talking about, D?"

"Let's see, John. General lightness of spirit. Relaxed shoulders. Goofy grin." She plucked my Coke off the table and took a long swig.

"You got laid! Finally! So, who *was* it? Tell Auntie D all the details!" She pulled her legs up off the floor and sat cross-legged on the chair, cornflower blue eyes wide with excitement.

"Yes, little bird, by all means, tell Auntie D," agreed Juliette with an evil smirk.

"Darlene, I didn't have sex," I explained mournfully, aware that every vampire within a hundred feet could hear our conversation.

"But the smile! The relaxed..." Darlene's eyes narrowed, and she glanced between Juliette and I. "John, has Lady Middleton been snacking on you?"

"It wasn't me," protested Juliette. "Other than the one time, and—" She polished off her second beer. "—to hear him tell it, he didn't even enjoy it. Not that you can believe *anything* he says."

You and Juliette? mouthed Darlene to me.

I waggled my hand and shrugged, knowing she'd interrogate me later.

"I just finished formalizing my relationship with the House," I told Darlene with an intentionally overblown infusion of gravitas.

"I have no idea what that means," she said brightly, "and I'm more interested in hearing who's been feeding on you. Did you and Anastasia...?"

"No!" Juliette smacked her empty beer bottle onto the table. A few of the more obvious eavesdroppers suddenly found reasons to go elsewhere.

"It was Her Majesty," I said, before matters could get more heated. "Lucia, I mean. Part of the ritual to make me an ally of the House."

"Oh." Darlene's face fell. "Was that really a good idea?"

"I didn't have much choice." I recounted the events of the last twenty-four hours. Something about the werewolf attacks seemed *off*, but I couldn't quite put my finger on it.

"I guess if it keeps your parents safe…" Darlene's own parents lived somewhere in the Midwest, but her relationship with them had ended the moment they disowned her for what they described as her *deviant* lifestyle. Kayla had offered to fly out and *change* their opinions on that front, but D had yet to take her up on the offer.

"Yeah. I did what I had to do." I took another bite of sandwich.

"And it seemed like such a hardship too," sniped Juliette, still irritated for some reason. Juliette and Darlene didn't hang out much, if at all, but their past interactions had always been pleasant. Maybe something had happened between them recently?

"I can't explain it. Unless being Lucia's pseudo-thrall allows her compulsion to work when she bites me." I looked at Juliette. "And no, I'm not letting anyone else bite me to check."

"As if I would want her sloppy seconds," Juliette sneered. The expression was ruined somewhat by the fangs that had visibly extended.

"So, it was good?" Darlene was smiling again, revitalized by the opportunity to discuss one of her two favorite subjects.

"Closest thing I've had to sex in two years."

The sudden silence that accompanied my remarks told me I'd managed to shock an entire kitchen full of vampires.

I looked around the table at Juliette and Darlene, and then past them to the cluster of manpires who were studiously *not* looking in my direction. "What? The fact that vampire bites are pleasurable can't be news to any of you."

"I think they were reacting more to the *two years* part, John."

"Holy shit, little bird," breathed Juliette, "you must be primed to explode."

"It's not that big of a deal—"

"In fact, I'm amazed you didn't just pop on the spot!"

"We are *not* having this conversation right now," I declared. "Or ever." I reclaimed my soda from Darlene, and took a sip, very carefully not making eye contact with any of the gawking vampires.

"How long did the queen drink?" Darlene asked Juliette, now ignoring me entirely.

"Long enough for lover boy to grab her ass," came the reply.

"I'm sorry, John," Darlene said, meeting my eyes with a serious gaze, "but you're going to need a bigger sandwich."

ooo

I was polishing off my second sandwich—a significantly larger one that came with three stacks of sliced roast, a thin layer of spinach, and Darlene's grudging approval—when my wonderphone buzzed. I fished it out of my pocket and swiped across the screen.

"Hello?"

"John, this is Davis. I got your messages. Were you planning on meeting with Carolyn and I sometime today, or should I be looking for a new mediator?"

"Somebody's in trouble," snickered Juliette.

"I'm pretty sure I'm the *only* mediator available, Davis," I pointed out, firing a triumphant look at Juliette as I did so.

"If you are unavailable to continue, we are within our rights to contact the mundane mediators in the city."

"Point taken." Four months ago, all of the city's mediators had been killed by the karkino on Xavier's orders, but I was pretty sure that vacuum was on its way to being filled. I swallowed my remainder of sandwich and washed it down with the last dregs of soda. "I had a few unexpected issues crop up, but I think that's all taken care of now. I'll tell you about it at our meeting."

I wanted to look both him and Carolyn in the eyes when I told them about the werewolf attack. It was far too easy for someone to pretend surprise over the phone.

"So, you *will* be able to speak with us today?"

"Yep." What had crawled up his butt and died? The son of Odin and I were going to have ourselves a talk. A very courteous and carefully worded talk; I had no interest in being beaten to death with one of my own limbs. I checked the wall clock. "How does 3:30—"

Juliette shook her head.

"I mean 4:00—" I received a nod of approval from the femmepire. "—sound?"

"We'll be here, Mr. Smith."

Juliette reached over and muted my phone. "Tell him you're bringing a guest."

"Okay?" I unmuted the device and did just that. Davis didn't seem pleased. The big werewolf had been much less of an asshole face-to-face. Maybe he was having a bad hair day.

Maybe *every* day was a bad hair day for werewolves.

When the call was over, I turned to Juliette. "What was that about? What guest?"

"Queen's orders." She shrugged. "Your exhibitionism in the Tower has apparently earned you a temporary bodyguard until this mess is over."

"That almost makes it worth it." I nobly ignored her slanderous interpretation of what had, after all, simply been a vampire ritual. "And my parents…?"

"They are safe," Anastasia answered, sweeping into the kitchen like a black-clad angel of death. Her entrance triggered a mass exodus of the vampires who had been milling about the kitchen. By the time she reached our table, the room was almost empty. "The White Ladies have agreed to watch over your family. Kayla is recalling our own people now."

"White Ladies?" The term sounded familiar. "You mean… ghosts?" Darlene and Juliette both looked surprised. "I do read, you know. It would be kind of dumb to discover that vampires and werewolves were real and then *not* research what else might be out there."

Plus, with Mike in the honeymoon phase of his new relationship, I'd had a lot of free time on my hands.

"Well said, Mr. Smith."

"Thank you, Lady Dumenyova." I smiled at the lovely vampire. "But I thought White Ladies were solitary beings?"

"Usually, they are," confirmed Juliette. "As recently as forty years ago, our city's Ladies kept to themselves, and never left their hauntings."

"What happened?" I didn't point out that her version of *recently* was fifteen years before I'd been born. I had enough trouble getting the People to take me seriously without continuously pointing out my relative youth.

"Graciela happened." The spiky-haired femmepire shrugged and rose to her feet. It was bizarre to see the punk rock proponent dressed demurely in a suit while Lady Dumenyova—by far the more conservative of the two—wore shiny black leather. "Could you babysit John while I go get ready, Anastasia?"

"Actually, Lady Middleton," Anastasia replied smoothly, "our queen has requested your presence. I believe she wishes to review your progress on the mayoral negotiations."

"As much as I'd *love* to spend another three hours discussing pointless minutiae, I'm going to have to pass, this once." Juliette's sweet smile was in direct contrast to both her words and the sharpness of her voice. "I just don't know that I could trust anyone else to keep little bird alive for the day."

"Then you will be gratified to hear that Queen Lucia has assigned me that very task." Anastasia met Juliette's fierce gaze coolly and it was the younger femmepire who looked away first. "I will not let anything happen to Mr. Smith."

Juliette slunk away, figurative tail between her legs, but not before shooting me a vicious glare.

Why was she angry at *me?*

With Juliette's departure, Darlene, Anastasia, and I were now the only three left in the kitchen. It was astonishing just how quickly the room had cleared. Darlene rose from her own chair.

"I should go find Kayla." She paused on her way out of the kitchen. "Hey, we're going to hit the Bitter End tonight. Want to come? Nine-ish?"

"Sounds good. Invite Juliette too? It seems like she could use a few drinks to loosen up."

"And some dancing, I bet. Will do." Darlene smiled mischievously in the doorway. "In the meantime, you two crazy kids have fun. Don't do anything Kayla and I wouldn't!" She gave me a big wink and skipped out into the hall.

I met Anastasia's jade green eyes. "And then there were two."

"Indeed." She shrugged. "There is a reason I seldom come to this floor. My presence tends to put a damper on the usual socialization."

"Only because they're scared of you," I pointed out helpfully, "which they might not be, if you came to the floor more often." It was my turn to shrug. "But I'm going to tell you something that I tell myself every time one of my dates crashes and burns."

"And what is that, Mr. Smith?"

"It's their loss." I grinned. "Now, in my case, that's just a lie I tell myself over donuts to make everything better, but for you…"

She looked at me for a long moment. "Every individual in this House fears me, John, save the queen—to whom I have pledged my life—and Zorana, who fears nothing. Why is it that you do not?"

"Didn't we have this conversation already?"

"We started to, yes."

I shrugged. "You're hot and I'm an idiot." I was clearly still riding a post-bite high because I would never have said that out loud normally.

Anastasia remained expressionless.

"Oh. You want the truth?"

"If you would."

"Okay." I thought for a moment, while the lovely femmepire studied me. "As far as I can tell, most of your world operates on some sort of cosmic pecking order." Noting her blank look, I clarified. "Power hierarchies, I mean. At the top are the greater gods and demons, followed by the demigods, followed by... whatever. Right?"

"Yes."

"Well, if you keep following that line of diminishing power, past the elder vampires, and the young vampires, the pixies and the goblins and the gnomes, at the very bottom, you'll find humans like me." I leaned forward, trying to emphasize my point. "*Everything* in this big, bad world of yours can kill me."

"And so?" She didn't even try to deny it. Anastasia had never sugarcoated the truth. It was one of the things I appreciated about her.

"And so, if I were going to be afraid of Lady Anastasia Dumenyova, aka House Secundus, aka The Stone Lady, aka whatever other impressively inscrutable titles you've accrued over the past four centuries... I'd *also* have to be afraid of that dick of a manpire who's currently guarding the gate. I'd have to be afraid of a werewolf with a mullet. I'd have to be afraid of ten-inch-high pixie entrepreneurs. And all that fear," I concluded, leaning back and crossing my arms, "would give me prematurely grey hair."

That surprised her, and I reveled in the musical notes of her all-too-rare laughter.

"I certainly would not wish such a terrible fate upon you, John," she noted primly, eyes sparkling, as she glanced at my untamed—but dark—mop of hair.

"Because you are a gracious and luminous creature," I said cheekily, depositing my plate in the sink and my soda can in the recycling bin. "But really, that's only part of why I'm not afraid of you."

"I believe you said something about me being hot," she teased.

"You have *no* idea." I let my grin fall away and regarded her soberly. "But I also remember who spoke for me when the Council wanted me dead. I remember Xavier with his sword at my throat, and I remember who stopped him."

I offered her a short bow, looking just as stupid as I had feared I would. And that was okay. Sometimes, gratitude was more important than pride.

She returned the bow with a nod, jade eyes intent on my face.

"But yeah," I admitted, "a lot of it's because you're hot."

INTERLUDE

You'd think it would be difficult to fall asleep while cold, bleeding, and under the threat of a hungry femmepire, but I managed it just fine. After all, we'd been imprisoned for more than a day, which meant I'd been without coffee for at least that long.

Vampires weren't the only creatures with dependencies.

Juliette had dozed off too at some point, although I could still hear the occasional clink of metal as she twitched in her sleep. I had learned two things already from my imprisonment. First, vampires did, in fact, sleep—Kayla had always said so, but everything with her and Darlene was so loaded with innuendo, that it was impossible to be sure—and second, Lady Middleton snored. Loudly. I was going to give her endless amounts of shit over that little fact… assuming we were rescued before she broke free from her chains and drank me dry like the world's largest juice box.

I was pretty sure it was her snoring that had woken me. I stared up into the darkness and took a careful inventory of my body.

Still naked and tied up? Check.

Still unable to see a damn thing? Check. In another blow to high-school Biology, my bat-like radar had yet to manifest.

Hungry? Thirsty? I was getting there. My mouth was dry but I managed to work up a little bit of drool at the thought of a nice burger and ice-cold soda.

And fries. Fries would be key.

Shoulder bleeding?

Huh.

I couldn't see my shoulder to tell if the blood flow had stopped, but the pain had dissipated. I rolled the shoulder. Still no pain. I rolled the other shoulder too, in case I'd somehow mistaken which one was injured, and got the same result. As far as I could tell, my wound had healed. Which was suspicious but also awesome.

"Things are looking up," I told myself hopefully. Maybe high-school Biology had been right after all.

Which was when I realized it wasn't Juliette's snores that had woken me. A muffled pounding could be heard. I focused my—still distressingly mundane—hearing on the new noise, and it resolved into something very much like heavy footsteps, somewhere above us. Those steps continued for a short time, and then there was the unmistakable sound of a door opening nearby.

The footsteps resumed, but they were louder now, coming in an odd staccato rhythm. I felt them drawing closer.

Something was coming toward us.

Something was coming, and I remained entirely helpless.

Helpless and still naked.

Waiting as the unseen beast drew closer, I felt a little bit like Monty Python's Black Knight, except that I couldn't even threaten to bleed on my attacker. I tensed up, hoping a sudden burst of adrenaline would give me the strength to put up a struggle. I even wiggled my jaw, trying to stretch out the muscles. If anything got near me, I was damn well going to bite it.

As plans go, it was one of my better ones. If necessity was the mother of invention, then maybe mine had graced me with the tactical skills of Alexander the Great or that Ender kid from the sci-fi books.

Unfortunately, my genius plan hadn't accounted for the fact that I was unable to see or move. Before I knew it, I was pinned to the floor by a massive weight on my chest. It felt almost like a kettlebell… if a kettlebell had pokey things on the end of it.

Juliette would no doubt have been shocked to hear I even knew what a kettlebell was. The truth was, I'd seen them in sports stores, struggled to lift any but the smallest of them, and moved on to the shoe department. Still, knowledge was knowledge.

Fetid breath bathed my face, and I gagged. Death-by-halitosis seemed a particularly terrible way to go. I tried to twitch away, but couldn't even manage my dying fish impression, thanks to the weight that felt like it was slowly pushing through my ribcage. I settled for turning my face away and almost immediately felt better.

"I don't know who—or what—you are, but you're in really big trouble," I told the creature, gasping the words out despite the difficulty I was having breathing. "If you let us go now though, we can pretend this never happened. I'll even get you some toothpaste—"

Heat erupted in my shoulder, followed almost immediately by a rush of pain, like magma coursing through the limb. Although the sound must have started at the same time as the pain, I didn't parse it until a few endless seconds later; the crunch of teeth tearing into flesh.

"Son of a bitch, did you just bite—"

A disgusting crunch interrupted me, as the creature bit even deeper. Because I had so little breath left, my scream was a tiny, whimpering, pathetic thing, but it was heartfelt all the same.

CHAPTER 20

IN WHICH A MEDIATOR IS NEVER RIGHT AND
RARELY ON TIME

"Do you remember that time I said you were hot?" I had to shout to be heard over the wind as we weaved our way through slow-moving traffic.

"Given that it was less than an hour ago? Yes, John, I do."

God, I loved hearing Anastasia say my first name.

"That's practically a lifetime for humans," I assured her. "Anyway, however hot you were back then, you can damn well double it now." I tilted my face up to the sun and sighed contentedly.

"I am beginning to suspect that you are simply using me to get to my car, Mr. Smith."

"I would never do that, Lady Dumenyova… but the Jag definitely does not suck."

We were doing ninety on the 15, with the top to Anastasia's Jaguar down. I'd had a dream like this once, but neither the car nor the woman from that fantasy could compete with their respective realities. The engine roared as if it was alive, and I found myself running my hands up and down the buttery soft leather.

Of the car's interior. Before we left the House, Anastasia had changed into a deep blue blouse and black pants. And even if she hadn't, I wasn't insane enough to pet her. There was *not being afraid* and then there was *being willfully obnoxious.*

I sent a superior smile to the popped-collar, polo-shirt-wearing BMW driver we'd just blown past. *Nice driving gloves, buddy!* Perhaps the only downside to having the top down—and it seemed blasphemy to sully an experience like this with complaints—was that the wind was messing up my already messy hair.

"You're sure Jee Sun will be okay?" I asked for the fifth time.

"She told you so herself, did she not?"

"Yeah." Apparently, the choice between an afternoon with her new friend, Tea Leaf, or a cookie-less afternoon with her old friend hadn't been much of a choice at all. The tiny traitor. "It's just…"

"Mr. Smith—" I don't know how Anastasia could make her voice heard without raising it at all, but she managed, and its chocolate-cheesecake richness seemed equally unaffected by the wind and noise. "—Queen Lucia spoke the truth when she told you the House has no designs on Lord Beel-Kasan's ward. And Summer is the treasure of our House; Jee Sun will be safer with her than perhaps anywhere else in this city."

"I know that, in my head, at least. I'm just finding that fatherhood—even pseudo-fatherhood—can be irrational." I eyed the vampire, watching the wind toy with strands of her silken hair. Her eyes were hidden behind wraparound shades, but a small smile told me she could feel my gaze. "On that note, have you ever… you know…"

"Been a father? No, Mr. Smith. I lack both the temperament and the equipment for it." Her mouth spread in a wicked grin. Behind the wheel of her Jag, she was considerably less reserved than the femmepire whose mere presence sent lesser vampires running.

"Thank you for clarifying," I said with a laugh, "but you know what I meant."

She sobered slightly. "I have never borne a child, John. Nor have I sought to. Offspring are a rare blessing for the People, but since I was young, my life has been dedicated to Lucia's reign." Her head tilted, and I knew she was looking at me out of the corner of her eye. "And you? Has your recent time with Jee Sun sparked a fresh interest in fatherhood?"

"Just the opposite, really. I do want a family at some point, but I have plenty of time. I'm only twenty-five."

"In my day, you would quite likely have had children already."

"Well, sure… but I also would have been assigned a bride."

"Only if you were a noble."

"I *would* have been a noble, Anastasia. Trust me on that!"

"Perhaps." Her lips quirked as she hid another smile.

I tried to picture myself with children… but that daydream quickly devolved into the mental image of a horde of Jee Sun clones, each of them brandishing a shiny revolver. I shivered.

"I'm *definitely* not ready for fatherhood yet. I guess my new phone isn't the only reason I'm grateful for the modern age." I patted the pocket containing my wonderphone. "Which reminds me… you never did give me your number."

"As I recall, we agreed you would discover it on your own," she replied. "And on that front, I have already spoken with Celeste, Akiko, and Kayla. They will not be assisting you in the matter."

"Now, that's just downright unreasonable," I protested. "The House operators were the linchpin of my strategy!"

"I assumed as much." She sounded smug. "If the task is beyond your capabilities…"

"I didn't say that. I'll figure something out. I *always* do." And by *always*, I meant roughly thirty-five percent of the time. I gestured to the sign ahead. "We'll need to get off at the 52."

"And then head east to Tierrasanta. Yes, I am aware." She cut across traffic and into the exit lane. "Mr. Hawthorne is a key player in the San Diego Pack, Mr. Smith. I know where he lives."

With that somewhat ominous statement, she cut to the right. We rocketed up the circular on-ramp and onto the 52 at a speed that could not possibly have been safe.

ooo

Almost as quickly as we turned onto the 52, we were turning back off onto the residential streets of Tierrasanta.

"When I was here on Wednesday, I was taking pictures through the back window of my Corolla. What a difference two days can make."

Anastasia nodded silently, waiting at the light to turn onto Portobelo.

"I did the right thing, didn't I? With Lucia and the House?"

She considered my question for a moment. "It was not a development I had anticipated. There is no question that it strengthens your position…"

"But?"

"But it also ties you more closely to my queen, which is something you were trying to avoid." The light turned green, and we started to move again.

"Well, I wasn't exactly spoiled for choice," I pointed out. "I had to do whatever I could to protect my parents."

"Indeed." We pulled into Davis' driveway, and parked behind a sea green Prius that hadn't been there on my previous visit. "And yet…"

"Yes?"

She pressed a button and the soft top began to close. I really did love this car. "If you had wanted to preserve your independence, there were other ways to protect your parents."

"Like what?" I felt myself getting defensive.

The sounds of the outside world cut off as the roof closed, and the scent of Anastasia's perfume strengthened within the confines of the car. The femmepire's lovely face was expressionless.

"To the best of our knowledge, neither of your parents shares your resistance to compulsion. It would have been a simple matter for me to move them to a hotel, where the Infected would be unable to find them. I also own a house by the ocean where they would have been welcome. As for your own safety," she continued, "if Queen Lucia were to lose prestige for killing her wayward thrall, what do you think would happen if she allowed that same thrall to be killed by someone else?"

"Wait… are you saying she *had* to protect me?" I had never even considered that possibility.

"Indeed. The House lacks the numbers to guard your residence, but a single bodyguard remains well within our capabilities. And if you kept Lord Beel-Kasan's ward with you, the child should have been protected by association."

"It would have been nice to know all of that before I agreed to exchange bodily fluids," I muttered. Blood *was* a bodily fluid, right?

"The first I heard of your difficulties was when my queen informed us that you were coming," Anastasia pointed out. "Did it not occur to you to call me, or Lady Middleton, or even Kayla before throwing yourself upon the queen's mercy? The operators would certainly have directed your call."

"Well…no," I admitted. "Since I had promised to call Lucia anyway, it seemed like the perfect solution."

"If you have a weakness, Mr. Smith—"

"What do you mean if? I could list at least a dozen."

"—it is that you have no real grasp of tactics or strategy."

"One may know how to conquer without being able to do it," I quoted smugly. "That's Sun Tzu."

"There are no words to express the abyss between isolation and having one ally." She removed her sunglasses, and gazed at me steadily, her jade green eyes solemn.

"I don't recognize that one."

"Chesterton."

I shrugged. We hadn't covered him in school, but he sounded British. "What does it mean?"

"That you have friends, John. And allies, both within the House and without. You need to learn to utilize the resources available to you."

"You're saying I *shouldn't* have agreed to Lucia's deal?" Out of the corner of my eye, I saw the front door to Davis' home open. The werewolf was no doubt wondering what was taking me so long… and where I'd gotten my sweet new ride.

"*Queen* Lucia, and not at all. I think an alliance with our House could be beneficial for both parties, provided you and she are able to coexist. I am simply saying that you should not let others dictate your decisions. Otherwise, this world will use you until nothing remains."

"Things were way less complicated when all I had to do was take pictures through motel windows." The shape in the doorway twitched; Davis was getting impatient. "But speaking of complicated messes… shall we?"

"After you, Mr. Smith." Anastasia followed me up the walkway to the werewolf's door.

Davis met us at the door, wearing another tank top, khaki shorts, and a scowl. "You didn't say that your *guest* would be a vampire, John." His eyes cut past me to Anastasia. "Lady Dumenyova." His voice was a growl.

"Mr. Hawthorne." Anastasia's voice was quiet but firm, not giving an inch. "I am simply here to protect the House's investment in Mr. Smith."

He looked back to me, confusion warring with irritation. "What happened?"

"Can we come in? I'll explain to you and Carolyn both." When he didn't move, I offered my own scowl. "For someone who was so pissy about me rescheduling, you don't seem to be in any great hurry to get started."

"Fine." He stepped back, as if to allow us entry, and then stopped. "But the vampire had best remain silent." He looked back at Anastasia, and the color drained from his eyes. "Using your glamour would be… unwise." The teeth he bared looked very much like those a dog might sport. But bigger and sharper.

Anastasia did not move or speak, but her stillness deepened, until she seemed like a part of the stone path she was standing upon. She met his gaze coolly.

"Alright, you two." I interposed myself between them. "Let's not start a war today. It's the kind of thing we mediators consider counterproductive."

The interior of the house was nice: well-furnished and decorated in a sort of high-tech lumberjack style. We found Carolyn in what appeared to be the living room. A large fireplace dominated one wall, with a couch and stuffed chairs oriented toward a huge plasma television. I was starting to think I was the only person in the world who still had a CRT.

Carolyn had swapped her jeans for a patterned floral skirt but was otherwise dressed like she'd been the day before. Wooden bangles rattled as she stood to greet me. Davis' enormous dog Brutus napped at her feet.

"Hello again, John. Why are you dressed like an undertaker?" The young werewolf was far more composed than she'd been out in the desert, although she blinked when she saw the woman behind me. "And who is this?"

"Carolyn Hawthorne, meet Lady Anastasia Dumenyova, Secundus to the San Diego House." Carolyn's eyes widened, but she did not otherwise react. I guess she'd gotten all of the leaping-at-and-trying-to-kill-people out of her system. Or maybe she just recognized that Anastasia was a much less vulnerable target than I had been.

"As for today's outfit… let's just say it's a loaner." I was, in fact, wearing the uniform of the House Watch; black slacks and a black button-up shirt. While the clothes left me looking like the world's preppiest goth, they had the distinct advantage of being clean.

"Mr. Smith was going to tell us what exactly is going on," rumbled Davis. "Apparently, it's linked to his unprofessional behavior today." He walked over and dropped heavily into one of the chairs.

"Dude, what is your *deal?*" I asked. "You being a dick isn't helping anyone."

Before he could reply, Carolyn piped up. "He's right, Uncle Davis. This won't work if we don't give it a chance. Isn't that what you told me last night?" She met his scowl with an unrepentant grin, looking like the teenager she was.

"You're right." Davis looked in my direction. "I'm not myself, today. If you will excuse me?" Without waiting for a reply, he rose from the chair, and left the room.

I waited to make sure he was gone, and then took a seat on the couch. Anastasia stood behind me, playing her bodyguard role to the hilt. Smiling at Carolyn, I gestured in the direction of her departed uncle. "Should I ask?"

She shrugged. "It's that time of the month."

I blinked. Did women make those jokes too? About dudes? How did that make any sense?

Carolyn saw my confusion and clarified. "The full moon is on its way."

"Oh. *That* time of the month. Okay, that makes more sense. Are you two going to… you know… wolf out?"

"Uhm, no?" From her tone, I might have been asking if red was blue. "It doesn't work like that," she explained. "But the men get a little fidgety around this time. They tend to change more often to relieve the stress."

As she spoke, a red-furred wolf the size of a bear padded back into the room and lowered itself to the carpet, where it dwarfed Brutus. Even supine, the wolf's back was level with Carolyn's chair. Bone-white eyes pinned me to the couch.

"Nice doggy," I breathed.

Behind me, Anastasia stifled a snort. Everyone's a critic.

"He can understand you," said Carolyn, her voice nonchalant, "but he'll be calmer in this form."

"And the wolf will protect him from vampire mojo," I recalled.

"That too." She rearranged her skirts and fixed me with a steely gaze. I could finally see a resemblance to her uncle. "Before we talk about my pack's problem, my uncle said you had something to tell us?"

I filled them in on what had happened after our last meeting. Carolyn was every bit as horrible at masking her thoughts and emotions as I was, which did a lot to improve my opinion of her. As I talked, I watched concern give way to consternation. By the time I had reached my discovery of the wolves outside my parents' house, the dominant expression was anger.

"It has to be Jason and his crew," she spat. "If you die, the mediation is over. With the strength of the New Mexico Pack behind him, he would be able to dictate terms."

"Wait…" I turned to look at Anastasia behind me. "The Concordat is satisfied simply by the hiring of a mediator… even if the participants then turn about and kill that mediator?"

She nodded, honoring her agreement to not speak.

"Well, that's some serious bullshit. I can see why it was left out of the mediator's handbook." Not that there *was* a mediator's handbook… but I rarely allowed reality to get in the way of my complaints.

On the floor, Davis grinned wolfishly.

I looked back to Carolyn. "Maybe you can put the word out that I've been declared an ally of the House? Further attacks on me will be considered attacks on the People."

I really hoped that would work as a deterrent. As great as it was to know that I'd be avenged if I contracted a bad case of death-by-werewolf… I'd still be too dead to enjoy it.

"Anyway… that was *my* night," I continued, donning my metaphorical mediator's hat. "Let's focus on you. Why don't you tell me how you and Jason first met?"

CHAPTER 21

It was your typical werewolf-girl-meets-werewolf-boy story. Or so I assumed. The two had been introduced by their respective fathers when they were still children, but the marriage arrangement hadn't been finalized until much later. While Carolyn had been the daughter and sole heir of San Diego's Pack leader, Jason was the third son of the ruling New Mexico family, making him important but also disposable. The goal had been to maintain the two packs as separate organizations, while solidifying their alliance through intermarriage.

"Were you in favor of the marriage?" All the political stuff made for a good story, but it didn't tell me a lot about Carolyn herself.

"Yeah." She toyed with her skirt for a moment, then shrugged. "Jason was *different* from everyone else I'd known growing up. Of our kind, I mean."

"Was it important to marry a fellow were?" I pressed. "I understand that you guys—" By *you guys*, I meant naturally born werewolves. "—can have children with humans or the turned."

"Just because we *can* doesn't mean we would want to." She wrinkled her nose, and I had to swallow my usual complaints about anti-human racism. "No offense."

"None taken. You're not my type either."

It was her turn to look offended.

"Anyway, whenever possible, naturals are paired with other naturals. It keeps our bloodlines strong and undiluted."

Because that worked so well for royal families, I very carefully did not say. Instead, I contented myself with a nod.

"So sure. He was exciting, and he was cute, and our marriage would strengthen the pack. Daddy thought it was a great match, and I didn't disagree."

"What went wrong?"

"Apparently, *exciting* and *cute* aren't the best starting points for a marriage." Carolyn smiled crookedly. "Have you ever been married, John?"

"Not yet." I didn't point out (again) that I was *only* twenty-five. It would just sound like I was making excuses.

"Have you lived with a girlfriend? Or boyfriend?"

"I'm straight, and no." This was the point in the conversation where Juliette would have said something snide. I really appreciated Anastasia's silent presence.

"Ah." The werewolf looked at me curiously, as if I were a carton of milk well past its expiration date. "Well, if that ever changes, you'll find that there's a big difference between dating someone and living with them."

"So, once you two were around each other all the time…?"

"Cuteness starts to pale the twentieth time you trip over the messes your husband keeps leaving around the house."

"Messes?" Maybe it was the wolf at her feet, but my mind immediately flashed on a dog that hadn't yet been housebroken, and the disgusting gifts it might leave behind.

"Dirty clothes, video game wrappers, trash… You name it, I probably stepped in it."

Yeah, that last part didn't help get me away from the poop theme. I struggled in vain not to smile.

"Did I say something funny?"

Only to someone with the mind of a third grader.

"Of course not." I rubbed my stomach. "Just something I ate for lunch disagreeing with me."

Mollified, she sat back in her chair.

"Did you try talking to Jason about any of this?"

"Obviously. And it turned out that there were things he didn't like either. We both agreed to work on them. Like adults," she concluded proudly.

"Glad to hear it. But I'm guessing things didn't get better?"

"Actually, they did… for a while, at least. We weren't entirely clicking, other than the—" Here, she mouthed the word *sex* with a glance down at her canine uncle. "—but we weren't driving each other crazy either."

"What changed?"

"Jason got bored. According to him, the San Diego Pack is rustic to the extreme." She rolled her eyes at her ex-husband's words. "Because New Mexico is *such* a paradise, you know?"

Having never been there, I didn't know. Luckily, Carolyn Hawthorne was on a roll, and no longer needed my careful prodding.

"First, he wanted to go out all the time. Then that wasn't enough, so he convinced some of his buddies from the New Mexico Pack to move out here too. And just like that, instead of tripping over dirty clothes, I was tripping over empty beer cans and discarded bongs."

"Did you know he smoked pot?"

"Oh sure." She waved her hand, dismissing the question. "Who doesn't? But there's a big difference between getting a nice high before—" Again, she glanced down at Davis. "—*you know* and sitting around in your boxers getting baked all the time."

It was hard to argue with her on that front.

ooo

Two hours later, Carolyn and Davis walked us to the door, the latter still in scary-big wolf form. Anastasia slipped out ahead of me and gave the all-clear. I turned to Carolyn.

"I'll need to talk with Jason next, so I can hear his side of things. When Davis is human-shaped, could you ask him to set up the appointment for tomorrow? He can text me the time and location." I hoped letting the werewolves set the schedule for our next meeting might in some way make up for my—entirely understandable but still unprofessional—tardiness.

"John, you can ask him yourself. Like I said, he understands you, even as a wolf."

"Sure, but I'd feel ridiculous speaking to a dog, even one the size of a house." I looked at the huge wolf, and pretended I was addressing a toy poodle. "Who's in the well, boy? Who is it? Bark twice if it's cousin Sally!"

When a werewolf barks, it sounds… *wrong*. Not just because of the volume—something that big can produce an exceptional amount of noise—but also because there's a harmonic undertone to the sound that you'll never hear with a dog. That didn't keep Davis from doing it twice. He then let his mouth fall open in what was either another doggy grin or an intentional exhibition of both the size and sharpness of his many teeth.

I blanched.

"I'll wait to hear from him." I retreated to Anastasia's Jaguar, where I buckled myself in and waited for the goosebumps to go away.

"Have we learned our lesson about baiting werewolves, Mr. Smith?" They were the first words Anastasia had uttered since we'd entered the Hawthorne home. A healthy dose of amusement was mixed in with the usual rich tones.

"Nobody likes a smart ass, Lady Dumenyova, but yeah. I'm a quick study when it comes to furry hell-beasts that can eat my face." I slowly relaxed as we left Davis' house behind.

"And did you find this meeting productive?"

"Yes and no." I shrugged, although she couldn't see the motion. "When I first met Carolyn and Jason, they spent the whole time sniping at each other. *That* was unproductive. Right now, I'm just trying to get to know them both. Once they're talking to me, I can work on getting them to talk to each other. And when that happens, maybe we'll find a compromise they can both accept."

"You make it sound simple."

"I wish it was." I smiled. "I like Carolyn though. She's… spunky. And nice enough, now that she's not holding me responsible for her father's death."

"She does seem spirited," Anastasia agreed, "but very young."

Through the grace of a God that apparently still loved me, I realized—just in time—that Anastasia might not appreciate me pointing out that we were *all* young compared to her. I fumbled for something to fill the silence.

"Were you watching when I told them about last night's attack? What was your impression? Were their reactions sincere?"

"You are the detective, Mr. Smith, not I," she teased.

"Sure, but you worked security for three of my lifetimes," I retorted. "A friend of mine recently told me that I needed to start utilizing my resources."

That startled another short laugh out of her. We reached the freeway, and the Jaguar flexed its automotive muscle. "I would say that Ms. Hawthorne's reaction was honest," Anastasia finally concluded, "or she is an excellent actress. As for Mr. Hawthorne... I do not know."

"Yeah. Not being a dog whisperer, all I got out of Davis was *drool, pant,* and *stare creepily at the tasty human.*" I sighed. "But I agree with your take on his niece." As open as she'd been about her personal life, I wasn't sure the young werewolf even had a *filter,* let alone the ability to lie convincingly.

"Do you believe that her ex-husband and his *crew* are responsible for the attack?"

I rolled that idea around in my head. "It's possible. But there were a lot more than four werewolves after me last night."

"Are you certain? Wolves *do* excel at camouflaging their numbers."

"I'll have to take your word for that." Again, I reviewed the attack. "There were at least four wolves chasing my car. Add that to the two by the ATVs, and the two in the car at my parents' house... and that's..." I did the math. It was more difficult than it should have been, both because I was exhausted, and because I was unwilling to use my fingers and toes as a counting aid in front of the femmepire. "...eight?"

"Perhaps they have acquired allies within Carolyn's pack," she mused, "or perhaps there are more of them here than the Hawthornes know." She drummed her fingers lightly on the leather-wrapped steering wheel as we slid into the left lane to pass a burnt orange vanagon that was in even rougher shape than my Corolla. "It would have been helpful if you had gotten the license plate of the car parked by your parents' house. Perhaps next time."

"I had that same thought, about twenty minutes too late." I wasn't sure it would have even been possible, as occupied as I had been with keeping Jee Sun's cries from alerting the watching wolves. "By the way, the ancients who came up with the Concordat need to have their heads examined. This whole *it's okay to kill your mediator* thing seems like a loophole they really should have considered."

"It is not quite as simple as Ms. Hawthorne suggested, actually. If there is proof that one of the parties is involved in the death of the mediator, the consequences are severe."

"No puppy chow for a month?"

"Something closer to the eradication of the offender and their entire bloodline. There is a reason we all follow the Concordat." She smiled chillingly. "I suspect that may be why your assailants tried to simply run you off the road. A dark night. A dirt road. A notoriously unreliable car. Accidents do happen."

Notoriously unreliable? I wanted to defend my Corolla's honor but the muted roar of Anastasia's rocket-propelled luxury-mobile was lulling me into complacency. "Well, they took their shot and missed. With the House protecting me, it's going to be a cold day in hell before they even think of trying again."

I was right.

About the temperature, if nothing else.

CHAPTER 22

San Diegans may think they've been to the Bitter End before, but they really haven't. Yes, there's a bar downtown—now known as the Tipsy Crow—which used to bear that name, and yes, it's a great bar, but it isn't and never has been the real Bitter End, despite serving as the other establishment's facade for years and years.

The real Bitter End is also a bar—albeit on one floor instead of three—and a club, and a revolving menagerie of the sort of oddities you'll never see walking around the city proper. It's easy enough to find—the portal is located at the bottom of the outside stairwell at the Tipsy Crow, after all—but almost impossible to enter.

If a random local wanted to give it a shot, they'd need to find a likely vantage point on F street that gave them a view of that stairwell. They could toss salt over their shoulder, rub fairy dust under their eyes, or whatever other bizarre ritual they thought might help them see through a glamour. If they waited long enough, they might spot some unusual people pulling aside the gate at the top of the stairs, and if they hurried, they could slip down the stairs after them.

If they were truly lucky, those other beings, who would most certainly have heard or smelled them, wouldn't be in the mood to do something about it, and would instead simply activate the portal and disappear. And if the random local had been born under a shining star with a silver spoon in their mouth, that portal—which spends most of its time masquerading as a stone wall—would still be active when they reached it.

They'd have to hurry though; the portal only stays open for a short time and has a history of eating humans.

Once through the portal, they'd find themselves at the top of another flight of stairs, in an underground cavern that—judging by the gold-laced obsidian walls—is a long, long way from San Diego. A line of white-flamed tiki torches would light the way down to an enormous iron-bound door and the mountain of a man standing next to it: grey skinned and grey haired, two ivory tusks jutting upward and outward from his lower jaw.

If our upstanding San Diegan, flush with their unexpected success and the thrill of discovery, tried to walk past that fine gentleman into the bar itself, they would find themself stopped by one meaty hand, informed that the Bitter End was a private establishment, and then torn limb from limb.

So I assumed anyway. I'd never actually seen the bouncer do anything. It was entirely possible he would instead treat interlopers to a complementary strawberry milkshake and a rousing discussion of San Diego's woeful sports teams. But I sure as hell wasn't going to be the one to test that hypothesis.

As a result, this was only my second trip to the Bitter End. Both times, someone else in the party—someone who smelled a little less like a *human*—had vouched for me. If there really was some measure of prestige inherent in being San Diego's mediator, it didn't hold any weight with the management of the city's number one monster bar.

The six of us formed a line at the entrance.

Juliette led the way, barely clothed in a one-shoulder, black crop top and a blood red miniskirt that was way more mini than skirt. High heeled stiletto boots completed the outfit.

God loves a badass in boots, and so do I.

She was followed by Kayla and Darlene, walking hand in hand. The House Captain was lean and lovely in a long grey tank of some sort of shimmery material, which she had paired with a tight black skirt. That skirt was far more modest than Juliette's, but looked almost as short, due to Kayla's mile-long legs. Darlene, for her part, was simply dressed in dark, loose slacks and a deep green blouse, but after their car ride from the House, only a few of that blouse's buttons were still closed. Kayla seemed to be enjoying the frequent flashes of cleavage and belly.

I was next, feeling seriously underdressed in the same Watch uniform loaner I'd been wearing all day, but Steve, Kayla's second-in-command, followed close behind me. My designated bodyguard for the night wore the same uniform as I did, but somehow made it look both fashionable and menacing. Maybe it was his serious bodybuilder musculature, or his mohawk, or something else entirely, but he looked like he'd just stepped out of a photo shoot for Stone Cold Killer Magazine.

Last was Brenna, a seriously fit femmepire who seriously didn't like me. Her chin-length, curly brown hair had been slicked back with gel and she had on a vintage black leather jacket, and beneath that, an equally black dress. The dress was nothing special, in and of itself, but the sculpted lines of her figure turned the scrap of fabric into a statement all its own.

I had found, over time, that prolonged exposure to vampires led to an inevitable depreciation of my own self-image. Nobody likes being the ugly duckling. Even so, it was kind of a rush to crash a bar with a group that looked like mine.

I just wished Ana had agreed to come with us.

Juliette finished talking to the bouncer and led our small party inside. He gave Darlene and I the *lesser species* evil eye but made no move to stop us from entering. It was good to have friends in low places.

The Bitter End was—in form, at least—not all that different from human establishments. There was a long bar along one wall, behind which several bartenders were hard at work. Directly in front of us was a seating area full of circular tables and mismatched chairs, while booths lined the left wall. Further in—although my eyes hadn't yet adjusted enough to the bar's strange atmosphere to see it—was a dance floor, and to the left of *that* were the private rooms.

What made the Bitter End different—beyond the fact that it was accessible only via dimensional portal—was its staff and clientele. Spheres of light floated about the room, glowing in blues, purples, and greens. A look up at the high ceilings revealed dozens more of those spheres, clustered together above us. They were the sole source of illumination in the Bitter End, sentient creatures that Juliette had called Mistborn. The closest thing I'd found in mythology books and D&D monster manuals was the will o' wisp. Whatever they were, they were curious; several spheres floated down to observe our group.

The bar was full this time, and I looked about me with wide-eyed interest. A pile of oversized worms squirmed about on the tabletop of one booth, and it wasn't until the iridescent, bug-eyed waitress brought a bowl to the table that I realized those worms were customers instead of food. A trio of tall individuals in black robes conferred around a single steaming mug, their hooded heads bowed. Next to them, a minotaur, one horn cracked from tip to root, sprawled out across three separate chairs, a steaming mug of… something, clutched in its clawed fist.

Juliette sashayed past the minotaur to stake her claim to one of the few empty tables. There were only four chairs to start with, but the spiky-haired Duchess of Snark swiped another two from the child-sized amoebas to her left. The amoebas didn't seem to care, not that I'm sure how anyone would have known if they did. Explosions or bloodshed, I was guessing; one of those amoebas seemed to be carting about a World War Two era grenade in the center of its amorphous, translucent body.

We took our seats. Five of us did, anyway. *Where was Steve?* I craned my neck and found that the mohawked manpire remained at the door, where he was striking up a conversation with the bouncer. In fact… I watched as he leaned forward with a laugh, clapping the bouncer on one shoulder.

"Is Steve hitting on the bouncer?"

"Well, duh," grinned Kayla. "As a teetotaler, he sure doesn't come here for the alcohol."

"A teetotaler is someone who doesn't drink, John," explained Juliette helpfully.

"I already knew that, but thanks." I was lying. I'd seen the word once or twice in books but had never bothered to look it up. And now, I didn't have to, proving yet again, the benefits of laziness.

"But still," I said, horror leaking into my voice, "the *bouncer?*"

"Easy there, mate," Kayla cautioned me, "Barry is a sweet guy."

"And Steve likes them butch," added Darlene, who made it her business to know everything about everyone in the House.

"Steve *is* butch." And he was, for a manpire anyway. The dark brown skin and the aforementioned mohawk—not to mention the short-handled axe he wore in a sheath on his back—all made a winning case for butch…iness.

Was that even a word?

"Yeah, but he likes them *really* butch."

"I guess Barry fits the bill." I shivered.

Steve said something else, and this time it was Barry's turn to laugh. Even the strange pig-man had more game than I did. I turned back to the table.

"Are they a thing?"

"Kind of." That was Kayla again. Juliette had already gotten bored of the conversation and was flagging down a waitress. And Brenna… well, Brenna was staring daggers at me from across the table. You kick someone out of the locker room, mid-shower, *one time*, and they never let you forget it. "Barry can't leave the bar, and Steve is busy with the House, but they sneak in what time they can together."

"He can't leave *ever*?"

"He's a wereboar, little bird." Juliette rejoined the conversation as a familiar red-skinned waitress started making her way to our table. "The oldest one in history, in fact."

I eyed the bouncer again. He looked like he was pushing fifty. Hard. "Late forties?"

"Try one-hundred-and-twelve."

If I'd had a drink, I would have spat alcohol across the table. "I thought the Infected went crazy and died in their forties?"

"Assuming they even make it that long," agreed Juliette.

"Then how…?"

"You've met Lord Kala—" she began.

"Wait, you *have*?" Darlene asked excitedly. Even Brenna and Kayla looked impressed. "What was he like?"

I shrugged and tried not to preen under all the attention. "He seemed nice enough for a skeleton in a robe. He and Lord Beel-Kasan are old friends, I think." Lord Kala was another immortal and the owner of the Bitter End. Our interaction had been short, but he'd been considerably more rational than Bill. Turning to Juliette, I asked, "What does Kala have to do with a centenarian wereboar?"

"What is Lord Kala the demigod of, you moron?"

Brenna laughed openly at Juliette's form of address.

"Death and Time. So what?"

"So, just as Gehenna is Bill's private territory, the Bitter End is Lord Kala's. Within these walls, his power is absolute."

I still didn't get it.

"He keeps Barry from aging any further, John," explained Kayla, "which means he'll never go mad and have to be killed, unlike most Infected."

"And since he has to stay here anyway to maintain that state of affairs, Barry has become the bar's permanent bouncer."

"And if he leaves…?"

"Best case scenario would be that the madness progresses normally, and he would have to be put down sometime in the next six to ten months." Juliette shrugged. "Worst case scenario is that all those years would catch up with him the instant he steps through the portal. Nothing would remain but bones and dust."

"Jesus." I eyed the wereboar—and Steve—with greater appreciation. "That's rough."

"It is," agreed Kayla. "On the other hand, it's given the two of them a lot of time together that they might not otherwise have had." She very carefully did not look down at her human girlfriend, a woman who, despite being only twenty-three, would die long before the femmepire.

"Ugh," protested Juliette. "It's too early for us to be getting maudlin." She smiled as the red-skinned, hairless waitress—elegantly clothed, as always, in a white chiffon halter dress—finally reached our table. "I'm here to get my drink on!"

ooo

"What I don't get," I complained, "is how all of this is secret."

"All of what?" Steve had joined us at the table sometime around my third beer, as Barry's attention was taken by a steady stream of new arrivals. My last time at the Bitter End had been on a Tuesday. The Friday night crowd was both larger and considerably stranger.

"All of this!" I waved my arms around, gesturing at the entire place. I was sober enough to avoid knocking any of the empty glasses and bottles off our table… but just barely. Juliette had ordered a round of shots, and they'd given me Steve's. "I get that you guys and the pixies and the goblins all have your mojo… and I guess the werewolves can pass as human, but what about the other races? Like the amoebas, or that dude?" I motioned to the minotaur. "I'm pretty sure these people would stand out in a crowd."

"If they walked around San Diego, sure." Steve took a sip of soda. *Diet* soda, not that vampires had to worry about calorie counts. (Superhuman metabolism was just one more reason to hate them.) Our alcohol consumption didn't seem to bother him, but he'd shown no interest in partaking. There was a story there, I was sure, but it was late, and investigation was my day job. I was happy to leave it alone.

"Correct me if I'm wrong," I drawled sarcastically, "but isn't the entrance to this place on F and 5th, in the heart of downtown San Diego?"

"Ah. I figured Juliette would've told you."

I followed his gaze to where the femmepires and Darlene were dancing. While my eyes had adjusted to the bar's interior—as much as human eyes ever could, anyway—I could only barely make out the shapes of our companions. It was like they were a hundred feet away, instead of thirty.

"Steve, does Juliette strike you as the *patient explainer* type?"

"Point taken." He clinked his glass against my bottle.

"So then…"

"Well, the Bitter End isn't *in* San Diego."

"Right." I knew that already. "It's in its own little dimension. But the *entrance* to it is."

"Just one of them," he assured me. "The Bitter End is older than San Diego. There are portals to it from all over the world. And other worlds, for that matter."

Maybe the beer was finally hitting me, but I was having trouble following his explanation. "Other worlds?"

"Or dimensions, or planes of existence, or whatever it is you want to call them." Steve shrugged. "A lot of the more unusual looking species don't make their homes on Earth."

"You're kind of blowing my mind here, dude."

"Human literature has all sorts of nonsense about faerie mounds and stuff, doesn't it? Not to mention heaven and hell? This is the same thing, really."

I carefully set down my empty bottle on the table. The conversation had gotten weirdly theological, and *that* called for another beer.

Forty minutes later, I was polishing off my fifth beer, and had decided to no longer even think about heaven, hell, God, or alternate worlds. It was safer that way. For my peace of mind, I mean. Instead, I was people-watching, or monster-watching, or whatever you wanted to call it, safe within the warm amber glow of an ultra-heavy beer buzz.

Two slender arms squeezed me from behind, heralding Darlene's arrival. "Jooooooooohn, why are you sitting here by yourself?" Before I could answer, she stepped past me to take a seat. "You could do *that* anywhere!" She beamed over at me with the bright cheeks and slightly manic smile of someone in their cups.

"D, are you wasted?"

"Pshaw!" She blew a raspberry in my direction. "You wish, Mr. Smith! Now then," she began, snagging my bottle off the table and checking it for any dregs of beer, "tell Auntie D why it is you're sitting by yourself looking all constipated and stuff!"

"Eh. Just trying to process the God-bomb that Steve dropped on me."

She waited, a sympathetic look on her face.

"Seriously… that's it. My parents raised me Catholic, and even though I stopped believing in that sort of thing back in high school, it's weird to hear about heaven and hell being actual places, or dimensions, or whatever it is they actually are." I rapped my head with my knuckles. "That sort of thinking bakes my noodle."

"Bakes your noodle?"

"It's something my dad says," I explained sheepishly. "And Bill, oddly enough."

"Well, I can't do anything for *that* noodle, but if you want to do something about the other one…" She grinned cheekily and winked at me.

Okay, she clearly *was* blitzed. "I'm flattered, Darlene, but you and Ka—"

I stopped talking when a tiny fist struck my arm. I think Kayla had been teaching her how to throw a punch, because it hurt a lot more than it should have.

"Ew! Gross!" She scowled at me. "I don't care what you've read on the Internet, John, alcohol won't make a girl straight. And I'm a one-woman person!"

"Thank God. But then… what are you talking about?"

"Brenna," she replied brightly. "She's not going to wait for you all night, you know."

"Darlene," I said slowly, feeling for all the world like I was back in junior high, "Brenna doesn't like me. In fact, she kind of despises me."

"Oh, I doubt that very much, John! Why else would she have come along, if not for the chance to hang out with you?"

"Let's see." I ticked the reasons off on my fingers. "To get away from the House. To go to a bar and dance. To meet other people at the bar and dance with them." I looked over at Darlene and shook my head. "None of those reasons involve me."

"Only because you're sitting on your ass over here, thinking about God and stuff," she replied firmly. "You know what hell is, John? Hell is wasting your life when there's an uber hot single babe dancing thirty feet away from you."

I thought about it for a moment. Maybe it was the beer, but my pint-sized friend was making a lot of sense. If I were going to dance with anyone, I'd have preferred it to be Anastasia. But the Secundus wasn't here, was she?

I rose to my feet, accompanied by Darlene's whoops of excitement, and casually strolled toward the dance floor. If you couldn't trust a lesbian to know these things, then who could you trust?

The house band was, as always, a vaguely elephantine creature, purple skinned, and smartly dressed in a tuxedo. Its mouth yawned wide open, and from that orifice came the sound of pulsing bass and electronica. On my previous visit, it had sung/played jazz, which had been even more impressive, albeit kind of difficult to dance to.

This time, I would remember to tip the guy.

There were a dozen people dancing, but it was easy enough to pick out the femmepires. Kayla and Juliette had created a space for themselves, and woe to any dude—tentacled or otherwise—who wandered into that area. As for Brenna…

Oh. I spotted the fit brunette in the far corner, grinding on a four-armed, two-headed bodybuilder-type dude with skin the color of eggplant. As I watched, she turned and gave first one head, then the other a deep kiss. Two of his hands wrapped around her.

"Huh," said Darlene, just now coming up beside me. "I guess I was wrong." She shrugged. "As long as you're up, let's dance!"

CHAPTER 23

IN WHICH THE LINE BETWEEN TODAY AND
TOMORROW IS A LITTLE BIT NEBULOUS

Sometime after two in the morning, my buzz had worn off to
the point where I could feel the exhaustion that had been building in
my legs all night. Contrary to popular belief and spiteful posts on
random internet blogs, I was an okay dancer. My sense of rhythm
tended to take unexpected vacations, but I'd never let that stop me
from enjoying myself, and half of dancing was just letting your body
move on its own. Even so, my donut-and-alcohol diet had left me ill-
prepared for multiple hours on the dance floor.

I collapsed into my chair and took a much-needed breather.
Away from the music, I could hear myself think again, and those
thoughts were telling me that it had been a long day and that tomorrow
would probably be even worse. I fished out my wonderphone and
checked for messages. Davis—a presumably non-dog-shaped Davis—
had done as I asked and scheduled a meeting with Jason. For noon,
which meant I was going to get to sleep in.

It felt like Christmas come early.

The address for our meeting looked familiar, and when I
googled it, I found out why; it was a small taco shop near the Torrey

Pines beach. Probably not the best venue for a heart-to-heart, but I wasn't going to argue with the choice. Jason would be more likely to talk if he was comfortable, and if that took cheap Mexican food… well, a sloppy chorizo burrito sounded good to me too.

Steve was back by the door with Barry, angled so that he could keep one eye on me. Lord Kala wasn't going to let anything happen in his bar, making the manpire's vigilance unnecessary, but it made it easy to get his attention. I waved him over.

"Hey man, I'm done for the night. I think I'm going to split."

"No problem, John. We can leave at any time." He didn't even look in the direction of his boyfriend. It was like a switch had been flipped, and his personal life had been neatly packed away so he could resume his role as bodyguard.

"Dude, I don't want to cut into your time with Barry. Why don't you stick around a while? I can take a cab back." My Corolla was still at the House. So was Jee Sun, who was no doubt driving the Watch insane while she and Tea Leaf enjoyed the first sleepover of their young lives.

"No can do. I was assigned as your bodyguard for a reason."

"Yeah, and that reason was that Lucia had stuff for Ana to do, and Juliette was unwilling to forgo alcohol for the night." I grinned. "Seriously, it's not a problem. By now, the spook squad is guarding my home and the werewolves have heard I'm off-limits. I'm good."

I watched the internal debate rage within my manpire guard, professionalism facing off against the very honest desire to spend more time with his other half. Finally, he settled on a compromise. "I'll walk you out and call the cab. If everything seems okay when it arrives, you've got a deal. And John? Thank you."

"That works." I stood up on wobbly legs. "Do you mind giving the ladies my farewells when you get back? I'd give them myself, but…" I waved one arm weakly in the direction of the dance floor. "Too damn far."

"I'll let them know where you went." He very carefully did not laugh at me, which just proved yet again that he was a good dude. "Shall we?"

I followed Steve up the obsidian and gold-laced stairs. We reached the portal at almost the same time as a skinny-looking humanoid with enormous ears and a grand total of two wiry hairs on top of his head. An elf? A brownie? I shrugged. There were more things in heaven and earth than had been dreamt of in my mythology books.

The little guy—whatever he was—stepped out of Steve's path, giving us the right of way. Smart bugger. I followed Steve through the portal—as disappointed as ever by how mundane teleportation felt without Hollywood special effects—and up the significantly less shiny human stairway.

The Tipsy Crow had closed at two, and we had the street to ourselves. The day's heat was a distant memory, and a cold wind whistled down the street. I shivered, wishing I'd brought my leather jacket with me. After a lifetime in San Diego, any temperature below seventy seemed less like an inconvenience and more like a crime against nature.

As Steve waited patiently, stoic in the face of the wind that had me shivering, I dialed the number for a taxi service. "Shouldn't be more than a minute or two," I told the manpire. "You don't have to wait out here, you know."

"You don't have a very good grasp on this whole bodyguard thing, John." He grinned, teeth looking very white against the darkness of his skin. "A few minutes aren't going to—"

A shadow the size of a pony hurtled through the air. I had a glimpse of large white fangs and bone-pale eyes, and then something drove me to the ground.

I rolled to the side to dodge a blow that never came. Steve was standing over me fending off a slavering wolf that was almost as large as Davis' form had been. In the dark, it was hard for me to see what exactly was going on, beyond the flash of teeth, and the sound of heavy paws on the pavement.

The wolf's stubborn attempts to bypass Steve to get at me certainly made my bodyguard's life easier. Finally, he caught the wolf with a kick to the side that launched the beast fifteen feet down F street. It gave Steve the time he needed to unsheathe his axe.

Still lying on the ground, I shot the werewolf a victorious smile. Someone wasn't going to get their kibbles and bits.

Instead of charging back in, the werewolf snarled from a distance, then tilted its head back and howled. I blanched. That howl was every bit as horrific as Davis' bark had been, complete with the odd, unnatural undertones, but I was way more concerned with the numerous howls that came back in answer.

Before I could even blink, additional shapes slunk around the corner. Some were on two legs, and some were on four, but they were all fur-covered engines of destruction.

"John," murmured Steve, still standing above me, "I'm going to need you to get up and run back down to the portal."

"What about you?" I hissed back.

"I'll be right behind you," he assured me. "But there's no way you'll make it unless I can slow them down." He swung the axe easily in one hand, but I no longer found the weapon reassuring. Not against what looked like eight freaking tons of werewolf.

I *knew* there'd been more than four of them attacking my car!

At Steve's whispered "Go!", I sprang to my feet and raced back toward the stairwell. Behind me, I heard the growls of werewolves attacking *en masse*. I hurtled down the steps, taking three or even four at a time, and charged the portal.

It was only after I bounced off the all-too-solid wall that I remembered humans couldn't activate the damn thing. I picked myself up off the ground with a groan, ears ringing. Next to me, the little dude we'd passed on the way out of the bar crouched silently, ears wiggling. We both watched the stairs in silence, but Steve didn't show.

"Shit," I told my companion. "Without him, we can't get back in—Oh. Never mind." The alcohol had clearly killed off my last few brain cells. I grabbed the brownie and hauled him to his feet. "Look, I need you to re-open the portal, okay? There are half a dozen werewolves up there, and they're going to eat our faces otherwise."

Either my words got through or the fact that I was physically shaking him did. I didn't really care which it was. What mattered was that, as soon as I set him back on his feet, he scurried to the wall I'd just bounced off. Almost immediately, the portal began to form. He darted through. Muttering a tiny prayer that the portal would allow me entry twice on the same night, I hurried after.

I was still an arm's length away when a thickly furred claw grabbed my ankle. Before I could scream, the werewolf had pulled me back and tossed me away. I hit the wall of the stairwell at something close to Mach three.

In its bipedal form, my attacker must have been seven feet tall, but all I was conscious of were the length of its claws, and the fangs that sprang from a dark furred muzzle. It stalked toward me, relishing my fear.

"Come and get some, dickhead," I babbled, still on my back, fumbling for something I could use as a weapon. My hand found an object, and I held it aloft in triumph, before recognizing the shape of one of my permanently stained Air Jordans. When had I lost a shoe? I glanced from the non-weapon to the stupidly deadly monster. "What are your thoughts on playing fetch?"

Judging by the snarl that exposed a forest of teeth, it was less interested than I'd hoped.

I threw the shoe at its face, but the beast snatched it out of the air with one bite. What fell to the ground bore no resemblance to footwear of any kind. With a single bound, the Infected loomed over me. It pulled a clawed arm back for a strike that couldn't help but eviscerate me.

I closed my eyes and tried to think of happier things.

A loud crash was followed by an even louder roar, and I cracked open one eye to see that Steve had thrown himself down the stairs and tackled the werewolf. The manpire was in seriously bad shape— uniform shredded and golden blood everywhere—but his axe was slick with blood of a darker shade.

"Kick his ass, Steve!" I shouted encouragement to the mohawked vampire, glad he had decided to stay with me while I called a cab. If we had followed my original plan, I would never have surviv—

Behind and above me, additional growls could be heard. I turned enough to see a wolf of the four-legged variety slip past the gate and start down the stairs. Other shapes followed.

Well, shit.

I limped back down the stairs to Steve, who was still struggling with the werewolf already below. The portal had gone dormant again, not that there was much chance of us reaching it. "Don't look now, but we've got company."

"I know," he replied, grunting as a blow got through his guard. "I left them to come save your ass."

"You mean you didn't just kill them all? What kind of a badass ninja vampire are you anyway?"

He chuckled softly, which might have been encouraging if it hadn't taken a detour to burble weirdly in one of his lungs. "Juliette was right," he gasped, "you really can be an asshole."

"Only to my friends," I assured him. The click of claws on the stairs informed me that the other werewolves, injured or otherwise, were closing in. And that was when I had my great idea.

I watched as Steve swung his axe weakly. The werewolf dodged the blow easily and darted in to bite at the vampire's side… when I lowered my shoulder and charged into it.

It was a little bit like tackling a brick wall. Still, this was Earth, and physics held *some* sway; my impact was just enough to nudge the wolf past Steve. The wolf and I bounced onto the steps—painfully—but for one moment, the manpire had a path to the portal.

"Go!" I yelled. I had no chance of making it there myself—tangled in one werewolf, with a half dozen more almost in slobbering distance—but at least the tragic love story of Steve and Barry would survive.

The manpire looked at the portal for less than a second, anguish on his normally stoic features. Then, hefting his axe, he stepped away from the portal and back toward me.

God damn it. Even my attempts at noble self-sacrifice were crashing and burning. I yelled something at the vampire, completely unaware of what exactly I was saying.

Steve shrugged in silent apology and threw his axe. It whistled by to embed in the werewolf next to me. From the sounds the creature made, even that blow hadn't been fatal, but it had at least given the wolf something to think about. Then, Steve advanced past me, barehanded, to duke it out with the wolves who had already kicked his ass once.

By this point, the stairs were slick with blood and other things I didn't want to think about. I wound up in a tangled heap at their base, at which point my body went on strike and stopped listening to my brain's frenzied commands.

And then, less than ten feet away, the wall began to glow.

The portal shivered, and discharged the big-eared brownie I'd just recently sent in. I looked to see if he was carrying anything that might help us—like a thermonuclear warhead—but he remained unarmed.

"Welcome back," I told him weakly, dredging up just enough energy to begin crawling in the portal's direction, "to the worst night out ever."

The little man cocked his head and stepped to one side. The portal shivered again, and a four-armed, two-headed creature charged past me with a roar. He was followed by a lovely femmepire in a black dress, and another in black and blood red.

I felt like I should know who those last two were, but it was too great of an effort to think of their names. Instead, I let myself slowly slip into darkness.

INTERLUDE

Finally, the crushing jaws released my shoulder. I received another blast of horrible breath, directly in my face, and then the weight on my chest vanished. The footsteps—whose odd rhythm I now recognized to be the result of four legs instead of two—retreated up what seemed to be stairs. Soon after, the door banged shut, and the sound of something walking in the room above us slowly faded.

"Yeah, you better run," I muttered, barely recognizing my own voice. I tasted salt on my lips and took it for a sign that we were near the ocean.

It definitely wasn't because I was crying. Not John Smith, hard-bitten gumshoe. He was the kind of guy who could take three slugs in his chest, pour a shot of whiskey on the entry wounds, and then return to his conversation as if nothing had happened. He was the sort of man who would crawl over broken glass just to spit in the devil's eye, the sort of guy who…

More liquid trickled into my mouth.

Okay, maybe I was crying. I gave myself a pass, given that my shoulder felt like it had been doused in kerosene and lit on fire. Except even that would have been better because fire would have meant I could see.

"Are you okay, little bird?" Juliette sounded awful—like she was speaking through a throat full of gravel and razor blades—but she was at least coherent. For now, anyway.

"No," I gasped back. "Why do things keep biting me?!?!"

"You know what that was, right?"

"I'm thinking werewolf?" I took her lack of response as confirmation. "Easy guess, given everything that's going on." I focused my mind on blocking out the pain in my shoulder. It didn't work at all. Stupid mind. "Could you smell who it was?"

"I don't go around cataloging werewolf scents, John. The odor tells me the species, but otherwise? No clue."

"Awesome." Not that the identity of our captor really mattered at this point. "What the hell are they doing? First, they go out of their way to try to kill me, but now that I'm a prisoner, they're content to do it one bite at a time?"

"You're the detective, not me." A shade of concern entered that ghastly voice. "Just be glad you haven't bled out over the last day."

"Not going to happen," I reassured her. "My last bite healed weirdly fast. I think this one will too."

The statement sounded oddly familiar, like I'd heard someone else say something similar, and recently. But who? And when?

And then it hit me.

"Oh, shit," I breathed, forgetting even my shoulder pain in that epiphany. "I know what they're doing."

CHAPTER 24
IN WHICH YOU CAN'T GO HOME AGAIN

I'm told it wasn't much of a fight once the customers of the Bitter End took up arms to defend us. Apparently, the werewolves just turned tail—literally, in this case—and fled, like the flea-bitten cowards they were. I'd have loved to see it but was suffering through a mild bout of unconsciousness at the time. I woke to Juliette looking down at me.

"Welcome back, little bird."

"Is Steve okay?" Behind her, I could see black-clad figures scurrying back and forth, all of them armed with medieval-era weaponry and angry expressions. There was no sign of my mohawked bodyguard.

"He's alive, and kept his limbs," she told me with a shrug. "It'll be a while before he's one-hundred percent, and his blood donors are going to look like cadavers in the meantime, but he should be fine."

"Thank God." I sagged back to the concrete. "And the werewolves?"

"Once they decided to run, we didn't have a prayer of catching them. Four legs are faster than two, and nobody wanted to chase them into another ambush. Brenna's boy toy got you a souvenir, at least." She pointed to an object leaning against the wall.

Was that…? Yes, yes it was. Somewhere in San Diego, a werewolf was running about with only three legs. Sucked to be him.

I carefully sat up. My head pounded, and I was going to have a spectacular collection of bruises in new and interesting places, but nothing seemed broken, which was a minor miracle.

Juliette smiled proudly, like a physical therapist pleased with her patient's progress. "You somehow made it through too. Are we sure there aren't any leprechauns in your family tree?"

"I just got the crap kicked out of me by a pack of werewolves!"

"And lived to walk away," she replied, still smiling. "That sounds remarkably lucky to me. Too bad you ruined your victory by fainting at the very end."

"I didn't faint!" I protested. "I slipped into unconsciousness, struck down by terrible and grievous wounds."

"Uh huh." Despite her words, Juliette's touch was gentle when she helped me to my feet. The world spun about, but I managed not to throw up. That was huge; I'd developed something of a reputation in the House for being a vomiter.

"Are you well enough to travel, John?" asked Kayla as she joined us. Unlike Juliette, the femmepire Captain was a mess, sporting deep wounds in her arms. At least one slash had left the belly of her tunic in ribbons.

"Whoa. I thought the wolves didn't put up much of a fight?"

The ash-blonde Aussie grimaced. "These were from Barry. When the gremlin came and told us what was happening, I had to restrain him from charging out to protect Steve." She shrugged painfully. "My number two didn't need to lose his boyfriend, on top of everything else."

"The little dude was a gremlin?" I looked about but he was nowhere to be found. "Aren't they supposed to be green?"

"We really need to go, John." Kayla's voice was terse. "I had to pull a lot of the Watch away from the House to secure this scene, which means Queen Lucia is vulnerable."

"Just have Zorana stand at the gate. Nobody would be stupid enough to attack then." I was apparently the only one who found that funny. "Sorry. I'm ready when you are."

I took my first fumbling step and managed not to fall over. That was progress, right?

In short order, I was bundled into one of the House's Escalades, with two Watch members in front, two behind, and Juliette in the seat to my left. Kayla and Darlene rode with another four Watch members in the second Escalade, while the third vehicle—or the first, I guess—was already on its way back to the House with Steve.

As we pulled away from the curb, I cursed.

"What is it?"

Every Watch member in my Escalade was suddenly brandishing a weapon, their usual hyper-vigilance instantaneously amped up to DEFCON 3.

"Sorry," I said again, waiting for the cutlery to disappear, "I just realized I'd forgotten to tip the elephant. Again."

ooo

We were headed toward the 15 when a thought struck me. "Juliette, we need to go to my parents' house."

"No can do, little bird. I'm taking you straight to the House, where we can hide you away in a bomb shelter, surrounded by a dozen guards armed with rocket launchers." She had found a stick of gum somewhere and blew a bubble in my direction.

"As delightful as that sounds, I'm serious." I leaned forward between the two front seats. I'd seen the driver—a squat, Samoan vampire—once before in the House gym, but didn't know his name. "Hey dude, we need to make a quick detour to Chula Vista."

The manpire didn't give any indication that he had even heard me. I turned back to the Duchess.

"Juliette… please?"

"*Why* do you need to go to your house?"

"If the wolves attacked me, they could easily have attacked my parents too."

"Your parents are fine," she assured me. "Lucia arranged protection for them."

"She arranged protection for me too, but if it hadn't been for a gremlin and Brenna's booty call, Steve and I might *still* have died." The femmepire said nothing, but I could see her mulling it over. "I won't even leave the car, I promise. I just want to make sure that everything is okay."

Juliette sighed. "This is officially the worst Friday night out ever." She met the driver's eyes in the rearview mirror and nodded. "Go ahead, Tupa."

We made it to Chula Vista and my parents' house without incident. I was relieved to see that the cars parked nearby were empty of occupants. The lights in my house were out, which was to be expected at four in the morning. Nothing stirred.

"Satisfied?"

"Hardly. Where are the White Ladies?"

Irritably, Juliette instructed Tupa to pull into the driveway. The Escalade's lights illuminated the front of the house.

"There's one." She pointed to the porch bench, where Anastasia and I had talked Thursday morning.

At first, I didn't see anything, but a figure slowly took shape, seated on the bench, and kicking its heels. The more I looked, the more solid that figure became, until I was regarding a young woman with long, dark hair hanging like a curtain in front of her face. She was barefoot and bare-armed despite the cold, her skin as white as the conservative 1950s-era cotton nightgown she wore. As I watched, deep spots of darkness appeared on the front of that nightgown and began to spread, dyeing the fabric black.

"Holy shit, she's bleeding!"

"She's fine, dumbass. She's a ghost, remember?"

Even as Juliette spoke, the blood stains disappeared, like they had never existed, and the nightgown returned to a pristine white. Moments later, the sequence began to repeat itself. The woman turned to regard our vehicle, extended one hand toward us, index finger pointed to the sky, and wagged it back and forth.

"That's our cue to leave, Tupa," Juliette told our driver, and the Samoan manpire was happy to oblige. As we pulled out of the driveway, she looked at me. "All good?"

"Was that Graciela?" My voice was hushed. It was one thing to know ghosts existed, and another thing entirely to see one.

"I don't think so." She scowled at my look. "Do you think I make it a point to hang out with ghosts? The less I have to do with their kind, the happier I am. Nobody screws with the White Ladies, John. Not more than once, anyway."

I spoke up again as we left Chula Vista. "Could we swing by my office too?"

Juliette reached over and smacked the back of my head, something that didn't really help my post-battle near-concussion symptoms. "There is something seriously wrong with you. We're going back to the House. Now. End of Story."

I let out a heavy sigh. Being on top of the furry world's most wanted list was even less fun than expected. "Fine. But can you send someone there in my place? I need something from my office safe."

"If it will buy us even a minute of silence, then yes. Fine. Whatever!"

One of the Watch members behind me snickered. Most of the Council might find me irritating, but I was an endless source of amusement to the House's rank and file.

Juliette was already speaking quietly into her phone. After a moment, she looked back at me.

"What is it you need retrieved?"

"My gun." Technically, it was Jee Sun's gun, which meant it was Bill's, but my wrestling match with a werewolf had convinced me I needed to arm myself with something more than a shoe.

"Did you get that?" Juliette asked the phone. The answer must have been satisfactory, as she ended the call without another word.

"Don't they need my keys and the combination to my safe?" I thought back to the number of times my office had been broken into over the past month. "Well, the combination, anyway?"

"Oh, please." She flashed a smug smile my way. "We're not amateurs."

"Cool. Next time I need to break into someone's house, I guess I know who to call."

"John?" Her tone was strangely serious.

"What's up?"

"Now would be a great damn time for that minute of silence."

This time, at least two of the other vampires in the car laughed. I waited for a half-beat and then responded.

"Did you mean *now* now? Or like ten seconds from now? Is someone going to be timing this? I don't want to overshoot my mark."

Juliette just shook her head and went back to staring out the window. Either she was grinding her teeth, or she chewed gum a lot more intensely than the rest of us.

CHAPTER 25
IN WHICH THE RULE OF THREE GETS REDEFINED

By the time we reached Scripps Ranch, I was ready for a shower and a bed… and not necessarily in that order. Instead, I was ushered up to the fourth floor and down the hall to one of the conference rooms the Council used for their meetings.

I would say something about how vampires had more meetings than Fortune 500 executives, but I'd never worked a nine-to-five at all, let alone for a Fortune 500 company. I had no basis for comparison. Maybe executives did nothing *but* attend meetings, squeezing in the maximum amount of corporate facetime before they headed off to their golf outings and private airplane caviar extravaganzas.

What I *could* say was that the Council had a lot of meetings. But even for them, half-past-four on a Saturday morning was ridiculous. Nevertheless, they were all present, looking as fresh and fashionable as if they'd just stepped out of a magazine photo shoot.

Freaking vampires.

Kayla and Zorana were there too, the former looking better than she had at the Bitter End, the latter casually shaving slivers off the wooden table using her thumb. I offered Anastasia a smile from across the room, but the auburn-haired femmepire's features were carved stone, her jade eyes dark and unknowable.

Lucia was at the head of the table. Usually, the sight of her sparked mixed feelings of attraction and repulsion, but this time, the repulsion was slow to come. Apparently, I was even more tired than I'd thought.

"With Lady Middleton present, we can get started."

"Started with what?" Nobody had offered me a seat at the table, but I took one anyway. I'd just survived a close encounter of the furry kind; I was not in the mood for exclusionary race politics.

"The war council, Mr. Smith. The Captain has already given her report, and what details Stephen was able to provide. What can you add, Lady Middleton?"

Juliette launched into her description of what had happened. I'd heard most of it before, and experienced the rest, so I focused instead on Lucia's words. My tired brain was having difficulty equating sounds with their respective meanings.

After a long moment, I deduced that Stephen must refer to Steve—which made me question why Lucia had never called me Jonathan. My full name actually *was* John, but there was no way she could have known that.

Then, the rest of what she had said sank in.

"Wait… what do you mean, war council? What war?"

Juliette shot me a dirty look for interrupting her tale.

"The Infected have openly attacked someone deemed an ally of this House, Mr. Smith," Lucia patiently explained. "Not to mention one of my own. The Concordat permits us retaliation, and we will demonstrate to the wolves and the rest of the world why we sit atop this city's power structure." She waved Juliette to a seat. "Secundus?"

Anastasia's cool eyes met mine for a moment. "We remain severely under strength. I recommend kill squads of no fewer than four.

If we withdraw from the estate grounds and patrol only the House interior, how many squads can we field, Kayla?"

"Five," the Aussie replied, after a moment's thought.

"So few?" queried Lucia. "What if we disabled the elevators, and closed off the third and fourth floors? Surely, that would help?"

"It would," mused Kayla. "If we *also* shut down the sublevels—everything but the security room—we could increase the number further. Maybe seven squads of four?"

"Better." The queen turned back to Anastasia. "Continue."

"We have the addresses of the pack elders. Two squads per house, plus one squad in mobile reserve." The femmepire's voice was flat and empty of emotion. "Cutting off the head works almost as well on packs as it does individuals."

"Wait a second," I began, but Marcus spoke right over me.

"And if they've already gone to ground?"

"We will hunt them down," hissed Lucia. "Marcus, how long will it take to freeze their financial assets?"

"Twelve hours, no more."

"Including those accounts off shore or in Mexico?" The manpire didn't bother with a verbal response; his look of insulted pride was more than answer enough. "Excellent."

Anastasia turned to Juliette. "Lady Middleton, you will liaise with the local police. We lack the forces to canvas an entire city, so we will have to use the humans as our eyes on the ground."

Juliette began to say something, but I'd heard enough.

"Wait just a second!" I had risen to my feet.

"Do you have something to add, Mr. Smith?" Thrall and honored mediator or not, the queen was back to looking at me like I was a bug on her windshield.

"Yeah," I replied heatedly, "that's why I'm standing up and shouting."

"Then by all means, speak." Lucia's voice could have taught an iceberg tricks.

"Don't you think starting a war is a *bad* idea?"

"That's human gratitude for you." Marcus sneered. "It is a pity that one of ours was wounded saving you."

"I'm grateful to Steve," I said through gritted teeth, "who was out actually putting his life on the line while you did whatever glorified vampire accountants do."

"Enough!" Lucia's voice cracked like a whip, quite possibly the only thing that kept Marcus from launching himself at me. "You squabble like children, and I *will not have it!*" In the fullness of her rage, the queen's eyes glowed.

She took a moment to see if we were going to reply, but I wasn't stupid, and Marcus… well, I guess his sense of self-preservation had the same effect.

"Now then," Lucia spoke quietly, but if anything, her words grew even sharper, "you will both sit down."

We sat. I took a quick survey of the room, and found Kayla concerned, Juliette irritated, and Anastasia stoic. Zorana, as usual, seemed greatly amused. Hugging her knees to her chest, the Blood Witch watched us with wide, cheerful eyes.

The gold around Lucia's pupils formed tiny suns in the cold blue sky of her eyes. "Tell me, my thrall, what is your objection to my House defending its honor and prolonging your life?" Her tone suggested my reason had better be a good one, the menace so blatantly obvious that I didn't even think of reacting to her having called me a thrall *again*.

"It's a problem of scope," I said carefully.

Zorana rolled her eyes and went back to whittling her way through the table.

"In what way?"

"We don't know who wants me dead. Going after the entire pack is epic overkill." And stupid. I hadn't said that last part out loud. At least, I didn't think so.

"There are times when overkill is warranted, Mr. Smith. If someone strikes you, then you should strike them back three times. Once in retaliation and once to balance the scales."

"Uhm." I was tired, but I was pretty sure that one plus one equaled two, not three.

"The third time is to show them that there is no limit to the potential reprisals for their action."

Okay, that was just scary. My mom believed very much in the maxim of an eye for an eye—to Father Peter's dismay—but this was more like an eye, a leg, and an arm for an eye.

"If the bulk of the pack must pay for the actions of the few," Lucia continued, "then so be it. The fault is theirs, particularly these so-called Elders who could not control their own subjects."

"It's a good thing Bill didn't feel the same way back in July," I pointed out quietly.

"Excuse me?"

"You don't see the parallel? A theft and attempted assassination by one of your subjects? By your logic, Bill would have been perfectly in his rights to burn this whole building down."

Next to me, Juliette choked on her gum. Dead silence filled the room, but I kept my eyes fixed on Lucia. One advantage of being so tired that I couldn't even sit up straight was that I lacked the energy for emotion. It made dealing with the queen a little bit easier.

After a long moment, she spoke again, biting off each syllable. "Your objection is noted. But the honor of my House is at stake, and the importance of that honor is something we have already made painfully clear to you." She turned back to Anastasia, dismissing me. "Is there anything more for us to discuss?"

"Your Majesty…" Again, I blinked. I really needed to scrub that honorific from my vocabulary. For some reason, I'd used it more on Queen Crazy-Pants in the past twenty hours than in the entire previous mediation. "What honor is there in allowing yourself to be used?"

A loud crunch sounded, like a gunshot in the small room. The queen's hand had clenched reflexively on the edge of the table and punctured the thick hardwood.

At this rate, they were going to need a new table.

"What the hell are you *doing*, little bird?"

"Mr. Smith." Anastasia had finally entered the conversation. "I understand that you are tired and did not come through the attack unscathed. For that, you have our sympathy. But perhaps you would like to explain your question, in words less likely to be mistaken for insults?"

She had thrown me a lifeline, and I gratefully took hold.

"Of course." I spoke to Anastasia, very carefully not looking in the direction of the now-irate queen. "As you know, my current mediation involves members of the San Diego Pack *and* the New Mexico Pack. We don't know which group wants me dead—"

"Probably both, given your track record," muttered Juliette.

"—but it seems more likely that it would be the New Mexico weres, given that the San Diego Pack hired me."

"And what does this have to do with the House being used?" Something told me Anastasia already knew where I was going with this. For all I knew, she had figured it out before I even arrived. She was so damn smart it was scary sometimes.

"The two packs are involved in a dispute over the San Diego territory. If I were a New Mexican furball and wanted a quick end to the argument that left my hands clean…"

"...you'd arrange for someone else to destroy the pack for you," Marcus finished triumphantly.

"Gold star for the flying accountant." I didn't have anything against accountants—my own father being one—but Marcus seemed to resent the label, and I was happy to use that to my advantage. After all, the dude was a total dick.

Lucia remained quiet, so Anastasia continued the questioning.

"But the New Mexican representative, Jason, is here, within our reach. Why would he adopt a course that will surely get him killed?"

It was a good question. Luckily, I had been nineteen not all that long ago, and knew the answer. "He's a kid. And kids not only have inflated opinions of themselves, they're convinced they are immortal."

"I can't believe *you* just called someone a kid." That was from Kayla, which was a little bit unfair, considering Darlene was two years my junior. If I was a kid, then Kayla was robbing the damn cradle.

"It seems to me that the simplest solution—" These were the first words Zorana had spoken since my arrival, and as usual, her voice caused my guts to twist in on themselves. She picked at a tooth and smiled around her child-sized hand. "—would be to destroy both packs."

Trust the Blood Witch to go for maximum carnage. Thankfully, salvation came from an unexpected source.

"We lack the resources to wage a war on two fronts," murmured Lucia, her eyes distant as she thought over the situation. Or of the many ways she could kill me with her bare hands; it was difficult to be certain. "And the New Mexico Pack is one of the largest in North America." Arctic blue eyes drilled into me. "How reliable is your information, Mr. Smith?"

"About the land struggle? Pretty reliable. That it's Jason who wants me dead? That's just a hypothesis."

"I trust that you would not trouble us with guesswork if you did not also have a suggestion?"

"Sort of." I took a deep breath. "As the still-breathing mediator for their dispute, I have a meeting with Jason tomorrow morning. I want to go and see if he shows up."

"And after he kills you, we'll know who to target!" Marcus smiled broadly. "I like it!"

"Funny." I rolled my eyes. "I didn't say I was going without protection. But if he doesn't show, it will tell us a lot."

"And if he does?" That was from Anastasia.

"It'll still tell us a lot. Especially if he's missing a limb. And maybe I can get some information out of him that will point us to whoever is responsible." I frowned. "There's something off about Thursday night's attempted car-icide, but I can't put my finger on what it is."

I turned to Lucia. "I'm not against you killing the bastards who banged up the Corolla and jumped Steve and me. But give me a day so I can figure out who those people are. Surely, a surgical strike would be more impressive than just randomly annihilating everyone?"

"You've *clearly* never witnessed total annihilation, monkey."

My stomach cramped again, and this time, I couldn't tell if it was from Zorana's voice, or the words she was saying.

ooo

In the end, Lucia granted my request. I wasn't sure if it was my logic that convinced her, or if she just had a deep-seated desire to not be anyone's patsy. Then again, it was my logic that had revealed the potential patsy-ness of the situation in the first place.

I was clearly one hell of a mediator.

"Mr. Smith?" I had almost made it out of the conference room, but Lucia's voice stopped me in my tracks. "Stay a moment. I would speak with you."

Juliette was already halfway down the hall, but her voice drifted back to me. "Somebody's in trouuuuble…"

"Sure thing," I told the queen, stepping aside to let the other Council members past.

When they had departed, Lucia shut the door, and a cold wind from nowhere rushed through the room. If there had been any papers on the conference table, they would have blown away like leaves. Ice formed on the door's surface, thickening as it spread, until everything from the top of the frame to the floor was entirely encased.

"I need to go *through* that door if I'm going to shower or sleep," I pointed out mildly. I'd moved past exhaustion into a state of numb disinterest.

"In time," came the reply. "Now sit."

And so I sat… again. It beat standing.

Rather than return to the head of the table, she took a seat beside me. She was no longer dressed in her leathers, and whatever she *was* wearing made absolutely no impression on me. If that didn't communicate, once and for all, how tired I was, nothing could.

"How did you do it, Mr. Smith?"

"Do what?"

"Do not play stupid with me. You know of what I speak."

"Here's what I'm going to do," I told her tiredly. "I'm going to put my arms on the table, like this. See? And now I'm going to lay my head down on top of those arms." They made a remarkably good pillow. "And I'm going to get some rest until you start making sense."

I closed my eyes, which kept me from seeing Lucia's open hand slap the table directly in front of my face. At any other time, I would have probably fallen out of my chair, but I simply cracked one eye and looked sideways and up at the queen.

"I'm speaking of our bond," she hissed. "How are you hiding from me?"

"What?" Absolutely nothing she was saying made any sense. I felt around for her presence in my mind and located it almost immediately. It quite helpfully told me that she was located less than two feet to my right. "I don't know what you mean."

She studied my face intently. "Since the moment you became my thrall, I have had a sense of you. Your moods, your actions—"

"That's pretty damn creepy," I told her, desperately trying to review anything I might have felt or done in the past seven weeks.

"—and, most of all, your whereabouts," she finished. "Today, you disappeared. The bond remains, yet it tells me nothing. I ask again, what did you do?"

"Lucia," I finally told her, "I know you aren't going to believe me, but I didn't do anything. Besides, you hid from me just fine at Mister A's."

"With active effort, once I realized you were using our bond to avoid me. An effort that you are apparently not expending." She scowled. "It is intolerable that my thrall can sense me, yet I cannot do the same."

I barked a short laugh. "You drank my blood to make me your thrall. Maybe me drinking your blood made you mine."

"I see now what you mean about needing your sleep. You are speaking nonsense." It sounded like the queen had taken a step back, but I'd closed my eyes again and couldn't be sure. "But I suppose it is possible that my blood in your body is causing a momentary interference."

I heard the chair legs scrape the floor as she rose. "We will revisit this issue in a few days, my thrall. Either the situation will have resolved itself, or I will dig deeper for the answers."

I didn't even pay any attention to the threat. I just turned in my chair and watched her de-ice the door and depart.

Her Talent really was ludicrously wasted in San Diego.

By the time I got up to follow, the hall was empty. I didn't see another living soul as I took an elevator down to the second floor and made my way to the same temporary bedroom I'd been previously assigned. The shower would have to wait; I barely had the energy to remove my clothes before I toppled into bed.

At least, I told myself—as my consciousness slipped away, like water through a sieve—*I get to sleep in tomorrow.*

CHAPTER 26

I was in the middle of a dream where a three-headed cow, the Michelin Man, and I were trying to climb Mount Everest, when the cow looked in my direction. Its many mouths fell open to sing the instrumentals to the theme song from Kill Bill. I turned to ask the Michelin Man what was up with our cow friend, but he wasn't there anymore. Nor was Mount Everest… which was, honestly, an even more alarming development.

Instead, I saw a lushly furnished room, with the first hint of sunlight creeping through the window. An open door in the far wall led to another room, but that room's lights were off. Why did this all look familiar?

The theme song from Kill Bill started to repeat, which was when I realized I wasn't being serenaded by a three-headed cow after all. I scrambled out of the world's softest king size bed, and over to the nightstand to grab my wonderphone.

"Y-wuh?"

"Is this John Smith?" A woman's voice, slightly familiar. It was difficult to tell through my just-woken-up-from-the-world's-best-dream haze, but she sounded concerned.

"Yuh." Sometimes, it took my mouth a little longer to wake up than the rest of me.

"Oh, thank God. I found your number in Phil's papers. You have to help me!"

As the post-sleep haze lifted, I realized that the woman didn't just sound concerned. She sounded frantic.

"I'm sorry? Who is this?"

"This is Melissa. Melissa Thompsen? We spoke just a few days ago?"

I rubbed my eyes tiredly. "Hi, Melissa. What has you calling me at—" Oh good lord. "—eight in the morning?"

"I'm sorry," she wailed, which would have immediately gained her my sympathy, if the sound of her cry hadn't pierced my head like an icepick. I held the receiver at arm's length for a moment. When I brought it back to my ear, she was already in mid-sentence. "—Phil. He never came home last night. And he's not answering his cell. I think something's wrong."

This was not a phone call I was prepared to have *ever*, let alone after an attempt on my life and less than four hours of sleep.

"Mrs. Thompsen," I began carefully, "is it possible he got hung up at his job? Or maybe went out for a drink or two afterward and wasn't in any shape to come home?"

"I called the construction company already. Phil didn't show up for work yesterday." Her voice quieted. "He's still… processing all the stuff you made me tell him."

"Hold up there. I didn't *make* you do anything," I pointed out.

"You're right. I don't know why I said that." Her voice started to rise again.

"It's okay. I get that you're worried. So, do you think he's just gone somewhere to kind of, you know, think about all of this. Or…"

"Or has he left me for good?" I could hear footsteps in the background of her phone, as if she were stomping around the crochet wonderland of her living room. "Or has something else entirely happened to him? I don't know! That's why I need your help."

"I'm sorry?"

"I need you to find my husband, Mr. Smith."

I rolled out of bed to look out my suite's bedroom window. Another beautiful day in San Diego. It was the sort of day to be spent at the beach or drinking coffee at one of La Jolla's overpriced gourmet shops or… pretty much anything that didn't involve a possible war between the House and the pack, a distraught werewolf's missing husband, and an incredibly early wake-up call.

"Melissa, if Phil needs some time to himself—"

"You don't understand, John! What if the pack thinks my husband is leaving me? Do you think they'll let him live, knowing what he knows?"

She kind of had a point. The first rule of Fight Club might be *don't talk about Fight Club*, but the first rule of the supernatural world seemed to be *kill any human that knows about us and isn't absolutely necessary to our plans for worldwide domination.*

It didn't really roll off the tongue, but it's not like anyone said it out loud anyway. It was the unspoken kind of rule. I'd only avoided that fate by lucking into the position of mediator, an event that was feeling less fortuitous with each passing day.

That said, I already had a metric shit ton of work on my plate. Between werewolf assassins, vengeful vampire queens, a vegetable demigod's child ward, and my mediation between two college-age divorcees, I didn't have the time or energy to take on something new.

"Please, Mr. Smith," Melissa whispered into the silence. "Phil is all I have."

Well, shit.

"I'll do what I can," I heard myself promise. "The good news is that I think the pack is a little too busy with other stuff to be chasing after your husband. And on that note, you really might want to stay home for the next few… well, until you hear back from me."

"Is something going on?"

"Possibly," I equivocated. "I'd tell you more, but I can't break mediator-client privilege."

"I'm not sure that's a thing."

"It is for me. Anyway, San Diego's a big city, but I'll do what I can to find Phil. Can you send me a list of his local friends, including their phone numbers?" I gave her my email address. "Any common hangouts would be good too."

"Of course. I'll do that right now. Thank you, John! I'll pay you whatever it takes!"

Those were the sort of words a private investigator dreamed of. When not dreaming of Everest anyway. Unfortunately…

"I'm still under contract to Phil through the end of the day," I admitted. "So, why don't we just call it even for now?"

Mrs. Thompsen seemed reluctant to let me go until I reminded her that I needed the list if I was going to track down her husband. Then, she couldn't get off the phone fast enough. I placed the phone back on the nightstand and sighed.

"Did I just hear you accept a new case, Mr. Smith?"

I was leaping back into bed, pulling the sheet and comforter around my mostly naked body, even before Anastasia had finished speaking.

"Holy crap! You nearly gave me a heart attack!" If I was going to spend nights at the House, I really needed to buy some pajamas or something. It was one thing to know you were a little bit overweight; it was another thing entirely to have others constantly bearing witness to that fact.

Especially femmepires I wanted to impress.

"My apologies." Anastasia didn't *sound* sorry. In fact, she sounded very much like she was trying not to laugh. I glared at her from within the safety of my bedding. "When I heard you on the telephone, I assumed that you were up and—" Her lips curved into the small smile I found so devastating. "—presentable."

"If it hadn't been for that phone call, I'd still be scaling Mount Everest." She quirked an eyebrow, but I didn't bother elaborating. "And to answer your question, yes, I took another case. But I'm hoping I can get some help from the House on it, while I deal with Jason and the pack."

"I assume you would like us to run a credit check and attempt to trace Mr. Thompsen's phone?"

I blinked. I wasn't surprised that Anastasia knew the details of the case. If she were close enough to have heard me talking, she was also close enough to have heard everything Melissa said. That was par for the course with vampires. No, I was more impressed with the simplicity of her solution.

"You can do that?" Damn it. Between this and Juliette's safecracker, I should have been sub-contracting to the vampires for years. Or for the few months I'd known of their existence, at least.

"Our IT staff does have the capability. However," she continued, tapping a finger against her lips in thought, "I would recommend using our contacts in the police department instead. There is no need to get more of the People involved than absolutely necessary."

"Ana, you're amazing. Having the cops locate Phil would be fantastic!" A new thought occurred to me. "Why were you down here on the second floor anyway?"

"To talk to you, of course, Mr. Smith."

"I only talk to gorgeous femmepires when they call me John," I teased. A total lie, of course. "Could it wait until after my shower though? After last night, I can't imagine I smell very good."

"You smell like a human," she replied with a shrug, "and not unpleasant. But I am happy to wait until you have completed your morning ablutions." She took a seat at the full-sized table in my room and regarded me calmly.

"Uhm." I was reasonably sure she couldn't see my blush through the pile of sheets and comforters I continued to hide under. "Do you mind looking away while I run from here to the bathroom? As you saw, I'm kind of undressed."

"I don't know, John," she replied, a twinkle in her jade eyes. "It has been said that you give quite the floor show."

She was referring to my previous stay at the House, when Juliette had surprised me in the act of getting out of bed. The result had been my mostly naked self getting tangled in the sheet, tripping, and sprawling out, limbs spread, onto the carpeted floor.

Vampires popping in on me in the morning seemed to be a theme. I really was going to have to buy those pajamas. But for now… Lady Dumenyova showed no sign of closing her eyes, or even pretending to look away, so I climbed out of bed, wrapped the sheet around my body, and began the trek to the bathroom, head high, shoulders back, and gut firmly sucked in.

It went surprisingly well, until one end of the sheet caught on the nightstand. At that point, I had little choice but to leap toward the relative safety of the bathroom, boxers, beer gut, and all.

As I closed the door, Anastasia's sweet voice carried to me, thick with amusement.

"For once, I believe Juliette was right."

ooo

As I left the bathroom, dressed in yet another of the apparently endless supply of Watch uniforms, I was greeted by the sweet smell of that heavenly ambrosia known as coffee. And just like that, everything was right in the world. There was a reason coffee was its own food group at the very top of the FDA's dietary pyramid. At least I assumed it was. I'd never actually looked at the chart. Two large steaming mugs were waiting for me, along with a plate bearing croissants and pastries.

Laundry service *and* in-room catering?

Life at the House had its perks.

Anastasia looked up from another of those perks, a glossy, ultra-slim tablet. Her outfit today mirrored the one I'd first met her in; a blue silk blouse paired with long black pants and low-heeled boots. She swiped a finger across the tablet's surface and the screen darkened. "I took the liberty of getting us some breakfast. I am sure you must be hungry."

"Always," I agreed, taking a long sip of coffee, and diving into my croissant. "Aren't you going to have anything?"

"I have already fed but thank you for asking."

"Do you mean fed, or... you know, *fed?*"

"Both, of course." Her gaze was level. "I do not require blood every day, but when I do drink, I generally do so upon waking."

"You have donors?"

"Of course."

I found myself envisioning a roomful of young, athletic, and mostly naked men, lined up for her daily selection. Just like that, the pastry in my mouth lost its flavor.

"Gustavo and Teresa are a lovely couple who live at my private residence in Cardiff. They insisted on joining me in this country several decades ago when Gustavo's own parents passed."

"Several *decades* ago?" The bare-chested male harem blinked out of existence in my mind, replaced by a pair of Italian… septuagenarians?

"Indeed. If you wish, I will introduce them to you. I believe they would enjoy that greatly, although their English remains limited."

"That's very kind of you," I said, taking another large bite of pastry to avoid having to say anything more. How weird a meeting would *that* be? "Anyway, I'm surprised you're already awake. It was a late night. Or morning. Or whatever it was."

She shrugged her strong shoulders. "At a certain age, sleep becomes less necessary for the People. I rarely rest more than four hours a night and can function adequately on less."

"I seem to be headed in the opposite direction. Five years ago, I wouldn't have blinked at an all-nighter. These days, anything less than six hours of sleep leaves me feeling like I'm swimming through molasses." I rolled my arm about in its socket and winced. "And minor scrapes and bruises take forever to heal."

"Yes, John." Anastasia's eyes sparkled again, as she teased me. "Having reached the venerable age of twenty-five, you are indisputably an old man. Or perhaps there were just fewer attacks on your life back then."

"That's a good point." I'd already kind of forgotten what we were talking about and was instead marveling at the way the morning sunshine—streaming through the bedroom window—reflected in her eyes, making them appear even larger and more luminescent than usual. How many humans had thrown themselves at Anastasia over the years? Was I the fiftieth or five hundredth? And did she ever get tired of that sort of adulation?

The femmepire took a sip of coffee from her own mug, and I tried not to stare at the way her lips molded to the container's edge.

"Anyway, thank you for breakfast. Today is going to be busy."

"Yes. That is what I wished to speak with you about."

"Don't worry. I'm not going to do anything dumb when we meet Jason. If you tell me to sit, I'll sit. If you tell me to run, I'll run." I winced again, although this time it was in memory of the previous night's attack. "I learned my lesson last night."

"That is good to hear, but—"

"In fact, you should probably change into your Valkyrie biker outfit." I waggled my eyebrows in what my dad had assured me was peak flirtatiousness. "I imagine it takes quite a while to get into that."

"You would be surprised," she murmured, and I found my heart rate spiking like I'd just run ten miles.

Okay… one mile. Ten miles would kill me.

"However, that is what I came here to tell you, Mr. Smith."

"Oh?" Her words were calm and crisp as ever, but I felt my heart sinking, as if part of me already knew what was coming.

"I will not be accompanying you to meet with Mr. Diaz."

"Mr. Diaz?" The only person I knew with that last name worked as a bagger at the Albertson's on Third and J. Good dude, but kind of a talker.

"Jason Diaz. The Infected with whom you will be meeting?"

"Right… him." I made a mental note to start getting the full names of the supernatural creatures I mediated for.

"You did not know his surname?" Again, her lips quirked.

"You're not supposed to call me out like that, Lady Dumenyova," I said primly, spoiling it with a grin. "But no. I've only met the guy once, after all. You're not coming?"

"Queen Lucia has assigned me other duties," she explained. Which really wasn't much of an explanation at all. "You will be accompanied by Lady Middleton and as many members of the Watch as can be spared."

I chewed on that for a while, along with another pastry. I liked Juliette a lot. She was the annoying, much older friend I'd never had. And smoking hot in her own right. But she was also a relatively young member of her species, and even with another century or two under her belt, I doubted she would be a match for Anastasia in terms of pure cold-blooded competence.

Considering my life was on the line, competence seemed kind of important.

"You think I'll be in danger?"

"Of course. Even if young Mr. Diaz is not responsible for these attacks, you are exposing yourself by going to meet with him." Anastasia took another sip of coffee. "The White Ladies protect your home. The Watch protects this House. The pack's best opportunity to eliminate you is when you are away from both locations." She gave me a pointed look. "Or drinking at a bar."

"Yeah. That wasn't the greatest of ideas. Although if you had accepted my invitation to come along…" I shrugged and moved on. There was no point in dwelling on past mistakes. Especially when they were mine. "So, do you think meeting Jason is a bad idea? Weren't you trying to nudge me toward that very decision last night?"

"Actually, it was not a course of action I had considered."

"Seriously?" It was like finding out that the moon landing had been faked or that Santa's naughty and nice lists were just wild-ass guesses. Or that vampires were real.

"Why does that surprise you?"

"You're usually nine steps ahead of the rest of us. I assumed any idea I had would be something you'd already thought of, dissected, and discarded as being stupid."

"Your mind moves along unpredictable routes, Mr. Smith. It is one of the things that I like about you. As we age, too many of us become mired in the same patterns of thought that we have utilized for centuries."

I'd felt a lot more confident about the day's itinerary when I'd thought it was all Anastasia's idea. Even so, I couldn't stop myself from smiling. "*One* of the things you like about me?"

"Indeed." She took another sip of coffee and didn't elaborate. "Your plan is undoubtedly dangerous, but I agree that the risk seems warranted if it will allow us to avoid outright war."

"Especially when the alternative was Zorana's clever idea to *bomb them all and let someone else pick up the pieces.*" I eyed the single remaining pastry on the plate. My stomach said yes, but my ambitions to one day see my abs said no.

The internal battle was brief but fierce. I scooped the donut off the plate and took a large bite.

Mmm… Jelly.

"Zorana does favor extremes, and she is not alone amongst the People. But I have had my fill of unnecessary bloodshed. A general assault on the pack costs strength we cannot afford to lose."

"It's great to hear you say so."

"I will always favor intelligent action over unreasoning reaction."

"So, the commando assault strategy you unveiled last night…?"

"Focusing on the pack elders would minimize casualties, while still meeting my queen's demands for immediate reprisal." She reached across the table and plucked the last remaining piece of my jelly-filled donut off the plate. "It remains a viable fallback option. While you meet with Mr. Diaz, I will be working with Queen Lucia to lay the groundwork for that strategy."

I watched the last bite of pastry disappear into her lovely mouth. Somehow, Anastasia even made eating look good.

"Well, I hope it doesn't come to that. And I really wish you were coming along today." And not just because I'd trust her to keep me safe over the rest of the House put together.

"As do I, John. I would be there, were I permitted." She regarded me levelly, but there was something in her gaze that added deeper significance to her words.

At least I thought so. My track record at deciphering non-verbal messages wasn't great.

"Well, at least if I do get in trouble, I know you'll be just a phone call away. Especially since I got your number from Marcus."

She gave me a look of polite disbelief.

"You make an excellent point," I acknowledged. "It's possible he gave me false information." I glanced over to the nightstand, where my wonderphone remained. "You should probably give it to me again, just so I can be sure."

"Am I to understand that, despite your repertoire of professional skills, you have yet to attain that small piece of information, Mr. Smith?" She shook her head in mock sorrow. "Perhaps you should consider abandoning these other—purely trivial—distractions, to give the retrieval of my phone number your complete focus?"

"After all," she continued, with that smile that made my heart do somersaults, "I will not be young forever."

CHAPTER 27

IN WHICH BURRITOS ARE PROBABLY A METAPHOR FOR SOMETHING

Several hours later, after checking separately on Steve, Kayla, *and* Jee Sun, I found myself packed into another of the House's Escalades with Juliette and four Watch members. I didn't know any of the black-clad guards, which said a lot about how many casualties they had been suffering recently.

Since my introduction to the People that summer, virtually every Watch member I'd met had either died or been gravely wounded. Not all of it had been my fault—hell, almost *none* of it had been my fault—but I still felt a little bit like a walking plague vector.

Which would have been kind of badass if the consequences weren't so apparent.

"Tell me again why you're bringing that?" asked Juliette. The femmepire had yet to earn her Valkyrie biker-babe merit badge, and in place of Anastasia's or Lucia's war garb, was wearing a long black Bukowski t-shirt and her usual skintight jeans. After so many days of seeing her dressed in suits or dresses, it was almost a relief to see the casual attire.

Except none of it screamed *ready to kick ass and take names.*

"This?" I looked down at the large caliber handgun I'd tucked into my waistband and patted the grip reassuringly. I'd found it on the dresser in my bedroom, my office safe clearly no match for whatever professional burglar Juliette had dispatched. "Just a little protection, in case things get crazy." I smirked. At least *one* of us exuded badass.

"It's going to be hard to protect you when the gun discharges and blows your nuts off," she pointed out sweetly.

I assumed she was joking but wasn't willing to bet my life on it. And, looking down, the gun did sort of point toward my... I eased it out of my waistband, and held it on my lap, barrel pointed carefully to the side.

"Does anyone have a holster? Or anything?"

"I don't know what you think a gun's going to do anyway, little bird." Juliette yawned, giving me a nice view of her partially extended canines. Either she was hungry, or angry, or bored. Or half a dozen other things. Sometimes, she just liked to flash fang. "The Infected heal from that sort of wound even faster than we do."

"It's still a better option than flailing at them with my nonexistent kung fu." I shrugged, which aggravated one of the muscles I'd pulled being flung through the air like a dish rag.

"If you say so." Juliette's voice was dismissive, but she was kind enough to drop the debate. Which was good since I was losing. "But if you accidentally shoot me, I swear I'm going to shove that gun right up your ass. And then pull the trigger."

The taco shop we were meeting Jason at was less than a mile from Torrey Pines, which made parking difficult on a Saturday. The size of the Escalade didn't help; we had to pass up at least two spaces that my Corolla could have squeezed into with a bare minimum of bumper-on-bumper action. When we did find a stretch of curb long enough to accommodate the car, it was almost four blocks away.

It was another oddly hot November day. I glared up at the cloudless sky and a sun that seemed to be taunting me for my lack of sleep. "Wouldn't it have made sense to drop the two of us off at Roberto's?"

"I'm not splitting our forces," retorted Juliette. "And thanks to *someone*, we don't have a human driver to stick with the hassle of parking the car."

I sighed, already out of breath, and starting to sweat. Whose brilliant idea had it been to dress the Watch in black? And why wasn't there a warm-weather version of the outfit? Were shorts beneath a vampire's dignity? Or flip flops?

The security precautions taken by my guards were less elaborate than those I'd seen for Lucia, but in the cheerfully pleasant surroundings, they still seemed excessive. So too did the weaponry every vampire had strapped to their back or hanging from their waist. The ability to control what humans saw made weapon permits a little redundant, but we looked like a weird fusion of modeling agency and Renaissance fair. Throw in the tiny taco shack waiting for us, and we were a joke just waiting for a punchline.

"So, what's the plan?" I asked as we approached Roberto's. Ahead of us, one of the Watch was walking point. Two others were flanking us, while the last member served as rear guard. It would have been ridiculous, if I hadn't recently been made aware of my own complete vulnerability.

It would've been awesome too, except for that same thing.

"Brian and Charles will go in to confirm that Jason is present and alone. When they give the all-clear, you and I will follow. Juan and Diego will stay back and cover our escape route."

I gave Juan a nod. "Don't worry, dude. I'll get you both something for the drive back."

The manpire—another disgustingly good-looking, impossibly fit individual with flawless olive skin—looked grateful. My plan to ingratiate myself with every vampire in San Diego was progressing, one sloppy burrito at a time.

"Don't distract the Watch, little bird," Juliette muttered, eyes trained on the door to Roberto's.

After a long moment, Brian poked his head back out. He gave a short nod and disappeared back inside.

"Looks like we're good. Let's go talk to your werewolf friend. And John? Try not to get us all killed."

"No promises," I whispered back.

○○○

It had only been a couple of hours since breakfast with Anastasia, but I was hungry again. I placed an order for a carne asada burrito with extra guacamole, paired it with a large Diet Coke—to make up for the calories I was about to consume—and headed out to the seating area.

Roberto's seating was all outside, consisting of a handful of tables and benches on the corner of Carmel Valley and Via Aprilla. The beach, just up the hill from us, wasn't visible, but the western sky was wide and open, the way only an ocean horizon can be.

I spotted our two manpires first, seated at a table to the right, but it took another moment to locate Jason. A nudge from Juliette turned me to the left, where the werewolf was eating. We tromped over to join him.

Jason looked up as our shadows fell upon him. "Hey, bro." He gave me the barest of acknowledgments before turning to the femmepire at my side. "Please tell me you're single." His nostrils flared, and a shadow passed over his face for just a moment before the cocky smile returned. "I don't normally bang vampires, but for you—" His eyes darted up and down the length of her body. "—I'd make an exception."

"Come on, man," I said. "You're still more or less married, and the lady's not interested."

"I don't know, John," purred Juliette, taking a seat at the table with sinuous grace. "I bet he's a real animal in bed."

"Lady, you have no idea." Jason's grin only widened.

"Unfortunately," she continued, "I don't date puppies."

"Who said anything about dating?" The male wolf waggled his eyebrows suggestively. Now that I'd seen him do it, I deeply regretted doing the same with Anastasia.

Dating advice from my dad was always dumb. One of these days, I'd remember that in time.

"Good lord," murmured Juliette, unknowingly echoing my own internal dialogue. "I think he's even dumber than you are."

"Not that I'm complaining about the eye candy," Jason told me, "but what's she doing here?" His nostrils flared again, and he looked past us to where the other vampires were seated. The grin disappeared like it had never existed. "And the muscle?"

I tensed, feeling utterly exposed out in the open. If the werewolf was going to spring his trap, now would seem to be the time. Instead, he scowled across the table.

"Whatever my old lady's paying, I'll double it if you let me go."

I blinked in confusion. "What old lady?"

"Carolyn, bro. If she wants me dead, it seems like there'd be easier ways to do it… but nothing with her is *ever* easy."

"You think *we're* here to kill *you?*" I kept my voice quiet, conscious of the traffic of other customers in and out of the taco shack.

"No, I think you just hang out with a bunch of bloodsuckers for fun." He rolled his eyes, before pasting a smile back on his face. "No offense, babe."

"Why would I take offense?" Juliette seemed genuinely confused. "It's what we do."

"Jason, I'm a mediator, not a… well, you know." I pantomimed a stabbing motion, ripped straight from the movies. "I'm just here to talk."

"Then what's with the Count Chocula spook squad?"

"Now *that's* offensive," decided Juliette.

"They're here for my protection." The werewolf's confusion seemed genuine. "Are you telling me you don't know anything about the attacks of the past two nights?"

"Attacks? Is that what happened to your face? Why would I know anything about that, bro?"

"Well—" I began, but Juliette cut in.

"Bored now." She made eye contact with Jason, her yellow eyes glowing faintly. "Tell us what you know, Kibbles."

Jason's reaction was instantaneous, his eyes lightening to the color of pale bone. "Did you think I'd sit down for lunch with a blood sucker and *not* have my wolf ready to block your tricks?"

"On second thought," Juliette told me, "he might be a little bit smarter than you are."

And I'd thought *Jee Sun* was the worst possible person to bring to a mediation. I sighed and turned to the angry werewolf. "Sorry, Jason. I had no idea she was going to do that." I rolled my eyes. "The People can't seem to help but meddle."

Jason shrugged. "I've been married for almost eight months, man. Vampires don't have anything on wives."

"I'll take your word for it." Jason still seemed sincere. If anything, he was even more of an open book than Carolyn. But if he wasn't behind the attacks… who was? I shook my head and pivoted to the reason for our meeting. "Speaking of wives, are you cool with talking about what went wrong between you and Carolyn? As well as what it is you want to get out of this mediation?"

"I didn't just come for the carnitas." Jason took a drink of what looked suspiciously like beer. "If little miss sexy over there wants to hear about my epic love life, who am I to say no?"

We talked for a little over an hour, and by the end of it, almost the only thing I had gained was a new appreciation for what Carolyn had been through. Jason was like the annoying and brainless younger brother I'd never had. Or wanted.

Once you got past all the bravado, his side of the story wasn't all that different from his ex-wife's. Basically, two young kids had been *encouraged* by their parents to tie the knot, only to eventually realize they weren't ready for that sort of commitment. Especially not with each other.

"What do you think, Mr. Man?" Jason polished off his second beer. "Can you fix it so I get the land I was promised? And maybe make it happen soon?"

"What's the rush?" I asked, my suspicions flaring back to life.

"I'm headed home for Thanksgiving, and Georgie is going to give me all manner of shit if I'm empty-handed."

"Georgie?"

"My hermano, bro. The last thing I want is to sit through another family meal while that asshole tells everyone what a disappointment I am."

"That's not really how mediation works. I'm just trying to help you and Carolyn come to an understanding. But I have a better handle on where you both stand. I think we might be ready to try another joint meeting."

"Whatever it takes." He chewed on his lip, brow furrowed.

"Are you sure this is what you want? I mean," I clarified, "if you took your brother and the pack out of the picture—"

"Spoken like a human." He shrugged. "I am the pack. It exists through me, and long after I'm dead and buried, I'll continue to exist through it. That's what we're taught almost from the moment we're born."

"If things had worked out with Cara," he continued, "everything would've been cool. Now, I have to go with plan B, which means getting what was promised to me." Jason shook his head. "Eight months ago, I thought we were forever."

"Sorry, man. Relationships can be tough." Finally, a topic I knew something about.

"Word." His face cleared, and he tossed another grin to Juliette. "See? I'm a romantic at heart, babe. We should do dinner or some dancing and shit."

Juliette was at a loss for words, but her open sneer said a lot on its own. I hurried to fill the silence.

"I do want to point out that, if someone kills me in the meantime, any chance of this mediation working goes right out the window."

"Really?" Jason snickered. "You mean mediators are actually an important part of mediation? Who'd have thought?"

"I'm just saying…"

"Like I told you, I don't know anything about any attacks, man. And most of my pack is back in New Mexico. Honestly, you don't seem worth the effort to me." He waved off my injured protest. "But I'll ask around. Maybe you pissed off my old lady by not wiping off your feet before entering the house or something. She's totally anal about that shit."

And with that parting comment, Jason rose to his feet, gave Juliette a smoldering look that was probably supposed to be sexy, and departed. He'd managed to find a spot right next to Roberto's for his motorcycle, and the entire restaurant was treated to the loud roar of his bike's engine as he peeled out and headed east.

It turned out *he'd* been the owner of the Harley I saw out in Santee, not Emilio. Go figure.

"Interesting kid," I said dryly.

"Yeah, he's a regular charmer. So, what now, Mr. Mediator?"

"Back to the House, I guess. Lucia gave me the day to figure things out, so I'll make some more calls, and see what turns up. And in the meantime, we can track down Phil Thompsen for his wife."

"The missing husband? My minions are looking for him."

I gave Juliette a look.

"What?"

"Minions? Really?"

"Hell yes, minions," she replied. "If I have to spend half my life doing paperwork, then I'm going to call the House's human assets whatever I damn well please."

○○○

We dumped our plates and stowed the trays above the trash can, and then I re-entered the restaurant to order burritos-to-go for Juan and Diego. Traffic had picked up, and there were a number of impatient diners waiting for our two tables.

Brian took point again. Juliette and I followed him around the corner and ran directly into the manpire's back.

"What is it, Brian?"

"No sign of Juan or Diego, Lady Middleton. We need to get to the car."

"Oh, come on!" I protested. "It's broad daylight!"

"And our team's numbers have already been halved." Brian broke into a light jog. Juliette's hand at my back was an unsubtle—and unnecessary—command for me to follow.

So, we ran. As soon as we had left the restaurant behind, Brian unsheathed his sword. Behind us, Charles did the same. I groped about for my gun before remembering I'd left it in the Escalade in order to keep my dude-parts safe.

It was a decision I was now regretting.

"Still think Jason is merely *interesting?*" Juliette was breathing lightly and running easily beside me. Freaking vampires.

"I might—" I wheezed, "—have been mistaken." My breath was already loud in my own ears. The blocks we had left to traverse might as well have been miles.

"We're almost there, little bird," she lied. "Don't have your heart attack until we're safely back at the House."

"Right." I focused on putting one foot in front of the other. "Wouldn't want you to get in trouble."

"Exactly." We crossed the residential street at a dead sprint—or the closest I could manage—and the Escalade finally came into sight. I'd have sighed in relief if I had the free air to do so. Whatever was going on, we'd at least made it—

An enormous shape flashed by in front of me, burying Brian in a mass of muscle and grey fur. As the manpire fell, his blade flashed, and the werewolf growled in pain.

"Don't stop!" Juliette's voice was harsh in my ear.

I didn't need to be told twice. I veered past Brian and his attacker and made a beeline for the car. Behind us, additional growls announced the presence of other wolves. The sounds of battle announced Charles' entry into the fray.

I couldn't believe Jason had set us up. I really needed to stop being so damn trusting.

We had almost reached the car when yet another werewolf— black-furred and ugly as sin—rose in front of us. Juliette hip-checked me to the side, and launched herself at the newcomer, a short silver blade in her fist. She rode him down to the pavement, her dagger stabbing again and again into the wolf's chest. That flurry lasted until the wolf got an arm up, and then the femmepire was airborne, thrown right into the trunk of a nearby tree.

Just hearing the impact made my bones ache.

I rolled to my feet, leaving Juan and Diego's burritos in the dirt where they'd fallen, and made it to the car. I took hold of the door handle and tugged.

No love. We'd locked the car when we left it.

Behind me, the sound of growling echoed like thunder. How many damn werewolves had Jason smuggled into San Diego? I held my keys in one hand, metal extended, and slammed them into the window.

For once, something I'd seen in the movies actually worked. The glass shattered, raining down on the exposed skin of my hand. I ignored it, unlocked the door, and dove inside, groping under the chair for my gun.

I had just managed to grab the weapon when, for the second time in a day, a werewolf caught me by the leg. I was dragged bodily out of the car, gun in hand, and tossed face-first into the pavement. Pain lanced through me as I turned over and brought the gun to bear...

...but my attacker was nowhere to be found. I tried to convince my trigger finger to fire anyway, but my limbs were refusing to cooperate.

Which was when another werewolf, this one with fur the color of rust, came into view. I never saw the blow that hit me, but damn if it didn't hurt.

INTERLUDE

"What do you mean, they're trying to turn you?"

"It's obvious when you think about it." And I was thinking about it. Better that than the pain in my shoulder. By this point, I was so used to the darkness that I barely even noticed I was blind. Even my nudity had ceased to be a distraction. "Melissa Thompsen told her husband that she was changed by a werewolf who bit her on three consecutive days."

"And?" Lack of blood was making Juliette grumpy. And sluggish.

"And unless we've been unconscious longer than you guessed, that was bite number two."

"But why would anyone want to turn you?"

"I said I knew what they were doing. I didn't say I knew why." It was possible I was starting to feel a little bit grumpy myself.

"So why has Jason been trying to kill you all this time? That hardly seems conducive to making you one of them."

"I don't know."

"And why did they kidnap me along with you?"

"I don't know."

"And what's with them keeping you nude?"

"I don't know, Juliette!" I shouted, exasperated, thirsty, and still naked.

"I'm just saying… it doesn't make any sense," she muttered, for the first time sounding like the eighty-year-old creature she really was.

"We're not dead," I pointed out, "and I've been bitten twice. If you have a better explanation, I'd love to hear it."

Silence.

"That's what I thought." I nodded sharply, feeling vindicated.

"John?" Juliette's voice was growing weaker. At least she hadn't slipped back into her blood hunger yet.

"What?"

"You're going to make a really lousy werewolf."

"I know," I admitted, "but I clearly wasn't much of a mediator either."

ooo

"Juliette? Are you there?" I listened to the pitter patter of little werewolf feet above us. It had been at least an hour since the femmepire had spoken. Or a week. In the darkness, it was difficult to be sure.

"No, dumbass." Her voice was tired and thin. "I busted out of here months ago and decided to leave you behind to be eaten by the big, bad wolf."

"Except for the leaving-me-behind bit, that sounds pretty good."

Her only reply was a sigh and the clanking of chains.

"Anyway," I continued, "I've decided you're right."

"And?"

"This doesn't make any sense." I twisted about on the floor to look in the direction I thought her voice was coming from. "Why try to kill me if the goal was to turn me?"

"And?"

"Uhm…" Some tiny spark of intuition told me she was looking for more than just my theories on the matter at hand. In fact, her tone of voice sounded suspiciously like my mother's when my father had done something wrong. I took a wild stab at what she might be expecting of me. "And I'm sorry?"

"For what?" Her voice had no give to it. It was impossible to tell if I was on the right track.

"For yelling at you?"

"Damn straight you're sorry."

Whew. Proof that even a blind batter could hit one out of the park every now and then. Relieved to be on solid ground—conversationally speaking—I continued. "Yeah, I didn't mean to shout. Of course, I also didn't mean to get kidnapped…"

"Do you know what the worst sort of apology is, little bird?"

"An insincere one?"

"Right. But just behind that is an apology immediately followed by justifications. 'I'm sorry I shot the sheriff, but he totally had it coming.'"

"Hey, I actually know that song."

"Hush. It's just an example."

"The real question," I continued, "is whether or not you shot the deputy." That tricked a laugh out of her, and I pressed my advantage. "I'm not justifying anything. I'm just pointing out that this is only my second kidnapping, and I would appreciate it if you would cut the naked, bleeding man a little bit of slack."

"You're not bleeding anymore," she shot back.

"You'd know better than I would."

"And as for you being naked, while that would be a great source of amusement and hilarity to me, I don't see why it matters right now in a pitch-black cellar."

"It just does."

"I'd also like to point out," she continued, voice hardening as she gained momentum, "that your worst-case scenario at this point is getting turned and having to go wolf a few times a month."

"And losing forty to fifty years in life expectancy!"

"Eh. What's the difference between dying at forty or ninety?"

"Fifty years. Like I literally just said."

"Meanwhile, I'm starving over here, and every time you get bitten, I end up being tormented by the smell of delicious food that I can't eat. And if I die, I'm going to lose a lot more than a few piddling decades!"

"Huh." I mulled that over for a moment, rolling onto my back in a desperate search for comfort. "That raises an interesting question."

"What?"

"Exactly how delicious would you say I am?"

"You're such an idiot." I could hear the smile in her words.

"Maybe when Jason or one of his wolves comes to bite me next time, we can get you some blood?"

"I hope so. It's taking everything I have to not just zone out." She sighed again. "Anyway. What were you saying earlier, about me being right?"

"I have no idea." I spent a long moment trying to recover my train of thought. "Oh yeah. This doesn't make any sense."

"I'm pretty sure we already said that."

"I know. The thing is, since all this started, I've just been reacting. Between the mediation, and the House, and Phil and everything else, I really haven't had time to stop and think."

"I forgot that it takes a hell dimension or some form of imprisonment for you to actually start using your brain."

"It's a character flaw," I admitted. "Anyway, there are some questions we need to ask."

"If you start telling me about the five Ws of journalism again, I'm going to—" Another clank of chains, followed by a long silence. "—do nothing, I guess. Fine. What lesson should we take from community college today?"

"I hadn't planned to bring up Journalism 101 again, but now that you mention it…" My voice trailed off. I was so hungry that I couldn't even remember all five of the Ws. What, when, where, Winnebago? That wasn't right, was it? "Anyway, that's not what I meant."

"Oh?"

"Yeah. First, why try to kill me at the Bitter End if the goal is to turn me?"

"If you're just going to repeat what I said—"

"Second, how did they even know I was even there?"

"You hadn't said something to Jason?"

"Until this morning's meeting… or yesterday morning's… or whenever it was, I'd only met Jason once," I pointed out, "and that was a solid day before I knew we were going out."

"So we don't know how they found you at the bar. Is that it?"

"Not quite. Something about the attack the night before was weird too." It had been bothering me for days, but I'd continued to push it to the back of my mind, choosing to deal with more important things.

"Like the fact that your junker of a car outran werewolves?"

"No," I said irritably. Only I was allowed to speak about the Corolla that way. "If they were focused on killing me before I reached the freeway, why was there a car of wolves waiting at my home?"

"Maybe they were covering all their bases? Maybe Anastasia has an anal-retentive counterpart in the pack?"

"I don't buy it. An extra car could have made all the difference out in the desert. And how did they know where my parents lived? Jason hadn't even heard of me before Davis introduced us."

"If we ever get out of here, I'm going to introduce you to an amazing invention called the Internet."

"Clearly, you haven't met my wonderphone." I held a quick moment of silence for my dearly departed device, lost when we had been taken. *"Anyway, there's a much simpler explanation."*

"Just tell me what it is, John. And it had better not involve aliens. Or singing."

Aliens. The thought gave me pause. What if?

"I wish, but no. I think we're dealing with multiple agendas."

"Oh." Juliette gave that some consideration. *"Makes sense. How does that help us?"*

"It doesn't, I guess. But isn't knowledge a good thing?"

"Fantastic," she muttered.

"I'm doing the best I can, Duchess."

"Your best is going to get us killed." She sighed. *"It's my fault though. After the car bomb this summer, I should have known to stay as far away from you as possible if I wanted to live to a hundred."*

"This isn't my fault!"

"No? Isn't this your mediation? I'm starting to see what Lucia means when she calls you the worst thrall in the—"

Juliette's voice cut off. Could vampires have anger-induced heart attacks? Or brain embolisms? When she finally spoke again, I let out a breath I had been unconsciously holding.

"We've been here a day?" The anger was gone from her voice.

"More, I think."

"So where's Lucia? She tracked you all the way across San Diego on the night of your stupid date. Unless they smuggled us out of the state, she shouldn't have any trouble finding you."

"Well, actually—"

"I mean… maybe she's finally gotten sick of you, but I'm a member of her Council. I matter! There's no way she'd just abandon me… not when she could use your bond to find us."

"Yeah. About that." I took a breath and then explained that something about the ritual to formalize my relationship with the House had left Lucia unable to locate me.

There was a long silence.

"You really do suck, little bird."

CHAPTER 28

IN WHICH THE PAST BECOMES THE PRESENT

And so there I was, naked and bound in some underground prison, waiting to be bitten again by the werewolves who had captured us. I spared a thought for Brian and the other manpires. Hopefully, they'd survived and were stashed in another cell.

For the tenth time in as many minutes, I mentally probed at the lump that was Lucia's presence in my brain. The queen was a long way away from us, somewhere off to my left, and exactly where she'd been every other time I'd checked.

"—can't believe your bond failed just in time for us to get captured." Juliette had been making her displeasure known for those same ten minutes and showed no signs of slowing down.

I tuned her out and focused back on the bond. At Mister A's, Lucia had been able to mask her location from me. Was it possible I could do the opposite? And if so, how?

I squeezed my eyes shut and envisioned astral fingers untying a knot in my mind. When that had no effect, I switched metaphors, and pictured a steel door swinging open. Still nothing. I lowered a drawbridge, knocked down a wall, and even built up a mental bonfire to send smoke signals with. Not that I had the tiniest idea of how to send smoke signals.

None of it was any use. I might as well have been trying to fly.

"—even listening to me?" Juliette's voice broke in again. She sounded angry.

"Of course I am," I said. "I'm a mess and a screw-up and it's all my fault somehow."

"Oh. Well, good," she replied, clearly nonplussed.

"On the other hand," I pointed out, "I'm twenty-five-freaking-years old. Maybe the centuries-old queen should have seen this coming *before* pressuring me into her little blood ritual."

"You don't get it, little bird." Just like that, Juliette's anger had run its course. "The House has never dealt with a human with your talent. Ever. You're…"

"…an anomaly?"

"I was going to say a weirdo, but anomaly works too. If we do somehow survive this, you might want to keep your little gift to yourself. There are a lot of groups that would happily vivisect you to try to reproduce your immunity."

"Thankfully," I grumbled back, "it looks like you'll starve to death, and I'll become one with the furry, long before that happens."

Above us, the ceiling creaked, as something or someone moved about. We'd been hearing those noises off and on for a while now. Whoever it was, they were a lot lighter than the werewolf who'd come and bitten me; where those footsteps had been heavy thumps, these instead sort of skittered across the surface.

Assuming that what I was hearing could be called a skitter; I'd only been effectively blind for a day or so.

They did seem to be nervous or worried about something though. Maybe the fact that they had people tied up in the basement? I could hear them pace back and forth above us in a frenetic cycle that charted a course across what was our ceiling. Whenever the footsteps stopped, I found myself holding my breath, waiting for the thump that would mean one of our captors had keeled over from a heart attack or stroke. After all, stress *was* the silent killer.

For the first time ever, I *did* hear a dull thud. Unfortunately, it sounded more like a distant door being closed than an evil and heartless werewolf kidnapper falling to the floor. The smaller werewolf rushed across the floor above us toward that noise, and then I heard the heavy footsteps of the werewolf that had become my personal nemesis. Assuming nemesis was the appropriate term for a monster intent on inducting me into his own furry fraternity.

I heard a few short, sharp noises. Were they talking? Fighting? That almost sounded like…

"Damn it."

"Sounds like your Infected friend is back to finish the job," Juliette mused.

"So, you're hearing that too?"

"Obviously." The femmepire sighed again. "Maybe once you're furry, we'll get some answers."

"We might not have to wait that long," I informed her grimly. "There are two creatures up there, right? The first one, Mr. Bites-a-lot, and a second, smaller one. At first, I thought it was a werewolf, but now I'm thinking—"

"It's a dog," Juliette finished for me. "Or a wolf cub, maybe. From the sound of its footsteps, whatever it is only weighs about a hundred pounds. One-thirty at the most. No adult werewolf would be that small."

Well, shit.

"That's what I was afraid of," I replied. "And I think I know who kidnapped us, if not why."

"Seriously? Who?"

I heard the door to the basement swing open. Soon after, the werewolf began to descend the steps.

"The same dickhead who got me into this mess in the first place." I raised my voice, speaking to the descending intruder. "Isn't that right, Davis?"

The answering voice was deep and slightly amused.

"Very good, Mr. Smith. You should have been a detective."

ooo

"Davis? Davis who?" Juliette was even worse with names than I was.

"Juliette, I'd like to introduce you to Davis Hawthorne, San Diego Pack elder, retired architect, and apparent asshole." I eyeballed the dark corner where Davis' voice had come from. "Our contract doesn't give you the right to kidnap me, you know." I decided not to even mention my nudity. If we could all pretend I was clothed, I'd be much happier.

"I suspect I have less to fear from my breach of contract than I do from the vampire's House." There was a rustle of clothing, as if he had made a gesture in the vampire's direction. "I do apologize for your captivity, Lady Middleton. It was not my intention to involve you in this matter at all."

"It's nothing that can't be forgiven over a nice two or three pints of warm blood," replied Juliette. "Or were you planning to starve me to death?"

Above us, the dog scurried about again. Was there someone else up there? Once again, my hearing failed to live up to its supernaturally augmented reputation.

"It seems I must apologize once more," Davis continued smoothly, after a moment's hesitation. "It was my understanding that, by the time someone reached the position of Council member, they would have outgrown the need for such regular feedings. Have I been misinformed?"

Ha. Even in my captive misery, I took a moment to snicker at the fact that Juliette had been outed as a junior vamp…

"I will see to it that you are brought fresh blood as soon as possible," he assured her.

Again, I heard a noise from upstairs that didn't fit in with the noises I'd classified as 'dog-related,' and again Davis paused. On the off chance that whoever was up there was coming to save us, I did my best to serve as a distraction.

"Seems kind of pointless, dude. Why feed her if you're just going to kill her?"

"John!" Juliette hissed my name from across the room. Femmepires really did get crotchety when hungry.

"I'm just saying," I said, "it would be a waste of perfectly good blood."

"When I get out of here, I'll show you *perfectly good blood,* you ungrateful half-wit mongrel…"

"Mongrel? Really? I'm not even turned yet, and you're already starting in with the dog jokes?" Hopefully, we were making enough noise to provide cover for whoever else was in the house. Assuming someone else was in the house, of course. When you're naked and one bite away from a permanent five o'clock shadow, any plan at all sounds like a good one.

"I assure you, Lady Middleton," Davis cut in, his voice loud enough to drown us both out, "I have no intention of ending your life. Once John's transformation is complete, you will be free to go."

"You know the House will kill you for this," I said. "How could making me a werewolf possibly be worth that?"

"Yes, Uncle Davis." I didn't have time to squeeze my eyes shut before an overhead bulb flared to life, like a sun going supernova. After days of darkness, I now found myself blind for an entirely different reason. Still, I didn't need my eyes to recognize Carolyn's voice. "I'd like to hear your explanation too."

"Niece," rumbled Davis. "You cannot be here. I must be the sole target for the House's vengeance."

"I'm not going anywhere," she snapped back, "until you tell me what the hell is going on. Why have you kidnapped this vampire and our mediat—oh, dear goddess, is he *naked?*"

The sheer depth of her appalled reaction did my already terrible self-image no favors.

I blinked my eyes furiously, and shapes slowly began to resolve. Davis stood with his back to me, confronting the niece who had come halfway down the stairway from the main floor. Carolyn looked angry as hell, which cheered me immensely, even if her uncle outweighed her by a hundred pounds.

"I will tell you everything," Davis began, "but there is no time—"

"This is about John's gift, isn't it?"

All eyes snapped to Juliette. Whereas I was naked—as I may have mentioned once or twice—she practically had two outfits on… the clothes she'd been wearing when we were kidnapped, and a robe of tightly interlocked chains that could have restrained the entire San Diego Chargers offensive line. Davis may not have been intending to kidnap her, but he'd certainly come prepared for the task.

"What?" the femmepire asked sharply. "I have a brain, you know." Her eyes flickered over to take in my naked form, and she found just enough energy to smirk.

"What is she talking about, Uncle? What gift?"

"Mr. Smith has an immunity to mind magic, Cara." Davis turned back to his niece, dismissing Juliette and me like the entirely helpless prisoners we were.

"Good for him, I guess." Carolyn seemed confused. "What does that have to do with you forcibly infecting him? You and Papa were the ones who told me what a terrible crime that was!"

"In desperate times, the end does sometimes justify the means. The vampires believe his ability is genetic," he explained. "If he is turned, any children he spawns with the pack might inherit that ability."

"Seriously? That's your brilliant plan?" I sputtered incredulously. "Turn me into a werewolf and then *breed* me? On what planet does that seem like a good idea?"

"You and I both know," Davis told Carolyn, "that our pack is losing territory each year. Anthony sought an alliance with New Mexico, but that would have only been a temporary measure, at best. Four, five generations from now, their pack will be facing these same challenges. He sought to strengthen us through external ties, but what we *should* have been doing is finding ways to strengthen ourselves as a species. Mr. Smith's gift could be the first step down that road."

I couldn't believe I had once compared this guy to Thor, when he was clearly a cut-rate villain from some DC comic book. "Dude, I might not be able to stop you from turning me, but you're an idiot if you think I would willingly serve as some sort of breeding stud for your women."

Unless they were crazy hot, maybe.

"As you will soon discover, John," Davis replied, "the wolf wants what the wolf wants, and cannot always be denied."

"Well, that's just unfair." And gross.

"Uncle," said Carolyn, "John's right. This plan is absolutely insa—" Her voice cut off suddenly, and I watched realization dawn on a face I could finally see in detail. "How long? How long have you been fighting the madness?"

"I saw the first signs just before Anthony's death," he admitted. "I had planned for my farewell gift to the pack to be a mediator who allowed us to avoid war and retain our ancestral territories. Then, Mr. Smith told me about his ability, and I realized I could give the pack something even greater."

"Yeah, like a hefty dose of assured destruction. Or do you not remember when Anastasia told you that the House had my back?" I looked entreatingly to Carolyn, having already abandoned the idea of negotiating with her apparently insane uncle.

"They cannot hold my pack responsible for what I did on my own, Mr. Smith. And Lucia's anger will be lessened when Lady Middleton is returned unharmed. I will surrender to face the People's justice, and my death will be the end of the matter."

"What you did on your own?" He really had gone mad. "Davis, you and your wolves have been after me all week!"

"Those were not my wolves. Until I took you, I had done nothing but observe."

"Right. So, when you kidnapped us, it just happened to be in the middle of another assault by unknown werewolves? How dumb do you think Lucia is?"

"I admit I took advantage of the distraction, but the House will have to look elsewhere to avenge its fallen. I saved their Council member and all it cost them was a single human."

Either Davis' brain was starting to rot from werewolf dementia, or he didn't understand vampires at all. Whether there really were two groups or not—Jason's group, trying to kill me, and Davis', trying to kidnap me—wasn't something most of the Council would even bother to consider.

"Carolyn…" The young werewolf refused to look in my direction, but that may have been because I was still naked. "You know this is crazy. Stop your uncle before he makes things even worse for your pack. Please."

"Think, niece," Davis countered. "A future where our pack does not have to fear the magic of our enemies. A future where *we* protect our wolves!"

I watched numerous emotions parade across Carolyn's face, chief among them indecision. Finally, she squared her shoulders, and took another step down the staircase.

"Uncle, he's right. This must end. In trying to help the pack, you've only made things worse."

"I'm sorry you feel that way, Carolyn." Davis shrugged his heavy shoulders. "But you can't stop me." He turned toward me, a mist coalescing around his form.

"Then it's a good thing," his niece said to his broad back, "that I didn't come alone."

Behind her, two more werewolves descended into the basement, much to my relief. Then, the first of them stepped into the light, and my joy was immediately replaced by fear.

"What's up, bro?" Jason grinned widely at me from over his ex-wife's shoulder, his teeth sharp and entirely inhuman. "I've been looking for you."

CHAPTER 29
IN WHICH YOU CAN'T SPELL EPIPHANY WITHOUT PAIN

Davis turned to confront the newcomers, but Jason stepped right past the older werewolf, hopping down the remaining stairs and crossing the basement floor to me, his steps quick and confident. He squatted over my squirming form and pinned me to the cement floor with one hand and a strength disproportionate to his scrawny frame. Mist formed around the other hand and curved claws—each the length of my pinky—replaced human fingernails. He looked down at me, grin somehow widening even further.

"This will only take a second, Mr. Man."

I'd like to say that, on coming face-to-face with my own unavoidable death, I handled it in as heroic a way as possible, matching glares with my would-be killer while saying something cool and portentous in a voice of steel. Something like "I'll see you in hell." or "I'll be back." or even "Look out! Behind you! It's a…!"

Instead, I just closed my eyes, and waited for it to be over.

I clearly needed to watch more action movies.

Several moments later, I cracked open one eye, wondering why I wasn't dead yet. Jason wasn't even looking at me. As I watched, he ran a clawed hand down my side, heavy ropes parting easily under the razor-sharp nails. Within seconds—as promised—I was free of my bonds.

"But… you… what…?" I stammered.

"You all right, bro?" Jason peered at me closely. "You're not making any sense."

"I am *so* confused," I whispered back.

"Happens to me all the time," he assured me, taking one of my hands in his—I was relieved to note that the claws had faded back into mist—and pulling me to my feet. "I think it's the weed."

I stood upright for all of a second before my legs collapsed under me. My werewolf bites may have been healing me and keeping me from starving to death or dying of dehydration, but my body was still one enormous, limp noodle. I felt pinpricks up and down the arm Jason was still holding, as those nerves slowly came back to life.

"I guess you're not going anywhere for a bit, huh?" He shook his head sadly. "Humans."

"Is one of you going to unchain me here, or should we all just keep babbling?" Juliette was as anxious to be free as I was.

"No worries, babe," Jason assured her. "I'll have you out of those in no time." His eyes darted around the basement for a moment, before he sighed, and turned back to Carolyn. "Any idea where he keeps the keys?"

I looked back to the stairs and saw that little had changed there. Carolyn was standing on the second-to-last step, putting her at an equal height with her uncle. The third werewolf—who I now recognized as Chains, the least ridiculous of Jason's cronies—stood behind Davis, ready to restrain the elder.

It didn't look like such measures would be necessary, however; the older werewolf stood in his own world, shoulders slumped, eyes staring down at his feet. I tried to dredge up sympathy for the man who, at forty years old, was already falling prey to werewolf dementia. Could I blame someone who, when faced with their own swiftly approaching death, had sought only to improve the lives of their family members?

Yes. Yes, I could. And did. Sympathy had gone right out the window when the dude bit me. And leaving me naked on the floor had damn well sealed the deal. Speaking of which… "Where are my clothes?"

"Good point; the keys can wait," agreed Jason. "This man needs some pants, and I need someone to pluck out my eyes so they never have to see anything like that again."

"Funny," I muttered, although I didn't think he'd been joking. As life came back into my arms, I rubbed my legs, reawakening the nerves and muscles. Meanwhile, my eyes scanned the room. A little over ten feet away from me was a long table, presumably made of mahogany, and on top of that table was a pile of black clothing, Juliette's dagger, and… my gun?

"Never mind," I announced. "I see them. Could everyone please just… you know, turn away so I can stand up without exposing myself?"

"That ship already sailed, Mr. Smith," Carolyn informed me with a sad shake of her head. "You might as well just—"

And that was when Davis made his move. I didn't see how it started, but Chains flew backward like someone had punched him in the chest with a sledgehammer. Carolyn tumbled to the floor and Davis was airborne, leaping toward me in an impossibly long jump, his form reshaping into that of a bipedal, rust-colored wolfman, jaws wide and drool dripping from needle-sharp fangs.

To be fair, I didn't actually see drool. But with those fangs, it seemed like a safe assumption.

I scuttled back on my hands and legs, but I might as well have been trying to outrun a tornado. So instead, I tried to roll out of the way.

Maybe if I'd done that from the beginning, I would have succeeded.

The expected crunch came, but it was—miraculously—unaccompanied by pain. I looked up to find Jason standing over me, grappling with Davis. It was a little bit like the biblical tale of David and Goliath, if David had disdained his sling in favor of hand-to-hand combat with a man twice his size.

It went about as well as might be expected. Davis batted Jason's hands aside, and then hurled the younger werewolf the length of the basement and into the far wall.

I scrambled to my feet, praying that my legs would hold me this time, and ran for the gun. I was almost to the table when Davis roared, the kind of sound that set your teeth vibrating and caused the hair on the back of your neck to stand up of its own accord. Great, now he *really* sounded pissed. I snatched up the gun and spun about.

Chains had regained his feet and was attacking Davis with the weapon I'd named him after. Three to four feet of heavy interlocked rings gave him the advantage of reach on the older werewolf. That advantage lasted until Davis stepped into the blow, letting the chain smash heavily into one of his arms. The other arm came through in an uppercut that made *my* jaw ache in sympathy, and Chains dropped like a sack of potatoes. Or bricks. Or a sack of anything heavy, I guess; mostly, he just dropped.

"I don't want to hurt any of you young fools," Davis growled, the words difficult to comprehend, shaped by a mouth that had never been designed for speech. "But I will not let—"

A loud twang echoed in the basement, and the werewolf staggered. From behind him, I saw the tip of a heavy arrow or bolt punch its way through his back. On the stairs, a newly arrived wolf, Travis of the infamous mullet, pulled back the string on his crossbow and loaded another over-sized quarrel.

If a gun couldn't stop a werewolf, I really doubted a crossbow would have any real effect, its obvious awesomeness notwithstanding. Sure enough, Davis shrugged off the shot with a growl… which was when the next bolt took him in the throat.

Even then, the older werewolf seemed unphased, but the delay had given the others a chance to recover, and Jason and Chains rushed Davis as a third bolt flew. Blood and fur sprayed everywhere, but the young wolves had Davis pinned on his back by the time Carolyn had stumbled to her feet.

I let out a breath I hadn't realized I was holding, and put my gun back on the table, swapping it for a pair of pants. In no time at all, I was fully dressed, and feeling much, much more comfortable with myself and the world at large.

Carolyn stalked over to Davis, her face angry. She was joined by Travis who left the unloaded crossbow by the stairs. The smaller werewolf's eyes remained bone white.

"Travis, what are you doing here?" Jason had one knee in the small of Davis' back, and a foot pinning the werewolf's sleeve to the ground.

"I called him," rumbled Chains, who was mirroring Jason's pose on the other side. Despite their combined weight, Davis continued to writhe about in an unsuccessful bid for freedom.

"I couldn't let you guys come by yourselves," explained Travis. "A dark cellar. Angry werewolves… You never know what could happen." He reached between the two to hold Davis down with a hand on the Elder's head. "People might get hurt."

There was a flash of silvered steel, and Davis howled, his legs kicking ineffectually, before sagging to the floor. I was still trying to figure out what had happened when Travis straightened back up. In one hand, a long blade dripped with dark blood. In the other hand, he held Davis' newly severed head.

"See what I mean?" he asked.

ooo

Carolyn threw herself at Travis with a scream of rage, knocking the other werewolf to the floor before Chains was able to pull her off.

Blood ran down Travis' face in rivulets from deep tears in the skin, but as I watched, those wounds disappeared. With a sneer, he stepped up to the struggling female wolf, blade in hand.

"Bro, what are you *doing*?" demanded Jason. "We had the old guy pinned. There was no need to kill him."

"That's where you're wrong, J." Travis kept his gaze fixed on Carolyn, the blade in his hand weaving in random geometric patterns through the air. She stayed utterly still, her wide eyes tracking the path of the blade even as tears trickled down her face. "It's time we got what's coming to us."

"You've finally snapped," growled Jason, starting forward to wrest the blade away from his friend. He made it three steps before Chains let go of Carolyn to intercept him. "You too, Chuck?"

"You need to listen," Chains—or Chuck, I guess—rumbled back. "For once."

"Fine." Jason's reply was sharp, his gaze clearly angry, but he stopped trying to advance. "Explain it to me. You have thirty seconds."

"It's simple," said Travis. "Insane werewolf elder snaps and kills his niece and the mediator before succumbing to his own wounds. The bloodsuckers will wipe out what's left of this sorry little pack in revenge, and when the dust settles, we expand our territory into California." He snapped his fingers. "It's a shitload more elegant than the original plan to just murder the mediator. And to think, we have the old dude to thank for making it all possible!"

"Wait… *you've* been the ones trying to kill John?" Jason's eyes looked like they wanted to bug out of his head. He started again for Travis, only to be stopped by Chuck. "This is treason! You both are so dead."

"We've known each other since we were pups," mused Travis, "but I still wasn't sure how you were going to react. Looks like Georgie was right." He shrugged. "I can't say I'll miss you. And you sucked at Madden. Chuck?"

The large werewolf hammered a chain-wrapped fist into Jason's ribs, and the loud crunch clearly spoke of bones being broken. Jason stumbled back, clutching his chest. Chain in hand, Chuck struck the other werewolf again and again, face impassive.

"Stop!" I was shocked when they actually listened. Maybe it was the tone I used; the sort of command voice that my mother routinely employed to such great effect. Or maybe it was that I'd picked Jee Sun's gun back up and had it pointed at Travis.

Yeah, it was probably the gun.

"Really, human? A pistol?" Travis rolled his eyes. "It's time you learned your species' place at the bottom of the food chain." He gestured to his companion. The big werewolf left Jason in a heap on the floor, closing in on me like a hunter stalking his prey. Neither wolf seemed particularly impressed by my weapon.

Well, shit.

I turned the gun on Chuck, who yawned and continued forward without even breaking stride. I sent a quick prayer to the local demigod of doomed last stands and an even quicker goodbye to the handful of people who might miss me.

Almost as an afterthought, I squeezed the trigger.

I'd fired a gun before. I'd even shot a vampire once, a lucky shot that partially paralyzed the manpire, causing his own leader to execute him for incompetence. That small amount of experience didn't make me an expert in firearms, but all the same, I was pretty sure what happened next was not normal.

Instead of a bullet, a torrent of crimson flame leaped from the barrel of the gun, like an old-school flamethrower or a miniature comet. The fire struck Chuck dead-on, and then continued right through him and over Jason and Juliette to splash against—and thoroughly blacken—the basement's far wall. When my eyes had adjusted yet again, the first thing I saw was a pair of legs teetering by themselves. As I watched, they fell to the ground. The rest of Chuck was nowhere to be seen.

"Holy shit," I breathed. And *this* was the gun that Jee Sun had been waving about in my office?!? Bill and I *really* needed to talk.

But first…

I turned my gun on Travis, who was nothing if not quick on his feet. The bastard was already at the stairs, running as quickly as his legs could take him. Even in human form, that was damn fast. Nevertheless, I aimed at his unprotected back, and pulled the trigger.

Nothing happened.

Travis disappeared up the stairs and was gone from view. From upstairs, I could hear shouting, and the sound of new bodies entering the house. This whole thing with wolves running in packs was starting to wear thin.

Jason had made it to his feet, but the damage he'd taken was taxing even a werewolf's absurd recuperative abilities. Nevertheless, he staggered up the stairs and out of sight. He came back just as quickly, accompanied by the sound of a door closing.

"Damn it! How much of my old pack is here, anyway?" The young werewolf looked desperately around the basement, and then hurried to the table that had held my clothes and gun. Despite his injuries, the table's weight, and the awkwardness of trying to maneuver something that size, he carried it over and wedged it into the stairwell, forming a makeshift barricade.

"One table's not going to be enough," he muttered. "Grab any furniture you can." He looked over at his ex-wife. "Cara! Unless you're hurt, I need your help!"

The other werewolf hadn't moved since being menaced by Travis' knife. At Jason's voice, she stirred to life, wiping tears away from her eyes. At her feet, the headless body of her uncle remained.

"I'm *still* waiting for someone to remove these chains," rasped Juliette, who had remained conspicuously silent while everything had been going down.

In retrospect, keeping quiet seemed like a pretty good strategy. I decided to give it a try the next time I was at the mercy of a bunch of werewolves.

"Right," muttered Jason in response. "Carolyn, you help me with the barricade. John, look for a key and let the vampire free. We're going to need her to break out of here."

"Can't you talk to your pack?" I looked about the basement for wherever Davis might have kept the keys. If they were upstairs in a drawer, we were screwed. I could only hope that—like me—the former werewolf would choose to keep his keys close to the doors or objects they unlocked.

"I didn't even know they were in town! They must be here on Georgie's orders. You'd have a better chance of talking them down than I would." He eyed me hopefully.

"You really have no idea what a mediator does, do you?"

Between the two of them, Jason and Carolyn carried an enormous, dusty armoire to the stairs. As they struggled with it, I heard the slightest of noises.

"Did you guys hear—" I began to ask.

"Keys. On a ring against the wall," Carolyn interrupted, nodding her head to something I couldn't quite see.

I decided not to be irritated by yet another demonstration of werewolves' superior senses and hurried over to grab the keyring. It held eight keys, none of which were helpfully labeled as 'the key to chains used for binding vampires.' Oh well. I'd just give them all a try.

Juliette looked awful. Her features were drawn and gaunt, her eyes showing a solid ring of gold around the pupil—almost invisible against the yellow of her iris—and her canines were fully extended.

"You're not going to go all batty on us if I let you out, will you, Duchess?"

"If you take more than thirty seconds to release me, little bird," she breathed back, her words slightly mangled, "I am going to break every one of the bones in your right hand. Given your track record with women, that should be enough to make sure you never have an orgasm again."

Alrighty then. I fumbled the keys in one hand and began inserting them into the massive padlock at double speed.

The fifth key was the charm, which was a damn good thing, as I was way too close to Juliette's deadline for comfort. The padlock popped open, and I helped unwind the chains.

The femmepire suffered through my assistance for a few moments, and then nudged me aside, and tore the chains off her with a muffled cry of exertion. While I'd had trouble standing upon my release, it was nothing compared to Juliette's struggles. She swayed like a drunken sailor still trying to regain their land legs. Two days without blood had taken their toll.

"You're going to need to feed," I told her quietly, trying not to wince as her too-bright eyes snapped to my face. "Maybe one of the wolves…?"

"Need human blood," she muttered, shaking her head, although her eyes remained focused on my face. No, not my face. My throat. Awesome. "Can't process theirs."

Well, shit.

"Alright." It was a measure of what depths my life had sunk to that I didn't even hesitate before rolling up the sleeve of my freshly donned shirt. Or maybe it was the memory of the thrill ride that had been Lucia's bite. I extended my wrist in front of the femmepire. "Just try to be—"

She bit in savagely, and I tried—and failed—to stifle my cry of protest. It hurt every bit as much as it had the last time she'd fed from me.

"—gentle," I finished lamely, gritting my teeth through the pain. I raised my voice. "Jason, if she doesn't stop on her own, I'm going to need you to pull her off." Although the pain continued, I wasn't feeling lightheaded yet, which meant she had a while to go before draining me dry.

"Gotcha, bro." The werewolf set aside whatever piece of furniture he had been planning to add to the makeshift barricade and came over.

It turned out he could have stayed by the barricade; a few agonizing seconds later, Juliette released me, her canines sliding wetly out of the flesh of my wrist. Her eyes fluttered shut for a moment, and a pink tongue darted out to lick the remnants of blood off stained red lips.

"Thank you, John. I needed that." Her eyes opened, and she was again the Juliette I recognized. For a moment, she clung to me, but this time it was in a 'seeking comfort' sort of way, and not the 'I'm going to drink you like a juice box' manner I was learning to recognize and fear.

I returned the hug.

"We good now?" Jason looked between us both and nodded, as if reassured by what he saw in our faces. "Okay. The barricade's not going to hold them for long when they decide to come down here after us, but at least it's given us the time we needed to get Miss Fang back on her feet."

Juliette rolled her eyes at the name but said nothing.

"So, here's the plan," continued Jason. "We remove the barricade, and then Cara, the vamp, and I clear a path to the car. Anyone gets too close to us, and you," he nodded in my direction, "ash them with the pistol from hell." He eyed Jee Sun's gun—which I had tucked back into my waistband, against all advice to the contrary—with a new level of respect.

"There's one problem with that," I told him.

"I know you're new at this, but believe me, it's an awesome plan—"

I drew the gun and pointed it at the far wall, carefully away from everyone. It didn't stop the werewolf from diving for cover as I squeezed the trigger.

Again, nothing happened.

"It seems to be out," I informed him coolly.

Awesome plan, my ass.

"Can't you like… reload it or something?"

"Sure. All we have to do is figure out what the hell it uses for ammunition, then we can organize a trip to get it, and then… oh wait," I exclaimed, as if the thought had just occurred to me, "we're not going anywhere, because we're trapped in a freaking basement!"

"Nobody likes a smartass, bro." Jason shook his head seriously, completely missing the irony of someone like him making that statement. "Well then, maybe we could… no. Well, how about… shit." He shrugged. "Time for someone else to come up with a plan."

"It's amazing your two species have lasted this long," Juliette told us with a sigh. "Where's my phone?"

"I didn't see it on the table. Given that the House would have been able to track it, Davis must have ditched it before bringing us wherever the hell we are now."

"This is a safehouse," Carolyn supplied absently. "A few miles away from where you first met us."

"Awesome." That explained why vampire storm troopers hadn't kicked down the doors already and rescued us.

"I have my phone though, if you need it," the werewolf continued, her eyes still distant.

"Obviously, we do," sniped Juliette. I shot her a look, and in the miracle of all miracles, she moderated her tone. "By which I meant, *yes, please.*"

Carolyn picked up the purse she'd dropped by the stairs—although calling it a purse was like calling Mt. Everest a hill—and rifled through its contents until she extracted a gleaming chrome masterpiece, the twin to my dearly departed wonderphone.

"Who are you calling?" I asked Juliette, but she replied with a raised index finger. A moment later, she spoke into the cell.

"Hello, Lucia? Damn it. Lost connection." She scowled down at Carolyn's phone. "One bar? What the hell? It's not like we're in freaking South Dakota or something."

"Reception sucks out here," I informed her, before inspiration struck. "Try Anastasia?"

"If I can't get a signal, calling a different number isn't going to do a damn thing, little bird." Despite her words, the femmepire dutifully punched in a telephone number, and listened for the ring. She shook her head. "Nothing."

"What about her cell?"

"That *was* her cell, moron." She looked over at the two werewolves. "What about the San Diego Pack? Will any of them come looking for you?"

"Most of them don't even live in San Diego anymore," explained Carolyn. "And the few that do… well, Uncle Davis told us all to go to ground yesterday. I guess we know why now."

"That's why we came to speak to him," added Jason. "That and the fact that nobody had encountered John since we broke bread at Torrey Pines. I totally didn't see *this* coming though."

"Stick around," I told him. "This shit happens to me all the time. So, what now? No cavalry, no secret escape tunnel, and no bullets. Any ideas?"

"I guess we have two options," announced Juliette. "First, we can make a suicidal charge up the stairs into an unknown number of enemy wolves—"

"I haven't even heard it yet, but my vote is for option two."

Jason nodded his head in silent agreement.

"—or we can hold out down here for as long as possible, and hope that either the signal improves, or the House is able to track us via the one call that almost got through."

"That sounds like the winner." Jason returned to his makeshift barricade and wedged a small stool into one of the many gaps. "What?" he asked, noting my stare. "Every little bit might help."

CHAPTER 30

IN WHICH ALL THINGS END IN FIRE

"What the hell are they waiting for?"

We'd been sitting in the basement for at least ten minutes, but other than the occasional bang on the basement door, the other wolves had yet to make their move.

"Bro, the longer they wait, the happier I am."

"True." The problem was I was getting *really* sick of that basement. And without my daily infusion of werewolf cooties, I was starting to get twitchy too. Maybe my body was starting to flush out some of the lycanthropy virus?

"They're probably trying to figure out a plan of attack," said Carolyn, "and who has to lead the charge against someone armed with a werewolf-ashing revolver."

"Travis didn't strike me as a lead-from-the-front general."

"General?" Jason snorted. "More like *general pain in the ass.*"

We bumped fists.

"While I don't disagree—and need I remind you that he was *your* friend, Jason?—he came up with a pretty good plan. And people have died because of it." Carolyn's gaze darted over to the corner, where we had draped a tarp over Davis' body… and his head.

"There's no way Travis came up with this on his own," said Jason, shaking his head. "Dude can barely hold his position in Call of Duty. No, this is all my brother's fault."

"Don't you mean your *bro's* fault?" I asked.

"Dude, my brother is *not* my bro."

I decided to just let it go. "If we get out of here, maybe you can speak to your dad and get him to muzzle your brother." I mentally snickered. It was good to see that not even imprisonment and torture—and being stripped naked *clearly* counted as such—could dull the razor-sharp edge of my humor.

"Don't bet on it." The werewolf let out a long sigh. "This may blow your minds, but I'm kind of the black sheep of my family."

"You don't say," muttered Juliette. The spiky-haired femmepire was making a slow circuit of the basement, seeing if she could get a better signal. Judging by the frustration on her face, she wasn't having much luck.

For my part, I was back to poking at my bond with Lucia. I'd worked my way through a new set of psychic metaphors—gleaned from fantasy books this time—without success and was currently envisioning myself next to the bond with a megaphone in hand, shouting for the vampire queen. If she didn't show up soon, there was no telling where my overactive imagination might take me.

"This sucks." Jason dropped onto the cold floor, resting his back against the bottom tier of our barricade.

"Weren't you just saying you were happy to wait?" Upstairs, we heard furniture being moved. It sounded like the werewolf version of Extreme Makeover: Home Edition was happening above us.

"Only because the other option was having my arms torn off. That would be awful, but come on, this is only slightly better."

Several feet away, Carolyn just rolled her eyes.

"Well," I said, "as long as we're here, with nothing to do—"

"Sorry, bro," Jason interrupted, "I don't do foursomes." He paused and reconsidered. "Not with dudes, anyway."

"*So* not my point," I muttered. "I meant that we could continue with our mediation."

"*Now?*" Carolyn seemed singularly unimpressed with the idea.

"We're kind of busy here, man," agreed Jason.

"Doing what?" My question was met with silence, and I smiled triumphantly. "Exactly."

"What is there to talk about?" huffed Carolyn.

"If Jason's no longer representing the New Mexico Pack—"

"Then he loses all claim to my territories?" Carolyn smiled for the first time that day. "You're right!"

"Hell no!" protested Jason. "Two of my friends just tried to kill me on my brother's orders. You're not taking my land away from me too!"

"It's not *your* land," began Carolyn.

"Enough!" I didn't raise my voice—too much, anyway—but the quarreling werewolves silenced almost immediately. Maybe it was the way I was caressing the grip of Jee Sun's gun.

"I understand you don't get along. Great. Whatever. But you," I gestured to Carolyn with the gun, and—bullet or no bullet—she flinched back, "need to recognize that, thanks to your dad, Jason has as much right to the land as you do. And you," I rounded on Jason, "need to realize that this woman and her pack may be the only home you have left!"

"So, what are you suggesting, John?" Carolyn's voice was tight. "There's no way in hell we're getting back together."

"Hell no," agreed Jason.

"At this point, I don't think anybody wants that. Least of all me. But is there a law that the pack leaders have to be romantically involved?"

"Not necessarily."

"Then I have a suggestion. Take it as you will; we're probably going to all die in this basement anyway."

"Great sales pitch," murmured Juliette, still waving Carolyn's phone about in search of a signal.

"The territory stays with the San Diego Pack. Jason becomes a member, and—" I silenced the male wolf with a wave of my hand. "— the two of you *share* leadership. Jason gets a new pack with wolves *not* trying to kill him, and Carolyn doesn't have to worry about her lands being absorbed by New Mexico, since Georgie and his family will lose all legal claim to them."

"If that all works out," I continued, somewhat reassured by the lack of angry tirade from either party, "Jason could even reach out to some of the other wolves in New Mexico who have fallen afoul of the pack. New blood for San Diego, without any political fallout."

"Like making our pack an asylum for disenfranchised wolves?" Carolyn seemed equal parts dismissive and intrigued.

"It's worked for the House," I said.

"Sort of." Juliette really *was* the worst person to have around for a mediation.

"Joint rule," mused Carolyn. "It *might* work."

"Until we disagree. And you *know* we will, Cara."

She thought about that for a moment and nodded. "He's right. If I said the sky was blue, J would immediately declare it yellow, just to spite me."

"I'm a free spirit, woman!" Jason grinned. "I refuse to live in a world where blue can't be yellow."

"Well, I guess you'd have two options at that point. If you two ended up deadlocked on an issue, you could always get a third party to mediate—"

"Oh hell no!" they both exclaimed at the same time.

I tried not to let them see how badly that hurt.

"—or," I continued, eyes narrowed, "you could open the question to the pack as a whole."

"Like a vote?" Jason seemed confused.

"Sort of a representative democracy, only without the elections?" Carolyn's eyes lit up. "A truly progressive pack?"

"This is the point where she'll start ranting about environmental conservation," Jason told me.

"And what's wrong with taking care of the land we live in? It's not going to kill you to recycle. Or to swap out that nasty motorcycle for something green."

"You're not touching my bike—"

"Quiet!" Juliette stopped in the dead center of the room and cocked her head. "Do you all hear that?"

I didn't hear a damn thing, but the two wolves nodded.

"It sounds like water?" Jason wrinkled his nose. "But it smells more like—"

"Gasoline," finished Carolyn, springing to her feet to walk over to the barricade. From under the pile of furniture, a small stream of liquid was making its way down the stairs.

"I guess the moron came up with a plan after all," said Jason.

Well, shit.

ooo

"Is it too much to hope that they're just trying to slowly drown us?" I asked, watching gasoline continue to run down the stairway.

Nobody dignified my question with a response.

"Now we know what was taking them so long," mused Carolyn.

"Yeah. Someone had to go get a full tank of gas so they could burn us out."

"They're just going to light a fire, and wait for us to die?"

"Or to try to escape." Juliette nodded. "Our time just ran out."

"Well, that's unfair." Disney had taught me that villains were all mustache-twirling egomaniacs. It was deeply distressing to have a werewolf with a freaking mullet outthink us.

"I'm not going to stick around to be barbecued," Jason declared. "Better to go out swinging. Are you all with me?"

Two heads nodded, but I waved my gun in protest. "I'm a lover, not a fighter!" I ignored Juliette's snicker of disbelief. "Seriously, I need a better plan than *run up and die heroically.*"

"There's nothing heroic about death," said Juliette. "It's just death."

"The fact that you've seen every movie ever made and can *still* say that makes me feel sorry for you, Duchess."

"There's not much point in a plan," Jason said with a shrug. "I'll lead, and we'll try to make a break for it. Get to a car and get away or something. Maybe one of us can—" He paused, and all three of them reacted to something I couldn't hear.

"That was a match, little bird," Juliette supplied helpfully, moments before fire roared down the stairs toward us. She took one step closer, and casually hoisted me in her arms. "Let's make sure you die to the wolves with the rest of us, and not in the fire." She then nodded to Jason.

"I don't think this is such a good idea—" was all I got out, before the male wolf charged up the stairs, followed closely by his ex-wife, a femmepire, and the human she was carrying like a baby.

It would have been an awesome setup for a joke, if it hadn't meant I was going to die.

○○○

Our desperate charge wasn't much of one, since Jason and Carolyn had to deconstruct what remained of the barricade that was now on fire. There was plenty of desperation though, so that part at least was true.

I wrapped my face in a sleeve and tried not to breathe. The fire had started quickly, and spread even faster, and the basement was already filling with smoke. If Juliette hadn't been carrying me, I would have never made it up the stairs. I found myself vaguely grateful that our impending death at least meant I wouldn't have to owe her, yet again, for saving my life.

Finally, we reached the top of the stairs. Jason lowered a shoulder and ran straight through the door, smashing it open, and we found ourselves in a narrow hallway. This floor, too, was already burning.

"Back door! To the right!" Carolyn called to Jason, but a quick glance showed that passageway had been clogged with a far more impressive and far more solid version of our own makeshift barricade. We turned to the left and were greeted with a similar obstacle. It was clear what the other wolves had been doing with their time.

This was, by far, the worst home makeover ever.

Again, Jason lowered his shoulder, and charged into the burning pile of chairs, tables, armoires, and whatever else it was that barred our path. This time, he bounced off, almost knocking the rest of us into the burning barricade on our other side.

"I guess we get to all die by fire anyway."

Jason started digging at the barricade, his skin blistering, blackening, and healing again in a process that was probably as agonizing as it was disgusting. Juliette set me down, pulled a metal table leg out of the pile with a hiss of pain, and started whacking at the barricade over Jason's shoulder. And I… well, I mostly hopped around, trying to find a spot that wouldn't burn my feet, while also holding my breath as smoke flooded the hallway. Carolyn's deep racking coughs suggested she'd had less success on the latter front.

Moments later, I blinked my eyes back open, surprised to find myself lying on my side. The heat from the floor was almost soothing, which seemed wrong somehow, given the blisters and burns I saw appearing on my exposed skin.

A large shape fell to the ground next to me, but the smaller figure continued whacking away at the barricade with her pole. *Good old Juliette*, I told myself, as my lungs screamed for air, and my eyes started to drift shut again. *Won't go down without a fight.* And then, almost as an afterthought: *She always said I was going to get her killed.*

Juliette was readying one last blow when the flaming barricade shuddered. That was wrong, wasn't it? Barricades were only supposed to move *after* you hit them. Was the furniture collapsing under the fire the werewolves had set?

Things weren't making a lot of sense right about then.

Juliette stumbled back as the barricade shuddered again. Then, the heavy oak table that served as its centerpiece literally exploded, showering us all with molten fire and wooden splinters. In the resulting gap, a figure appeared, standing in a hallway dripping with ice.

A stone angel, I thought, *like in those pictures of Rome. How nice. I always wanted to see Rome.*

And then I passed out.

CHAPTER 31

I woke to find myself being carried into blessedly cool air and lowered onto dirt that, despite the heat of the day, was a far cry from the fire-scorched floor on which I'd laid down to die. I blinked up in time to see Anastasia—but an Anastasia that had been transformed entirely into stone, hair included—lower me to the ground, and spin back to the house.

A stone angel, indeed.

I raised myself on my elbows, surprised to not be hurting worse than I was, and looked at the house that had held me prisoner for days. There wasn't much left of it, really. The fire the enemy wolves had set was devouring the building, and what remained was a black-walled shell. Fire was visible through the open door and the gaping, glass-less windows on the second floor, bringing to mind a Jack o' Lantern or flame-scorched skull.

Only the front door was clear, ringed with ice that reformed as fast as it melted.

As I watched, Anastasia disappeared back into that tunnel of ice and re-emerged, moments later, carrying two other burdens. I only recognized Jason and Carolyn after they had been deposited next to me. The former was a mass of scorched skin, but both were breathing. Under my gaze, a large patch of blackened flesh flaked away, exposing fresh pink skin below it.

"Juliette?" I croaked up at Anastasia.

She made a gesture to someone I couldn't see, and then crouched beside me, her skin regaining its usual porcelain beauty. Hair crinkled audibly and then fell softly about her face in auburn waves. Her clothes were scorched and streaked with ash, but even with the burning house as a backdrop, she was, without question, the loveliest sight I had ever seen.

"Lady Middleton is to your right, Mr. Smith," Anastasia said in answer to my original question. Her face was composed, but her jade eyes glittered with emotion. "Please, do not speak. You inhaled a lot of smoke and have been burned badly."

"I actually don't feel so bad," I said, then caught a glimpse of the blistered mess that had been my arm. "Okay, *now* I feel bad."

I blinked and looked again. Had some of the blisters disappeared? As I watched, skin visibly healed. It was a far cry from what Jason's body was managing, but still…

"That should not be possible," murmured Anastasia, taking a bottle of water from someone behind me and urging me to drink from it. As it trickled down my throat, the lukewarm water tasted like ambrosia, or mead, or really good beer.

"Werewolf bites," I told her.

Her eyes widened. "Have you been…?" She left the question dangling.

"I don't think so. I only remember two bites," I told her. "But I must still have it in my system for the time being."

"Either that, or Lucia's blood has had its own strange effect," she agreed.

We were out in the middle of nowhere, as Carolyn had suggested, but there were at least a dozen vampires milling about. In the distance, I saw a familiar white-clad figure. Next to her was a squat, pot-bellied man with a mustache I'd recognize anywhere.

"Emilio?"

"He led us here," she explained, "although it was almost too late."

"And the other wolves?" Given the lack of activity, I was assuming whatever battle had taken place was already over.

"Many had already departed," she confirmed, "but we slew those who remained. My Queen will be dispatching our forces momentarily to rid the city of werewolves." She spared a glance for Jason and Carolyn, but her expression didn't waver.

"No! She can't do that…" I struggled to my feet and began staggering toward the blonde vampire queen.

Anastasia caught up to me, her hand at my elbow the only thing keeping me from falling on my face as we approached Lucia and Emilio. The mustachioed werewolf stood stiffly, arms pinned behind him by manacles that must have been designed with the supernatural in mind.

"Mr. Smith." Lucia's white leather outfit was free of ash or soot. "You have a knack for staying alive. I had thought we would be avenging your death, but it seems you shall yet be of service to my House."

And hello to you too, I very carefully did not say. There were more important things at stake than our habitual clashes. "Lucia," I told her urgently, "the San Diego Pack had nothing to do with any of this. You can't just hunt them down."

"No?" The queen's plush lips thinned at the suggestion that there was anything that she could not do. She waved one tanned hand at the burning shell before us. "Is this not one of Davis Hawthorne's safehouses?"

"Well, yes…" Maybe I should have figured out what to say *before* I came over.

"And did he not, in fact, kidnap you and one of my Council members, and hold you both prisoner for the last two days?"

"You've already talked to Juliette," I concluded.

"Indeed."

"Did she tell you that he acted alone?" Mostly, anyway. I remembered the car that had been parked outside my parents' house. With the New Mexico Pack busy trying to kill me out in the desert, those two wolves must have been working for Davis. Maybe he'd been meaning to kidnap me right off the street that night? "And that the actual attacks on my life and on your subjects," I stressed, "were perpetrated by the New Mexico Pack?"

Inwardly, I managed to dredge up a smile. Find me another human who's been bitten by a werewolf, fired a hellgun, almost died in a fire, and still managed to correctly use the word perpetrate in a sentence. I didn't care what anyone said. I was a hell of a mediator.

"The same wolves," I continued, "who just killed Davis and tried to burn Juliette, myself, and the two leaders of the San Diego Pack alive?"

Emilio's shoulders slumped. Even his mustache drooped.

Oops. Apparently, he hadn't known that Davis was dead.

"The insult to my House must not stand, Mr. Smith." Lucia's eyes blazed, and talons of ice formed over her fingers.

"Which insult?" Skin on my arms continued to flake away. "The kidnapping? Davis is dead. You could try to find the body and kill him a second time, but it's probably ash by now. The attacks? Like I said, those are the fault of the New Mexico Pack. Should the wolves responsible be punished? Hell yes! They shouldn't even make it out of

San Diego alive. But who's better suited to hunt down a wolf than another wolf?"

Lucia was many things, but stupid was not one of them. Comprehension dawned in her glacial blue eyes, momentarily dampening the fury. "You suggest an alliance then?"

"I'm just a mediator," I said with a humble shrug, "but given that Anastasia just saved all of our lives and neither Jason nor Carolyn wanted a war with the House in the first place, I suspect you'll find them agreeable. Once they're conscious, at least."

Lucia nodded slowly and reached behind Emilio. A moment later, the werewolf's hands were free. He cocked a curious eye at the vampire queen.

"See to your packmates, wolf," she told him.

I watched the burly man cross the scrub grass and dirt, and then turned back to find Lucia eying me strangely.

"What?"

"You are an interesting creature, my thrall," she said simply, turning on one heel and stalking away.

"Why does that worry me?" I asked the afternoon sky.

"Because you are not a stupid man," the auburn-haired femmepire at my side told me.

"It was a rhetorical question, Ana."

"Sometimes, even rhetorical questions deserve answers."

○○○

I stopped to check on the werewolves before we left. Both Jason and Carolyn were on their feet, and while they were moving gingerly, there was nothing to show they'd been on the edge of death less than an hour prior. As I'd gotten to experience so recently myself, werewolf healing was awesome stuff.

All the same, I was happy to keep muddling along as a human. Without the third bite, the virus would eventually be flushed out of my system, and I wouldn't have to worry about turning furry.

Lucia had already left, starting the trek back to where the House Escalades were parked, but the werewolves still had slightly dazed expressions on their faces, as if they'd just been run over by a five-foot-tall goddess in skyscraper heels. Given the way Lucia negotiated, that probably wasn't too far from the truth.

"Are you guys okay?"

Jason nodded. "I don't know how or why, but—for the short term, anyway—we're now allied with the vamps."

"Was that your work, Mr. Smith?" asked Carolyn quietly.

"I may have suggested something along those lines, but nobody tells Lucia what to do. Not more than once, anyway." I lowered my voice. "Any idea which of our attackers made it out alive?"

"Travis, for one," grumbled Jason. "As far as we can tell, he and a bunch of the others took off before the fire started." He nodded to the corpses that had been neatly deposited into the still-burning remnants of the house. "They left a few wolves behind to finish off anyone who made it through the fire."

"Well, that sucks." Travis was one werewolf I'd really hoped was already dead.

"Nah," said Jason, "it's better this way. It would have sucked not getting to kill him myself."

Emilio, standing just far enough away to give us the illusion of privacy, cleared his throat. I looked over and saw that the area was rapidly clearing of vampires.

"Are you two ready?"

Carolyn took a moment to look over at the burned-out house, her eyes shadowed. With a sigh, she nodded, and the three of us departed. Emilio followed close behind in his self-appointed role as rear guard. A handful of black-clad vampires were pacing us, but the older werewolf didn't seem inclined to trust his pack's security to them.

It may have been the werewolf virus still in me, but the walk back to the cars was less strenuous than I'd expected it to be. In fact, I kept up with the others just fine, which was why I was able to hear Jason's heartfelt curse as we cleared the last hill.

"What's up?" I looked warily down at the parking lot. Lucia and Juliette had already departed, along with many of the House vampires, but two Escalades remained.

"Goddamn former packmates stole my bike," he growled.

"*And* my Prius!" Carolyn's tone clearly conveyed which of the two she considered to be the greater loss. "Your old pack *sucks*."

"All the more reason to hunt them down, right?" I tried to be comforting, but inwardly, I was just glad that my Corolla remained safely stashed in the House garage. It was a pile of junk, but it was mine, and I wanted it back.

I was halfway down the hill when another thought brought me up short. Soon, my curses joined the wolves'.

"Your car too, bro?"

"No." My shoulders sagged. "The gun. I must have left it in the house somewhere."

"Ouch," offered Jason. "That blows."

"Yeah." Even if the weapon had somehow survived the inferno, the chances of finding it in the wreckage was minimal. Especially since the place was now a mass grave.

"Maybe you can order another one?" Carolyn had grown a lot more considerate over the past day. Life threatening experiences sometimes had that effect on people.

"I don't think there's a website for shit like that, Cara," snickered Jason, before cocking an eye in my direction. "Is there?

Where *did* you get the hell-gun? And can you get me one? Something in black? Maybe a semi-automatic? I've got standards, bro."

And then, there were those people who seemed immune to change. I shook my head as we stepped onto the beaten dirt of the parking lot.

"It wasn't *my* gun," I told them. "It was Jee Sun's, and as far as I know, *she* got it from Bill."

"Bill?"

"Lord Beel-Kasan, Demigod of Nightmares, Terror, and Vindication," clarified Anastasia, waiting for us at the nearest Escalade. "Mr. Smith has been watching the lord's ward."

At Anastasia's words, both wolves visibly blanched. Apparently, they'd heard of my asparagus friend. Emilio alone remained unruffled, every bit as cool as the mustache that graced his weathered face.

"You've... *met* Lord Beel-Kasan?" asked Carolyn.

"He was the other party in my first mediation. Since then, we've kept in touch." I grinned. "Bill's actually hilarious for someone that could at any moment send you to Gehenna to burn for all eternity." I flashed back to a recent Sunday afternoon when Bill, Jee Sun, and I had watched Winnie the Pooh on the houseboat. Theirs was, without question, the weirdest family dynamic I'd ever seen, but they made it work.

I looked up to find two werewolves staring openly at me. Behind them, Anastasia just shook her head, a small smile on her lovely face.

"What?" I fought down the sudden urge to make sure that my fly was closed. After two days of nudity, I shouldn't have cared, but... I blamed the whole ingrained reaction on a particularly unfortunate experience in fourth grade.

"It's nothing, John," Carolyn told me soothingly.

"Like hell it's nothing!" said Jason. "Don't take this the wrong way or anything, but I think you might be nuts."

I shrugged. I was starting to think he might be right.

We piled into the last Escalade and began the long drive to the vampire House. Apparently, Lucia didn't want us wasting time with pleasantries like food or showers or sleep… not when she had rogue wolves to kill.

I waited until we'd reached the 52, and then leaned over to whisper in Carolyn's ear. She gave me a look that suggested Jason wasn't the only one beginning to doubt my sanity, then shrugged and handed me her phone. Unlike my own wonderphone, lost when Davis had kidnapped me, hers had survived both the attacks and fire unscathed.

I glanced up at the front seat, where Anastasia rode shotgun with Tupa, and very quietly swiped across the phone's screen. Then, I brought up the call log. Juliette had tried calling Lucia a half-dozen times before the fire started, but in between that chain of numbers and the first time she had called it, there was another unknown telephone number. I tapped on it and pressed redial.

Anastasia stirred as her phone buzzed audibly. She glanced down at the device questioningly, and then, with a shrug, answered the call.

"Yes?"

"So," I told her, speaking into the borrowed phone, "how about that date?"

In the seat next to me, Carolyn choked on water that had apparently just gone down the wrong pipe. Behind me, Jason whistled.

"Baller move, bro."

CHAPTER 32

IN WHICH A SHOWER, A NAP, AND A SANDWICH
ARE TOO MUCH TO ASK FOR

For once, I wasn't invited to the House war council. I guess Lucia was worried that I'd try to talk her out of mass slaughter or something. Maybe I should have, but I was dying to spend an hour or three in the space-age shower of my House-provided suite. After two days as a prisoner, I was redefining the word smelly. It was a wonder that the vampires and werewolves who'd shared a car with me hadn't made any comments on the stench.

It was an even greater wonder that Anastasia had said yes.

I tried to relax under the luxurious cascade of water from no less than six apertures in the shower ceiling, but my thoughts kept returning to the past few days. There was so much I still didn't understand about werewolves. Their shortened lifespans, for one. It seemed weird that super powerful healing would result in a shorter life rather than a longer one. It didn't matter as much, now that I wasn't going to become one with the furry, but why would turning me into a werewolf have cut my life expectancy in half?

Come to think of it, while Emilio was probably early thirties at best, and Davis had looked much younger than forty, I remembered seeing a handful of werewolves amongst the crowd at their base camp that had been pushing fifty at a minimum. Assuming that the werewolf dementia was related directly to the reality of *being* a werewolf… was it possible that the turned could live longer lives than those naturally born? Did the doomsday clock only start once the transformation was complete?

I waved my hand under the automatic dispenser for body wash and shrugged. There was no point in trying to puzzle it out mid-shower, not when I had two wolves upstairs to pester on the subject. But if I was right, maybe we would revisit the question of my turning at a later point… like, say, when I was sixty or something. Spending my final few decades as an uber-healthy furball didn't sound half bad.

It also meant Melissa Thompsen wouldn't be dying and leaving her husband alone sometime in the next ten to fifteen—

Shit. I tapped the wall and the water flow shut off with a promptness that would have been highly satisfying if I'd been paying it any attention whatsoever. In all the excitement of once again almost dying, I'd completely forgotten that I was supposed to be tracking down Phil Thompsen for his wife.

I clambered out of the shower and dried off, pulling on a fresh Watch uniform as I moved to the phone on my bedside table. I flipped it over and pushed the single button in its center.

"John!" Akiko's cheerful voice rang out, as the House operator picked up on the other end. "Welcome back! How are you feeling?"

"How did you know it was me?" I asked her curiously.

"Who else is going to be calling from your room?" she pointed out. "We do have cells, you know?"

I felt a momentary pang of sorrow. The loss of my wonderphone still stung. It was kind of nice that the People considered this room to be *mine* though. Akiko being audibly happy to hear from me didn't suck either.

"I'm surviving, and still more or less human," I assured her. "I hope you and Celeste are both doing okay, despite all the recent craziness?"

"Well, Celeste is *pissed*," replied Akiko, her tone merry, "because her second-favorite donor just got called out of town on business, but that's got nothing to do with anything. I keep telling her she should collar and leash the boy, like I did my two. Put a bell on the collar, and you always know where they are!"

"Yeah, that does sound… smart?" I really hoped *collar and leash* was some sort of sexual euphemism I'd never heard before. "So anyway, I'm guessing you heard about the whole kidnapping thing?"

"Of course, John! You know that your misadventures are one of our primary sources of entertainment around here."

"Of course they are." Another thought occurred to me. "Hey, did anyone other than Juliette and I survive the attack at Torrey Pines? Charles? Brian? Juan? And… uhm, anyone?" I didn't want to admit that I couldn't remember the fourth manpire's name. In my defense, I'd been having an awful week.

"Believe it or not," she told me, her tone slightly less merry, "they all did. Between the four of them, I don't think they had enough blood to fill a shot glass, but the Infected left once you were taken, and Brian was able to pull himself together long enough to drive the Escalade home."

"They *all* made it? That's great!" Given that Juan and… (was it Donald?) had been removed from the scene even before the rest of us were attacked, I couldn't fathom how Brian had managed to find them *and* get everyone back to the House. It really spoke to how freaking tough their species was.

It was a shame that, unlike werewolves, vampires couldn't turn humans. There wouldn't be much of a downside to *that* transformation. Other than the whole drinking blood thing, maybe, and if the vampire got even a fraction of the pleasure their donors experienced, even that would be an easy habit to become accustomed to.

"Anyway…" I shook my head, dismissing that train of thought with a yawn. I was having a lot of trouble staying focused, and the bed was looking more and more inviting. "This is a bit of an odd question, but do you by any chance have the number for Melissa Thompsen on file? I lost my phone and need to call her back. Maybe see if she's listed online or something?"

"Is that the Infected whose husband is missing?"

I whistled. It really was amazing how quickly information spread through the House.

"Celeste and I are two of the People assigned to look into the matter," Akiko explained. "I have all the information you might need on Mrs. Thompsen: height, weight, blood type, social security number, internet browsing habits…"

"Just the phone number will be fine."

"Are you sure? She's been visiting some *very* naughty sites…" Akiko teased, before resuming her professional demeanor. "Okay, I've pulled it up now. I'll connect you to her immediately unless you need anything else?"

"Actually, you said you were part of the Thompsen task force?" Thompsen task force sounded like it could have been the name of a television show on Fox. "Were any of you able to find Phil?"

"Of course," she said brightly. "He's over at the Marriott in Kearny Villa, actually. He's also been spending a fair amount of cash at the Elbowroom, just north of there. I don't want to tell an Infected how to manage her marriage, but maybe Celeste isn't the only one who should think about the whole leash and collar thing."

"I'll pass the suggestion on to her," I lied, increasingly curious about just what sort of life Akiko's boyfriends and donors led. "Thank you as always."

"My pleasure! You'll have to come visit Celeste and I down here on sub-level two at some point," she told me. "We could do with the entertainment!"

ooo

"Hello?" The voice on the other end was tired and dispirited.

"Mrs. Thompsen? This is John Smith—"

"Mr. Smith! Where have you been?!" Melissa demanded. "I've left *at least* a dozen messages for you."

"I'm sorry," I told her. "I lost that phone and have been out of touch the last few days. It's… a really long story."

"Given that I don't have a job and seem to have misplaced my husband, I've got nothing but time to listen."

I winced. "So, you haven't heard from Phil yet?"

"No!" Her voice was almost a howl, painfully loud even over the telephone. "I was going to file a missing person report, but *you* told me to keep a low profile, and I was worried that involving the police might make things worse. And then you *disappeared!* Where the hell have you been?"

"Like I said, it's a really long—"

"Don't give me that! Just tell me what was so important that you couldn't even *call* me!"

"What do you want to hear about?" I asked, irritation bubbling to the surface. "The multiple attacks on my life by werewolves from New Mexico? That your friend and mentor decided to kidnap me and keep me in his basement so he could infect me and pimp me out? That the New Mexicans then tracked us both down, killed him, and tried to burn me alive? Or that I haven't eaten anything—that I know of, and I can't tell you how *insane* it is to have to qualify that statement—since a burrito on Saturday afternoon? A burrito," I told her witheringly, "that was supposed to come with extra guacamole, but barely had even a spoonful of it!"

On the other end of the line, Melissa sniffled, and my irritation transformed into guilt. The last thing a recently turned werewolf in the middle of marital difficulties needed was to be snarled at by the college dropout detective she'd hired to find her husband.

"I'm sorry," I said, speaking into the silence. "It's been a difficult few days. I didn't mean to snap at you."

"Davis is dead?"

"Yes." *That* was what had bothered her? Apparently, my being attacked and kidnapped simply didn't rate. To say nothing of the guacamole. Freaking werewolves.

"What about his niece?"

"Carolyn is fine," I told her. "She and her ex-husband Jason both survived and I think you'll be seeing some positive changes with the San Diego Pack in the next few months." And speaking of ex-husbands… "But that's not what I'm calling you about."

"Have you found Phil?" Melissa's voice went from morose to hopeful so quickly it gave me whiplash. "Is he okay?"

"I have and he is," I told her. Akiko and the others wouldn't mind me taking the credit for their work, would they? I thought about that for a second, and decided clarification was in order. "While I was out of commission, some associates continued the search. I can give you the information now, if you'd like?"

"Yes, please," she said excitedly, before her voice fell again. "Only… what if he still doesn't want to see me?"

How had she still not picked up on the fact that I was the *last* person to go to for relationship advice? I reminded myself, yet again, that Melissa was going through a hard time.

"Maybe he should speak with someone else first," she said. "Someone still human, who could give him a fresh perspective." And then, in case I hadn't already put the clues together like a proper private investigator, she dropped the last one right in my lap. "Man to man. What do you think?"

And somehow, I found myself agreeing to be that person, exactly as she'd hoped, placing myself once again in the middle of their marital difficulties. Maybe it was guilt over the fact that I'd sort of caused their breakup in the first place. Or guilt that I'd snapped at Melissa over the phone and made her cry. Or guilt for continuing to lie to my parents about my second career.

Maybe it was all three; Catholics—even lapsed ones—do guilt very, very well.

Whatever the reason, I found myself committed. I needed to gather up some Watch members, put together a convoy, and get myself over to the Kearny Villa Marriott.

But first, I was going to make myself a sandwich.

CHAPTER 33

I'd taken one step toward the hall when a red-haired missile streaked through the door and tackled me.

"John!" Darlene cried up at me, while doing her level best to hug the life out of my freshly showered body. "You're alive!"

"Why… so I am!" I agreed, blinking in mock astonishment.

She released me, and then, before I could move, hauled back and punched me in the arm. Hard. I was going to have to talk to Kayla about the lessons she was giving her girlfriend.

"You need to stop getting yourself blown up, or kidnapped, or all of the rest of this crap!" For a moment, her blue eyes welled up with tears. "It's really *very* inconsiderate of you!"

"You're preaching to the choir, D." I rubbed my arm, hoping that any lingering werewolf virus in my system would heal the bruise. "Unfortunately, it's the rest of the world that needs convincing."

"Are you okay?"

"I'm surviving… but what are you doing here? Don't you have classes on Monday?" I rubbed my face in tired confusion. "It *is* Monday, right?"

"Yeah, it is, and yeah, I do, but I decided it made more sense to stick around the House and support my girlfriend," she told me. "Kayla was *pissed* that she had to stay and guard the House today, but Queen Lucia has the Watch on a strict rotation, and K was already out looking for you on Saturday *and* Sunday."

"They've been searching all this time?"

"Uhm, yeah?" Darlene shook her head ruefully. "The House has been sending out teams since Brian and the others reported that you and Juliette had been taken. How do you think they captured the werewolf that finally led them to you? Ernie or something?"

"Emilio."

"Whatever." She waved a tiny hand dismissively. "It seemed a solid enough lead that Lucia herself went, and she took half the House with her. But Kayla got stuck guarding the building in their absence. Anyway, I'm just glad you're alive."

"Me too. I'll be happy to give you the full rundown," I promised, "but now that I no longer smell like raw sewage, I'm freaking starving. Can we continue this in the kitchen?"

We turned to go, but another, even smaller figure was blocking our path.

"Mr. John!" shouted Jee Sun excitedly, her superman cape flapping in a nonexistent breeze. She had done… *something* to her hair and was now sporting at least three braids and no fewer than a dozen bows and strands of colored ribbon.

I detected the not-at-all subtle hand of Tea Leaf in that arrangement.

"Hello, Tiny Flower." Inwardly, I suppressed a sigh. It was gratifying to realize how many people cared if I lived or died—so many more than I'd been able to think of with Chuck charging at me in the safehouse—but right then, Jee Sun and Darlene were just human-shaped impediments, standing between me and my rightful sandwich.

○○○

Elbowroom was a sports bar in Kearny Villa, just east of the 163. It had the distinction of being the home of the Browns Backers, a fan club for one of the few NFL franchises whose recent history was on par with our own woeful Chargers. On this particular Monday afternoon, Browns jerseys were nowhere to be found, but there were still a fair number of people there for Happy Hour.

We'd stopped by the Marriott first and left a message for Phil at the desk, but I hadn't seen any downside in looking for him at the bar as well. The worst-case scenario was that he wouldn't be there, and I'd get to sneak in a beer or two.

Actually, the *real* worst-case scenario was the one I was currently in; having found Phil, I now had to talk to him.

I kind of missed the days where I just took dirty pictures.

"That's him," I told Kayla, who sent Watch members to take up stations near the bar's exits with a curt twitch of her head. When I'd announced that I needed to leave the House, she'd put together a two-squad escort and had insisted on including herself in that number. If any of the New Mexico Pack tried to make a play, the wolves were going to find themselves seriously outgunned.

"We'll keep watch," she said, voice uncharacteristically serious. "You don't have the best safety record with bars."

There wasn't much to say to that because it was true. I patted her on one muscled shoulder and made my way to the table where Phil drank alone.

I know he was aware of my approach—mainly because I bumped into a waitress on the way, and we very barely avoided a glass-shattering catastrophe—but the construction worker didn't look up, even when I took a seat across from him.

I ordered a beer, and sat back, content to wait him out. He looked like I felt, with deep, dark circles under his eyes, and a multiple-day growth of mostly white beard. I'd thought he looked old and defeated when he first hired me… but this was so much worse.

I was halfway through that first beer, and already contemplating a second, when Phil finally sighed. "What do you want?"

"Just checking in to see how you're doing," I told him. "Melissa is worried about you."

"Sure she is."

"I don't know why, honestly. She's been going out of her mind thinking that something happened to you, and you've been slobbing it up here in Kearny Villa."

"You wouldn't understand," Phil said tiredly, downing the remainder of his own beer, and signaling to the waitress for another.

"Understand what? That your wife had a horrible thing happen to her, and when she finally got the courage to speak about it, the one person she thought she could rely on for support ran away instead?" I rolled my eyes. "I understand just fine."

His face darkened with anger, but I wasn't concerned. It's easy to be brave when you're backed up by eight near-immortal death-dealing creatures of the night.

"I don't need some kid telling me how to live my life. Finish your beer and get the hell out of my face," he told me.

"Sure thing." I took another sip. "So, how was *your* weekend?"

"Didn't you hear what I said—"

"Yeah, I did." I shrugged. "And that's what I'm doing. Finishing my beer. And when I drink beer, I talk. Go figure. Now, if you want, you can try to force me to leave—"

"Okay." He shifted, as if to do exactly that, and I hurried on.

"—but I don't think you're going to do that."

"No?"

"No." I met his tired eyes across the table. "Like you said, I'm just a kid. But I've been in this business for a while now, and I've learned a lot in the process."

"Yeah; you're a regular Sherlock Holmes," he muttered.

"I wish. That guy didn't have to sit front-and-center for a lot of failed marriages. Most of the time, the evidence I find on the job is the final nail in a relationship's coffin."

"Well, you're batting a thousand," he told me, nodding his thanks to the waitress as she brought the replacement beer he'd ordered.

"Am I?" I caught the waitress' eye and glanced down at my empty glass with a smile and a significant nod. She left to get me another one… hopefully. My nonverbal communication was notoriously poor. "Obviously, neither of us expected me to find what—"

"You know, John," he interrupted, "I'm still waiting to hear what's to keep me from kicking your ass and throwing you out of here."

"Well, first of all because it would be a waste of good beer." I grinned. "But secondly, and more importantly, because you don't really want to."

"What?"

"Your wife isn't cheating on you," I told him bluntly. "Yeah, she has a medical condition that she kept from you, but the important thing is that she still loves you. Only you freaked out and ran away, and now you don't know what to do or how to fix it."

"Is that what your experience as a detective tells you?"

"It sure is. You know what people do when they're done with a marriage? They end it. Sometimes, they clear the bank accounts out first, sometimes they hire a lawyer to make sure their bases are covered, but inevitably, they call it quits. They don't go hide in a hotel and spend their days drinking with—" I gave a theatrical shudder. "—Browns fans."

That startled a grin out of him. "Well, they're not Vikings fans…"

"You're living in San Diego, dude. It's Chargers now or nothing." I took a sip of my new beer, deciding it was a good sign that Phil hadn't objected to its arrival. "The real question is something only you can answer."

"And what's that?"

"Do you still love Melissa?" My question dropped like a stone into the sudden silence.

"She was really worried?"

"Of course. She's clearly still in love with her husband. Now personally, I think she could do better. Attractive, intelligent woman like that? Do you think she'd be interested in a mid-twenties private investigator?"

"Not on your life," Phil growled, sounding suspiciously like a wolf himself. He shot me a hard look before it sank in that I was joking. "So, what do I do?"

"You shower and check out of the hotel, go back to Clairemont, and spend the next week, month, or year working your way back into your wife's favor. As for her condition… I know some people you can talk to, if necessary."

"The whole thing is kind of insane."

"Tell me about it. It's a weird world and it's getting weirder all the time." If he only knew. "Which is why we need to hold on to the people we love, right?"

"Yeah. You're smarter than you look, Mr. Smith." Phil rose from his chair and started looking for the waitress.

"Go take care of your marriage," I told him. "I'll get the check."

With a curt nod, he turned and left the bar, walking like a much younger man, even if that horrible eyesore of a beard gave away the lie.

"How did you know what to say to him?" asked Kayla, melting out of the crowd to join me at the table.

"I didn't. I was winging it the whole time. And I think some of that was from a book. Or a movie." I *had* watched a truly depressing number of romantic comedies over the years, but I wasn't going to volunteer that information to anyone.

"Well, it did the job." Her brown eyes looked in the direction Phil had left. "Do you think he'll really go back to her?"

"If he's smart." I shrugged again. "Either way, I'm done for the day. I killed a werewolf, escaped a burning building, helped create an alliance between the pack and the House, *and* may have just saved a marriage. Do you know what this situation calls for?"

"Ice cream?" Kayla guessed.

"Damn straight. That and a long night of sleep." I swallowed the last of my beer and rose to my feet. "Shall we?"

"Uhm…" Kayla nodded at the bill.

I hadn't even seen the waitress deposit it on our table. Was Elbowroom hiring ninjas now?

I patted my empty pockets. "I don't have my wallet on me. I don't suppose we can charge this one to the House?"

"That was the plan all along, wasn't it? I wondered what would possess you, of all people, to offer to pay."

"There are times," I admitted, "when my innate generosity conflicts with my ongoing financial status."

"You've been spending way too much time with Lady Dumenyova," she said, extracting two crisp twenties from her wallet. "You're starting to sound like her."

CHAPTER 34

IN WHICH BLACK IS THE NEW BLACK

Phil did, in fact, go back to his wife, and I'm told she was so happy to see him that she didn't even make him suffer too much before forgiving him. The two were still going to have their ups and downs, but that seemed true for most relationships, supernatural or otherwise.

A week later, I was at my office desk, grinding my way through the paperwork I'd been letting slide for far too long. The November heat wave remained in effect, and I'd dressed appropriately in an old t-shirt and board shorts. Jee Sun lay sprawled on the floor, working on another of her all-black masterpieces, occasionally muttering 'Shit' under her breath as she scribbled.

The little girl and I had fallen into something of a rhythm, where she spent her weekdays at the office with me, and her nights and weekends back at the House with her new best friend. It was an arrangement that worked far better than having her stay at my house with my parents.

As was starting to become my habit, I leaned back in my chair and glanced out the window, scanning the street. The sight of the gleaming black Escalade parked outside remained reassuring. The combined forces of the San Diego Pack and Lucia's House had swept through our city over the past week, but there were still a few of the New Mexican werewolves at large.

Unfortunately, Travis was one of them. The asshole had to be at least half weasel. I doubted he was anywhere near San Diego at this point, but Kayla wasn't taking any chances. It was good to have friends in high places.

"Mr. John?" Jee Sun's voice broke into my thoughts. She was on her feet now. In her outstretched hands were a few tattered shreds of paper, all that remained of the black Crayola. As usual, she had managed to smear crayon all over her hands and face, in addition to the formerly pristine sheet of paper.

"I'm sorry, sweetie," I told her, "but we don't have any more crayons of that color." Her face fell and I hurried to reassure her. "Maybe we can pick some more up on the way back to Tea Leaf?" Did Crayola make entire packs of black crayons? I hoped so; it was expensive having to buy new cartons every time the little girl used up the one color.

"And ice cream?" she asked hopefully.

"Yes, definitely ice cream," I agreed. "And whipped cream, but only on my sundae."

"Where is it that we are GOING for ICE CREAM?" asked a voice I hadn't heard in some time.

"Mr. Bill!" Jee Sun was quicker on the uptake than I was, and was already sprinting across the room, knocking one of my client chairs to the floor in the process.

I looked over and there he was, standing just inside a closed door whose newly installed deadbolt remained locked: Lord Beel-Kasan, a seven-foot-tall asparagus with charcoal eyes, a carrot nose, and a mouth drawn on his green stalk with permanent magic marker. He had grown two arms, as he sometimes did, and was hugging his small ward, his mouth twisted up into a smile. And he was… smoking?

Not puffing on a cigarette or one of those funky electronic vapers either. He was *literally* smoking. Tendrils of smoke curled lazily into the air above him, and parts of his green stalk were scorched and streaked with ash. That was new.

I would have worried about him setting off the smoke detector if I hadn't scavenged its batteries during one of my firm's leaner months.

"Bill!" I said with a smile. "Welcome back, amigo!"

"Howdy doody, Johnny Appleseed," he replied, growing a third arm to toss me a wave. "WHERE have I BEEN?"

I had no idea how to answer *that* question. Thankfully, he didn't wait for a reply.

"Tiny Flower, do you need more WIGGLE FACE time with John-o-rama, or are you ready for ICE CREAM?"

A question like that only had one possible answer, and Jee Sun's excited squeal told us exactly what that answer was.

EPILOGUE

I watched the taillights of Anastasia's Jaguar disappear into the darkness with a happy sigh. Finally, a date that *hadn't* crashed and burned.

The food had been every bit as good as Ana promised, but I couldn't even remember what I'd eaten, my memories of the night filled with jade green eyes and that smile that warmed my soul. The femmepire had worn a simple, figure-hugging dress in deep green silk, her auburn hair up in some sort of complicated do that highlighted the graceful lines of her neck and shoulders.

I'd worn my suit—freshly dry cleaned, at Kayla's suggestion, and paired with one of Steve's swankier ties—and the light in Anastasia's eyes when she saw me had more than validated the extra effort. It was only as I walked back up the driveway to my house that I loosened the tie. How the hell people could wear one of those things daily was beyond me.

The light on upstairs told me that my parents were still up. I knew they'd want a full report as soon as I entered. Kayla and Darlene were, no doubt, waiting by their phone back at the House.

I wasn't ready for interrogations just yet though, no matter how well-intentioned they were. I wanted space to myself, space and the time to savor what had been one of the best dinners—and evenings, for that matter—of my life. I took a seat on our patio bench and stretched my legs out with another happy sigh. It had taken until almost Thanksgiving before we were certain that San Diego was free of foreign wolves, but the date hadn't suffered for its delay. Lady Dumenyova could stop traffic on her worst day; tonight, she had very nearly stopped time itself.

I undid the top button of my dress shirt, tugged my tie off altogether, and turned to place it on the bench next to me, when I realized that seat was already occupied.

"Good evening. Still here, I see?" I kept my eyes carefully on the ghostly woman's face, which allowed me to ignore the wound that continued to appear in her chest, soaking her nightgown with blood before fading back away.

When Lucia's deal with Graciela and her White Ladies expired, I'd been surprised to discover that our assigned guardian had stuck around. She had yet to tell me her name—I wasn't sure she could even talk—but her presence was a surprising comfort. Yes, she was a little bit spooky, and the bloody nightgown thing was plenty gross, but she was an excellent listener, and my parents couldn't have asked for a better guardian. I even had some hope that she might keep my nosy neighbor, Mr. Brown, in line.

"I hope you had a lovely night," I told her, and she cocked her head in a manner that I'd decided meant she was listening. "Mine was amazing."

We sat together on the bench, looking out into the darkness, and I told her all about the date as we watched the lights in our neighbors' houses turn off, one by one. The air was crisp and cool now that the heat wave had finally passed, and I felt the nervous energy slowly drain from my body as I spoke.

Almost five months after I'd met her, Anastasia remained a riddle, with a wicked sense of humor hidden away beneath the cool reserve and iron self-control of a trained diplomat. The highlight of my night had been hearing the musical chime of her laughter, bubbling up at unexpected times throughout the evening.

"Does she like me? Or *like* like me?" I shook my head. "I know; this isn't high school. But still…" I drummed my fingers on the bench while working through my own thoughts. "Maybe she just enjoys talking to someone who treats her like a person instead of a weapon or a threat, but it feels like we actually have something…"

I kept talking and the White Lady sat patiently next to me for all of it, as was her habit. When I found myself detailing for the fourth time the way the femmepire's jade green eyes had sparkled in the candlelight, I forced myself to stop. I rose to my feet and gave our ghost a smile.

"I'll stop rambling now. Thank you for listening, as always. Can I get you anything?" I'd asked her that every night since the first. One of these times, she was going to take me up on the offer.

But not tonight. The ghost shook her head, dark eyes big and intent upon my face through a curtain of hair.

"Okay then. I'm going to call it a night. I'll see you tomorrow."

As I turned to leave, she held up one finger.

"One second?" I sucked at charades.

She nodded and rose to her feet, the lower half of her body passing right through the bench, as if it wasn't there. She walked along the porch to the far corner and motioned for me to join her. When I arrived, she pointed at the portion of our yard that butted up against the house.

"I'm sorry… I don't understand. Do you want me to do something to the yard? Plant a shrub or some flowers?" It seemed like an odd request for a spirit to make, but with Bill back in my life, I was kind of used to odd.

She rolled her eyes in a disturbingly human gesture, and waved one hand, as if she were pushing books aside on a shelf. As I watched, grass, topsoil, and dirt just… flowed away, leaving a deep hole behind, almost three feet wide, and six feet long.

Uh oh.

"Nobody told me you could do that," I admitted, although I was mostly trying to delay the inevitable. I really didn't want to see what had been buried in a coffin-sized hole. Not even Mr. Brown deserved that fate.

The hole was deep and dark, but the combination of the streetlamp and our own porch light were enough to illuminate the very surprised, very scared, and very dead faces of a mullet-wearing werewolf and two of the vampires that had escorted Juliette and I to our ill-fated meeting with Jason at Roberto's.

"These three came here together?" I asked her. "And you stopped them?"

She nodded.

"That explains a lot." Like how Juan and Diego—and yes, that was the other vamp's name—had disappeared outside Roberto's without a peep, only to show up alive again after the fact. "I can't believe I bought Juan a burrito," I grumbled to my ghostly friend. "The House has a serious traitor problem. These two must have been helping Travis stay hidden for the past few tweeks."

"If you'd just gone back to New Mexico," I told the dead werewolf in a quiet voice, "you'd probably still be alive. Instead, you came looking for revenge, and all it got you was a permanent home in Chula Vista."

I stepped away from the porch railing and nodded to the White Lady. With a wave of her hand, the hole filled back in. When she was done, there was nothing at all to show that my parents had three very bad dudes buried in their front yard.

"Thank you," I said. "I don't know what they were planning to do, but my parents and I owe you our lives."

She smiled suddenly, the first time I'd ever seen her do so, exposing black gums and surprisingly white teeth. I suppressed my shiver and returned the smile. It wasn't *her* fault she was dead, after all. With a wave, I said goodnight.

Even the subsequent hour of interrogations, first by my mom, and then by Darlene, couldn't diminish my sense of satisfaction. I lay in bed, waiting to fall asleep, smiling up at a ceiling I couldn't quite see. It seemed impossible that someone like Anastasia might be interested in someone like me, and yet… what other explanation was there?

My tired mind spun fantasies of dates to come, dreams of the sort of life that Kayla and Darlene already shared with one another. And who knew where it all might lead to? I fell asleep with that smile still on my face.

Lady Anastasia Dumenyova Smith. It had a certain ring to it.

ooo

I wouldn't see her again for almost six months.

John Smith will return in Summer 2021
with *Ghost of a Chance.*

In the meantime, keep reading for a short
story starring everyone's favorite demigod
of nightmares, terror, and vindication,
Lord Beel-Kasan.

This story's events take place between
Investigation, Mediation, Vindication and
Blood is Thicker Than Lots of Stuff.

THE GOOD, THE BAD, AND THE ASPARAGUS

CHRIS TULLBANE

GHOST FALLS PRESS

NEVADA

CHAPTER 1

"Howdy, partner! What's a tall drink of water like you doing in a little frontier town like this? My name is Lord Beel-Kasan, Scourge of the Zoroastrians—"

"Mr. Bill?"

"—Lord of Gehenna, God of Nightmares, Terror, and Vindication. But you can call me—"

"MR. BILL!"

I look down and find the cutest little cowpoke ever punching me in the leg. Jee Sun is just about three buttons tall, with glasses like coke bottles and a shiny red cape over her dungarees.

"What is it, Tiny Flower?" I ask.

"Who are you talking to, Mr. Bill?"

"Our readers, of course! They've come to WATCH OUR FACES WIGGLE!"

"But… there's nobody there!" Tiny Flower has an adorable pout. We've put her black hair in pigtails today in honor of Pooh's bestest buddy.

"They must be invisible then," I decide.

"Oh phooey. Again?"

"Worry not, little lady! I'll make sure they're right proper enchiladas. Nobody will dare mess with Outlaw Bill, fastest gun in the west!"

"Are we in a Western today?"

"You bet your last silver dollar we are!"

"Yay!" She frowns suddenly, and I look about to find who's responsible for stealing her smile. We don't stand for that sort of malarkey around these here parts. No we don't, no we don't. Not at all. "I don't think we can be outlaws today though, Mr. Bill!"

"We can be anything we set our MINDS to, Tiny Flower!"

"But we're supposed to be helping Mr. John with the oranges!"

For a second, I think she's talking about the fruit. Which would be AWESOME but also a bit of a mess. Especially out here away from civilization and such. But Jee Sun is a special little non-outlaw. She can't see things that aren't there the way I can, but she does see monsters in color.

Not human monsters though. They're the sneaky sort.

Yellow is vampire. Purple is pixie. Green is me. And orange? Orange is…

"Why is John-o-rama meeting with GOBLINS, Tiny Flower?"

She shrugs.

"Doesn't he know they are dangerous? And possibly CONTAGIOUS?"

"You told me that already, Bill," says a new voice. "And maybe ixnay the insultsway, considering the oblinsgay are right here?"

I swivel around and find the human himself, Johnny-come-lately, standing three feet to my left.

"John-and-the-beanstalk! When did you get here? And how did you learn to SPEAK IN TONGUES?"

"I was here when you arrived, Bill, and… I don't know what you mean."

"Of course you don't. Ha ha!" Johnny-on-the-spot looks silly when he wiggles his face, but he's a true compadre. He helped Tiny Flower and I get back our magic box from the vampires, and we've had ice cream together and everything.

The goblins next to him though…

Them I can't vouch for.

"Are you going to introduce us to your orange friends, John?"

"But we already…" He stops and waggles his head, like he's trying to shake something loose in it, and then motions to me and the goblins by his side. "It's fine. Lord Beel-Kasan—"

"And Jee Sun!" announces Tiny Flower.

"—and Jee Sun, this is Chief Tikky-Wokka Tomlinson, of the Superchargers tribe. And his wife, Rihanna Mariah Kardashian."

"Howdy-doo," I tell them, tipping my cowboy hat at the missus. I don't spend much time with goblins because they don't have nightmares like normal folk. And also because they're dirty rotten scoundrels that tarnish the good name of even a wild frontier town like San Diego. Why, there isn't a saloon for miles around that would serve them a lemonade!

They aren't really orange, of course, although you shouldn't tell Tiny Flower that. Goblins are small and grey with big, staring eyes and only three fingers on each hand. Tikky-Wokka is all in powder blue and yellow which is nice but a bit strange, and Rihanna Mariah Kardashian is wearing a dress that appears to have been sewn together from fluffy towels.

Towels from a motel, by the looks of it. I do Johnny-boy a solid and avoid making a dismissive sniff. Jee Sun and I get our towels and robes and dishes from the Marriott. *Far* higher quality.

"Chief Tomlinson hired me to mediate an issue between the Superchargers and the Padres," says John-of-the-dead, "but we ran into something weird along the way."

"Are you being Sheriff today?"

"Sheriff?"

"This is the Wild West, good buddy," I tell him. "Every town needs its own Johnny Law."

"Okay…" He gives it some thought while I wait patiently. "Yeah, I guess I am being Sheriff in a way. Which would make you and Jee Sun my deputies for the day."

"Are you sure? I really wanted to be Outlaw Bill. Wild Bill, even. Wild Bill and Tiny Flower, the FASTEST HANDS in the west."

"We need you on the side of law and order this time, Bill."

"Oh phooey," says Tiny Flower.

"Whelp." I adjust my belt and pistols and tip my hat again at Rihanna Mariah Kardashian. "I guess sometimes a demigod's gotta do what a demigod's gotta do."

CHAPTER 2

"You understand what we need, right?"

Just like that, we're indoors again, although I don't remember seeing a sign or a door or even the owner of this establishment. I hope it's not one of *those* houses. Jee Sun is TOO YOUNG to learn about gambling.

I give Johnny Dangerous my best dead-eyed stare. "Of course I do, John. I'm here, aren't I?"

"Cool. I'll be downstairs with the Chief and his wives then. Thanks again, Bill. I really appreciate your help on this."

"We're amigos, Jonathan Skywalker. Amigos don't let good fences burn."

"Right."

I wait for him to leave, walking through a long hall with too many doors and down the staircase at the far end, and then I look down at Jee Sun.

"What did he want us to do, Tiny Flower?"

"Mr. Bill!" She giggles. "Weren't you listening?"

"I was," I admit, "but I think the I that I am might not be the I that was listening at that time."

"Oh." She thinks about that a little bit while chewing what I hope is bubble gum and not tobacco. "The orange man said his orange son was having bad dreams and waking up in weird places."

"But goblins don't have NIGHTMARES," I tell her, feeling nervous for no reason at all.

"That's what you said!" she agrees. "But you also said a deputy's job was to investigate it anyway."

"That is EXACTLY a deputy's job." I polish the star on my chest and then look back at her. "But if I am going into their dreams, you cannot come with me, Tiny Flower. You are too young and it is too dangerous, even with your six-shooters!"

"Oh." Her little face falls and I find myself suddenly angry that the goblins have intruded on our fun day of cartoon watching and cookies. "Can I stay in the room at least?"

"That is allowed! And you will be safe because I will keep you safe and I will look at the orange dreams and tell Johnny-be-Good about them, and then we will all have cookies and ice cream!"

"And milkshakes?"

"Of COURSE milkshakes! What sort of Pooh party would it be without such a delicious thing as milkshakes?" I send her a wink. "I will have BANANA this time."

The door that we have been standing outside of opens easily, like all doors do. Inside is a small bed with a small figure and a large number of colorful pillows. I don't have to check if he is asleep. Some things I just know.

I pick up the only chair in the room and put it in the corner facing both the door and the bed. "You sit here, Jee Sun, and if any varmint shows up, you fill them so full of lead they'll give a prospector a heart attack, okay?"

"Okay!"

"And in the meantime, your old pal and fellow deputy will be going on a little vision quest."

"Like a witch doctor?"

"Or a shaman. YES!" I do not normally bring Jee Sun with me when bringing dreams of retribution and terror to the people of the west, but she is very smart and knows what to do.

And not do.

I drop to a seat next to the small bed, brush off some of the dust from my vaqueros and close my eyes.

When I open them up again, the vision quest has already begun. Hurray! Ice cream for everyone!

○○○

The goblin's dream swirls about me for a moment or two, and then that swirling becomes dust and wind as the world beyond solidifies. As you'd expect from a city slicker, his is a dream of modern buildings and asphalt roads, but it also has delicious crunchy taco stands, so not everything is bad.

I adjust my gun belts again and walk through the empty streets to the building in the distance. It's big and concrete and mostly circular, ringed by other much smaller and more circular circles, and square in the middle of an empty parking lot big enough to park a herd of cattle in.

I am not a great follower of human sports other than dodgeball, but I once took Tiny Flower here on a field trip for hot dogs and nachos and sodas and ice cream sundaes, and there were little men in helmets competing in a game called football that predominantly involved hands.

Humans are delightfully weird.

The stadium is still a long way away, but this isn't my first time ponying up to the table. I reshuffle the deck a bit and just like that, I'm inside the stadium walls, down in the center area where the players play their game.

The field is not the way I remember it: green and white and full of frantic humans jumping on pigskins while wearing bright colors like orange and white and blue and yellow. The grass under my feet is now brown and dry and crunches like the straw put down in a stable. The yellow Y's at each end of the field are gone, as are the white stripes that made the space look like a jealous zebra.

I like it better this way, but the little goblin crouched in the center of the barren field does not seem to agree. The fear pouring off of him is mixed heavily with grief, and that spoils the whole flavor, like anchovies and pineapple on pizza or apple pie without balloons.

I am close enough to hear his sobs, and though I do not like goblins, this one is small like Tiny Flower, and that is enough to wrinkle my noggin.

Even worse, goblins do not have nightmares. It is what I said to Johnny Banana and Tiny Flower both and I said it because it is true and it is true because it is how things are. So, for this sad city slicker to be having one now can mean only one thing.

Banditos.

I draw my pistols and spin around, and sure enough, there they are. Three varmints, with bodies of smoke and eyes that burn, ringed around the crying goblin. Their voices whisper, but it's not the whisper of watching movies and not wanting to miss the best part. It's the whisper of snakes slithering through the sands of my home in Gehenna.

"Gone," says one.

"Why did they leave?" asks another.

"No more," says the third.

And then, all together: "San Diego Superchargers!"

It's not a spell that I am familiar with, but I am a shaman gunslinger not a spell caster, so this does not surprise me. Still, the effect on the shivering goblin in the center is immediate.

More fear. Delicious.

More grief. Far too salty.

Johnny Sunshine is the sheriff, but he's not here. Which means it's time for his deputy to set things right and bring law to this lawless town.

I shuffle the deck again so the shadow people can see me.

"Howdy, PARTNERS! I'm gonna have to rightly ask you to stop wiggling your faces and vamoose in an easterly direction until you fall right out of this here dream."

They spin about, seeing me for the first time, and one and all, they recoil. Even the crying little goblin on the ground. I wonder what it is I have appeared as. Everyone sees me as their biggest fear, except for the sheriff and Lord Kala, and of course, Tiny Flower, who no longer has anything at all to fear because I have saved her and will protect her and will BURN anything that thinks differently.

"What *is* that?" asks one of the smoke people, his whisper forgotten.

"I didn't summon it," says another, her voice dry and scratchy like she's been drinking bleach.

"I am not a something that is to be summoned by the wiggling of faces or the crushing of bone or even the smell of hot cocoa," I tell them. "Unless the hot cocoa also has MARSHMALLOWS in it, in which case I will come with two mugs of my own."

"Whatever you are," says the third shadow, in a voice like Ralph from Wreck-It-Ralph, "this dream is our construct, and that makes you our prey." He looks to the other two shadows. "Kill it."

ooo

Something like lightning comes at me from the shadow on the left, but this isn't my first rodeo. I'm already dodging to the side, and my pistols roar as I send lead downrange in response. Thirty-six bullets in a handful of seconds, because I have a six-shooter in each hand, and Jee Sun's book says thirty-six is a multiple of six.

The shadow man doesn't even try to dodge, but my shots pass through him without any effect.

The shadow on the right sends an incantation of his own, something green and slimy that hits the dried grass around me with a snake's hiss and sets the brown field ablaze. The shadow that my bullets couldn't touch sends another lightning bolt my way. And the third shadow has disappeared.

I may be the fastest draw in the west, but this gunfight isn't going my way. I send another forty-two bullets at the shadow spewing venom, but this one is just as impervious as her fellow bandito. And now my snakeskin cowboy boots are on fire, after I just got them shined by the nice old blind man outside the saloon.

Luckily, this former card sharp turned outlaw turned unexpected lawmaker *always* has an ace up his sleeve.

I pull that ace and everything changes.

Lightning stabs at my body, venom splatters against the star on my chest, but it's the banditos' turn to be surprised. I catch the lightning in one hand and it becomes a fistful of daisies. The venom turns into steam and my star is left shining as brightly as ever.

I holster my smoking six-shooters because they're not needed anymore.

"Dead or alive, you're going to hang from your wiggly faces," I tell them.

"This isn't possible," mutters the one on the left.

"We created the dream," shrieks the one on the right. "It's ours to control!"

"I reckon you're right, Smoky-the-bears," I tell them both, before pointing to where the sobbing goblin at the center of the stadium has started to disappear, "but this here isn't your dream anymore."

Above us, the sky fills with purple clouds, wreathed in lightning. The grass of the stadium becomes red sand, and the stadium itself is nowhere to be seen, replaced by row after row of twenty-foot-high, brightly burning candelabras.

"We're in my home now," I say, as the shadows blow away, revealing two goblin shamans with just the right mélange of terror, "and hell's coming with me."

ooo

Two sparkly new candelabras later, it's time to be a proper enchilada and return home. I've searched high and low—but mostly low—for the third goblin shaman, and he's nowhere to be found. Unless he's an actual snake, that means he vamoosed out of the dream before I brought the rest of his gang of cattle rustlers and dream pirates into Gehenna.

I'll let Johnny Appleseed figure out what to do next. Tiny Flower is probably ready for a post-gunfight milkshake.

CHAPTER 3

Tiny Flower is happy to see me and I am happy to see her and we are happy together and the goblin that is just now waking up in his bed faints as soon as he sees me but I am certain it is a happy faint and so there is nothing but happiness in the small room with the one bed and the one chair and the two deputies.

I tip my hat at Tiny Flower, and she hugs my leg, and we mosey out into the hall and down the stairs and past another hall full of goblins that cower and run away, until we finally find Sheriff John, talking again to Chief Tikky-Wokka.

"Johnny-come-marching-home-again! Your deputies return victorious!"

Tiny Flower pokes me in the leg.

"Mostly victorious!" I correct myself. "One of the banditos got away, but the cattle-rustling gang's power is FOREVER BROKEN in this territory, or my name isn't Doc Holiday!"

"Your name's not Doc Holiday, Bill."

"Not with *that* attitude, John-o-rama."

"What is Lord Beel-Kasan saying?" asks the chief, offering a nervous bow in my direction.

"I think that he took care of the issue."

"Boom," adds Tiny Flower, taking a long sip of a milkshake that is strawberry like the shortcake.

"Wait. Where did you both get milkshakes?"

"At the saloon, of course, Johnny Rotten!" I wave my banana milkshake about. "Where they serve lemonade and milkshakes and the occasional pie."

"Right." He waggles his head again, but I am too polite to comment on that fact. Sometimes, brains do get stuck after all. "Can you explain exactly what you found?"

"I thought I just did that, John."

His face wiggles but no words come out. After a moment, he tries again. "Okay. So… there were banditos?"

"YES!" I am so pleased he finally gets it. "Banditos in the dream that they created to give to the goblin who is happily fainted in the bed that is upstairs!"

"Right. And do you know who the banditos were?"

It is Tiny Flower's time to answer. "Orange!"

"Other *goblins* were creating a nightmare for Chief Tikky-Wokka's son?"

The goblin chief makes an angry face that is not so threatening on someone so small. I step between him and Tiny Flower, just the same.

"My son fears nothing!" he declares. "What nightmare could they give him that would affect him like this?"

I shrug again, which causes the Chief to flinch, even with my pistols holstered. "There was an empty concrete stadium with dead grass and no FEET or BALLS."

Johnny-on-the-spot just stares at me blankly, like he sometimes does, but the goblin goes pale like paint in a television house flip.

"Qualcomm stadium? The Superchargers?"

"Boom," says Tiny Flower again.

"It was just a nightmare," says Johnny Camaraderie to the chief. "The Chargers aren't going anywhere. They're an institution here in San Diego."

"So were the Clippers!"

I don't know if they are talking about the human sports teams or the goblin tribes, but either way, I am not paying attention, partly because I have a banana milkshake in my hand, and partly because voices are coming closer. And I have heard both voices before, although I cannot be entirely certain when. I will have to ask Tiny Flower when she is done with her milkshake.

After a minute, Johnny-be-good and the goblin chief hear the voices too. They turn as Rihanna Mariah Kardashian enters the hall, followed closely by a male goblin in powder blue robes. She bounces over to the chieftain, but the new goblin stops in his tracks, big eyes going even bigger as he sees me.

And just like that, I remember where I heard his voice before.

The shaman bandito dives toward Chief Tikky-Wokka, but I am the fastest gun in the west. I already have both hands extended, one with a milkshake and one with a six-shooter, and the one of those two that is not a delicious frozen beverage makes a loud noise and kicks in my hand like a bucking bronco. Eighteen bullets hit the goblin right between the eyes.

And this is not the dream he created or a dream at all and so there is very little left of his head when the gun smoke clears.

Rihanna Mariah Kardashian screams and faints. I slip my six-shooter back into its holster and turn to John-and-the-beanstalk. "All banditos are now accounted for, Sheriff."

"The Superchargers' High Priest was one of the bad guys... err... bandits?"

"That's a 10-4, good buddy," I tell him. "Have fun flying the increasingly friendly skies."

There's a momentary pause, as everyone looks at each other and I drink my banana milkshake.

"Are we not in a western anymore, Mr. Bill?" asks Tiny Flower.

"Roger that! Now we're on a highway to the danger zone!"

"Oh goody!" She takes another long sip of milkshake. "I like this game."

I do too. I adjust my aviators, she straightens her bomber jacket, and together, we head for the door, leaving Johnny-boy and Chief Tomlinson to wrap things up.

I'd stick around longer, but I feel the need.

The need for speed.

AUTHOR'S NOTE

Thank you so much for reading!

In defiance of the publishing timestream, *Blood is Thicker Than Lots of Stuff* was actually the second book I ever wrote, although it has gone through any number of edits in the ensuing years. *The Good, the Bad, and the Asparagus*, on the other hand, is almost brand new, written at fellow author Kerri Davidson's request in late 2020.

I know, I'm as confused by my scheduling as you are.

I hope you enjoyed both stories! John and his ever-growing cast of friends are a lot of fun for me to write. The next book, *Ghost of a Chance*, kicks things up a notch, as John's dual roles as investigator and mediator continue to get him into trouble. It's a longer story but it's already in editing and should be out by summer of this year.

In the meantime, if you're looking for something a little darker and more expletive-filled, please check out *See These Bones*, the first book in my post-apocalyptic superhero trilogy, The Murder of Crows. It and its sequel, *Red Right Hand*, are already out and available, and I'll be finishing the trilogy with *One Tin Soldier*, later this year.

If you enjoyed *Blood is Thicker Than Lots of Stuff*, please consider leaving a review. As an indie author, I depend heavily on word of mouth and the feedback of readers like you.

Thank you!

ABOUT THE AUTHOR

Chris began life as a gleam in someone's eye, but birth and childhood were quick to follow. He's been fortunate enough to live in Spain, Germany, and all over the United States of America, and is busy planning a tour of the distilleries of Scotland.

A graduate of the Johns Hopkins University's Writing Seminars program, he put that degree to ill use for twenty years as a software engineer but has finally circled back around to the idea of writing for a living.

Chris currently lives in Nevada with his angelic wife and ever-expanding whisky collection and occasionally ventures outside to peer upwards, mutter to himself about 'day stars', and then scurry back into the house.

Blood is Thicker Than Lots of Stuff is his fourth novel and the second in *The Many Travails of John Smith*. Chris frequently shares updates and new content on his author website at https://christullbane.com.